THE BLOOD OF THE SEER

BLOOD-RITES SERIES

BOOK 1

LEISL LEIGHTON

PERMIEN PRESS

Published by Leisl Leighton as Permien Press. For more information, email: leisl@leislleighton.com

First Published 2023 as a first draft early release serialisation on Leisl's Legends Subscription service via Ream

ebook ISBN: 978-1-922836-23-6; print ISBN: 978-1-922836-24-3

Cover design by Samantha Marshall

Edited by Brooke Halliwell

 Formatted with Vellum

PRAISE FOR LEISL LEIGHTON

I found the premise very cool...I recommend to all shifter and witch fans because this is an intriguing story with tons going on and a new spin that you will love! I can't wait for the next book!

— **CASSANDRA LOSKOT - CASSANDRA LOST IN BOOKS BLOG/BOOK REVIEWS**

"So good! I will always love paranormal romances, they just have so many different types, and themes, and never get boring. Leighton delivers a great one!"

— **TAPNCHICA – GOODREADS AND BOOKSPROUT REVIEWER**

I absolutely love this ... Leighton is a master at world building, character, plot, and oh...those sex scenes are pretty damn hot. You'd be crazy not to read this series!

— **LAURA BADHUS – GOODREADS REVIEWER**

I loved this! ... This is a very good book and is most definitely worth reading.

— **A SCHOFIELD - GOODREADS & BOOKBUB REVIEWER**

THE BLOOD OF THE SEER

My love of vampires began with Lestat and was brought to even larger life with Dracula and Buffy the Vampire Slayer. Buffy's and Angel's love made my heart sing and cry and started my mind percolating over so many what-ifs. Shows like The Vampire Diaries, The Originals and books like Vampire Academy, just cemented my love and kept things percolating. It took 20 years until it solidified into characters and a story, but here it is, finally. My own little take on the ultimate vampire boyfriend and the witch soulmate who is strong enough to put up with his shit.

This is dedicated to all the vampires, their lovers, and the legends that came before Gabriel and Ardenne.

CHAPTER I
GOODBYES

All is Dark. A pinpoint flash. Light is born, minuscule and powerless. Dark surrounds Light. Another spark flares. Light meets Light, glows, grows, warm and welcoming to all but Dark. Velvet and cold, Dark envies Light for the warmth and love that surrounds it always. Pushed to the edge, unwanted and unseen, misunderstood and mistrusted, Dark hurts.
Dark is not evil until Light makes it so.
Extract from The Middleton Manifesto, Preface, Book 1

VALLE D'AOSTA, ITALY

Ardenne made her way down the hall, away from the wails of her sister bemoaning the injustice of today to Cook. Cook was the best person to deal with Mia's tantrum. She could always bring Mia to reason. Although, Ardenne wasn't sure anyone could make Mia listen to reason over this. Certainly not her. If *she* didn't understand why she'd been chosen to go for special training to the Cousins in *Firenze* while her elder sister was overlooked, how could Mia possibly be made to understand?

1

And now the day had come for her to leave.

Well, she couldn't go in and say goodbye to the kitchen staff with Mia there, so she'd start her goodbye with someone else she'd miss with everything in her.

Listening intently, she continued to walk toward her cat's favorite haunt. "Where are you, you rascally thing?" she whispered under her breath. "I don't have time for hide and seek today. I have to say goodbye."

She only had an hour or so left until it was time to go.

The thought made her pause as realization struck. She was leaving the only home she'd ever known and would not be back for years. Her chest thrummed with excitement at what lay ahead as her lip trembled at the thought of all the goodbyes she must utter today.

She'd always longed to travel but as the daughter of the Bartolli Prime, for security reasons, she hadn't been allowed. Now she was finally getting her wish, a part of her didn't want to leave. Especially given she had to leave so early on her birthday and wouldn't even get to share lunch with Papa and Lord Hei. But Lord Hei said today was the day, so today it must be. Lord Hei never did anything without a reason.

She only wished that this time, she knew what that reason was. It might make things a little easier to bear. She swallowed hard. Actually, no. Nothing would make some of these goodbyes easier to bear. But make her goodbyes she must.

First though, she needed one last cuddle with Miss Kitty—a terrible name for a tomcat Mia was forever telling her, but that couldn't be helped. The moment she found him cowering in the garden outside her room on her fifth birthday, she'd anointed the kitten Miss Kitty. By the time they discovered he was a boy a few days later, it was already too late to change the name. He answered to Miss Kitty and no other. Not even Mr. Kitty—the name Mia suggested.

A soft pad of paws over floorboards told her where Miss Kitty was hiding and before the cat pounced, Ardenne had her arms out, catching him up against her chest with a laugh.

Miss Kitty let out a soft, happy meow and began to purr in her arms as she stroked him from head to tail. "You like that, don't you?"

She liked it too, the texture of his soft fur under her hands, the bits of outside she always found tangled in it telling her the journey of his day. She sat on the wide windowsill behind her, Miss Kitty nestled on her lap, the sun warm on her back. The moment filled her with contentment tinged with sadness. Sadness because it was unlikely Miss Kitty would still be here when she finally came back in five or six years after her training was completed. Papa said they usually didn't allow the Bartolli Prime-in-training to come back home during their training, so they would visit her, although not for at least a year.

Miss Kitty though would not be brought with them.

Before the sadness could overwhelm her, she lifted him up, nestling her face against his head. "You'll have to find someone else to play with when I'm gone. And to stroke you like this." Her fingers pressed into his back as she stroked him, just how he liked, his fur soft and cool against her skin.

She wished she knew what color he was. Mia said he was an absurd orange. It was hard to imagine orange. People sometimes described the sun as orange; a sunset could be orange; and of course, the sweet, juicy fruit she plucked from the orchard with the thick rind that smelled clean and fresh and tart was called an orange. But all those things were incredibly different. She was left with the impression that orange was hot and bright, enhancing the scent of the grass and the flowers and trees and soil that were all around, but was also mellow, a color of quiet and reflection and a beauty that made people make a soft sigh as that color lit the sky.

Miss Kitty was none of those things. He was fluffy and warm, and his purring vibrated through her chest in that blissful way that made her sigh a smile. And he was as stealthy as night creeping up on twilight and engulfing it without a sound. "Although, you're not as quiet as you used to be," she said, kissing his head. "I heard you long before you pounced."

"I don't think that's him, *mia cara*. I think your hearing has improved again."

Miss Kitty yowled and hissed, then jumped from her arms, scratching her as he went. "Ow." She rubbed at the scratch.

"Sorry about that. He really doesn't like me, does he?"

Ardenne stood to face Tomas Bartolli. "It's not you, Papa. He doesn't like any men. Except for Lord Hei. He turns into a gooey mess for Lord Hei."

"Well, that's no surprise. All animals love Lord Hei."

Ardenne frowned as she crossed to where he stood in the doorway to his study. "I've never understood that."

"Why? Don't you think Lord Hei is loveable?"

"Of course he is. Everyone loves him." She turned her face up as if really looking at him. Not that her papa cared where she looked when she spoke to him, but she'd learned most people did. It made them more comfortable. "It's just ... he feeds on animals. You'd think they'd sense he is the hunter and they are the prey."

Tomas' chuckle rumbled in her ears. "I've never really thought about it like that." The chuckle died and his warm hands cupped her face. "It doesn't worry you, does it?"

She smiled. "No. It's just something I thought."

"Always thinking, aren't you?" He pressed a kiss to her brow. "It's one of the reasons you were chosen to go."

Ardenne's smile stiffened and she shifted, moving her face out of the warmth of his grasp. "Will Mia hate me forever?"

She heard the sigh in his chest before it was exhaled. "No, *mia cara*. Her talents lie elsewhere and she will come to understand this is for the best."

"Is it?" Ardenne gripped her hands tightly in front of her, her thumb worrying the fresh scratch. "Am I the right choice?"

"Hey ... Where is this coming from?" Tomas' arms went around her, and she tucked her head under his chin, winding her arms around his back and hanging on like she'd done when she was a child. "I thought you were excited to go to the Cousins. To have the Prime training to take over from me when I'm ready to step down."

"I am." Her voice was muffled and thick with tears. She pressed her face against the soft wool of his jumper, willing the tears to stay in the sightless orbs they gathered behind. "It's just that ... Mia is whole, and I am ... not. I—"

"No." He pulled back and cupped her face again. "I will not hear you say that. You are brilliant and insightful and thoughtful and beautiful and so full of life it sometimes hurts to watch you. What you lack in sight, you make up for in so many ways that if I began to list them now, you would be late for your journey."

A laugh bubbled out of her at his tone. "I don't think one person can be all those things, least of all me. You make me sound so perfect."

"You *are* perfect."

She shook her head, pulling away from him. "You and Lord Hei look at me with rose-colored glasses, Papa. I love you for it, but sometimes I feel ... I feel ..." Her hand pressed against her chest as she struggled to tell this dear, kind man who had adopted her when she was a baby and had never treated her as anything but his own, about the thing that bubbled away in her heart; bubbles that were like acid, cauterizing joy, making her always aware that there was something different about her.

Something other.

Something not entirely encapsulated by the fact she was the only blind person at *Casa Cinque*.

"What do you feel, *mia cara*?" He took her hand in his, pressing it against his chest, over his heart, its slow, steady beat a comforting thrum through her palm.

She struggled to say the words, to tell him the doubts in her mind. While she could do so many things, she couldn't see. She knew she shouldn't feel like this. She'd read many books where the blind protagonists were proud to be blind, and she tried to be. But ...

Maybe if she lived a normal life it wouldn't feel like such a weakness, but when you were surrounded by perfect beings like Lord Hei and his vampires, how could it be anything but that? What use was she with all her intelligence, her thirst for knowledge, her agility and supposed beauty if she couldn't see the danger when it was coming? And it was coming. It was always coming toward Lord Hei and his people.

But she couldn't say that to him. Knew it would hurt him, too. So, on an exasperated sigh, she said, "I worry I can't be all you expect me to be."

Tomas' fingers squeezed around hers. "I don't expect you to be anything other than what you are: my daughter who I love with all my heart."

"Papa." This time, no amount of willing the tears away stopped them from spilling out, and she allowed him to wrap his arms around her. As she burrowed into his broad chest the way she'd done when she was little, the certainty of his love surrounded her. "I'm going to miss you, Papa."

"And I you, *mia cara.*" His lips, soft and warm, pressed against her forehead. "More than I can possibly say."

"I wish I had more time."

"As do I, but Lord Hei chose you and you must go. Which reminds me ..." He set her away. "He sent me to find you. He would like to see you now. He wishes to say his goodbyes in private."

"He's not coming with us to the station?" Disappointment weighted her chest. "What happened?"

"There's been word of Wild on the outskirts of Lake Como."

"But why must he go? Why can't he send a few of the others?"

Tomas' sigh brushed over her face as he captured her hand in his, squeezing lightly. "There are issues here I can't explain to you yet, but he must go. Which means I must stay here in his absence."

She clutched his hand. "No, Papa."

"You well know it's part of my role as Bartolli Prime to run things when he is absent. If there was another choice, I would make it, but I'm afraid there isn't. I can't come with you to *Firenze*."

"No. This isn't goodbye." Her voice felt choked in her tear-thickened throat. "It can't be goodbye yet. I don't want to say goodbye now."

"This is not our goodbye, *bella*. I will walk you out to the car when it's time for you to leave and say goodbye then."

"But, Papa, who is to be my Guardian on the journey. I thought you were—"

"Other arrangements have been made."

Tension filled the space between them, his voice strained. Normally she would have backed off, not pushed him further when he was so obviously upset. But today wasn't a normal day. "What arrangements? Who is coming with me?"

"Matteus."

"Really?" She clasped her hands together. If Matteus was with her it would almost make up for Papa and Lord Hei not being there.

"And Gabriel."

She gasped, a thrilling shiver chasing through her. "The Lonely Angel is here? He's coming with me to *Firenze*?"

"Yes."

She wanted to ask Tomas so much more—what was Gabriel like? If the legends were true? Was he the fierce warrior vampire he was painted, tracking down and killing the Wild and the Dark Brethren like an avenging angel, or was he the kind man from her memories of fifteen years ago, when he had held her on his lap through the long funeral service for Uncle Yuri. She'd been so bewildered and frightened by the rending of her good dress, of ash being smeared on her face and the sobs and cries of the adults around her as they expressed their grief for a life cut too short, but Gabriel had held her hand and talked to her and told her stories and all of that had disappeared. "But, Papa, I thought he was on business for Lord Hei far away."

"He was. Now he's back. To be your Guardian on your journey."

She frowned. Why wasn't Papa happy that the Lonely Angel was going to be her Guardian? Gabriel was legend among vampire kind. She could not have been safer if Lord Hei himself journeyed with her. But something about the tension in him now made her swallow all those questions. Instead she asked, "Am I to meet him before I go?"

"I don't know. But Lord Hei is waiting for you, so no more wasting time with questions about Gabriel. Go to our Lord and bid him a proper goodbye."

Ardenne nodded. "Where is he?"

"In his study."

"Then you'll come to take me out to the car?"

"Yes." He kissed her cheek. "Now go."

She turned and headed down the corridor that led into the oldest part of the villa, aware somehow that he watched her go until she disappeared around the corner.

The softer pad of her shoes on the floorboards turned to the hard slap of shoes on stone. The air changed, became colder and full of a scent she could only put down to the passing of centuries; moist and old. But despite the cold and the scent, she wasn't unsettled. This part of the villa always seemed more like home than any other, the history of it whispering stories long forgotten. Stories she wished she knew.

She loved these old rooms, but she especially loved Lord Hei's study in his private apartments. She'd spent many happy hours there learning of a world she would never see.

As she walked, the echo of her footsteps lighting her way through familiar corridors, she became aware of voices.

Tight, unhappy voices.

She began to move softly, silently, her attention solely on the voices—one deep and so thoroughly familiar she knew it as well as her own, the other familiar through memory and dream.

Gabriel.

The quiet husk of it thrilled through her despite the clipped coldness of its tone. The owner of that husky tenor was not happy.

She knew she should stop. Knew she should wait where she couldn't overhear. But she was too curious. What was he saying? Why was he unhappy? It was suddenly essential she knew. Holding her breath, she paused right outside the door, listening.

CHAPTER 2
HARD TRUTHS

The child with blood, both Dark and Light
Born into the world, sans sight
A herald of the war to come
She must be trained to see the sun
Four and Five oppose Two and Three
First's will over all, so mote it be.
Extract from The Middleton Manifesto, Verse 13, Incantations,
Book 1

"Sit down, Gabriel, and let's talk about this."

Gabriel ran his hand through his hair and kept pacing. "I can't believe you called me back for this. You know why I need to stay away." He spun around and was across to Lord Hei's desk in the blink of an eye. "I was this close to catching her." He held up his hand, thumb and forefinger held slightly apart. "And then you called me back and now she's gone. *Cazzo!*" He slammed his hand down on the desk, ignoring his Sire's wince as the marble inlay split with an audible crack. "Who knows what the hell she'll do next."

"You know what she'll do next, Gabriel," Hei said as he came around the desk and placed his hand on Gabriel's shoulder. "That's why you're the one to hunt her."

"And yet you call me back for this!"

"You know why I called you. You're Ardenne's Guardian."

"And I was doing my Guardian duty the only way I can, by hunting down those who would hurt her. I don't need to be turned into a bloody babysitter." He broke from his Sire's hold and began pacing again. Hei leaned against his broken desk, for all the world looking as serene as he did in the painting behind him; five centuries old, it had been painted by a fledgling artist a year before they'd rescued Mary Middleton. That artist had gone on to great things. And Mary, well ... she'd been grateful for her rescue but that didn't stop her prophecies from screwing with all their lives.

Despite how serene he looked right now, Gabriel knew his Sire, King of their vampire sect, Lord and Master of a vast empire of businesses, properties and charities, wasn't anything close to serene. He kept brushing his long white hair over his shoulder, and his lips, so often curved in enjoyment of life, were a flat line as he watched his sireling pace.

"You came, Gabriel. You did not have to end the chase when you did, and yet you came the moment I called."

Gabriel growled low in his throat. "Of course I did. You're my Sire."

Hei chuckled and crossed his arms over his chest. "And we both know how little sway that has over you, my son." He tapped his long fingers on his biceps, the diamond sharpness of his nails glistening in the dawn light streaming through the window to his right. "You know why you really came the moment you heard my call." He stopped tapping and stood there, statue-still as Gabriel halted, his back stiff, the nuances of his Sire's tone playing through him.

"I did not come because I was worried about her. She's here with you. Nothing could touch her."

"Of course it couldn't. Not here. I didn't say that you were worried. And she has a name, Gabriel."

"I know she has a name. I was there at her birth when her mother named her."

"How about you use it."

"Using it will not change my mind. I don't want to see her again."

A deep sigh. "You knew this day was coming—it's carved into your soul. And whether I'd called you or not, you would have been here, watching from afar, unhappy that Ardenne's safety was being left in the hands of others, no matter how capable they are. You would have interfered, upset those I put in charge and possibly even frighten Ardenne with your intensity. So, I saved us all the grief of that and called you here to take direct control."

"What about Carrington? And Vincente. I thought they were overseeing her future education."

"They are. However, we've decided it's best to train her powers in secret—I imagine you know why this is best. Vincente is fully versed. He will comply."

"And who is to be her Companion?"

"Sarita Cartelli."

Gabriel tensed, his gaze darting over his Sire's face, gauging the calm certainty there. "Is she the best choice?"

"She is the only choice. Given her background and circumstances, she cannot help but take care of Ardenne as aggressively as a leopard cares for her cub. Her understanding of the girl's unique plight will help set Ardenne on her path."

"Does Sarita know of your plans?"

Hei took in a deep breath then let it out slowly. "No. Ardenne cannot suspect Sarita of duplicity. We need her to trust her Companion."

"Why would the child not trust her?"

Hei shook his head. "Ardenne is no longer a child, as you well know given you have marked her every birthday with a secret gift."

"Not so secret if you knew they were from me."

Hei's lips twitched as if he found Gabriel's grumbling amusing, but he didn't respond to the comment, simply went on as if he hadn't heard. "She's grown into a savvy young woman despite the isolated nature of her upbringing. As a result, she's become too attuned to the secrets we keep from her. We cannot ask Sarita to do her job and lie to Ardenne at the same time. Ardenne will figure it out and that could lead to disaster. Sarita's motives must be pure and of her own design for Ardenne to trust her as she must."

Gabriel opened his mouth to say something, but nothing came out. It seemed there was no argument he could make to change his Sire's mind. A great tearing pain squeezed his chest, followed by a sensation of drowning, as if there was no air. He stared at his Sire's too knowing gaze and then sank into the chair behind him, clutching the arms. It turned into kindling beneath his fingers.

"When you've finished destroying my furniture, maybe we can talk about this."

Gabriel sprang out of the chair to stand by the tall windows. Gauzy curtains fluttered in the light breeze, shifting and sighing around him. For a long moment he stared blindly at the snow-topped mountains that surrounded Lord Hei's private home before turning slowly to face his Sire.

Usually, this room was an oasis to him, with its splashes of jewel-bright colors against the soft fawn of the walls, the eclectic furnishings and paintings that spoke of moments in time that brought happy memories. It was a place he came to when he needed calm and the presence of his Sire to soothe his soul. But now, it held nothing of peace. The furniture was not the only thing broken by his presence in this room.

Because his Sire was right.

Damn him.

He crossed his arms over his chest, fingers digging into his skin to stop him from picking up the priceless Ming vase he stood next to and flinging it across the room. Doing that would not make him feel better, and it would only serve to upset his Sire more than he already was on this terrible day. "I don't want this," he said through a throat as dry as paper.

Something glistened in Lord Hei's electric blue eyes, but was gone before Gabriel could name it. "I know, my son. And if I could choose for this burden to go to anyone else, I would, but I can't. You were marked by fate for this."

"You don't believe in fate."

Hei wagged his finger. "No. Do not misquote me. I do not believe that men should throw up their arms and blame everything on fate. I like to believe we are masters of our own destiny in most things. But there are certain things we do not have power over; nexuses in time that are fixed. And this, for you, Gabriel, is one of those. The more you fight it, the more it will hurt."

Gabriel ignored Hei's words, focusing on the painting that hung over the carved marble mantel above the fireplace opposite the desk. "Why do you keep that there? Aren't you worried she'll find out before you're ready to tell her?"

Hei looked at him curiously before saying as if to a child, "Gabriel, Ardenne sees nothing but what she terms a 'velvet dark'. She will never notice the resemblance between herself and the woman in that portrait."

Gabriel thought that Tomas wouldn't like it but kept that thought to himself. Tomas had played the role of Ardenne's father for so long that everyone but a few had forgotten the truth of her birth. "You know it's not a secret we can keep from her forever."

"So you have argued before, Gabriel, but now is not the time."

"And yet it is the time to send her away? You know what's going on out there. Know how dangerous it is."

"Gabriel." Hei shook his head, his expression full of the wisdom of thousands of years. "You know I must. Her power has begun to push beyond the spells that have bound her since birth. They are about to break free. She must be trained, or she will be a danger to herself and everyone else."

"Is she aware?"

Hei shook his head. "The shield placed on her just after her birth is still functioning but weak. If her magic surges, it will collapse. She needs to be educated properly. To be brought to an awareness of this world we live in by those who do not care for her like I do. I coset her. As does Tomas and everyone here. We cannot give her the kind of training she needs. She must go, and she needs you by her side when she leaves."

"So, she's not a Huntress like her mother."

"No. She promises to be so much more, as you well know. Which is why she needs you by her side."

Gabriel hissed and turned to pace again. There had to be some way he could get out of this. Some way to avoid the disaster ahead.

"Gabriel."

"Does the fact she's blind not concern you?" Gabriel asked after his last argument had failed.

"No more than it should. Why does it worry you?"

Gabriel threw his arms up and looked to the heavens. "You know why. You know what the prophecy says."

"You will not mention that to her or anyone. I do not believe in prophecy."

Gabriel choked on a laugh. "And yet you talk of fate and nexis! You hide your head in the sand when it comes to her. She. Is. Without. Sight. If your enemies were to find out the truth of that, she would never be safe, not even here, and yet you send her out in the world with only me as her Guardian."

"You will have an army to help guard her, Gabriel."

"That's not what I'm talking about, and you know it. She's blind. You of all people know what that means. And what makes it worse is you play into the fact she can't know. You allow her to stumble around in the darkness, ignorant and weak, and you ask me to babysit her and teach her and yet tell her nothing of—"

"Gabriel, enough."

Gabriel fell instantly silent at his Sire's quiet request, noting his attitude of listening, his tight, pained expression.

And then he heard it. Breathing so quiet just outside the door he'd not noticed until this moment. Someone was standing there, listening. He frowned. The person couldn't be human, because no human could be that quiet, and yet one of his siblings would have been free to enter at any time. There would be no need for them to stand outside a door eavesdropping.

Who was it? He breathed in and had his answer in the soft, intoxicating scent. Damn. "How long?" he mouthed to his Sire.

Hei mouthed back, "Just now." Then he said loudly, "Ardenne, come in."

A young woman entered, shoulders back, a pleasant smile on her face. He sucked in a breath.

Ardenne?

She'd been a mere child the last time he'd visited. Now ... Now she was most definitely not a child.

"My Lord. I hope this morning finds you well." Her voice was light and yet with a slight huskiness that made him think of honey with cinnamon and spice.

"I am, my dear. And you?"

"I am as well as can be expected given the circumstances." Her tone was even, giving no sign that she might have overheard their discussion. Her pale skin was slightly flushed, but that could be because she was wearing a heavy jumper in preparation for her journey. One would be forgiven for thinking she hadn't been listening outside the door, hearing things that were not for her ears, except, somehow, Gabriel thought she'd heard far more than even Hei knew. He couldn't put his finger on it, but he could swear she was upset. Hurt. Deeply.

Merda.

That was the last thing he needed right now—to deal with Ardenne's feelings on the long journey ahead. He wondered if she was going to be missish. Or was she one of those people who preferred to be nasty when faced with unpleasant truths? Perhaps she liked to pout and have a tantrum? Or would he be given the silent treatment?

The last he could take. The others ... he wasn't so sure how he would respond. He'd not had to deal with anyone's feelings for a very long time. Rolling his eyes to the heavens he muttered under his breath, "By The First, why now?"

"I'm sorry, my Lord. Am I interrupting something? There's someone here with you."

"You're not interrupting, my dearest girl." Hei came around his desk and took her hands in his, kissing her on both cheeks and then a third time for good luck. "I was just finishing up giving some instructions to Gabriel. He is to be your Guardian on your journey—and maybe for a little longer, if things go to plan."

Gabriel shot Hei a look, but then Ardenne turned to face him and oh, by The First! Her eyes. They were still like pieces of the moon with the blue at the heart of a glacier deep inside them, but rather than shining with a child's youthful exuberance as they had the last time he'd visited, they were glowing and intelligent and so full of expression it took his breath away.

But that wasn't the only thing that took him by surprise. She was tall and willowy with curves that marked her as a woman. She'd always had skin almost as pale as a vampire's and yet there was a scattering of freckles across her cheeks and nose. And despite being an innocent, she had a poise that belied her age. With her head tipped like that in challenge, the dark curls of her ponytail brushing over her shoulder, she looked like she was prepared to take on anything the harsh world might throw at her. And she was looking right at him as if she could see him with those astonishing eyes.

Che cavollo! She was beautiful.

He sucked in a breath. He shouldn't be surprised given who her parents were, but he hadn't been prepared for the impact of her after all these years.

Fanculo! What the hell was he doing here?

He realized she was talking to him and tried to focus on her words without looking at her lips.

"Yes. Papa told me." She bowed her head in acknowledgment, hands folded in front of her. "It's been a long time, Gabriel."

Gabriel stared. No tears or emotional outburst. Had she heard what he'd said at all? Maybe not. Maybe he'd been wrong about her being hurt by things she was never meant to hear. Gathering himself he said smoothly, "It has, Ardenne. It's good to see you again."

Her smile trembled a little. "How lovely of you to say—even though it's a lie." Before he could do more than gape, she turned to Hei and said in a gentle, sympathetic tone, "I'm sure Gabriel has far better things to do with his time than be Guardian to a weak and ignorant blind girl like me. I hardly warrant such extreme measures to keep me safe as to call on your greatest warrior against the cults. Matteus could be my Guardian."

"Matteus will accompany you to the station, but then he is going to Indonesia to take care of a problem best dealt with by him."

Gabriel's brow rose. This was the first he had heard of that.

"The Wild?" Ardenne asked, a slightly breathless quality to her voice.

"Yes. But I do not wish to sully your departure with ugly tales." He threw a warning look at Gabriel. "Or by bitterness caused by a chance word said that I know was misheard and misunderstood. Gabriel did not mean your blindness was a weakness. If it was, you would not be going to *Firenze* to learn all you must to become Bartolli Prime when your papa is ready to step down. I trust you know that, my dearest one."

Ardenne dipped her chin, her brow furrowed. "I trust that you believe in me. But Gabriel's views—"

"As I said, Gabriel meant no insult. Did you, Gabriel?"

"No."

She tipped her head in a way that made it seem like she looked at him. "But *you* don't think I should go."

"You misunderstood," he said carefully.

"Did I?"

"Yes."

A pause, then, "You are disappointed."

There was a hitch of pain in her voice, but there was also a note of defiance that made the hunter in him sit up and listen. Very carefully, aware his answer was crucial in putting an end to whatever thoughts were tumbling around her mind—the last thing he needed was for her to try and prove to him just how capable she was—he said, "Not disappointed. Just ... surprised. And ... misinformed. I did not know you had come so far in your studies, but I can see now my concerns were unwarranted."

"Because I do not stumble around? Or show that I am blind by using a stick?" Her voice was edged with something hard. "That's because Lord Hei and my father spent all their spare time training me to use my other senses, and some of your siblings, like Matteus and Corrina, have helped me to hone them. I don't need a stick. And I don't need you to pity or belittle me."

His brows rose and he stepped forward, hand stretched out to her before he realized what he was doing and snapped it back to his side. "I don't pity you. And I'm sorry if you think I was belittling you. I hope I can make amends on our journey."

"I suppose everyone deserves a second chance." Her lips twitched as she turned to Hei and held out her hands. "I came to say goodbye. Would you take me for one last walk outside in your private garden?"

"It would be my pleasure, Ardenne," he said, tucking her hand into the crook of his arm and turning toward the door. "And it would allow me to give you your birthday gift."

"Your trust in me is the greatest gift I could have."

"Prettily said, but I still would like to give you a little token to mark this special day."

Gabriel made a choking sound of surprise as they walked out the door that led into his Sire's private garden.

He'd been dismissed. Not only that, Ardenne had taken him to task! Nobody but his Sire had ever taken him to task before. It was a new experience.

One he liked far too much.

Fanculo! This journey was going to be hell.

CHAPTER 3
JOURNEY

She must journey
She must part
Leaving behind a broken heart
But the path ahead
She must tread
To face the monsters in her head.
Extract from The Middleton Manifesto, Prophecy 6, Book 1

The goodbyes were as excruciating as Ardenne dreaded they would be. Even Mia poured hot tears on her shoulder as she hugged her goodbye—although Ardenne thought maybe they stemmed from jealousy rather than actual sorrow. Her sister's words when they were told of the decision to send Ardenne still stung: *"Why did they choose you over me? You might be good at everything I'm not, but at least I can see. At least I could appreciate the paintings and sculpture and architecture and the beautiful landscape of Firenze. You can't. You never will. It's so unfair. It's ridiculous to think you'll understand any of it."*

Of course, she would wave Mia's words aside as she had many

times in the past if only other, more hurtful words uttered only that morning, didn't still echo in her head.

She'd obviously only heard the end of their conversation given so much of what she overheard didn't really make sense, but the fact Gabriel thought her blindness a problem was not something she'd misunderstood. He'd made his worries clear.

Damn Gabriel for ruining her excitement. The fear she'd been ignoring for the last week since she'd been told was now climbing up her chest, threatening to sink its claws into her throat and choke her.

"Are you okay, Ardenne? You look a little pale."

She started, aware that she'd been sitting in the back seat in silence as Matteus drove them down the mountain. A mountain she'd pictured many times in her mind and was now being bathed in the beauty of a sunny spring morning she could only imagine. "I'm fine. Just a little ..."

"Tentative?"

The warmth in the question made her smile. "I was going to say sad, but tentative works too."

"It's your first time away from home. It's only natural you would be both. But Lord Hei wouldn't have chosen you for this honor if he didn't think you were ready."

She nodded, taking a deep breath. He was right. Lord Hei and Papa had said the same. She had to trust their faith in her. Otherwise, they would not have given her the birthday presents they had —a pair of fighting daggers from Papa and a beautiful hand-carved crossbow she was to learn to use from Lord Hei.

If they did not think her capable, she would have received clothes and perfume like others her age received.

She was going to be taught to fight properly among many other things. She had no idea exactly how she could be taught to throw daggers or shoot a crossbow with any accuracy, but that was a worry for another day. Today, she just needed to concentrate on what the gifts meant and all the wonders she was to experience in the next few years.

But as she leaned back in the seat, she couldn't get her mind to concentrate on anything but ... "Where is Gabriel?"

"You know he's coming?"

"I met him at the villa."

"You don't sound impressed."

She screwed up her mouth. It wouldn't be polite to say anything uncharitable about Lord Hei's favorite protégé. "He was ... different from what I thought."

Matteus laughed. "That's not surprising. It would be hard for anyone to live up to the 'Lonely Angel' hype, especially given we're nothing close to angelic. Although," his voice became wistful, "the lonely aspect Gabriel has hands down."

Something about the way he said that made tears prick her eyes and a horrible sadness well in her chest. Blinking hard—she refused to feel sorry for him—she asked, "But where is he? I thought he was to be my Guardian."

"He's scouting. He'll join us later."

"At the train?"

"Perhaps."

She unclenched her hands—she hadn't realized she'd been gripping them so tightly together—relieved to be spared having to share car space with the vampire whose words had hurt her more than she cared to admit.

"Would you like me to play some music?"

"No, thank you. But I would like you to talk to me, tell me what you see." She listened for a moment to the sound of the car's wheels on the gravel road, the wind whistling by. "Is it beautiful, Matteus?"

"The mountains?"

"No. Well, yes." Ardenne laughed. "I know the mountains are beautiful. Lord Hei and Papa have described them so many times I think I can picture them in my mind's eye. But I meant everything else. The valley below, the road, the trees. Everything. Describe everything. I don't want to miss a thing."

"You never do." Matteus began to describe everything as she'd asked.

She concentrated on his voice, trying to build images from the pictures he created with words and intonations. But for some reason, all she could see was the velvet dark she'd lived with all her life, Gabriel's doubt echoing louder and louder in her head. She clenched her hands together then wiped them on her jeans, swaying as the car went round a tight corner. She simply needed to concentrate harder.

But after a few minutes of frustration, she said, "Stop, Matteus. It's not working. I can't picture it. I can't picture anything." By The First! If she couldn't picture something so simple, how was she going to cope when there was so much more going on around her?

"What's wrong?"

"I don't know. But—" She swallowed hard. "It's just, I know everyone at home, every inch of *Casa Cinque*. And I'm ... I ... I've never been out in the world before and I'm not sure I'm going to be able to do this."

There was a long silence, and then Matteus said, "If you think you're the first one to be nervous when being sent into the outside world for the first time, you'd be wrong. Knowing what you know about us, knowing what you must hide, and yet, trying to be a part of the world is difficult and confusing. I've seen many Bartolli go through that. Including Tomas when he was chosen."

"Papa was nervous when he left to study with the Cousins?"

Matteus chuckled. "He certainly was. In fact, as I was driving down the mountain, I had to pull over a couple of times so he could vomit. He said it was car sickness. But I could smell the nervous sweat on him."

Ardenne laughed and wiped her sweaty palms against her jeans again. She should have known Matteus would understand despite the fact he'd been a vampire for three hundred years. That's why he was one of her favorites of Lord Hei's sirelings.

Yet even though it was comforting to hear her papa had been

nervous about what lay ahead, there was still a huge difference between them. Her laughter died.

"You're still worried."

She pulled at the edge of her sweater, glad Papa had made her sit in the back seat because Matteus couldn't see the extent of her nervousness. "I've never been able to watch TV or surf the web like others do."

"I thought there was a computer program that could help you with that now."

"There is, but from how Mia talks, I know it's not the same. I've also heard all about tablets and touch screens and iPhones that do everything for you, but I've never even held one."

"Lord Hei doesn't like those modern conveniences being used at *Casa Cinque*."

"I know. But at least Mia has seen them and used the ones her friends own at the school she goes to. I haven't even done that." She sighed, then frowned. "I haven't even seen a movie."

"I didn't realize those things bothered you."

She twisted her sweater in her hands. "They haven't. Not at *Casa Cinque*. But out there." She bit her lip before saying, "I'm worried I won't fit in. That I'll stand out more than I already do."

"That's why you're going to *Firenze*. You'll learn to fit in. There'll be computer software you'll be able to use on all those devices. Vincente Solari will have you fitted out with the latest of everything you need to fit into the modern world and make sure you can use it. There's no need to worry."

She huffed out a laugh. "I wish it was as simple as telling myself not to worry."

"Just imagine it is, and it will be so."

She laughed outright this time. "You sound like Lord Hei. He says imagination is my greatest tool."

"He'd be right. Alongside your heightened senses, it will help to light your way."

He paused. Silence fell. The crunching of tires against gravel filled the car. However, Ardenne's hearing was acute, and she could tell from the way Matteus sucked in a breath that he had something else to say.

"What is it, Matteus?"

"I just want to say one more thing, *bella,* and then we'll drop this topic."

She sat forward, hands clenched on the seat. "You can say anything to me."

Matteus drummed his fingers against the wheel, every strike playing her nerves like discordant guitar strings. "I'm not saying you're wrong to worry about the real world and your place in it. People out there *will* judge you because of what they perceive is a weakness. Don't let them. Remember our true purpose is to wipe out the Wild and Dark Brethren and protect the humans. Don't ever let your lack of sight become more important than our mission."

"I'm not planning to." Her tone was more confident than she felt.

"Good girl."

She dropped back into her seat, the leather squeaking under her jeans. She wished she had his faith in her. She just hoped she could live up to their expectations.

No! Hope isn't enough. I will *live up to their expectations. I have to.*

The car picked up speed and she was pushed back a little in her seat as they wove down the curving mountain road. The nervous sickness she'd experienced ever since getting up this morning was slowly taken over by a bubble of excitement.

"How long will—"

The back passenger door opposite Ardenne opened and closed with a whoosh of wind. The car swerved. Ardenne screamed and clung to the door handle. The seat dipped next to her, and she cringed, waiting for an attack.

When Matteus didn't cry out in warning, heat flushed her face. The Wild or Dark Brethren wouldn't attack them with Matteus here —she was stupid thinking it even for a moment. It was probably just Corinna making a dramatic entrance. She forced herself to let go of the door handle, heart still clamoring in her chest, and took a deep breath.

A scent, like clear mountain air in spring, enticing and warm, filled her senses. It belonged to the vampire sitting beside her; definitely not Corinna's. It was the scent she'd smelled as she'd crept down the hallway earlier, overhearing what she wished she'd never overheard.

Gabriel.

"Lord's blood, Gabriel. Did you have to give the girl a fright?" Matteus snarled. "I would have stopped to pick you up if you'd flagged me down."

"You can't afford to stop. Besides, she'll get over it. Won't you, Ardenne?"

She managed to nod as she pressed her hands against her chest, heart beating wildly. He'd done that on purpose. To test her. To see if she'd act like some frightened human who didn't know vampires existed, or the hardened Bartolli she was supposed to be—now she understood why she'd been made to sit in the back. Her face burned as she realized how badly she'd failed that test, heart still pounding too wildly—a sound he could hear as clearly as she heard the car's engine.

He didn't say a word though. Just sat there. Was he looking at her, his mouth curled in disdain? Possibly. Probably.

She could picture his expression in her mind. She could do that given she'd traced his face with her fingers when she was younger, as she'd done with all Lord Hei's sirelings. She'd learned the shape of his features, the length of his hair, felt the shadow of a dimple beside full lips that had deepened when he smiled. A smile that was probably replaced by ill-concealed annoyance.

A strange kind of fluttering started in her belly as she thought of touching his face now, of feeling that soft press of his smooth, cool skin under her fingers then the ever so slightly rough scratchiness of where his beard might grow in. She'd felt the same on many of the Bartolli males when they'd allowed her to touch their faces to build pictures of them in her mind, but never on a vampire.

Strange.

Strange too was the way her fingertips tingled at the memory of brushing across his five o'clock shadow in a way they never tingled when she brought to mind the memory of tracing other male's faces. And the more she thought on it, that tingle intensified until she had to clench her fingers against her palm. It didn't help though. The tingle now raced up her arms and down her body, finally settling where the fluttering was in her stomach, turning it into a strange clenching.

She pressed her fist against the sensation, her stomach twisting in two. Was she going to be sick? By The First, she hoped not. That was the last thing she needed to do in front of Gabriel. Perhaps it was the swaying of the car as it drove down the winding mountain road? No. She hadn't felt this way until Gabriel had entered the car.

No. It was him and his disappointment that fell on her like a heavy cloak.

Well, let him be disappointed. She was disappointed too.

Gabriel was nothing like she remembered. He'd been kind then, and warm, like Corinna and Matteus and the others. Now he was just—

"Is there some danger?" Matteus asked, interrupting her wallowing. "Is that why you jumped into the car?"

"There's always danger, Matteus." Gabriel's voice, his English slightly accented, wove around her. "But no, the area is clear. I thought it best to play the role of Guardian close by rather than from a distance."

Ardenne tensed, his words a burn in her chest. He thought her so incompetent he didn't even think she could cope with a car ride down the mountain that had been her home all her life. A nasty little voice inside her head whispered, *What if he's right?*

No! He wasn't right. Nor was Mia, or the nasty voice. She *could* do what they asked of her. Matteus thought she could. Papa thought she could. Lord Hei thought she could. She wouldn't let them or herself down. *Just ignore him.* If she could do that, hopefully her heart would stop banging painfully in her chest, and the strange clenching in her stomach would go away.

Clearing her throat, she leaned toward Matteus' vanilla and burnt-cinnamon scent, and asked, "How long will it take to get to the train?"

"You should know," Gabriel answered. "It takes three hours to get to *Milano.*"

She stiffened. "How would I know that? I've never been there before."

"Haven't you studied the area?"

"Yes. But we don't take lessons on how long it takes to drive to the station."

"So, knowing timing and distances is beneath you? I would have thought, given your situation, that kind of knowledge would be all important."

"My 'situation'! You mean because I'm blind?"

"Especially because you are blind."

Her head jerked as if she'd been slapped.

The clenching in her stomach disappeared as anger took its place, burning deep inside her. But she wouldn't let it out. No. Yelling at him or saying something nasty would only play into his low opinion of her. Besides, she didn't have to stoop as low as some people.

She turned toward the window trying to ignore him, but it was difficult when his presence shouted that he thought her a dead weight—one who could never be the next Bartolli Prime.

Don't think about it. Don't think about him. He'll be gone soon enough.

She firmed her jaw, determined to follow her own advice. She'd been looking forward to this journey. Looking forward to learning new things. She refused to let Gabriel spoil it. She had to stop thinking about the strange, hot, edgy sensations racing through her.

Anger, that's all it was. She was angry. She had a right to be angry with him.

She tried a visualization exercise that usually brought calm. She imagined the sky as Papa had described it, sparkling and mysterious, the expanse punctuated by fluffy clouds like the froth on cappuccino. If she opened the window, she'd smell the forests and the snow that covered the mountains like a downy quilt even in summer. She knew snow. The numbing cold of it melting in her hand. The icy fresh taste on the tip of her tongue. The sound as it blanketed the land, bringing different echoes for her to learn. Echoes that bounced off the mountain range rising majestically behind *Casa Cinque*; mountains that were as old as time.

She sighed, a smile widening her mouth at the thought.

"What are you thinking about, Ardenne?" Matteus asked gently.

"Lord Hei told me he'd seen the mountains here rise and change over his lifetime. It made me wonder about immortality. To be able to have seen and experienced so much must be such a gift."

"Immortality is not a gift," Gabriel said. "And anybody who thinks so is an ignorant fool."

Ardenne sucked in a sharp breath. "I'm not ignorant."

"You're a child."

"Gabriel!"

"Keep out of it, Matteus."

Tears burned, hot and angry at his verbal slap. "I'm not a child."

The rustle of him shifting on the leather; the heaviness of eyes staring at her. "You're not an adult either."

"I am. Officially I'm a year past being an adult in most countries."

"Turning nineteen does not make you an adult."

"*Basta!*"

"Speak in English, Ardenne."

"*Perché?*"

"Because Lord Hei wants you to. Isn't that enough?"

"Gabriel. Don't be so hard on her."

"Somebody must. Lord knows you've all coddled her enough. She needs to toughen up now she's being sent to live in the real world."

"That's not your job."

"Isn't it?"

A heavy silence followed his comment. One Ardenne didn't feel she could break, no matter how angry his words made her. She swiped at her eyes, hoping he wasn't watching. She didn't want him to see her tears as weakness. They were only there because he'd made her so furious. Damn him!

She caught her lip between her teeth, and bit down. She needed the pain to stop her from crying.

The car jolted as it hit a rough bit of road, making her jerk and bite down harder than intended. "Ouch!" Blood welled from the cut —warm and salty.

Gabriel's sharp intake of breath gave her a start. The material of his pants slid roughly against the leather of the seat as he shifted away from her. Cool morning air washed across her face as the window mechanism engaged. The air was redolent with the scent of warming earth and the spiciness of forest ferns, and in the distance, the snow she knew was there. It mixed with Gabriel's mountain air scent in a most disturbing way. Her stomach began to clench again, and she pressed her fists hard against the sensation.

New sounds invaded the car and she tried to focus on that instead of the strange sensations roiling inside her and electrifying her skin: the wind as it whistled past; a bird's querulous call, the echo fading off into silence when no mate replied. But the sounds were like an echo coming through the tension that was a thick fog all around her. Tension emanating from the vampire sitting next to her. Tension that stroked over her skin, making her nerves fire, a horrible, needy ache building inside her.

A grinding sound made it through the fog of tension. Like something being crushed. By The First, what was happening? Cold prickled on her skin, chased by burning heat, fraying her nerves. She sucked on the blood welling on her lip. Her worrying at it made the cut bleed more. She wiped the blood away with the back of her hand.

Gabriel hissed, almost like he was reacting to the blood. But why would he? Lord Hei's children couldn't drink from humans for sustenance. That's what set them apart from the Wild and Dark Brethren.

A strange buzzing filled her ears and pressure built behind her eyes. Like a headache, but not. She'd felt that pressure on and off all her life; more often in the last few days. She had no idea what it was. All she knew was it brought a tingling sweatiness, and a sensation like she stood beside herself. This time was no different.

Rubbing her eyes, she tried to will the feeling away. It wouldn't go. In fact, it worsened as her throat dried, itching and hot.

Corinna had told her about how hunger felt to a vampire—an unbearable burning that if not assuaged, began to consume the whole body until it was all you could think of. This felt like that. But she hadn't even been slightly thirsty a moment before.

And there was a scent in the car, a delicious smell, slightly sweet but not cloying. It made the thirst worse. It wasn't Gabriel. His scent filled her with warmth and a strange tingling. This delicious ambrosia was different. Her mouth watered.

What on earth was going on? Nobody else had entered the car. She would have heard them or smelled them. So, where was that scent coming from?

She swallowed hard again. It made no difference. "Have we got anything to drink?"

The seat creaked. She knew Gabriel had turned to face her; she could feel his gaze boring into her for the longest moment before he spoke.

"You'll have to wait until we reach the train."

"You don't have to be so nasty, Gabriel," Matteus said.

"You have no idea what I must be. She can wait."

Hunching into the corner, Ardenne turned away from him. Only Mia had been so awful to her, and she'd always just ignored her sister. Unfortunately, Gabriel wasn't someone you could ignore.

She'd just tried and failed miserably. Matteus' presence didn't even help. The tension between the two vampires made her as edgy as prey between two circling wolves. Which she could cope with if only she wasn't so thirsty.

And pathetic.

And alone.

Rubbing at the tight pain in her chest as her heart pounded too fast, she leaned her head against the window. Closing her eyes, she tried to ignore the raw throb of thirst in her throat and the cold vampire at her side.

Spring sun warmed the glass as they left the mountain. In her mind she entered the golden glow of warmth and tried to become lost in the imagined beauty of the day.

CHAPTER 4
CONFUSION

*I met him. God help me, I met him and ... Forgive me for the pause.
I had to compose myself, because he walked through the room and
smiled at me and I lost all thought. I am certain I looked like the
simple man who stares too long at the sun. Yet he did not comment
or make me feel like I was less because of it. It is quite remarkable.
He is nothing like I thought he would be.*
Extract from Mary Middleton's Diary, April 1, 1535

When the car finally pulled up outside the train station, Gabriel leaped out. Breathing deeply, he rubbed at his chest where a pain hovered over his heart. He took in another breath, trying to fill his nostrils with something other than her scent.

Through the bond, he could feel the anger and longing pulsing in Ardenne's chest and swirling in her stomach. Nausea—a sensation he hadn't experienced for over eight hundred years—rose in him. Not for the first time since her birth he cursed the bond that enabled him to sense what she was feeling—the bond that forced him to be her Guardian when it was the last thing he should ever be. It was partly why he stayed far away—the further he was from her, the less he felt it.

He tried to ignore it but an insane thirst gripped him, making that impossible.

Fanculo! It was unacceptable to have lost control like that in the car. Matteus would be furious when he saw the state of his precious door handle—it had crumpled in his hand when he'd first smelled her blood. But the scent had been so unexpected. Unlike the rest of Lord Hei's sirelings, he was never comfortable around human blood; but he hadn't had *that* reaction for a very long time.

If only he could get away from her for a moment, he could regain his control. But there were too many opportunities for ambushes and other problems here. Besides which, Matteus was suspicious already. He'd been shooting warning glances through the rear-view mirror for most of the journey. If it hadn't been so annoying, Gabriel might have laughed. As if he'd hurt Ardenne! He'd allow himself to be torn to shreds by Dark Brethren before ever allowing harm to come to her.

Which was why he shouldn't be here. This protective instinct he had toward her was madness. He could expose them all and not give a damn if it meant keeping her safe. Which in the end, would expose her to more danger.

Damn his Sire for making him do this!

He sighed heavily. At least he only had to stay near until Ardenne was delivered safe to Vincente Solari and the Cousins in *Firenze*. And once inside the train with Sarita, she would be safe. He would leave her then and take up position at the front of the train. Just a few minutes more and he would be free.

He rounded the car. Matteus, still glaring at him, moved to open Ardenne's door. "I'll help Ardenne inside."

Gabriel waved him away. "No. You liaise with the guards and bring the bags. I'll accompany Ardenne to the train."

Matteus' eyes narrowed and his lip curled, exposing one of his fangs—something they usually did not do in public and a sign of just how angry he was with Gabriel. Thankfully though, instead of arguing, he said, "You're the boss."

"Yes. I am. And you have a job to do." Matteus nodded curtly then walked to the boot of the car, his lips moving as he spoke through the radio mics to the others who were scattered throughout the station.

Gabriel turned and opened the door for Ardenne, reaching for her arm to help her out.

She shoved his hand away. "I can do it."

He stood back, happy not to have to touch her—it made the bond sing louder when he did.

She climbed out of the car, the sun catching red highlights in her almost black hair. She was pale and slender, her features as finely sculptured as her birth father's, with a determined strength in her that was wholly her mother's. If he didn't know better, he would think her untouched by her surrounds, but through the blasted bond, he could feel her uncertainty as the sound of *Milano* hit her like a physical wave. Confusion roiled through her as the cars rumbled by, horns honked, stereos blasted. Dizziness swam in her mind as a multitude of feet pounded the pavement nearby, voices chattering at an exhaustive pace.

He shouldn't be surprised at her reaction. After all, she'd never been around so many people. Or in a place where sounds and smells pummeled her; oil and exhaust fumes and the tart scent of too many bodies pressed tightly together on the buses that roared past; the scents of freshly baked bread and the cups of *caffè* made by a barista only a few meters away.

She took a deeper breath just as a garbage truck drove by and choked as the scent of garbage filled the air. She went so pale he thought she might vomit, but she managed to fight the instinct to gag.

He stepped closer even though it made the burning thirst in his throat intensify.

She took a step away from him and stumbled on an uneven paving stone.

He caught her by the elbow, hauling her up. "You need my help." He changed his grip, fingers brushing against the skin of her forearm. A frisson, like a fine shiver, passed through her; the hairs on her arms rose, her skin flushing.

That was strange. Was she somehow sensing the admiring stares from the men who passed by on the footpath? He glared at one who looked a little too long; the human stumbled over his feet before rushing away. His fingers brushed over her skin as he pulled her closer.

She shivered again.

"Are you cold?"

"I'm fine." She pulled at her arm. He didn't immediately let go. "I'm fine." She tugged again.

He let go.

"Thank you." She moved her head as if looking around. He watched her closely, aware of how lost and exposed she felt in this unfamiliar place.

She turned those ice-blue eyes on him, uncannily like she could see him, and asked, "What? Why are you staring at me?"

"How do you know I'm staring at you?"

"I can feel the weight of it. So ... what is it?"

"I ..." Damn it, he shouldn't be the one to feel uncertain. Pulling himself together he said softly. "I simply wish to help you."

"Why?"

"Lord Hei would never forgive me if you hurt yourself."

"I'm not useless."

"I never said you were."

Her mouth fell open on a gasp. "You called me a child!"

"You are."

"I'm nineteen. When you were still human, a nineteen-year-old was considered a grown woman. I'd be married and have babies by now."

He paused, unsettled by how close to home her words were. He and his wife were merely sixteen when they married. "This is not the thirteenth century." He took her hand, meaning to place it on his arm, but she yanked it away again regardless. "Ardenne ... please. It is very busy here and the space inside is not known to you at all. In the interest of getting to the train as quickly as possible, it would be best if you allowed me to lead you. So stop pulling away and allow me to assist you."

She looked for a moment like she wished to argue, but then simply nodded and held her hand out, seeking his arm. He stood still while she situated herself beside him, her hand on the crook of his arm, then said, "Are you ready?"

She nodded, but did not raise her face to his once more, instead, bowed her head as if she was trying to ignore he was there at all.

"Bring the bags," he instructed Matteus. "Then scout around until we leave. Stay sharp."

"I'm always sharp." He scowled once more at Gabriel before taking off with the bags toward the platform where they were to meet Lord Hei's private train.

Gabriel sighed, then with Ardenne holding lightly to his arm, he moved from the curb into the shadow of the *Stazione Centrale*. Still obviously bewildered by the unfamiliar sounds and scents around her, she allowed him to lead her without another protest.

They walked into the cool, echoing space, their footsteps clicking on the hard, marbled surface. The mixed smells of dirt and oil and perspiration became stronger as they walked through the press of people hurrying to catch their train. A crackling voice announced the next train destinations at periodic intervals, adding to the buzz of noise. Ardenne's head jerked this way and that, fingers tightening on his arm.

"Are you okay?"

She swallowed hard. "You were right. It is very busy here. I never realized it would be like this. So full of sounds and smells and sensations. It's ... too full. I can't make a picture in my mind. Everything's too chaotic." Her head bent as she muttered, "You probably don't understand."

"Yes, I do. It's hard to hear the echoes, the dead sounds that tell you where walls and furniture lay. You can smell the people, but only *en masse*. In places like this, you lose the nuances that help you use the radar senses Lord Hei has taught you to use."

"How do you know that?"

He couldn't tell her it was because he could sense it directly from her. She had no idea about their bond and never would if it was up to him. So he shared the only truth he could. "My vampire senses are overwhelmed in places like this. My first time in the city as a vampire made my head pound, every sound a shriek in my ears, every scent an assault I couldn't ignore, the colors too vibrant and bright until all I heard and smelled and saw was a cacophony that made no sense. It took me some time to learn to deal with it, to draw back and be able to separate the parts until it all made sense again." He squeezed her hand where it clung to his arm. "You will make sense of it, with practice."

She nodded, inching closer to him.

He wished she wouldn't do that. It tore at the protective instinct in his soul that the bond was tied into. He wanted to pick her up and run through the station to the awaiting train, to save her from every possible danger and everything that distressed her. But he couldn't. What he'd said to Matteus was true. She had to learn to be strong.

He may not agree with his Sire in sending her away at this time —she was still so young, despite being the age he'd been when he'd become a father when human—but Lord Hei was right about her magic. It sizzled all around her. She needed to be trained or she'd give herself away to those who must never know she existed. He wished there was some other way, but there wasn't. She wasn't a Huntress like her mother and the only other cover they had for her training was that she was to be the next Bartolli Prime. And this was the way the Bartolli Prime had been trained since they came to serve Lord Hei centuries ago. Tomas had gone by train with a

Guardian and an armed vampire guard—they couldn't tip their hand that Ardenne was any different. They had to follow the usual protocols.

She was chewing on her lip again, the fresh scent of blood a torment he fought with every breath. He couldn't allow his fangs to show in a place this crowded. She needed comfort, and even though he was the last person she probably wanted comfort from, he was the only one here. He put his arm around her and kept moving forward.

She tucked her chin into her chest. At first, he thought she was trying to listen harder, but then he saw the blush redden the skin of her neck.

"Are you hot?"

"No." The blush deepened, the emotions battering him through the bond a riot of confusion.

Frowning, but aware he wasn't going to get anything more out of her by the way she'd hunched her shoulders, he kept silent and led her swiftly through the bustle and noise to the platform where Lord Hei's private train waited for them. He led her into the velvet quiet of a carriage and let go of her arm, desperate now because of the thirst to get away from her as soon as possible.

She swallowed hard, but lifted her head, an attitude of listening in the tilt of her chin. He smiled, encouraged by her resilience—his Sire had been correct about that, although it didn't make his unease shift.

It was good, though, to see that she was already trying to figure out her new surrounds.

A door opened and a woman with the warrior bearing of an Amazon entered the carriage, her dark hair cut short and choppy, sticking out at the ends in a style that made her look elfin despite her height. Her feline-shaped brown eyes sparkled as she took in the two of them standing there, and her generous mouth opened in a wide, delighted smile.

"Gabriel. How wonderful to see you." Her tone spoke of a

cultured English upbringing—no surprise given her branch of the family had been stationed there twenty years ago.

"Sarita. Charmed as always." Gabriel took her hand, appreciating the way her gaze met his, her grip firm.

She turned from him to the girl standing at his side. "And this is Ardenne?"

"Of course."

"It's lovely to meet you, Ardenne. I'm Sarita Cartelli."

She grasped Ardenne's hand in hers but didn't let go after Ardenne mumbled hello. Instead, she turned, placing Ardenne's hand on her arm. He sensed her powers flare—she was most likely reading Ardenne's emotional state and sending out comforting vibes. Ardenne relaxed; so did he. It was no wonder Lord Hei had handpicked Sarita for this job. His Sire was right—Ardenne was in safe hands.

And yet ... He had the insatiable urge to stay by her side, to not let her out of his sight. By The First, he had to go now, before the damnable bond made it impossible for him to leave at all. It had never been this bad. What was wrong with him? He shook that thought away and said, "Be good, Ardenne. Learn well. If you need me, I will come."

"You're going?"

"Of course." Forcing himself to turn away from her need, he gave Sarita her instructions.

CHAPTER 5
IMAGES AND IMAGINATION

There is a time she will start to see
Everything she could, or would, be
If only she has the courage to fly
She will surpass even the heavenly sky.
Extract from The Middleton Manifesto, Prophecy 9, Book 1

He was leaving her. Now?

Their conversation swirled around Ardenne, the words making no sense as she scrambled to understand the feelings that welled inside, swirling through her like a torrent out of control. Her heart beat faster and for one mad moment Ardenne wanted to grab his hand, hold on and never let go. He might have been awful in Lord Hei's office, following it up with a supreme bout of rudeness in the car, but he'd been nothing but kind as he'd ushered her through the train station and now she didn't want him to go. He was her last link with family, with home. She had no idea where Matteus was, didn't even know if she'd get to say goodbye. So the thought of Gabriel going was suddenly terrifying.

And there was something in his voice that made her think he didn't want to go either.

Oh, if only she could see his face, to read the play of emotion that would tell her more. But she couldn't. Frustration tightened her throat, burned behind her sightless eyes. Her fingers tightened on Sarita's bare arm.

If only she could see. If only she could—

She almost gasped as an image swam in her mind of a man, a beautiful man.

Gabriel.

She knew it was him. She'd felt those features under her childish fingers all those years ago and had built a picture of him in her mind in those few wonderful moments. But that had been an image with no life, no color. Not that she knew colors, but Papa and Lord Hei had helped her relate to them with her other senses.

This was not like that image at all. Color painted the shadowed picture of Gabriel she'd kept in her mind, and it was more wonderful than any image she'd created before.

He was beautiful. A beauty she could never have conjured from her imagination alone.

But how?

She didn't know. All she knew was that the image she saw in her mind now was Gabriel, his black clothes an imprint of darkness against the lush burgundy and deep, burnished redwood of the train carriage. She had no idea how she knew what those colors were, but it was a certainty in her mind she couldn't deny.

Not that colors mattered when his image took her breath away. The blood beat fast in her veins. The whole world centered on him; the light in the dark.

He looked younger than she'd imagined; why she was so shocked about that she wasn't sure. It was well known he'd been turned when he was twenty-four human years. Perhaps she'd expected the weight of the eight hundred years that had passed since his human death to show in some way on his features. But they didn't. Maybe it was because his skin was so pale with the smooth, molded quality of Lord Hei's finest Lladdro figurines. His lips were full like the cheeks of a plum but pressed closed. They were the color she imagined blood must be, thick and warm and full of the rich scent of life and love, dangerous and forbidden. Waves of thick hair caressed his upswept cheekbones, his neck. It was shorter than she remembered and dark yet held a reddish glow that sparked in the light, like the glow that appeared behind her closed lids when she'd turned her face to the sun for too long trying to understand the secret of colors hidden within the swirling lights. He was tall but not willowy, exuding strength and anger and something she couldn't grasp, something she could feel but not understand.

Then he turned from Sarita to stare at her. His cool, sparkling dark blue eyes—so dark as to look violet—pinned her to the spot. She stood, mesmerized, as they darkened to the deepest velvet with a glint of warmth the color of darkest purple—the color she lived with every day. In that purple there was something like a fire at their center, warming from a pinpoint flash of light. It grew as he stared at her.

Fire burned with equal intensity inside her.

Gasping, she let go of Sarita's arm. The image of Gabriel—that confusing, frightening, beautiful image—slipped away.

Trembling, uncertain now that what she'd seen had been caused by anything but a vivid imagination, she tried to push the memory of it aside. But a shadow imprint remained like light burning into the back of her retinas.

She shivered.

No. It was ridiculous. She couldn't have truly seen him. It was probably a trick created by her desperate need to not let him go.

A cold hand landed on her shoulder. She jumped.

"Ardenne. Did you hear me?"

"Don't touch me like that," she snapped, annoyed because of the searing heat that shot through her at his barest touch, the pounding of her heart and the weakness in her knees.

She wasn't weak. She'd been given a huge responsibility and she was determined to live up to it. Especially in the face of this vampire's condemnation.

He mustn't see her as weak. And he couldn't know of the wild fantasy that had just occurred inside her mind. Nobody could be as beautiful as the image she'd just conjured up in her imagination. It simply wasn't possible.

He pulled his hand away and she swallowed down the sob that rose in her throat at the loss of it. Determination helped her angle her head in what Lord Hei had termed her regal nod, and said, "You can go now. I'll be fine."

"As you wish." His tone held a hint of mockery.

She opened her mouth to retort, but the air felt different, like something was missing.

He was already gone.

Anger seeped out of her with a suddenness that had tears burning her eyes. She bit her lip to try to stop the tears. It didn't help. She pressed her fingers to stinging eyes, lost, defeated, despite her resolve of a few moments before. What did it matter if she collapsed now that Gabriel was gone?

"Ardenne?"

She jumped, turning toward the voice. She'd forgotten Sarita was there.

"I imagine you're feeling a little overwhelmed."

Despite the fact the woman's voice was warm and sympathetic Ardenne frowned, wishing she hadn't given so much away. "I'm okay."

A strange pressure pressed behind her eyes, breaking off as the woman spoke again.

"Yes, you will be." She sounded a little amused. "Shall I help you to a seat?"

Ardenne shook her head. It was bad enough that she'd allowed herself to be overwhelmed after getting out of the car and had leaned on Gabriel like she had. Lord Hei and Papa would be disappointed. Pulling herself up, she said firmly, "Thank you. But I can manage."

The echoes inside the carriage told her there was a bank of seats to her right. She began to move over that way but barked her shin against the edge of the coffee table. Damn it. Her radar hearing was still a little upset by the senses overload she'd experienced outside and by the unexpected feeling of loss when Gabriel left. *"Excuses rob you of the ability to learn."* Lord Hei's oft-spoken words rang in her head as she rubbed her barked shin surreptitiously and sank onto the plush velvet lounge, vowing to no longer give in to the overwhelm.

She was better than this. She had to make certain everyone else knew this too.

Sarita sat opposite her.

Silence reigned for long moments. Ardenne shifted once, twice, then asked, "Where's Matteus? Do I get to say goodbye to him?"

"I'm sorry. I think he had to run. I was told he had a plane to catch."

"A plane? Where is he going?"

"He's been posted to Indonesia from what I understand."

Of course. She'd been told that. "But if he's not here and Gabriel is gone, who is my Guardian? Is Corinna coming?"

"I don't think so. And Gabriel isn't gone. He's just taking charge of the security team. You can't travel without a guard. You are Tomas Bartolli's successor, after all."

No Corinna and no Matteus. Only Gabriel. Her heart sped up again at the thought. Trying not to think about it or him, she said, "I've always had two guards on the few occasions I left *Casa Cinque*. Is that why you're here, Ms Cartelli? To guard me too?"

"No. Although I am trained in defense, that's not my primary role. I'm the Cousins' representative and your Companion. I'm here to take care of all your needs. Outside of all that though, I would like to become friends."

"Oh."

Sarita laughed, a friendly sound, full and tinkling like the voice of a brook. "So … I'd like you to call me Sarita or any shortening of that you'd like. Is there a shortening of your name you'd like?"

Ardenne frowned. "Everyone has always called me Ardenne." She tipped her head. "But I've always liked Ari if anyone was ever going to shorten my name."

"Ari it is then." She clapped her hands. "Oh, we could be Ari and Sari!" She laughed. "Or is that a bit silly?"

Ardenne shrugged, her lips twitching into a smile. "I actually like that."

"Good. Now, refreshments? You must be thirsty after your long drive."

Funnily enough, the terrible thirst had gone. When had that happened? *When Gabriel left,* a voice inside whispered.

What? Why? How could Gabriel's presence cause her to be thirsty in a hungry sort of way? That didn't make any kind of sense. Although, much of what had happened since he'd jumped into the moving car hadn't made sense at all, least of all her rollercoaster of reactions to him and everything else.

"Ari? Would you like a drink?"

Sarita's voice snapped her attention back to the here and now. "I-I'm fine. Maybe later."

There was that strange pressure again, like the press of tears behind her eyes. Then her hand was taken by Sarita, followed by a comforting squeeze. The breeze of her movement brushed over Ardenne's face. She smelled of sunshine and flowers; familiar scents. She breathed in deeply and sighed with relief. Maybe, this woman could be a friend.

She smiled at the thought.

Sarita let go of her hand and as she did so, most of the strange pressure behind Ardenne's eyes faded. Before she could wonder about that, there was a change in the hum of the engine and a shunt as the train jerked then smoothed into a forward motion.

They were pulling out. Her journey had truly begun.

Excitement fluttered next to homesickness, creating nausea. She swallowed down the thickening sensation in her throat and sat up straighter as Sarita shifted in her seat, perhaps leaning back to get more comfortable.

Ardenne tried to do the same.

After a moment of silence, Sarita said, "Would you like to touch my face? I know not all visually impaired people like to do that, but I'm told Lord Hei taught you to use all your senses and that you can create an image through touch. That's remarkable."

Ardenne had to choke back a laugh. "Not so remarkable." At least, Gabriel didn't think so.

Pressure built behind her eyes again, making her wince. Then Ardenne jerked as the young woman's soft fingers brushed her cheek, cupping her chin.

"Never listen to the negative thoughts of others, Ari. They will only seek to harm you." She drew back. Ardenne felt her contemplative gaze. "You will learn your blindness can't be a hindrance. In fact, none of the Cousins will give you an inch because of it."

"I don't want them to," she said, her chin rising in stubborn defiance.

"I wouldn't either." Sarita grasped Ardenne's hand and led it to her face. "Show me how you do this."

Ardenne smiled, liking her new Companion's open friendliness. She'd never really had a female friend that was truly hers before. Mia had been the only girl around her age at *Casa Cinque*, and there was too much sibling rivalry to ever think of her sister as a friend. In fact, there was a definite lack of human females living at *Casa Cinque*. All of the Bartolli families with children lived elsewhere, either situated in the nearby village and traveling to *Casa Cinque* every day if they worked there; many lived in other cities where they did their work for the Bartolli Prime and Lord Hei. There had been a few families around many years ago, but after Mama died ten years ago, all had moved away, leaving only a few aunts, their sons and Cook as permanent residents aside from Papa, Mia and herself. Those women were all too old and busy to take the time to spend with a girl longing for some female interaction. She might have been closer to Mia if her sister hadn't gone to school in the village when younger and then to the high school in the valley, making friends there. Ardenne had not been allowed to go because they had no program for visually impaired people and so …

She shook her head. She wouldn't feel sorry for herself. It didn't matter what happened in the past. Here was a woman, perhaps not too much older than her, offering friendship. She might be the assigned Companion, but there was warmth in her tone that made Ardenne think that she was truthful in her wish for friendship and wasn't just trying to fill the requirements of a job.

Longing to know the features that went with that warm voice, she traced her fingers over Sarita's oval face, noting the high brow, straight, thin nose and pointed chin. Eyebrows shaped like constant questions arched over almond-shaped eyes with long, soft lashes. Her cheekbones were high, lips full, the bottom one especially so. "What color are your eyes?"

"Brown."

"Brown-brown, chocolate-brown or amber?"

Sarita laughed. "You know color distinction?"

She shrugged. "Papa and Lord Hei would describe things in ways I could understand so I imagine I can see them. Chocolate is warm and melting and rich. Brown-brown is like soil or bark, warm in the sun, cool in the shade, full of spicy, musty, nutty scents. Amber is sticky and thick, cinnamon and sweet."

"You do that for all colors?"

Ardenne nodded. "So which is it?"

"I suppose they're more amber than normal brown. Not nearly as pretty as your eyes which are—can I try?"

"If you want."

"Hmm, let me see. Your eyes are luminescent, the palest blue like the winter's sky or the blue you see in the depths of ice." She laughed. "That's no good. You can't see the sky or into the depths of ice."

"No. But I know the coldness of both."

"Well, that's not right at all. Your eyes are anything but cold." She laughed again.

The sound made Ardenne want to laugh with her. "So what about your hair? What color is it?"

"Black."

"Like silence and shadows and night." Ardenne felt Sarita's hair. Short and choppy, it swept over her brow in wisps and curled at the nape of her neck. "I like this."

"I like yours. It is so long and wavy and such a beautiful color. Night warmed by the glow of a fire. How was that for a description?"

"Good. I—" She jumped as the sound around them changed, echoing, enclosed.

Sarita touched Ardenne's arm. "We're in a tunnel. The line between *Milano* and *Firenze* is mostly underground now. No more unsightly tracks and wires to jar the eyes of tourists." She squeezed Ardenne's hand. "No reason to be concerned."

Ardenne nodded and was about to return to her exploration when the high-pitched sound of tearing metal screeched through the air, hurting her ears. The train shuddered but didn't stop. "What was that?"

"I don't know." Sarita's tone filled with worry. "Maybe something was on the track. Stay here. I'll be back." The door clicked shut behind her before Ardenne could protest.

Alone, a rarity for her, she sat still, scraping her fingers over the material of her jeans. Waiting.

A growling howl shattered the silence. The train shuddered again, swaying violently. The movement knocked her off the lounge. Brakes squealed. Ardenne pushed to her knees, heart clamoring in her chest.

Footfalls thundered along the roof of the carriage, one set, then another and another.

There were no heartbeats. She couldn't hear the heartbeats!

Vampires were attacking the train.

Shuffling scuffling sounds and tightly held grunts punched the air. A noise, like the whisper of dead leaves, rustled inside her mind. The rustling became clearer as the fighting continued, forming a vibration of words repeated over and over, *"Guard her well, Gabriel. Protect her from harm."*

"I will, my Sire. I promise."

The words made her jump to her feet, quivering, wanting to fight, to prove she didn't need protecting. A high-pitched wail rang in her ears. Then a beat replaced the wail. A low, thready thump-thump, a sound so familiar she didn't recognize it at first—a heartbeat, but not her own.

More shouting from the front of the train. Footfalls sped up, fading into the distance. The other heartbeat went with them.

Fear played along her nerves, shredding them like paper. But not fear for herself. For Sarita. For Gabriel. What was happening? Her heart squeezed in her chest as the sound of fighting outside intensified. Cries of anger, pain, and pleasure tore through the air almost covering the swoosh of sound as the door at the far end of the carriage slid open.

"Sarita?"

She knew as soon as the name left her lips this wasn't Sarita. There was no warmth, no heartbeat.

Vampire.

But it wasn't Gabriel, of that she was certain. He made her feel uncomfortable—all hot and tingly—but not the kind of uncomfortable this creature created.

A sweet enticing scent wrapped around her, calling to her, making her nerves tingle and flame, urging her to move toward it.

Something inside her mind shuddered in repudiation of the violation of that scent, the way it dug inside her. None of Lord Hei's sirelings ever made her feel that way, no matter how good they smelled. This vampire was not one she knew. It didn't offer warmth or comfort, only enticement and death and a horrible, creeping certainty that she was incapable of stopping it.

A whimper escaped her mouth as she heard it prowl toward her.

CHAPTER 6
ATTACK

She will be lost, she will be found
Hunted by all, tracked to ground
Mysteries always to be unwound
Caught in the sigh of a familiar sound.
Extract from The Middleton Manifesto, Prophecy 10, Book 1

The vampire stalked forward. It barely made a sound and yet menace pushed at her, stroked at her skin. Instinct screamed in her veins to run. But all Ardenne could do was stagger back as though her feet were caught in vines. Horror caught at her as she realized that she didn't have to see it to be caught in its hypnotic pull.

Was that a feature of one of the cults? The Wild? Dark Brethren? She didn't know. How could she? She hadn't been trained yet. Didn't truly know what distinguished one from the other or how to defeat them. All she knew was they were different from Lord Hei's sirelings: they killed and hurt people for food and pleasure. And now, one was here with her, prowling toward her and she was all alone with nobody to help. Her guards were outside, fighting off the others.

She had to help herself.

But how?

"*Mon Dieu*. You look like her."

Its voice was like nothing she'd ever heard before. It was a song of purest crystal with a slight sibilance of tongue against fangs. Strange that its fangs were down. Lord Hei and his sirelings' fangs never came out unless they were about to feed or fight.

Was it about to feed on her?

She should be frightened by that fact, but she wasn't. It wasn't just its crystal-clear voice—although it would have intoxicated and mesmerized alone—but the scent of it … Oh!

That scent! It fired along her nerves, pulling at her, making her tremble with want. She had a sudden longing to give in, to give over everything she was to its sweet seduction.

And she would have if the thought alone wasn't so alien as to snap through the fog shrouding her mind.

It was trying to compel her!

Lord Hei's sirelings were forbidden to do that to another being. It was anathema to all of them; a kind of mind-rape.

She shuddered, stumbled a few more feet away from the horror of the creature in front of her. Her foot caught on a cushion, and she fell, arms wheeling, and hit the ground with a painful explosion of breath. There was no sound of movement but suddenly the vampire stood over her, his presence pressing into her skin. His breath, sweet, intoxicating, brushed her face, making her want to lean forward, to draw closer to such an exotic scent; to breathe it in and never take another breath seemed like something she really should do.

"You will come with me now."

"Yes." She began to move, to get up. She had to do exactly what he said.

A shout from the front of the train made him shift away. With his breath no longer caressing her skin and twining through her veins, his voice no longer shattering her thoughts, reality crashed back in.

What the hell was she doing? She couldn't let it compel her!

She scrambled backward, shoving the cushions aside that impeded her flight. She had to fight it. Get away. If she didn't, she might not survive the hour.

"Ah, *ma petite*. Don't be shy. You want to come with me. I know you do."

It had turned back to her, its intent once again focused entirely on her. "No!" She gritted her teeth against the desire to do its bidding. "No!"

There was shocked silence. Then, "*Viens avec moi!* Come with me. Now."

"Not going to happen," she spat out.

She heard it move back, as if surprised. She took the opportunity to try to gain her feet—she didn't know much in the way of fighting, but one thing was certain: she couldn't fight while lying on the floor. But as she pushed up and back, her foot slipped on the wet carpet. Her temple hit the edge of the coffee table with a loud thwack, the pain a sharp white light behind her eyes. Dazed, she lifted her hand and touched, feeling the hot stickiness of blood.

The vampire sucked in a breath. "Mmm. *Ma petite*, you smell so sweet. Shall I take a little sip?"

She pushed back again, sliding sideways, head rapping against the metallic corner of the lounge. Pain spiked through her, a white-hot flare, the foam before the wake. And in the wake was darkness. A red, hazy darkness she'd never seen before; and in that red haze, dark images swam, foul and blood ridden. They surged through her mind: power, ego, and a desire tinged with the madness of blind lust. And thirst. A thirst like the one she'd experienced in the car.

Her throat closed over that harsh, parching thirst. A thirst that could only be assuaged by one thing.

Her blood.

Panic flared, her heart lurched, mind spun, slipped sideways like she was falling, falling. She tried to take a breath, to steady herself, and as she did, an image flared in her mind.

Like when she thought she'd seen Gabriel, the image was full of light and colors, but more intense and washed with the red haze of all-consuming thirst. Hunger.

Sitting in stark relief in the haze of red was a young woman with a pale face and pointed chin, large luminous white eyes, and crooked ponytail of dark hair cascading across her shoulder, a trickle of blood on her brow.

It was her! She knew it was because she'd felt it too often not to know.

But how?

She had no idea.

Her mind reeled as a white hand extended from her viewpoint, the nails like sharp, glistening diamonds—from the descriptions she'd been told, they were vampire nails.

The nails were tipped red with blood and the fingers stretched out to touch, to grab. Horror held the scream in her throat but didn't stop her from reacting. A terrible presence pushed at her mind and without thinking, she pushed back.

The vampire grunted, stumbled back. Her viewpoint jostled. But that hand remained outstretched toward her, its fingers curling into claws.

By The First! She was seeing from the vampire's eyes!

A hot wave surged through her, but she didn't have time to question the strangeness of this or what it meant, because the creature was obviously about to attack.

As it came at her, she did the only thing she could do from her position on the floor—she rolled back and kicked out with both feet aimed at what she hoped was its stomach. The impact jarred her, but she didn't let that stop her from pushing with all the strength and desperation inside her.

He was shoved back with such force that he flew across the room to hit the wall across the other side of the carriage with a loud smash and crunch of wood. In the corner of his vision, chunks of plaster and wood exploded around him.

By The First! How had she done that? She'd never been in a fight in her life and although she'd studied the basics of several martial arts as well as dance to help with her movement and fitness, she'd never actually used any of it. And she'd never had that kind of strength in her.

It had to be adrenaline.

But she couldn't sit there trying to figure it out. She had to move. Now. While it was occupied. She turned, scrambled to her feet, but before she'd made it more than a few stumbling steps, the red haze that was the vampire's mind deepened. The heat of his anger surged through her, mixed with a heady dose of blazing pleasure that fired through her veins and clenched between her legs. Gasping, she clutched her body, holding in the trembling euphoria and cried, "Get out. Get out of my head!"

The image snapped out of her mind as suddenly as it had come.

The vampire approached her, his steps cautious, voice somehow needy and uncertain. "How did you do that?"

Ardenne didn't know but wasn't about to admit it. "Don't come closer," she gasped, using the seats to support her as she moved back toward the door behind her. "I'll do it again."

He halted briefly before taking a taunting step toward her. "Oh, I wish you would. That was *délicieuse*." His voice was back to the enticing drawl, pulling at her, drugging her senses. "Now I really do have to taste."

"Don't touch me. Don't you dare touch me!"

His steps faltered. "What ... What are you ... doing?"

"Don't touch me. Don't touch me," Ardenne repeated, the phrase becoming a mantra in her mind, the force of it building, building, until a chilling heat flared out from inside her, bursting from her skin.

There was a crash, breaking glass. The vampire growled, frustrated, like he was fighting something. "*Non. Non. C'est impossible.* You weren't supposed ... to know how ... to use magic."

What? Magic?

He was insane. She wasn't doing this. To have magic ... it was impossible, forbidden, dangerous. No! This wasn't magic. It couldn't be. Nevertheless, she pushed hard against his presence, using her words like a shield. "Don't touch me."

He let out a frustrated roar.

She had no idea what was happening, but she hoped it lasted long enough for Gabriel to realize the vampires weren't just outside. He had to come.

Gabriel, help! she screamed in her mind.

The vampire's presence pushed into her mind again. She cried out at the crushing pain as she fought its compulsion, gritting her teeth, afraid she might pass out. A different kind of darkness wavered over her. Sweat prickled her skin, stinging the cut on her brow as she pushed against the sensation. She couldn't lose consciousness now. Not until Gabriel came.

Gabriel. Please help.

He'd promised he'd come if she called.

But he was outside fighting the others, thinking her safe. He wouldn't come.

Despair sank into her skin and the darkness crept over her. Whatever was stopping the vampire faltered, died. And he was there again, in front of her, his breath over her face, cold hand gripping her arm. "What did you do to me? What did you do?" he screamed, nails biting into her skin.

Ardenne's teeth snapped together, her head spinning with pain, white and black lights flashing in the darkness of her mind, but still she struggled, trying to break his crushing grip. His fingers tightened until she thought her arm was about to snap. She screamed.

"No!" Sarita's cry was like an echo of sound underwater.

"Sarita!" Ardenne gasped as the vampire let go of her, its fingernails slicing across her bare arm as it spun to face the woman who had entered the carriage.

It hissed, anger vibrating from it. "You should not have come, Companion. Now I will feed from you before I take her."

"Sarita, go. Run!"

"You will not touch either of us," Sarita said, voice menacing and filled with a power that made electricity tingle over Ardenne's skin.

An expulsion of breath followed Sarita's words, then a scream of rage and a crash—splintering wood, the crack of broken plaster. More blood scented the air.

"You dare!" the vampire screamed, its rage a shrill shriek.

"I do more than dare. I give you pain!" Sarita's voice was barely recognizable as the words hissed out of her throat, a wildcat protecting its young.

The acrid tang of lightning scented the air and the vampire cried out, the sound filled with both pleasure and pain.

Before she could try to figure out what was going on, glass smashed to Ardenne's left. She raised her arms, covering her head as the scent of mountain air flowed over her. Less than a breath later, an ice-cold hand brushed the hair from her face. "Ardenne."

"Gabriel. You came," she blubbered as he lifted her up so very gently before lowering her to a seat. "You came."

"I'm here," Gabriel breathed. "You're all right."

A screech of hatred sounded behind them, and Sarita cried out. "Gabriel! I can't hold him."

Gabriel left her side so quickly she wouldn't have known he was gone but for the breeze of his leaving.

"Sarita—a shield," he said as the sound of metal clashing on metal lit the air. "Stop the others from coming in."

The other vampire shrieked—rage and pain—but she could hear nothing from Gabriel as they fought. If the vampire got any blows in, he didn't respond, just fought with a silence that was menace and threat. Ardenne wished she could see what was happening, so afraid the vampire might get the upper hand in the tight space, that others would join it. And where was Sarita? Had she run out to get a shield? Was she fighting the others? Maybe she'd gone for help. Perhaps Ardenne should move, go for help, but her legs were weak as she pushed to her feet, dizziness and nausea swaying through her. She turned to grab the back of the seat before she fell.

"Ardenne!" Gabriel and Sarita's simultaneous cry was drowned out by a loud crash followed by a high-pitched scream that made her clutch at her ears and fall to her knees.

Then the screech was cut off by the sigh of something sharp slicing through the air—she knew that sound: a sword swinging swiftly through the air. She'd sat and listened many times when Lord Hei and Papa had trained others in warcraft and defense not to know it well.

The sound was quickly followed by wet warmth that sprayed across her face scented of copper and rot—blood, so hot, it stung—and two thumps hit the ground near her foot.

She scrambled back from what she knew were bits of the vampire but crashed into upturned furniture. There was nowhere to go.

Her skin burned where the vampire blood had splashed across her face, arms and chest, and everything hurt, especially her head. Although, that pain was quickly being overtaken by where the blood sizzled and burned on her skin.

She couldn't stop the sob from exploding out of her as she tried to wipe it off, but that just seemed to make everything worse.

Cool arms caught her, holding her against a firm chest.

"It burns. It burns," she said, trying to scrape it off with her nails.

"Stop. You're hurting yourself. Let me help." Then he lifted her, laying her down on something warm and soft.

"Sarita. A cloth. She's been sprayed by its blood." Cold hands cupped her head. A cool breath brushed over her face, enticing, chasing tingling warmth across her skin, taking away the burn.

"You came," she mumbled again, as he wiped her face with a wet cloth.

"Ardenne. Ardenne, stay with me."

But she couldn't. Not even when *he* asked it of her. The shock of what had happened and the blow to the head proved too much. And as darkness swept in, the vampire's voice echoed in her mind: *"Mon Dieu. You look like her."*

Like whom?

It was the last thought she had before darkness took her under.

~

ARDENNE BECAME aware of something cool and wet across her brow, and soft warmth beneath her head. Rising from the dark of unconsciousness, she pushed the wet thing off her forehead. "Gabriel?" She tried to sit up.

"Don't move, Ari." Not Gabriel. Sarita. "You took quite a bump to your head." The cold cloth was replaced, and a cloud wandered over Ardenne's mind, her limbs softened, and she sank into the warmth of Sarita's lap.

She sighed in relief, but relief was quickly swamped by terrible memories pounding like waves on the beach, thundering in and out of her mind.

She gasped, tried to sit up again, but fingers skated across her brow, combing back her hair, the rhythm of it making the wave disappear in the fog that enclosed her mind. "Shh, Ari. Rest. Just rest."

She wanted to do that, to sink into the soothing fog, but it turned to a red haze and the wave of memories came crashing back, a churning unintelligible turmoil.

Ardenne listened for any sound that might make sense of the memories crashing around inside her head. All she could hear was the train as it clacked along the track, the wind rushing in through the broken window, Sarita's heartbeat, slow and sure, and her own, still pounding blood through her veins with a resounding thud-thud-thud. Everything seemed normal, except her head hurt more than she'd ever remembered it hurting before and she seemed to have horrible memories of a vampire attacking her. Of accusing her of using magic!

But that couldn't be. Witches were enemies to all vampires including Lord Hei and his sirelings.

And yet, she'd somehow managed to see what the vampire saw. And Sarita had …

The fog pressed into her mind again, her memory of what had occurred becoming fuzzy once more.

The door opened. "How is she?"

Gabriel. He *was* here. He hadn't left her.

She tried to sit up again, heart thumping wildly in her chest, but cool hands pushed her back. "You have a nasty bump, Ardenne. Stay down."

The cool hands left her, but the nausea and pain in her head remained, so she stayed where she was. "What happened?"

"We were attacked by at least twenty Wild pairs—far more than we've seen together in many years. Half the human team was killed and two vampire warriors were injured badly." Sorrow drenched his tone, causing an ache in her chest. Did she know any of them? It seemed wrong to ask right now; she wasn't sure why. The loss wasn't only Gabriel's. But the words wouldn't form in her mouth. Instead, tears burned her eyes for those lost, sorrow and anger intertwined.

"The rest of the attackers?" Sarita asked.

"Dead or gone. I've rung ahead and Vincente is sending extra security for when we reach *Firenze*. You have nothing to worry about."

"Good."

Nothing to worry about? People were dead, vampires injured. Warriors who had fought to keep her safe. And there was something else. If only she could remember past the howling roil of sound and images thundering through her mind.

Sarita brushed her hand down Ardenne's hair, and with the movement, most of the pain faded. Without the pain muddling her thoughts, memories began to sift into place.

"We're safe?" Ardenne asked as a memory, a red haze of anger and sex and animal longing, separated itself from the confusion, making her shudder.

"For now." Gabriel shifted away. "I'll sweep the area. Make certain no more of the Wild are lying in wait. Don't leave her side."

"I know my job," Sarita said, her voice tight.

A tense pause. A deep breath. Then the sound of them moving further away to speak in hushed voices.

Voices she could still hear clearly.

"It needs to be done now," Gabriel whispered. "We can't wait until she's begun her training in *Firenze* as planned."

"No, we can't." Sarita sounded ... horrified? Fearful?

"You must."

"I-It's far safer to do what I'm doing."

"We are past lies."

"I have my orders."

"That may be true, but you are here because you can think for yourself. Do so now."

"I will do what's best." Her voice was flat, resolute.

Something more passed between them, something heavy and important before Gabriel said, "I hope that's true."

The door snicked closed, signaling Gabriel's exit.

What had they been talking about? It had seemed so important, but she couldn't make sense of their words, couldn't order her thoughts. They had the sticky, muddled consistency of a freshly mixed *panettone*.

She pressed a hand to her head and tried to sit up.

"Ari. No, don't get up." Sarita's hands were suddenly on her shoulders, gently pushing her back down, but she fought them, desperate to break the contact, to not allow herself to give in to the warmth and comfort offered. If she did that, she'd sink back into the hazy dark and when she awoke, she knew she wouldn't be brave enough to ask the questions that scared her to her core.

If she didn't ask those questions, she wasn't worthy to be Lord Hei's Prime.

Desperately trying to pull herself together, to fight against the fact her words wanted to stick in her throat, she managed to say, "That vampire ... he was going to ... he was going to—"

"You heard Gabriel. You're safe." Sarita stroked her hair, coaxing Ardenne to stay calm. "You're safe."

Ardenne shook her head. "He's still here ... with me ... inside my head. Evil and longing and lust and pain. It liked the pain. The pain excited him." She swallowed hard against rising nausea. "Gabriel killed it."

"Yes."

"Good." She paused, pressed her hands to her aching head, trying to make sense of what she'd experienced. She desperately needed someone to confide in. Sarita had been so kind. Could she tell her what had happened? Would she understand? Knowing somehow that her new friend would, she blurted out, "I saw something, Sarita. In my mind. It was like the vampire was in my mind and I saw some of what it saw."

Silence. Then, "You were dreaming, Ari."

"No. No. I kicked it away, made it fly across the room. How did I manage that?"

"Adrenaline?"

"No." She shook her head but stopped when nausea flared. Swallowing against it, she blurted out, "It accused me of using magic. I —" She snapped her mouth shut. Why had she said that? Magic was forbidden to anyone working with Lord Hei. If Sarita thought ...

But Sarita ... She'd stopped it, thrown it across the room. There had been that feeling of lightning that had swept past, that sensation of power and excitement as Sarita had grappled with it.

Sarita grasped Ardenne's face, her fingers pressing into her skin. The pressure behind Ardenne's eyes intensified. Her thoughts slipped, as if pushed aside by that pressure, while Sarita's hands remained firm and warm on her cheeks. Her words, slow, calm, gentle, flowed through that pressure. "You were dreaming, Ari."

"No, I—" Sarita stroked her cheek. The pressure expanded, fogging her mind. "But it said ... m ... magic. And you ... You stopped it with your voice. It was so strong ... b ... but you stopped it. There was this prickling sensation. I—" She gasped. "Oh, my head!"

"Sorry, Ari." Sarita's voice was strained as her fingers tightened. "By The First, you're so strong. Fuck! Gabriel is right. We have to do it now."

"Gabriel is right? About what? What do we have to do?"

There was a pause, tension thrumming in the air, before Sarita said, "Come, let's move to the next carriage where we'll be more comfortable, and I'll try to explain."

Confused, head aching again, she let Sarita help her to her feet and guide her through the carriage into another one. The sound of rushing wind cut off with the click of the door closing behind them.

"Sit down."

Ardenne sat, leaning her head in her hand. "Why does my head hurt this much?" It was like when she'd drunk too much *limoncello* with her cousin, Alexandro, last Christmas.

"It's because I tried to stop you from remembering. Gabriel was right. You're too strong. Too strong to be kept in the dark about your powers any longer."

"What? My powers? Wh-what are you ...? Th-that's not possible. Bartolli have no powers. Witches and vampires ... it's forbidden. I don't have powers—"

"Shh." Sarita sat beside her, taking her hands. "There's a lot to take in, I know, and it will be difficult to believe, but I need you to trust me."

"I don't understand." But as she said the words, clarity struck as the pain leached out of her, sliding through her fingertips, withdrawn into the woman who wanted to be her friend, who had just read her mind, not once, but continually since she'd arrived. Who'd tried to hide from her the words the vampire had uttered.

Ardenne gasped. "You read my mind."

"Yes."

"You're a witch!"

A pause, then, "And so are you."

CHAPTER 7
MAGIC

We are born with magic in our souls. It is not something we choose.
It is also not something that can be gained by learning. Although
we must learn how to use and control our magic, or our magic will
use and control us.
Extract from The Middleton Manifesto, Section on Magic,
Lesson 1

Blood pounded through her veins. She should be frightened. Instead, a longing surged to the fore within her. A longing for Sarita's words to be true.

But no ... "That's not possible." Witches had hurt members of the Family in the past to gain information about Lord Hei, one of the main reasons why magic—and associations with witches—was forbidden. She couldn't be a witch and yet ...

What had happened between her and the vampire, when she'd seen out of his eyes, when she'd held him back with nothing but desperation and her words ... The only thing that explained that was magic.

Then there was Sarita and what she'd done to the vampire to

hold him, to cause him pain until Gabriel arrived to kill him. There was no denying that had been magic because despite the fact she'd been injured and confused, Ardenne wasn't confused about the fact Sarita had been at one end of the train carriage and the vampire down the other end. She hadn't really processed it at the time, but she'd felt the magic.

So, Sarita *had* used magic with the vampire. Then she'd used it again to try to keep Ardenne from remembering any of this.

But how could a Cousin be a witch? Not only was it forbidden for any Bartolli or the Cousins to associate with them, but Ardenne had always been told they were evil.

Sarita didn't seem evil. Nor had she tried to hurt Ardenne. She'd tried to help her. Had saved her from the vampire. What's more, Gabriel had seen her do it and hadn't been surprised. It was ... unbelievable. And yet ...

"It's true, Ari. You know it's true."

Excitement overtook fear and disbelief as she tried to grasp the threads of what she was being told. She wanted to trust Sarita. But ... "It doesn't seem ... possible. Lord Hei. He'd kill you if he knew."

"No. It's our world's greatest secret but ... certain covens work with Lord Hei. They have for centuries. He would no sooner kill me than he would you."

Ardenne's mind spun with the enormity of what she was hearing. "You're lying."

"I'm not. You know I'm not. You know what I am telling you is true. You can feel it."

She did. Truth rang in Sarita's voice; truth that opened her mind, which made sense of so many things—whispers she'd heard between Papa and Lord Hei and some of the others that she'd convinced herself were her imagination or even dreams. And yet, knowing now what she'd heard was true ... well, it threw up even more questions. "It's ... it's so ... fantastical."

"I know but ... you believe me, don't you?"

She nodded. She did. She couldn't help but believe this woman who had treated her with such open warmth and then had put her own life at risk to fight for Ardenne, exposing her talents as she did. She'd trusted Ardenne with her secret by doing so, was trusting her even more now by admitting to it. And suddenly, more than anything, Ardenne wanted to live up to that trust. But ... "How? How can you be a witch? How can *I* be a witch?"

"You were born a witch, as was I. But you need training. That's why you are being sent to *Firenze*."

"No. I'm being sent to *Firenze* to train as Bartolli Prime, as Papa did before me."

"That's what we needed everyone to believe, but it's not true."

"I'm not going to be Bartolli Prime?"

"No ... I ... It's not the role ... Oh, I'm explaining this all wrong. I wish Carrington were here. He'd know what to say."

Her mind swam with everything Sarita had started to say, but the only question that came to the fore was, "Who is Carrington?"

"You'll meet Carrington soon. He's the leader of the Middleton Coven, one of the most powerful covens in the world. He had a vision about you and told Lord Hei, insisted you would need to be sent for training on your nineteenth birthday."

"Lord Hei knows about me being a witch?" Ardenne gaped, lost for words. Why hadn't he said something? Why hadn't anyone said something? Why keep this from her?

"They had to, Ardenne. For your safety and the safety of all those who know," Sarita said again, proving she was reading Ardenne's mind.

"But I ... how long? How long have they known?" Was it a recent thing? That would perhaps explain why they'd kept it a secret—because they didn't know how to tell her, or how to deal with it.

"It's not recent, Ari. He's known since your birth. As has Tomas. And Gabriel. And others like Carrington and the leader of the Cousins."

What?

Betrayal simmered inside her. How could they have kept this

from her? How could they have made her think magic was evil? How could they ...

Her mind jagged on something Sarita had said earlier and her anger died. "You said I was born this way as were you. But I thought being a witch was a genetic thing."

"It is. The gift runs through the Cousin's gene pool, which is where I get it from."

"And me? There are no witches in the Bartolli Family as far as I'm aware."

"No. There aren't. But you're not a Bartolli by birth. Your mother was a witch."

"She was?" She didn't know anything about her birth mother other than she died long ago. Tomas and Lord Hei never wanted to talk about her. She'd always assumed that was because the memories hurt too much, but maybe it was something else entirely. "Lord Hei and Tomas knew she was a witch?"

"Yes. But I don't know anything about her except for that. What I can tell you is, the reason your heritage was kept from you, the reason Lord Hei made everyone think he was against magic and witches, is because the vampire cults can't know. They can't know of the association between him and my coven. It was why the Cousins were set up like they are—to keep the magical training of Lord Hei's people a secret from everyone, but mostly the cults. They can't know that you, the next Bartolli Prime, is one. If they did, war would break out between all vampires and witches, and the humans would get caught in between. He cares too much about you, and us, and the humans, to ever let that happen."

"I ..." She shook her head. "This is a lot."

"I know." Sarita's hand grasped hers, squeezing gently. "But what's important now is that you know about your powers and the coven and that you are one of us. And that it's important you be trained in the right way—it would be terribly dangerous if you weren't. It's why Lord Hei sent me to be your Companion and has sent you to the Cousins for your training. The witch gene isn't strong enough in my family to have formed our own coven, but we have strong ties with Carrington's coven going back centuries."

"Lord Hei wants me to be taught to use magic?"

"Yes. Just like he did me. When my powers began to manifest, he sent me to train with the leader of the Middleton Coven himself."

"But ... why lie to me? To most of the Family? Why make us think magic is forbidden?"

"I can't answer that for him. I do know what Carrington told me when I asked him something similar."

"And that was?"

"That Lord Hei has long worked with those of us in the Middleton Coven to protect our world from the ravages of the Wild and Dark Brethren and to protect our most precious secrets from ever being discovered."

"Precious secrets? You mean that our existence must be kept from the humans?"

"In part. It would be a disaster if they were to discover that vampires, witches, magic, and the supernatural are real. But there are also other dangers that only a trusted few know of, and it must remain that way for the safety of all."

"Do you know?"

"Some. Not all."

"Will I ever be told?"

Sarita squeezed her hand again. "I think so. But there is much I don't know. What I do know is that everyone who cared for you wanted to give you as normal a childhood as possible and so your powers were bound so you couldn't use them."

"They bound my powers?"

"Behind a shield." Sarita patted her hand. "Do not be angry. A witch-child's powers are often bound until such a time when they can control them—usually around their eighteenth birthday, although it is different for every witch child. But the shielding that holds the bindings wear off, as yours has begun to do. And given they have, you are to be taken to the Cousins in *Firenze*. The truth was to be slowly revealed to you there after which you would be trained by both coven and Cousins. And continue to be shielded from those who might seek to use or harm you, until you can shield and protect yourself—both magically and physically." She sighed heavily again. "You weren't supposed to find out so abruptly. We thought we had weeks, if not months, to gradually introduce you to what you need to know to deal with this secret. Unfortunately, your powers broke through with this attack, stronger and quicker than anyone imagined they would. In fact, you're proving too strong for me to shield without bonding to you. If we don't do something about it now, the cults will be able to track you. Unshielded power is a lodestone to them."

Ardenne's mind whirled.

She understood why Papa and Lord Hei would want to keep her safe but was this the best way? To keep her in the dark so completely? Surely a hint over the years, some suggestion, would have given her something to grab onto now, to steady her, to make all of this seem not so terrifying and insane.

"Ari, I know this is difficult, I know you probably feel betrayed—I felt the same when the truth was explained to me when my powers began to push through the bindings that had been placed upon me —but we don't have time for your doubts if I'm to keep you safe. We must shield your mind now and I need your help to do it."

Ardenne's mouth dropped open. "My help?"

"Yes. Your help."

"B-but how? I don't even know how I did what I did."

"That won't matter for now. Not if we're bonded. But I can't do a bonding without your consent. Do I have it?"

There was something of pleading and desperation in Sarita's voice. But before she agreed to anything, there was more she needed to know. "Is this what Gabriel was talking about before he left?"

"Yes."

"So he knows too?"

"He's always known."

"Of course he has." The words were full of surprising bitterness —a bitterness she never knew was in her. Although, some of what she'd overheard between him and Lord Hei now made sense. And maybe even some of Gabriel's behavior made sense too.

"Ari, we don't have time for this." Sarita's words and the sharp tug on her hand pulled Ardenne out of her spiraling thoughts. "The pull of your magic is too enticing. They will find us and attack again if we don't shield your mind and your magic. Will you consent to the blood promise?"

Something unblocked inside Ardenne, so that the whisper of Sarita's fear was suddenly hers, filling up her bones, making her want to give the Companion anything to allay that fear, to make it go away. But ... "A blood promise?" It was what Lord Hei used to tie the Family and the Cousins to him, a promise that was as much give as it was take. It was used carefully and strategically and was endlessly powerful because it was ...

Blood magic!

Why was it only now that it was dawning on her that Lord Hei used magic in this special rite? Why did no one ever question him using magic in that way while telling everyone magic was evil?

She shook her head. That wasn't a question she could answer now. No. The only question that mattered was why Sarita thought it was necessary to use now.

"Because it's the only thing strong enough that will allow me to shield you in such a way that will make it impossible for others to see your power for what it is until you've been taught to shield yourself."

"I'll be able to shield myself?"

"Of course. That's what we're all here for. To teach you. To make you strong."

Despite everything, despite learning she'd been lied to all her life, Sarita's words sang through Ardenne, a sweet melody, thrilling and dangerous, bewildering and bewitching.

"Come into my home" said the spider to the fly.

But unlike the spider, whose intent was to eat the fly, there wasn't anything sinister in Sarita. She wouldn't ask for a blood promise unless there was need. Would she?

Of course she wouldn't. She was one of the Cousins. One whom Lord Hei, through this mysterious Carrington, had sanctioned to be here.

And incredibly, she was a Cousin who knew magic!

There were things she could teach Ardenne. She would know how Ardenne had managed to push the Wild vampire away and cause him pain. She would show her how to shield her mind from the intrusion of others. She could teach Ardenne to defend herself properly and not just with untried martial arts skills.

And if she could defend herself, who knew what else she could do? Maybe she could then make them see that cosseting her, thinking to protect her by keeping things from her, was always the wrong way to go. That she was strong enough to face all the truths.

And maybe, just maybe, she could even convince a certain cold vampire that she was more than a child. Much more.

Sarita gripped her hand, voice urgent as she said, "You'll learn more than you ever dreamed. I promise. So, do you agree?"

There was only one answer. "Yes."

At Ardenne's assent, the strumming tension that had built up between them swept away in a sudden current of euphoria. She felt almost giddy.

Sarita let go of a loud sigh and released Ardenne's hand from her tight grip. "Thank you. You don't know what this means. Stay here. I'll fetch my athame."

An athame! A sacramental knife.

She'd only ever come across one before. Lord Hei's. He'd let her feel its weight and the carvings in the handle only a few months ago. She'd had no idea at the time why he might show it to her or let her hold it. She'd been equally ignorant as to what she'd felt tingling through her as he'd placed it in her hands. She knew now it had been magic she'd sensed. But in that moment, she'd simply thought the sensation was caused by the excitement of being allowed to hold such a sacred implement and the fact that it would be used in the ceremony that would bind her to his service once she returned from her training.

A ceremony that used the blood magic that was the heart of a vampire's power.

Blood magic.

The very thought of it made her shiver because regardless of its source—vampiric or witch—blood magic was incredibly powerful; one of the most powerful and lasting kinds of magic. All the Bartolli knew this just as they were taught that magics were forbidden.

But that had been a lie. Had what they were told about blood magic been a lie too?

No. She knew it was powerful. It was a magic that was equally of light and dark for it could bring life and death. It was binding. Eternal.

This was why the thought of it thrilled her now. Had always thrilled her if she was truthful. The idea of magic and blood magic and what it could do ... it spoke to something deep inside her. She knew she should be wary of something so powerful offered to her by someone she had only just met.

But she wasn't. Not now.

Not with Sarita.

It seemed right, as if it had always been in her destiny. As if she was about to fill the void that had always been inside her despite the love she'd been showered with all her life.

She'd never realized just how big that void was until now. Until Sarita told her she had magic and that she would be trained in it. That knowledge alone helped fill the void. She was being offered something that would make her everything she'd ever dreamed.

If agreeing to tie herself by blood promise to Sarita was her way to get all that, then she was willing to do it.

She was willing to do far more.

She sensed Sarita return, so wasn't surprised when the witch said, "Put out your hand."

Ardenne flinched as the knife scored her palm but held steady.

Sarita's sharp hiss joined hers as she made the matching cut on herself necessary for the binding ceremony. Then long, slender fingers wrapped around Ardenne's hand, the sticky warmth of Sarita's blood mixing with hers.

A buzz thrilled through her as Sarita's voice, low and intense, intoned words filled with power:

"I call the spirits with this knife,
The sacrifice of blood, combining life,
Blood is now mingled, its power rife,
An unbroken promise, or unending strife,
Our blood together: a sacred rite.

Your promise is bound, three times three,
Your promise now belongs to me,
Joined mind, body, spirit: the trinity
Combined forever, eternally,
We share the secret, so mote it be."

An electric jolt tingled across Ardenne's skin. The air prickled and tensed, like the heavy waiting before a summer storm. Lightning and fire seemed to strike at the core of her being. Breath gushed from her lungs. Her heart held onto its last beat before thumping painfully to a start once more.

Power curled inside her then burst, expanding ripples of sound in the broken air, her soul-song, and Sarita's, wavering away until it was gone.

"It is done," Sarita said, her voice jubilant and relieved. "You will be safe for now."

Ardenne nodded, unable to speak, her mouth dry, her throat full of something that didn't hold words.

"The blood promise pulls on your energy and makes you thirsty. Let me go get us a drink." Sarita left, but she was back a minute later.

"Here. Sip on this. It's an electrolyte drink. It will make you feel better." She handed Ardenne a tall glass with a cool liquid inside that tasted like water with a salty-mineral tang. "Now, let's bandage up your hand and then we can get to know each other better."

As Sarita wrapped the bandage around Ardenne's hand, she couldn't help wondering what she had just become a part of.

The 'more' she wanted to learn was no longer hidden around the corner. It was right in front of her. Breathless anticipation made her forget about the pain from the bump on her head and the cut on the palm of her hand.

It had begun.

~

It has begun!

Gabriel leaned against the other side of the door, the scent of Ardenne's blood once again strong in his nose, his mouth, burning his throat.

Fanculo! He'd almost failed in his duty in more ways than one today. He swallowed hard against the fear still lodged in his chest, squeezing his eyes closed against the press of thoughts flooding his mind.

She *was* safe. Sarita had blood-bonded her as he'd wanted. She too would always know where Ardenne was and shield her mind from others.

Then why did he feel so ... jagged?

"She is safe," he whispered to himself. "She is safe for now." However, that 'for now' was a driving pressure in his veins. The uncertainty of it.

Cazzo!

He didn't need this. Didn't want it. To feel such a sense of responsibility, to worry like this, was galling. With Lord Hei's help, he'd locked so much behind the door in his mind, even been able to mostly deny the bond. Until he'd seen the vampire in the carriage, fangs extended, the blood running down Ardenne's forehead, dripping down her arm. Rage had rushed to the fore, the bond pulled tight, and the door had slammed open. Knowledge—ancient, secret, some even forbidden—had rushed through him, firing his emotions. He hadn't just wanted to kill the creature in front of him, he'd wanted to kill every single one of them.

He'd wanted to rend until there was nothing and no one left who could endanger Ardenne. And for one wild, glorious moment, he'd given in to that impulse, letting out the savagery, the monster inside until he'd turned and seen Ardenne, her porcelain features screwed up in pain, confusion, fear.

The sight of her at that moment had been the one thing capable of stopping him in the middle of that madness; it was a horrifying reminder of the danger of his nature. A danger he had to keep well in hand because his nature was to tell her everything, and yet it was the one thing he could not do; the one thing guaranteed to cause more pain than any of them had ever known.

That bloody prophecy. It had ruined everything!

Mary Middleton's words echoed in his head as loudly as they had when he'd first heard them five hundred years ago:

> *The blind girl given sight,*
> *Forbidden knowledge her eternal blight*
> *Never can you allow her to find,*
> *That which will her anger bind,*
> *Dangerous secrets in the Lonely Angel's head,*
> *Discovering them will see all dead*
> *Three times three times three times three,*
> *Your memory bound inside of thee,*
> *First's will over all, so mote it be.*

At first, he had scoffed at her words. As had his Sire. Lord Hei believed Mary's prophecies were only one version of a possible future and had said so after she'd told them this one. Mary had looked them both in the eye and said, *"You think me a foolish woman given to idle fancies. Yet what I tell you will come to pass if you do not mind what I say. When you realize who I talk about, you may think to tell her about her heritage, about who she is and what she may choose to do, thinking this will stop her. And maybe, in other circumstances, you would be right because I foresee much good in her. However, telling her the entirety of dark secrets you know will lead you down the path to more darkness than you could ever encompass. Some you may share when the time is right. Others, not at all."*

"What you say is ridiculous," Gabriel had scoffed. *"All we have to do to stop this future from coming to pass is make certain she is never born."*

Mary had grabbed his arms, her fingers squeezing tight on his cold skin, eyes wild in her face, whirling with the dark and amber fire of a witch using her powers. *"She is fate's nexus. To her you will be bound. So keep your secrets underground."* Her eyes had rolled up into her head and she slumped to the floor.

Gabriel had stared at her unconscious form, a cold creeping prescience under his flesh warning him something significant had just taken place, if only he had the wit to figure it out.

At Ardenne's birth, he realized the true depths of what Mary had tried to tell him. No matter their meddling in fate, the child foretold in the prophecy had been born. And if that was true, then what about the rest?

In the years since, he had become certain that telling Ardenne everything, making her choose one terrible thing over another, would only hasten the darkness that would come. And yet, keeping some of these secrets from her was anathema to his soul. The bond sliced at him, demanding he help her, not hurt her, yet he seemed to be caught in a tide not of his own making, forcing him to do the opposite. And the pain-enforced mandates of the Forbidden that bound the rest of their kind from even thinking about those truths, didn't seem to work for him.

That was why he and Lord Hei had pushed it all behind the

locked door in his mind. If he didn't know, he couldn't tell—another part of Mary's prophecy that had come true.

The Wild's attack and the danger to Ardenne had shredded their plans into pieces. He had to keep her safe, and for now, she was safest if he wasn't around, particularly given he would struggle to keep his mind shielded from her because of the bloody Guardian bond that had been forged at her birth without the need for the usual blood magic rites.

He opened his eyes and lightning-quick, pushed away from the door. He had to get away from the torment of her. The push and pull she created inside him made worse by the knowledge flooding through him and the terrible thirst the scent of her blood created. Why must he thirst for her blood like this? It was a peculiar kind of torture.

Throat burning, he snarled, wanting to tear into something with fist and fangs until his need was sated.

He would hunt the Wild who had escaped.

He laughed, anticipation of the hunt firing his veins. Bursting out the last door of the end carriage, he leaped onto the track, the midday sun hot on his head as he rose and looked around.

From the scent, they had definitely run out of the tunnel and into these woods. He would hunt them down, drink from them, then ensure they could no longer be a blight on this world. And maybe, just maybe, knowing he was saving so many innocent humans by doing what he'd been reborn to do would make him feel better about the secrets he must keep, the lies he must tell.

The image of Ardenne's open, trusting face crumbling with hurt as she had turned from him in the train carriage flared into his mind, causing rage to fire inside him.

Fanculo.

He couldn't be tempted to tell her all of what he knew, even a little of what he knew, especially not before she was trained.

And yet he was. So terribly, viciously tempted.

He had thought that keeping her from her mother was the only way to keep her safe. Now he wondered if perhaps he was the greater danger to her soul.

By The First, how he hated anything that made him this uncertain. The word, 'uncertainty' had never been in his vocabulary until the day Ardenne was born.

Swearing under his breath, Gabriel ran into the woods, the burst of speed bringing a false sense of freedom. He *would* gain back his control. If he couldn't remain strong, couldn't close the door again, then they were all damned.

This vow of secrets lost to silence was one he dared not break.

CHAPTER 8
OUTING

The child of mixed blood will serve their Lord. This cannot be changed. She will be sent to his followers. But to hide her is not enough. Her blood is power.
To the Dark Ones, it beckons: a bright light to succor their lustful hopes.
Extract from The Middleton Manifesto, Prophecy 21, Book 2

There was much to discover and love at *Palazzo Maimoona*, the Cousin's stronghold outside of *Firenze*. So many things in fact that they kept Ardenne incredibly busy in the month after she arrived. There were people to meet, a library full of all their histories in braille for her to read, meetings with various Masters she'd study with during her time here, not to mention learning the *palazzo* and its garden's layout and working on strengthening her radar hearing in all the new places in and around the *palazzo*. There were also her workouts and fight training that took up hours of each day.

The one thing she hadn't started though was her magical training. After a week had passed with no talk of magical training, she asked Master Solari, but he just fobbed her off with, "All in good time."

Three more weeks flew by and still no magical training and only the same answer from Master Solari and her other Masters whenever she asked them.

So, she decided to ask Sarita if she knew.

"Why haven't I started my magical training yet? I thought you were all afraid it was going to bust out of me. Which according to you can't be allowed to happen."

"The blood bond allows me to shield you so there is no fear of that right now."

"Okay, well that's good. But it still makes no sense. I thought a large part of why I was sent to the Cousins was to train my magic."

Sarita sighed. "I know it's frustrating not to start right away, Ari, but we can't go ahead with your magical training until you've been assessed."

"Then why aren't you assessing me?"

Sarita took her arm and led her to a seat in a recessed window in the library. She sat even though she didn't feel like it, the sun warm on her back as it shone through the glass.

"I cannot do the assessments. Nobody here can. We are waiting for a specialist to be sent from the coven."

Ardenne frowned. "I don't understand why you can't start to teach me something."

Sarita took her hand and squeezed. "It is important to start you off in the right way. Different magics work differently and need to be trained differently. If I was to start training you in the wrong way, it could cause irreparable damage to the way you access and use your magic."

"Really?"

"Yes."

"Okay. But ..." She shifted to face Sarita more squarely. "Couldn't you at least give me some lessons on the history of magic so I know some of this stuff?"

"I'm afraid I am forbidden to start your magical education in any way." Sarita patted her hand. "Be patient. Someone will be sent soon. You are a top priority to the coven."

"Obviously not too much of a top priority if they are making me wait so long," Ardenne grumbled.

She felt Sarita's shrug and her own frustration through the touch of her Companion's hand on hers. "As I told you on the train, we thought we would have months to get you to this point. Things were set up to happen then. It's been ... difficult for some of those things to be changed including when the assessor can get here. But I promise, it won't be much longer, and in the meantime we can fill our time with other educational endeavors until your assessor arrives. Speaking of which, can you remember anything more about the nightmare you had again last night?"

Ardenne shook her head. "Nothing more than I have already told you. Gabriel was standing there, looking down at a woman's body lying on the floor. There was blood all around her and yet her chest shuddered with labored breaths. Then Gabriel muttered something about being sorry for what he was about to do and kneeled next to her. Everything went black after that." She wasn't sure why, but she couldn't tell Sarita or anyone about the voice that always came to her during or after the nightmare images that had been coming to her lately. It only ever said one thing: *"This is what they have hidden from you. Think about what they still hide."*

The sound of loss, of horror, of anguish in that voice always made her wake up screaming, her body full of need and longing, frustration and uncertainty; and a multitude of questions pressing at her mind.

And anger.

There was always anger.

Anger at those who had kept her in the dark for so long. Especially the vampire who was supposed to be her Guardian but who seemed to want only to skulk in the shadows and ignore her when she caught him at it. It was like he was trying to make her think she was going insane. But while he never answered her when she thought he was there, she could always smell his unique scent, so she knew he had been nearby, watching her.

"Ari? Are you all right?"

Ardenne realized she was squeezing Sarita's hand tightly in hers —too tightly. She pulled her hand away. "I'm fine." She took a deep breath to steady herself. "I—" She stood up, breathing in deeply. There it was again. His scent. Faint but definite. Like he'd been standing just outside the doorway to their left for a while, his scent wafting into the room and over to her. "Is Gabriel here?" she asked as she made her way over to the doorway.

"I don't think so," Sarita said from behind her. "Why?"

"I can smell him." She was about to move out into the hallway, when she bumped into a large figure as he made his way into the room.

"Oops," Master Solari said, chuckling, his hands moving up to her shoulders to steady her as she bounced off his very large chest. "Where are you off to in such a hurry?"

Swearing under her breath—she was annoyed at herself that she'd been so intent on following Gabriel's scent that she hadn't noticed Master Solari's footsteps approaching. She moved out of his grip and said, "Nowhere."

"Were you looking for me, Master Solari?" Sarita asked, coming up behind her.

"Yes. Actually, I was looking for both of you. We are going to *Firenze* for the *Scoppio del Carro* festivities tonight."

"We? You mean I can come?" All thoughts of following Gabriel rushed away. Ardenne hadn't been allowed further than the grounds of the *palazzo* and the surrounding fields since arriving. A heady mix of excitement and trepidation chased over her skin at the thought of going into *Firenze* to experience the crowds and the fun of the Easter Saturday festival. This was a step toward the freedom she'd always wanted, and yet, she'd barely coped when faced with *Milano*.

She curled her fingers at her sides. No, this time would be different. She was prepared.

"Of course you can come. This isn't a prison."

Something in his tone checked her excitement. "Is that why Gabriel was here just now? To guard me?"

"Why would you think that?" Master Solari asked. He took her arm, tucking it under his. He was a tall man with large shoulders and the broad, well-muscled chest of a fighter. But it wasn't his build that made her think of strength when she was in his presence. His title was 'Master' and the word suited him; his intelligence, his sense of purpose exuded from his every pore, making those around him seem small.

"I thought I smelled him."

"Did you?"

She nodded. Gabriel's scent—a scent she found difficult to forget—was still in the air, enticing her to follow. "I can still smell him."

He patted her hand. "Well, he must have walked down here on his way out after speaking to me. I trust that nose of yours." He took her arm and began to escort her down the hallway, Sarita joining them on his other side.

"You spoke to Gabriel?"

"Of course. He had some concerns about me taking you into *Firenze* for the festival."

She bet he had. She could just imagine the conversation being something like the one she'd overheard him having with Lord Hei. "Then why am I going?"

"Because if we don't let you out in the world, how are you supposed to learn about it?"

Exactly! "What did Gabriel say to that?"

"He agreed."

"Oh." Maybe he'd come to tell her that. But then, why hadn't he come in when she'd sensed him rather than slinking away? Why leave only the press of his presence and the frustration of his tantalizing scent in his wake?

They stopped at the stairs leading up to the private quarters and Master Solari said, "Sarita, can you please go out to the stables and make sure the driver and car are ready. Ardenne, you run upstairs and get changed. We'll meet you at the car in ten minutes."

Pushing aside any thoughts of Gabriel, she ran up the stairs and down the hall to her room. Slamming the door closed behind her, she flew to the dresser in the corner, pulling out jeans and her favorite peasant top—she liked the feel of the lace and embroidery. Dressing quickly, she slipped her feet into a comfortable pair of ballet flats, grabbed a light cardigan Sarita said went with everything, ran a brush through her hair and hurried out the door. She was in such a rush to get outside that she tripped on the last stair.

Catching herself on the banister, she hoped nobody had seen her. Face ablaze, she straightened her shoulders and, at a more sedate pace, walked out the front door of the *palazzo* to the car.

Sarita called out to her and she headed toward the sound of her voice, her Companion's floral and light musk scent greeting her as she drew near.

Sarita hugged Ardenne's arm to her as she drew up next to the open door. "You are going to love this."

Ardenne smiled at Sarita's words, hoping her Companion was right. She hopped in the car, pushing aside all her doubts, and breathed in deeply.

Gabriel's scent drifted by, faint enough so that she knew he wasn't in the car with them; but he had been here, maybe as little as ten minutes ago. "Where's Gabriel?" she asked Sarita.

"He's gone down to the city already," Master Solari said as he hopped into the front passenger seat.

"Oh." She frowned. He *was* obviously avoiding her.

"Ardenne, are you okay?"

She forced a smile to her lips and said to her friend, "I'm fine. Just excited."

"So am I. The festival is always fun."

Fun. That's what she needed. Not frightening dreams and endless thoughts about Gabriel. He was rude and cold and uncaring. Why couldn't she keep him out of her head?

Because he saved you. Because he held you. Because, after the vampire attacked on the train he said, "Ardenne, stay with me," and you so desperately want him to mean it.

The thoughts whispered in her mind now as they did in her dreams every night before the nightmares came, but she shook them away. Turning her thoughts to the night ahead she said, "I hope we can get close when the cart full of fireworks explodes in front of the *Duomo*."

"Not too close. You don't want to be deafened by it," Sarita said.

No, but the big bang might truly help to clear her head and push Gabriel out. Maybe it would make the nightmares, and the voice, disappear too.

The thought made her smile.

As the car picked up pace, winding down the road toward *Firenze*, she tried not to think and just enjoy the ride. The breeze from the open window cooled the heat on her face and as her ears picked up nuances of different sounds and smells, she pressed closer to the door, wanting to soak in everything as they drove into the outskirts of the city.

The noise of the traffic as cars and bikes zipped along the streets, horns blaring, the sound of people's feet hitting the pavement—so many voices, so much activity—made her smile in anticipation. Scents wafted in the air. Some were delicious—baking bread, tomatoes and pizza dough cooking, meat warming the air with its spicy scent, the full-bodied smell of early summer fruits and the sweeter smell of the gelato sold by the street-side vendors. Some were not so nice—sweat and grease and petrol fumes and garbage.

Behind it lay the scent of age, a scent that captivated her imagination. What had this city been witness to through the ages? What secrets were held in the ancient stone?

A thrilling shiver chased over her skin at the thought of unraveling those secrets. She took a deep breath, determined not to be unsettled this time like she'd been in *Milano*. This time she was going to be like a sponge and suck it all in, retain every scrap of new knowledge, allow it to change her shape. Change her.

They drew to a stop—she heard the click-click of the traffic lights; a sound, she'd read, that had been introduced to help those like her navigate the traffic safely.

Above the general noise she was able to pick out individual voices; a tour guide espousing the beauties of the architecture in heavily accented English to whatever group followed behind, hurrying them along so they could make the festivities; a child complaining of sore feet and hunger; a mother soothing a fractious baby; a curious one-sided conversation about someone's mistress making trouble at the family company.

Then the car moved on and the voices fell behind. Church bells rang the hour, a musical peel gliding above the cacophony of sound. Ardenne imagined that everyone would stop to listen to those beautiful bells she'd been told were the *Duomo,* but everything continued the same.

Expectation tingled on her skin, making it impossible to sit still. The car stopped and it took everything in her not to just open the door and dive out, losing herself in the crowds. She wanted so badly to test herself and experience *Firenze* in festival mode. Anything could happen tonight.

She hoped it would.

"This is as far as I can take you," the driver said. "The road is blocked ahead for the festival."

"*Andiamo.*" Master Solari clapped his hands together and hopped out.

Soon they were moving through a sea of people—at least, Ardenne thought this was what being in a sea must feel like. The shifting, moving, pulsing crowd pushed against her one way and then the other. Scents of food and alcohol and body odor pressed around her, sinking into her pores.

They wandered for a while, allowing her to get a sense of the shift and flow of the crowd, get used to the music, the scents, the sounds, the press of people all around. Disoriented to begin with, slowly she was able to use the mass of noise and scent and people to form an image in her mind of the narrow streets and wide *piazzas* they ambled through.

After a while, Master Solari made them stop at a store selling delicious smelling pizza. Ardenne burnt her tongue biting into a slice; the fresh tomato was molten hot under the layer of salty prosciutto. But she didn't care. What was a sore mouth in comparison with the delicious flavors swirling around her tastebuds?

She gobbled down the entire piece in a couple of bites and a laughing Sarita bought her some more.

"I'd think you hadn't eaten all day," she said, handing over another slice, the greased paper crinkling in her hand.

"This is delicious. I don't think I've ever tasted anything so good."

Master Solari's laugh boomed over her shoulder. "See Petra, my dear. Yet another customer you've spun in your culinary web. I've always said you were dangerous to a man's soul."

A light tinkling laugh. "Wait until she tries my *porcini*, chili, and sweet basil gnocchi. She will be my slave for life."

"I better move her away before that happens."

They waved Petra goodbye and moved on, Ardenne with another piece of pizza pressed into her hand by Petra just before she followed Master Solari and Sarita.

They wandered past other shops, tried wine at one, grabbed bottles of water from another and ate gelato from Master Solari's favorite gelato shop. They had fifty flavors, and it took Ardenne twenty minutes to decide what she wanted after trying about half of them.

"I thought we were never going to leave there," Sarita said as they stepped out of the shop.

"I didn't know there were so many different flavors of gelato." Ardenne licked up the drips of blood orange and *limoncello* gelato that dripped down her cone, making her fingers sticky.

"They are always trying out something new. I'll have to take you there next time they do English plum pudding—it's a favorite of mine."

Ardenne nodded eagerly.

They sat by the *Arno* eating their gelato, the music of the water playing an alternate beat to the music drifting from the city behind them.

"Are you having a good time?" Sarita asked.

"The best," Ardenne replied. "When will they light the fireworks?"

"Soon. We should go and try and get a good position."

"Okay."

They finished their gelato, washed their fingers with the rest of a bottle of water and then moved back into the crowd through the labyrinthine *vias* and *vicolettis* toward the *Duomo*. They'd walked around long enough for Ardenne to have a greater sense of the layout of the city and the flow of the crowds. So when Sarita and Master Solari stopped to watch a street performer she wasn't interested in, Ardenne felt free enough to wander toward the sound of a musician who was playing a guitar piece that pulled at her soul.

She knew she was in no danger. Apparently, Gabriel was around somewhere, although she'd had no sign or scent of him, and there would be a guard watching from nearby. She bumped into a few people, but she'd come to understand within minutes of them arriving, that wasn't an unusual thing, and kept on going, making her way with sure steps across the *piazza* to where she could hear the music emanating from.

The echoes of the music made it easier for her to keep her steps steady, the beat creating a constant flow of light and shade as it bounced off her surrounds. Very soon she'd found a place near a doorway where she could listen without being bumped into. She hummed quietly to the music, swaying a little in time to the beat.

This was exactly what she'd dreamed of. Freedom. The ability to spread her wings, try new things, experience the world and all it had to offer. The shackles of her existence were slowly lifting.

This was only the beginning.

CHAPTER 9

WILD FIRENZE

Curiosity is her blessing
Curiosity is her curse
Curiosity will save her
If it doesn't kill her first.
Extract from The Middleton Manifesto, Prophecy 31, Book 1

Ardenne hugged her arms around herself and took in a deep, satisfying breath.

A familiar scent slid past, causing instantaneous longing and a warm fluttering of excitement in her stomach.

Gabriel.

He *was* here. But why hadn't he shown himself so far? Why was he hiding from her?

She tried to find the scent, following it out of the doorway, but within a couple of meters, she'd lost it. Moving further down the street, she tried to pick it up again. There! Following, she stepped onto the cross-street and was immediately swept along in the current of the crowd.

Voices bubbled around her; cameras clicked. Rich smells

surrounded her, pizza and perfume and sweat, making it almost impossible to pick up Gabriel's scent again. Intent on picking apart the different smells to discover direction, it was a moment before she realized she was being jostled and maneuvered down the narrow lane away from that enticing scent.

Too quickly she lost it entirely.

"Damn!" she muttered. She really had wanted to follow Gabriel. Where had he been? Why had he left? Why avoid her? She needed him to tell her. Needed him to know he couldn't do that to a person. To be so nice and then ... not. Not to mention following his scent was a test. She wanted to prove something to herself. To him. To show him how well she could get around using her radar. That she didn't need his help at all. That she was worthy of Lord Hei's trust.

But he was gone.

And so were Sarita and Master Solari. She couldn't smell or hear them either.

Shit. She hadn't realized she'd moved so far away from them. She couldn't even scent the guard who had been a constant presence ten meters from them ever since she'd got out of the car.

Panic clawed her throat, making her breath speed up. Her head began to spin.

No!

She refused to behave like the frightened child Gabriel had accused her of being in *Milano*. She clenched her hands, pushing her nails into her skin, the bite of pain bringing clarity, allowing her to gain control. She might not know exactly where she was, but the crowd was most likely going to the *Duomo*, and once there, she was sure she could find a place she could stand where the others would find her. The guard couldn't be too far away. He'd be looking for her, surely. He and Gabriel could track her by scent easily enough. No doubt they would find her soon.

Besides, she'd read so much about *Firenze*, it seemed like a friend. She couldn't get lost here. She let herself move along with the flow of the crowd, concentrating on the sounds to help her step steadily along the cobbled streets.

She'd only made it a few meters when a red haze slammed into her mind. She staggered.

The sensation was overwhelming and it took her a moment to realize someone had grabbed her arm and was talking to her.

"Are you okay, pumpkin?" the woman said in twangy English, one hand on her shoulder, the other cupping her elbow.

"Fine," she managed to croak. "Thank you." And with a little tug, she freed herself to follow the red-haze sensation. In her mind she could see an image. A crowd of humans. Loud, colorful, vibrant humans who smelled of blood and sex and flesh.

Heat seared her veins. Her skin was sweaty and itchy and sensitive to the touch. Her breasts swollen, nipples suddenly distended against her bra. A strange tugging roiled deep in her stomach, like nausea, but not, and the flesh swelled between her legs.

She wanted something. Desperately wanted something, but what?

She rubbed her hand over her stomach, up her chest, but the parching thirst that suddenly ravaged her throat took precedence over everything else.

She wanted to drink.

She *had* to have a drink.

Breath shuddered out of her as fear traveled over her skin, ice melding with the heat.

She'd experienced this before. Only once. It was exactly like what had happened with the vampire on the train!

A cry on her lips, Ardenne whipped around, trying to smell or hear him. But there was nothing. Just that red haze, the sensation of what she knew now to be an insatiable thirst mixed with lust, and the image of the festival crowd moving along the street in front of him.

She moved forward, pushing in the opposite direction against the crowd, no longer interested in going to the *Duomo*. A part of her screamed to stop and wait for Sarita and Master Solari, to let the guard or Gabriel find her, but the greater part of her didn't care about the stupidity of following this vampire and how dangerous it was. She'd begun to doubt that what had happened on the train—that she'd seen with the vampire's eyes—was true! This was proof it had happened. For some reason she could see through a vampire's eyes.

Could she do it with any vampire? Or was it just the Wild? Was he projecting on her or was she somehow getting into his head? She didn't know. But she wasn't losing the opportunity to find out.

She knew he was dangerous, but she just didn't care. Besides, if he got too close, she'd back off, slip away into the crowd. It would be fine.

He was on the move. He looked back and over his shoulder and she caught a glimpse of the young woman she'd seen on the train, the one with the heart-shaped face, white eyes, and dark ponytail, dressed in blue jeans and a short sleeved white cotton peasant top, a black cardigan tied around her waist—herself. His gaze lingered on her for a moment, and she halted, but then he looked away, his eyes tracking the rest of the crowd hungrily.

He moved on.

She followed.

He moved quickly. The red-hazed images began to fade. No! She couldn't lose his sight now. Not when she'd just found it again, when she hadn't found out anything new other than it was real. But the sight was fading. It was going ... going ... gone.

No!

She almost cried out with frustration. No matter the nauseating sensations attached to that vampire's mind, seeing through his eyes had been a miracle. She needed to find out more. But she'd lost it, and she doubted the opportunity would arise again any time soon given she didn't know when her magical training would start—this had to be part of her magic, right?

Tears pricked her eyes. It wasn't fair. How could she be given the opportunity for sight and then have it cruelly torn from her simply because she was too slow!

She slumped against a nearby wall, breathing deeply, trying to hold back the urge to cry. She didn't want to be found crying in a crowd by Gabriel or her guard. How humiliating would that be? Besides, how could she explain her tears? They wouldn't understand. They'd act fearful and take away what little freedom she'd been granted so far. She'd never be allowed to go out again without being surrounded. She pushed her knuckles against her ribs and took in another deep breath, sniffled and swiped the tears from her eyes. She had to calm down and then she needed to find the others and pretend like nothing had happened.

A sweet scent brushed past her. Intoxicating.

Her head whipped up and she took in a deeper breath.

Oh! It was like the scent of the vampire on the train. The scent that had fluttered over her face, curled around her, stroked her like a caress and fogged her mind with desire. It had made her want to do whatever the vampire asked—that was until she'd hurt herself and found the will to fight the intolerable intoxication.

That scent was one she could easily follow. In fact, she wanted to follow it more than she'd ever wanted anything before.

Moving faster than was sensible, she pushed through the bustling crowd, using her senses, picking out the sound of her feet slapping against the pavement among the bustle of hundreds of other feet shuffling past. She was hurrying, not taking the care she should, but she didn't care about tripping. She just had to find the vampire's mind again and try to connect, to see if she could do it at will.

The sounds around her formed a shape of the cobblestones in her mind, the lay of the street, the area taken up by tables and chairs, the awning under which buckets of flowers stood, waiting to be sold. And the people. All the people, shuffling around, getting in her way, stopping her from getting to ...

The red haze slammed into her mind, and she could see with his eyes again.

Oh! It was wonderful. Despite the red haze, there was such clarity. He was moving, not so fast now, almost as if he was waiting for something. She could see how people looked at him as they passed, the wonder on their faces, the way they stopped and turned to watch him go. They got in her way as she followed, and she bumped into more people than she liked.

Seeing through his eyes was strange. It was difficult not to use his perspective to judge her movements by, but after a while, she got the hang of seeing and still using her other senses to light her way. She knew she wasn't moving as smoothly as she usually did, but that didn't matter. With practice, she was sure she'd get used to it.

She wondered where he was going. The crowd enticed him until his thirst was a burn in her throat. She couldn't read his mind but had the sense that he wanted to stay and 'play', but something far stronger suddenly called to him, leading him away.

The crowd thinned. The sounds of the festival dimmed behind her until the people and music were a distant echo. There were no people wandering past, just the vampire and his red-tinged sight making sense out of the shadows. She followed at a distance; some part of her mind still able to be cautious enough to know she couldn't get too close.

The vampire turned a corner and stopped. Ardenne skidded to a halt and pressed up against a doorway in the wall she'd seen through his eyes only moments before. Moving into the shadows, she focused on what the vampire saw.

Anger, mixed with a sadistic glut of pleasure rushed through her as the smell of blood spiked through the air.

He watched a fight. Not just an ordinary tumble of bodies she had read in recent weeks that the Wild often indulged in. This was a fight to the death.

And one of the fighters was about to die.

The vampire stalked silently toward the combatants; a female dressed in a long velvet dress of green—that was the word that flashed across her mind as his gaze skated over that dress, caressing every curve and dip of her body—and a man dressed all in black, his dark hair glinting in the lamplight like the glow she sometimes saw behind her eyelids when she turned her face up to the bright summer sun.

The female hissed, lashing out at the one in black, intent on tearing into his flesh.

The vampire she'd followed was almost upon them. Ardenne wondered who he was going to help—if he was going to help at all. He seemed to be enjoying the fight far more than was healthy. The lust that surged through him, the heat in his veins as he reached down and stroked himself through his pants made Ardenne gag.

She almost lost his sight in her revulsion. He was masturbating. What kind of a sick ...

The vampire in black turned.

Gabriel.

At least, she thought it was Gabriel. He looked remarkably like the picture she'd imagined in the train, except tinted with the red haze of the vampire's vision. But his face, rather than cold, was animalistic and vicious. He grabbed the female as her swing went wide then threw her from him. She crashed against the wall with a sickening crunch. He turned to face the male Ardenne had followed.

The male immediately stopped masturbating and with a vicious growl, pounced. Gabriel knocked him aside, but the male was up, the blood firing hotter in his veins. If he liked seeing the others hurt each other, he enjoyed his own pain even more.

She began to gag again and lost his vision.

No!

Desperately trying to ignore the sick sensation trembling through her, she lunged out with her mind and reconnected with him. For a moment, all she could see was a blur. The fight was fast and furious and over almost before Ardenne had a chance to draw breath. The male lunged at Gabriel, but Gabriel grabbed his arms, pulling them up behind him so he grunted in pain and held still. Then he sank his fangs into the male's neck.

The shock of it made Ardenne shudder. Before she could react further, Gabriel ripped out the male's jugular and dropped him to the ground.

His sight dimmed as blood gushed from him, but Ardenne saw the female pick herself up behind Gabriel, the hatred in her face so apparent she couldn't miss it even with the dimming sight.

She let go of the male's sight, stumbled around the corner and screamed, "Gabriel. Behind you."

CHAPTER 10
AFTERMATH

Confusion and betrayal. It is what she will live and breathe until she understands. What that is yet, I cannot see ... but it will mark her in ways that will make her wish to be in the dark once more.
The gift to See is not much of a gift—this I know.
Extract from Mary Middleton's Diary, April 16, 1534

There was a furious cry that turned into a screech of agony then utter silence.

A billowing wave of heat rolled over her a moment later, followed by the acrid scent of sulfur and ash. Her heart pounded painfully in her chest. She tried to catch Gabriel's scent, but all she could smell was smoke.

What had happened? Was he still alive? She wished she knew how she could see out of another's eyes but the skill seemed to be accidental at the moment.

Something else she really needed to learn quickly if only someone would teach her.

A cold hand grabbed her. Her scream never made it out of her mouth as another cold hand pressed over her lips, pressing them into her teeth. She was spun away and pushed up against a wall.

Gabriel's cool breath brushed over her face. Her heart stuttered in relief and desire as he demanded, "What the hell are you doing here?"

Shaking, Ardenne moved her lips against his hand. He dropped it so she could answer.

"I was following the vampire."

He swore softly, then his voice whipped her with impatience. "Where are the others?"

"I don't know," she choked out. "I stepped away to listen to some music and the crowd pushed me away from them. I didn't know where they were to make my way back."

Gabriel hissed. "That doesn't explain why you would do such a stupid thing. Or how."

His tone was harsh, frightening, compelling Ardenne to tell him even though she knew she shouldn't. "I smelled the same sweet scent from that vampire on the train and I just followed him. I …"

Breath punched out of her as his fingers tightened on her shoulders. She took in a gasping breath and said, "Gabriel. You're hurting me."

His grip loosened even as he said, "Do you know how much danger you were in?"

"I didn't think—"

"No," he cut in. "You didn't. Your father warned me you could be trouble, but I had no idea he meant you were subject to acts of suicidal stupidity."

"I wasn't in any real danger. You were here."

"You didn't know that when you followed the Wild male, did you?"

"I …" She went to move, to step away from the wall, but he held her in place with his superior strength. "Let go of me, Gabriel."

"I don't think I can. I don't think I can trust you won't do something equally as stupid as following a Wild."

"It wasn't—"

"You have no idea how dangerous what you just did was, which makes it even worse. I called you a child once, but what I should have called you is a stupid, ignorant little girl. What the hell made you think you could follow one of the Wild and escape unharmed?"

Tears pricked her eyes. The rough stone cut into her back as she cringed away from his anger, but that pain was nothing against his harsh words. She wanted to defend herself, but couldn't, because she couldn't explain why she'd followed the vampire. If she'd given it one moment of thought, she would have known it was too dangerous a thing to do, untrained as she was. Yet, she hadn't thought at all. She'd just ... followed. Despite the fact she knew his scent was a lure, she'd followed. She'd wanted to prove she could stay in control of herself. And she wanted to hold onto his sight for as long as she could.

But she couldn't explain any of that to the angry vampire in front of her, so she said, "I was careful. He didn't even know I was there."

Gabriel swore again, a stream of angry Italian and English, and let go so suddenly she stumbled and would have fallen to the paving stones if Gabriel hadn't caught her, holding her upright. Holding her close.

Too close.

A warm flutter began in her stomach despite his cruel words and anger, followed by a sensation of heat that rose over her skin, leaving little shivers and prickles in its wake. Her lips parted on a gasp.

He swore again. "Don't. Don't say a word. I'm so angry right now I'm not sure what I'll do."

"You won't hurt me," she breathed.

"Are you sure of that? I've already hurt you in ways there is no forgiveness for." The last was whispered under his breath, but she heard it. Had he forgotten how good her hearing was, or had he meant for her to hear?

Before she could ask, a voice hailed them, one she didn't recognize. Footsteps neared them.

Gabriel turned from her to bark an instruction. "Tell Vincente I've got her and not to worry. I'll return her shortly."

Sounds of footsteps retreated and they were alone once more.

His hiss of annoyance brushed over her face as he turned back to her. "How am I supposed to keep you safe when you act with such stupidity?"

"Stop calling me stupid."

"I will when you stop acting like you know no better. Those people at the festival have no idea what lurks in the dark, but you do."

"No, I don't," she hissed. "I don't know about this. About any of this. All I was ever taught at *Casa Cinque* was that the Wild and Dark Brethren are our enemies. You talk about their scent lure but I have never been taught anything about that or how to fight it. How am I supposed to serve Lord Hei if nobody ever teaches me about this world? All I've learned since coming here is about our histories and a few things about the cults, but nothing else. Nothing about my magic or the exact details of our enemies or how to truly fight them like you do." Her voice echoed unpleasantly shrill in the narrow confines of the alley as she shouted. "It's like you all want me to fail!"

From further along the alley, somebody shouted, "*Stai zitto! Io sono addormentato!*"

Ardenne almost choked on a laugh—how someone could sleep with the festival going on was beyond her. But Gabriel ignored him, grabbing her arm above the elbow. "You want to learn about my world so badly? Then come with me. I'll teach you."

He hauled her along beside him. She tripped and stumbled over the uneven cobblestones, unable to quiet her jangling nerves enough to concentrate on using her radar. He swore then picked her up as if she weighed nothing and took off with a speed that was breathtaking.

He kept to the quieter parts of the city as he ran. She knew they'd crossed a bridge—the rushing sound of the *Arno* jostling its banks sang to her like music—and then they were free of the concrete chasm and out into the open. She knew they were in the fields surrounding *Firenze* because the wind pushing against her face had changed from hot and close and full of the scents of humanity, to cooler with the fresher aromas of grass and trees and soil.

He put her down in a swift move but kept walking, pulling her along beside him. Shells crunched under her feet and the sweet scent of roses and night-blooming jasmine floated on the light breeze. It sounded and smelled like they were in a garden, moving along a path up a steep hill.

Finally, he stopped.

The damp soft smell of moss on ancient stone rose around her. Tree boughs rustled and creaked above her head. The babble of hundreds of voices at the festival was made soft by the distance.

Gabriel stood at her back, cold, tense—a presence as dark and frightening as death. She shuddered, but was proud of how calm her voice sounded when she asked, "Where are we?"

"A hill looking down on *Firenze*."

"Why?"

He leaned closer and whispered, "You wanted a lesson on the cults, and this is as good a place to start as any—the hill where everything changed for me. The hill where I died."

Ardenne swallowed, the sound achingly loud. "What ... what do you mean?"

His hand firm on her shoulder, he turned her back to face the direction of *Firenze*. "No more questions. You're here to learn." He cupped her cheeks with his cool hands, sliding his fingers along her skin, fingertips pressing—chin, cheek, temple—mirrored on both sides. Despite the coolness of his touch, warmth, like a lick of fire, bloomed. Leaning closer, he whispered, "Learn."

His voice slid through her like *cioccolato gelato*, delicious yet bringing a cold shiver, and the velvet darkness behind her eyes became inky black.

Into the inky black, images began to flicker past, lightning fast. Emotions swirled among them, frightening in their intensity. The images slowed, until one pulsed before her, calling to her, pulling her in. Ardenne leaned forward and ...

She was Alice in the rabbit hole. Falling. Falling. An arrow on its descent, she sped toward the earth, screaming. Her arms flailed like useless wings. She was going to smash into the earth, break every bone in her body, never to wake again.

Just before the implosion of body against earth, her downward spiral changed, and she slid along a path of sparking light that brightened until she realized she was standing on a hill. A young oak tree cast dappled shade over her back as she looked upon *Firenze* nestled into the valley below.

The *Arno* shimmered in the late afternoon sun. Orchards and fields spread out in all directions, a patchwork quilt over hills that looked like ripples in a giant's unmade bed. Pastures glistened in the distance, gold with ripening wheat and the bounty of jewel-tipped fruit trees.

"I can see," she gasped.

"You are in my memory." Gabriel's voice whispered to her on the wind. "You are seeing what I saw long past. Now, pay attention."

She looked out of Gabriel's memory with his eyes. Images flickered past, almost too quick to capture; a dark-haired pregnant woman; a fevered child; two little crosses; another larger cross. The vision blurred and then they were staring at the water from the rickety wooden bridge he stood on.

Oh, and there was a longing inside him; a longing to lose himself in the depths of that swirling water, let it embrace him as his wife's and children's arms would never embrace him again. She almost cried, his grief a horrifying ache, but the vision blurred again before the tears could manifest.

He was sitting on a hill. His aching sadness a constant companion as he looked down on the *Arno* wending its way through the green and dusky valleys, a golden serpent in the late afternoon sun, glistening and cool. The serpent's whispers still called to him, daring him to search its secrets. Months had passed and he still wanted to follow those whispers and surrender everything he was to that enticing voice, plummeting down into the cool green depths to be reunited with his dead wife and their children—oh Lord, she hadn't known! He'd been a father and he'd lost them all.

Ardenne wanted to sob, but the image shifted and changed once more with the passing of time.

He was on the hill again, looking down at his priestly robes. He had taken his vows, searching for meaning, and yet, even with the good he brought to his small flock, he longed for the arms of his wife and children, the simple life of love and laughter he once had.

Lost in his sorrow, Ardenne sank fully into the memory, becoming one with it. Becoming one with him.

His lips moved. A soft plea exhaled in a language that held a different, archaic cadence. But she understood. He wanted salvation from his pain. He invited death.

He sat there as dusk painted the sky blood-red then turned, knowing he needed to head back. Padre Patritsio would be looking for him. It was past the dinner hour.

Shadows rose over the ground, whispering close until they materialized as two men and two women. They were dressed in clothes of rich colors and expensive fabrics, their hands and hair dripping with jewels, indicating they were of noble birth. He stood to greet them, but a scent—oh! Such an intoxicating scent—made the words catch in his throat.

A voice whispered in his mind, *Run!*

But he couldn't run. The scent drew him toward them.

They were incredibly pale. Their skin glowed in the last embers of the sinking sun. And their eyes ... Gabriel knew there was something wrong with their eyes but couldn't quite figure out what, because they began to circle like wolves hemming in their prey.

"Look, Sandrine. A priest."

The one called Sandrine licked her lips. "Mmm. Delicious."

"This one prays for death," the other woman said. "Shall we give it to him?"

"I pray for nothing more," drawled one of the males. "But shall we have a little play first?"

Gabriel heard a low growl of pleasured anticipation.

Then they pounced.

His invitation to death had been answered.

CHAPTER II
BEING MADE

Violence is the way they're made
Souls are twisted, craven and afraid
Of what they once were, nothing is left
Their essence taken, the greatest theft
Hate inside like a canker grows
Its inevitable weakness, as darkness always knows.
Extract from The Middleton Manifesto, Prophecy 14, Book 1

The memory became hazed by pain and blood and excruciating pleasure.

For, despite the horror of the violation Gabriel had endured—not to mention the torture of breaking his solemn vows of celibacy—his body responded to them. He lay with the females as the males watched, writhing in pleasure, unable to find release as they found theirs. Then the men joined in, and he responded to them with equal desire. He'd only ever been with his wife; had never known a man could be with another man like this, and yet, he couldn't seem to stop himself from writhing with the pleasure of it, especially when their teeth sank into his skin and they drank. Something about that was utterly euphoric and he begged for more.

When they withdrew to play with each other, he pleaded to be included. Yet all the time, in his mind, a small part of him screamed and railed against his traitorous body, gagging at what he was doing, wanting nothing more than for it to end. For everything to end.

He was sobbing, half from pleasure, half from exhaustion, and yet it didn't stop; not their appetite or his reaction to them. Their 'play' went on and on. Even when he could barely breathe from blood loss and exhaustion, his body kept going, while inside he pleaded to his Lord God to bring death to him now.

"There is something special about this one," Sandrine said, taking her turn with him again. "He is lasting longer than any other."

"He is full of power," one of the men said, licking at the blood that dribbled from the bite mark on Gabriel's neck. "Can you not taste it?"

A long lick up his arm across the various bite marks there. Pleasured goose bumps chased over his skin as nausea roiled in his stomach. "I want more," said the other female.

"Then let's take it."

Fangs pierced his skin again as hands stroked and tongues licked. He screamed but his voice became a croaky husk as he pleaded for more pleasure, for mercy, for death. Dawn lit the horizon. He heard their conversation about having to go before the sun rose in full and whether to take him with them as vague murmurs in his head. He was too lost in a fog of blood loss, unsated desire and pain to care about what they did with him.

The sounds of *Firenze* awakening in the distance lifted to the hill. Life going on without him. He faded in and out, thankful that finally his body was shutting down and soon he would feel no more. He welcomed death. There he would see his beloved Isadora and their children, Stefano and baby Clisto.

Sandrine had just climbed on top of him again when there was a high scream and the sound of something being ripped and torn.

Suddenly Sandrine was no longer on him. Panicked cries and running sounded around him. More screams. A flare of flames then a wave of heat washed over him.

Silence.

In that silence the most beautiful face he'd ever seen crossed his fogged vision. "Are you an angel?" he asked, his voice a breathy husk barely recognizable as his.

For a moment, Ardenne, lost in the horror of what she'd just witnessed, didn't understand the significance of that beautiful face. But then, from Gabriel, a name arose:

Lord Hei.

Relief shuddered through her alongside her wonder at his angelic features, so like Gabriel's but so different. He would save Gabriel. He would take the horror of it away. She knew in some distant part of her mind which had somehow been separated from the horror of what Gabriel endured, that Lord Hei had saved Gabriel. He'd killed the Wild. Everything would be okay.

Wouldn't it?

She sobbed. How had he managed to survive the memory of what had been done to him? How could he dredge it up again to share with her? His strength ... It was astonishing.

Lord Hei caressed Gabriel's face, parent to child. "Do you truly want to die? Or do you want to stop what happened here from happening to anyone else?"

"I do not know how," Gabriel sobbed. "They were too strong ... too much. I could not say them nay."

"I can make you strong, my son. I can make you the thing that hunts them if that is what you wish. But you need to want to live. You need to want to survive."

"Will I remember ... what they did?"

"Always. But I will make it all fade away so it hurts no more. Is that what you want? If not, I can simply end it for you here. So you must tell me ... die or live to protect those who cannot protect themselves?"

"Live." The answer flew out of him before he'd even given it a thought. The angel in front of him smiled and nodded in satisfaction and then bent to place his lips against the pulse in Gabriel's neck.

A faint tearing sensation, but the pain was nothing compared to what he'd already been subjected to. The pain subsided, covered by a numbing sensation. Then ...

Joy. Unrelieved joy.

And as he was spinning in that joy, something was placed to his lips, wet, warm, inviting.

He drank.

The memory went blank, and Gabriel's words fluttered through her mind, like his breath on her cheek. "The transition was relatively quick in the scheme of things. My human death followed soon after Lord Hei shared his blood with me—a few hours at most I think, although I can't be sure. The pain was excruciating throughout the change, but it wasn't all physical. Everything I'd endured through my human life revisited tenfold on me. Grief and loss and pain were all I could see, a never-ending road before me. I think with the last of my strength I fought my Sire, desiring none of what he offered despite asking for it. Maybe in some way I knew his gift was flawed and fought simply to die. But it was far too late. And in the end, what he promised came true. His gift did end much of that suffering, but there are times, even now, when I wish he hadn't done it. When I wished I'd had the strength to ask for death instead."

Ardenne trembled at the idea of Gabriel dying—of not being turned into what he now was, passing into dust centuries before she was ever born. Despite her anger over the way he treated her, it was a terrible, horrifying thought. One she couldn't even contemplate. "No."

His fingers left her skin, and she would have tumbled to the grass if he hadn't caught her and lowered her to sit on the mossy stone of the ancient garden wall that had been new in his memory. But he didn't stay with her. He turned away, and she imagined he looked out on the land stretched before them just as he had in his memory. There had been so many changes and he could remember them all.

He sighed. She came instantly to attention.

"I'm sorry I had to show you that. I forget at times how carnal it was; the violation of the desire they drugged me with and forced upon me. The worst thing about remembering is the memory of that violation. How weak I was against it."

She didn't know what to say. 'I'm sorry' seemed so trite. 'Thank you for showing me that' even worse. She would never thank him for showing her that. It was horrifying. Simply horrifying. Despite him begging them to do what they did, it had been rape. Ugly and repulsive.

Tears in her eyes, she shook her head. "How do you endure it?"

"The memory isn't as strong as it was. Becoming a vampire makes many things that happen when we are human seem almost like a dream and much easier just to let go and never think about. Although, the things we choose to remember, we remember with vivid clarity."

"That ... rape ... is one of those things?"

"Strangely enough, no. As vampires, we can shut off our memories if we wish. I have done that with that memory. Until tonight."

Her lips trembled. He'd pulled that memory out just to show her? "Why would you do that?"

"Because I wanted you to know. To see. To truly understand the depravity of what we deal with every day."

"But why? Why like that? With such vivid clarity?"

"Sometimes words are not enough."

He was silent again for such a long time she would have thought he'd gone except his scent told her he was right there next to her. "Gabriel?" Her voice wavered.

"I'm here." His hand on her face, a swift caress, gone almost before she felt it.

Silence again, then, "I used to think the view from here was magnificent, but with my human eyes it was a mere painting of the reality I see now. Now I taste the colors and scents and textures on my tongue. Exotic, enticing, ever changing. The wonder of it calls to my soul. There are many things about being a vampire that are truly astonishing. But, Ardenne, you must never forget the darkness that lies at the heart of us all."

She frowned. "But Lord Hei's blood makes you different from the Wild and Dark Brethren."

"That's true. Because his blood gives life to my veins, I remember the importance of light and laughter, love and life. However, that is not all it gives me, and it isn't all of what forms me."

"All the vampires I've known at *Casa Cinque* have been nothing but good and kind."

"Of course they are. To you. And they mostly are good and kind to others, too. However, that is not the only side to our nature."

"Are you saying they ... you ... are vicious monsters like the ones you just showed me?"

"No, I'm not saying that. But there is a side to our nature that is essentially animalistic, and in the Wild and Dark Brethren this is even more true." He sighed, exasperated. "I'm not explaining this right. Perhaps I shouldn't have shown you."

She shook her head. It gave her an understanding of him she'd never have had otherwise. And it showed trust ... like he knew she'd never betray him with what she'd seen of his memories. "No. I'm glad you showed me."

"I don't want you to be glad. I want you to be horrified. I want you to see from my memory that those who were responsible for my human death and vampire life are unlike anything you imagine them to be. They're not simply dangerous. They are fanatics and they will never stop being what they are."

"I saw that." She fisted her hand against her chest. "I felt that."

"Good." He was there again, in front of her, his fingers gripping her arms, firm but gentle at the same time. He stood so close, his low voice vibrated through her chest as he said, "I'm sorry if it hurt you, but learning the theory is not enough. I want you to know why I was so angry with you tonight. I need you to understand that the one you followed tonight, the one in the train, the ones who tortured me—they know only the dark. I need you to feel what that truly means."

Ardenne pressed her fingers against her lips to stop them from trembling. His tone had changed; dangerous, with shadows and terror, of violence and a seductive pleasure she couldn't begin to fathom. She shuddered again, but this time fingers of ice, not pleasure, played up her spine. "You want to frighten me."

He let her go. "No. I don't want you frightened. I want you armed. I want to ensure you don't make stupid mistakes again. I never wanted you to come out into the world as ignorant as you are. It's wrong. It should never have been allowed. If I'd been half the man and Guardian I'm meant to be, I would have made certain it never happened."

Humiliation heated her face. He was right. She was a stupid, ignorant child because she'd been kept that way. But before she could sink into her dark thoughts, he continued.

"What I showed you tonight is only the tip of the iceberg. The Dark Brethren mutilate themselves to represent archaic ideals of terror. They enjoy the pain of mutilation as much as the terror their visage creates. Their need for pain is as strong as their need for blood.

"Humans are only herds to these cults. Theirs for the taking, for food, for amusement, to satiate their lust and the thirst-hunger that drives them to acts of torture and murder you could never understand. You saw. The Wild played with me because they could. Because they enjoyed it. And they made *me* enjoy it. The Dark Brethren would have done even worse."

"Then teach me. Teach me more. I've learned so much tonight. Nobody else has ever taught me what you have; showed me what you have."

"That's because they don't want to terrify you with the truth.

They never want you to truly understand what drives the vampire, the need that makes us all more deadly than almost anything else on this earth."

"And what is that?" she asked, unable to stop shaking.

"Blood."

She frowned. "I know you all need blood to survive. What's so shocking about that? Especially given all Lord Hei's sirelings only drink animal blood."

He hissed.

"What? What am I missing?"

"So very much." He turned away from her.

It was her turn to hiss. "I don't lack imagination like you seem to think. Besides, I imagine your need for blood is much like my need for food, for water, maybe even for air."

She got a sense he was shaking his head at her.

"It is much more simple and yet so much more complicated than that," he said, his voice distant as if he now stood further away from her. "Blood means more to a vampire than you should ever understand."

"But you could teach me. Like you did tonight."

He was suddenly in front of her again, fingers cupping her face. "There are things, Ardenne, you can never be taught. Things I would keep from you if I could, despite you longing to know all." He dropped his hands. "If it was up to me, I would keep you far from my world."

"Why?" The word was almost a sob.

"Because you don't understand what it is you ask for. Because there are some things that are too dangerous for y ... for a human or witch to know. Even one with power such as yours."

Her chest ached. The shuddering breath she took didn't help. She ached inside, ached in her very soul. But not in terror. No, this ache was something else entirely, although she wasn't sure what.

Fireworks popped in the distance—she was missing the festivities, but she didn't care. All she cared about was this moment with

Gabriel. He wasn't cold. Or mean. She'd seen that in his memory, felt it in the way he cared. He'd endured so much pain and yet he fought against it every day. The ache in her chest turned to a throb. She wanted so much for him to see her as more than a child.

When his silence continued, she dredged her voice from deep inside, pushing past the pain in her chest. "Are you trying to confuse me?"

"What do you mean?"

"You tell me I should never have been let out of *Casa Cinque* without being taught more and then tell me if it was up to you, I wouldn't be taught anything. Which is it? Am I to be taught or not?"

"Lord Hei says you must learn how much of a plague the Wild and Dark Brethren are upon this Earth and be able to help in the fight against them."

He sounded so indifferent. And it wasn't the answer she wanted. She wanted to know if *he* wanted her to be taught. If *he* wanted to teach her.

She longed to see his face right now, to see his expression so she could figure out more clearly what was going on in that mind of his. She didn't want to just extrapolate it from the sound of his voice. That sound was too nuanced for her to make anything out with any clarity. She had no idea what he was thinking. What he was feeling. What he was trying to say behind the words.

Her borrowed sight!

If she could tap into his sight as she'd done with the Wild, with just the two of them here, she would be able to look out of his eyes and see …

Nothing but her own face.

Her shoulders sagged. Her new ability had limitations. It was an amazing gift, but it still didn't make her whole. It made her once again reliant on others. She didn't want to be reliant. She wanted to be able to take care of herself. She wanted to be as strong and self-sufficient as Gabriel.

Then she'd just have to ask. "Are you going to teach me?"

"Master Solari has organized for you to have lessons in self-defense and on the vampire cults."

"That's not what I asked. Are *you* teaching me?"

"No."

Her shoulders sagged further and she couldn't help the petulant tone in her voice when she asked, "Then why did you do this?" She tensed as she waited for him to answer.

"You will meet your magic instructor tomorrow. He will also give you specialist warrior training too."

She let out the breath she hadn't realized she was holding; she should be excited about that information except ... he hadn't answered her question. She opened her mouth to ask it again but he spoke first.

"You will also be happy to know that Corinna will arrive in the next few days to begin properly instructing you on the cults."

She was happy to see her friend except ... "I learned so much from you tonight, wouldn't it be—"

He gripped her shoulders, giving her a little shake, his hands trembling as he did so. "Did you learn nothing tonight? My world is vivid and gruesome and real. I hunt and kill as those you followed tonight hunt and kill. I do not have the time or the inclination to teach you. You do not belong in my world. You can never belong in my world."

What if I want to belong in your world? The words were there on her tongue, but she held them back. Belong to his world? Why would she want that?

Because I've never wanted anything more.

By The First, it was true. She wasn't sure why or how given his attitude to her to date, but she had feelings for him. She'd somehow managed to romanticize him saving her on the train or something. Yes. That must be it.

Well ... if it was that simply started it would be simple enough to end. His attitude tonight should do it.

She tried to focus on when he'd pushed her against the wall and yelled at her, when he'd shaken her just now. But it didn't work. That feeling of need to spend more time with him, to find out more about him, to have him share more with her like he had tonight, was still there. It was because of what he'd shown her. It had to be. It had tied her to him in some way, feeling his despair and grief and then his anguish and terror like she had. She had *empathy* for him now.

And that empathy made her emotions where he was concerned far more complicated.

Damn him! Damn him and him sharing his memories to hell. She wanted to hate him but couldn't. She wanted to take him and shake him like he'd shaken her to make him see how cruel he was being. Crumbs to a starving person is what he'd given her. And she was starving. She knew that. Starving to know everything he did, to experience the world he lived in, to belong *there*.

But he wasn't ever going to let her belong. Not with him.

She shrugged away.

He let her go, the imprint of his cold hands remaining on her shoulders like a burn.

He paced away, his tread sounding somehow impatient. "I'm hungry. I must hunt. I've put it off too long. I didn't get the chance to feed properly and your maddening scent is more than I can endure."

The words ... they cut her more than any words he'd uttered before. Sucking in a deep breath, she pressed her lips together, trying not to give in to the urge to cry.

"Tonight is a good night to hunt for vermin. Festivals always are." He turned back to her, taking her arm once more. "Come. It is time I return you to Vincente and Sarita."

His silence was impenetrable as he picked her up and ran back down the path toward the city.

As he ran, she found herself wishing that she could be as cold, as hard as he was. Or at least find a way to sort out what she was feeling for him. But that was as useless as wishing she could see, now she'd seen part of who he really was.

Depressed and confused by what she'd seen and what he'd told her, she didn't want to return to the others. Instead, she longed to crawl into her bed and roll into a ball, cherishing the fissures of hurt in her heart.

CHAPTER 12

DREAMS OF MADNESS

I have come to understand that the magic I can see in the air around me is not what most witches see unless they look with their magical sight. I think maybe this is why the visions come to me like they do. I have a suspicion it is because she did something to me. While I will forever be thankful to have met and spent that secret time with her, I often wonder what my life would have been if I never had stumbled upon that place and her. And there are times, when the visions will not leave me any peace, that I wish I never knew she existed.

Extract from Mary Middleton's Diary, December 22, 1540

That night, Ardenne dreamed. It had always been a source of mystery to her and others that in her dreams, she reported she could see. The visuals were never clear, and they were in what could only be called a kind of dull blue-gray and white. But this dream was different from the others she'd experienced. The background wasn't hazy, she could see the faces *and* it was in full, vibrant color, even clearer than when she'd seen through the Wild males' eyes.

Gabriel stood beside a woman, looking out on the valley to *Firenze*. In the strange way of dreams, she knew the woman was her older self. Gabriel reached out, linking their hands, a warm slide of skin that was strange given his skin in real life had been so cool. But as his fingers linked with hers, there was a click, and she slipped inside the adult-dream-self.

Darkness surrounded her. She'd lost her ability to see.

But she could feel. And she could smell and hear. Gabriel's mountain air scent curled around her. "Are you sure?"

"Yes," Ardenne whispered.

He lifted her hand to his mouth.

His fangs were so sharp she could barely feel them as they sliced into her palm, but even so, the sensation filled her with a mixture of desire and dread. A lump of fear stopped the cry from escaping her throat. But before she could pull away, she heard the slash of his fangs across his own palm and the air was stung with the rich tang of copper and lightning that was the scent of his blood.

He melded his palm to hers. "Blood is my world. See with my blood."

Fire tore from her palm, up her arm, pumped around her body by a stuttering, surging heart.

"Open your eyes."

She didn't want to open her eyes. All she wanted to do was scream from the pain, but the lump in her throat had grown larger; too large to speak around let alone scream.

"Open your eyes. See what I see."

Trembling, Ardenne opened her eyes and gasped as all the pain and dread—and the lump in her throat—rushed away.

The world pulsed and vibrated with too many colors to name. The intensity of the rainbow-shot rays of sunlight brought tears to her eyes. Blades of grass on the furthest hills swayed in the breeze. She could see them as clearly as if she stood above them with a magnifying glass. A hawk, variegated colors from cream to darkest gray speckled with mini rainbows of the protective oils that coated its feathers, swooped out of the sky, aiming with deadly precision at the field mouse scurrying through those blades of grass. Deathly silent, its shadow was the only sign the mouse had of the violent end descending. The hawk dipped. A squeal of panic and pain stabbed the air. The hawk rose. The mouse flopped in its sharpened beak.

"The hawk kills to live." Gabriel's whisper fluttered in her ear. "Vampires view themselves little different from the hawk and humans little different from that mouse. Humans are nothing more than fodder. But some meals are better than others and you ... You are a delicate dessert." He tugged at her hand, forcing her to look at the mark of his fangs on her skin. "To me, your blood is ambrosia. The scent of it is almost more than I can bear. A kind of beauty that is painful to all my senses. And if I can barely suppress my need to taste, imagine what you would taste like to others who are less ... tame."

A tear fell down her cheek as she looked up at him. She knew what he meant about painful beauty. When she looked at him, her heart clenched and her soul shook. *He* was beautiful. So perfect as to be almost untouchable. Terror rode side by side with that kind of beauty—how could she ever match it?

But he wasn't talking about that kind of beauty. Turning her thoughts back to his words, she swallowed hard. "You aren't the hawk. And I'm not fodder."

"No. You are something more. Which means this life is even more dangerous for you. You are a temptation that many of our kind will not be able to resist."

"I don't understand. Tell me more."

He shook his head.

"Remember this, my child. Remember what they hide."

The voice whispered in her mind as Gabriel's smile turned into a frown.

"Who are you?" Ardenne asked to the voice in her mind.

"They tore us apart. But one day, I promise, we will meet and I will tell you the truth."

Gabriel's fangs glistened with venom, hatred a flashing burn in the depths of his violet eyes as he grabbed her shoulders and looked deep into her eyes. "Leave now."

"Why?" she asked, frightened by his intensity. "What did I do?"

"Not you, Ardenne. *Her*." His gaze intensified. "Leave now or I will kill you."

"Not if I kill you first."

Dark Brethren and Wild stepped from the shadows, their howls of exhilaration rending the air with needy desperation. Gabriel shoved Ardenne away. "Run!" he cried, turning to fight.

But there were too many. They covered him like ants on a carcass in seconds.

"Gabriel! Gabriel!" She leaped forward, ready to fight, but there was a flash of flame and the vampires fled.

And then she saw it.

Gabriel was caught in the flame; a flame almost too bright to look at, his form already a darkened silhouette imprinted forever on her retinas as he screamed in rage at the sky. There was a flare brighter than anything she'd seen before, so bright, she had to cover her eyes. A woof of wind hit her, lifting her off her feet to crash to the ground. Heat and molten hot grit burned into her skin as she scrambled forward to help Gabriel.

But only clumps of ash floated on the wind.

Gabriel was gone ...

A silent scream in her mouth, Ardenne struggled up from the remnants of the dream image, breath shuddering hard and painful in her chest.

"Gabriel!" His name was a sob in her throat as she shouted it out in the silence of her room, his beautiful face swimming into her mind: hatred and fear and desperation mixed in equal measure when he told her to run.

She clutched at the front of her pajamas, pressing her knuckles to her chest. It was a dream. It was only a dream.

But by The First, just the imagined loss of him felt like a gaping hole had been carved in her chest. How could she feel like this about him? Why would his death affect her so? She didn't even like him—did she?

Hell! She did.

Even though she'd tried again and again as he'd carried her back to the others in *Firenze*, then again as they'd journeyed back to *Palazzo Maimoona*, she pushed herself to remember how horrible he was; to tell herself he wasn't worth a flicker of her worry or concern or empathy.

But it hadn't worked. She still felt all the things she'd felt for him on the hill after seeing his memory; after seeing what he'd endured. The dream had just made it worse.

She had no idea why she should care for him in such a way, but she did. He was ... *necessary*.

She shuddered, torn, on the edge of something significant that she couldn't quite grasp. He shouldn't mean so much—especially when he'd mostly been cold and disdainful toward her, making her feel like she was useless and weak and a pain in his ass—but he did. He meant ... everything?

No. Not that. Not yet. Hopefully not ever.

But he did mean something. Something more than he should to her.

She puffed out a breath, trying to stop her heart from beating so goddamned hard it hurt. Tried to think logically about him. But after ten minutes of sitting there, her thoughts a tumbling, confused mess, she decided to give up. There was no logic to apply here. It had to do with feelings. She didn't want to have them for him, but she did.

In the dream, she definitely did. They had been friends in the dream. No. They'd been more.

She tipped her head, tapping her chin as she thought about this. She had no clear reason to think that, but she was certain it was true. In her mind, she'd built their story to include a relationship. Boyfriend and girlfriend were too trite to explain the feelings she'd experienced in the dream she'd just had. It had been something deeper, something more profound.

Or was she just reading something into it that wasn't there? Possibly.

Playing the dream over in her mind, she came up with no answers, but she did come up with some problems. The voice that had been coming to her more often of late was in the dream. She'd always assumed it was her subconscious, but now she wasn't so certain. It seemed too ... other. Like it wasn't a part of her at all. Not to mention, it had been aware of the web of lies that had been spun around her when she'd been rather clueless.

But if it wasn't her subconscious, what was it? And where did it come from?

Sighing in frustration—she didn't have a hope in hell of answering either of those questions now—she turned her thoughts to the other thing that bothered her the most about the dream: the fact Gabriel had told her to run.

Of course he'd told her to run because she was untrained, because she couldn't see, because she couldn't fight.

And then he'd died because she couldn't save him.

That was what truly upset her. That he'd been lost because she hadn't been what she could have been; what she *should* have been.

She almost laughed, but the laugh caught in her throat on a sob.

The desperation in the sound shook her out of the spiral she was heading down. She gripped her bedcovers in her hands and squared her jaw as she said, "No," into the dark. Her dreams might have revealed the truth of her greatest fears—about being lied to and being helpless—but that didn't mean she had to be that person she'd been in the dream.

Why couldn't she stand side by side with Gabriel and fight as his equal? He had told her yesterday that she would be taught to fight and how to use her magic. What about her ability to see through vampire eyes? That would have to make a difference. She could become as deadly to their enemies as Gabriel was if she could fight, had magic, and could see through others' eyes.

Breath punched from her lungs as the thought slammed through her, taking her on a turbulent ride of possibilities she wished were true. Could all of that together make her Gabriel's equal?

She didn't know.

Sarita said it would all become clearer when she met Carrington and began her training. Which, according to Gabriel, was tomorrow —at least her trainer in magic and fighting would be there tomorrow. If she learned to wield her magic and learned to fight, she would be a force to be reckoned with, even with the limitations of using a vampire's sight. Despite its inadequacies, it was better than nothing. And who knew, with Carrington's help, maybe it would almost be like truly seeing out of her own eyes.

Yeah right!

She laughed softly in the dark and dropped back down onto her pillow. It was a lovely thought, to be able to see out of her own eyes, but only a thought, a fantasy. As much of a fantasy as the dream where she had stood beside Gabriel as an equal. Where he had told her there was a part of her he found beautiful.

What wasn't fantasy was the red-haze-tinged sight of the Wild. Their perception of the world was ugly and was sure to bring on the nightmares again, but even so, she wouldn't give up the memory of them for the world. Because, apart from what she experienced in her dreams, now, they were her only hope of being able to see.

She turned her mind from the dream and kept it firmly centered on her memories. Except for one memory—Gabriel's denial:

"You can never belong in my world."

She couldn't allow those words to cut a deeper wound than they already had. They were probably why she'd had the strange dream tonight. She didn't want to remember either.

But as she slipped into sleep, the strange voice from the dream whispered in her mind, *"He will never let you belong in that world. But I will. All you must do is let me in."*

She opened her arms, ready to do the strange voice's bidding, but then Gabriel's voice slammed into her mind, "Ardenne. Run!"

His cry was so alive in her mind, it brought her to jerking wakefulness, "Gabriel?" she said into the silent room.

But he wasn't there. Nobody was there. It had just been another dream.

Not wanting to fall into another dream like the others, Ardenne decided to do some work. Getting up, she turned her computer on. The lessons loaded up about the history of the region and how the Cousins came to be based in *Firenze*, read by the slightly stilted voice of the computer.

But behind the computer voice, she heard another voice whispering to her still. Unintelligible words that pulled at her and left her shuddering. It kept on and on until she found herself huddled on the chair, her knees pulled up to her chest, her hands pressed against her ears, as she whispered, "Shut up. Shut up. Shut up," over and over until all she could hear was the echo of her own voice and the sound of the birds in the trees outside greeting the coming dawn.

GABRIEL'S HAND halted on Ardenne's door. No, he couldn't go in, no matter how much her distress pulled at him. It would cause more problems than it would solve if he went barging in there now.

Fanculo!

It seemed he'd made their bond stronger last night, not more fragile as he'd hoped.

She was in his blasted dreams now.

He choked down a laugh at the ludicrousness of that statement, particularly given she'd always been in his dreams. She was, after all, the nexus around which his nightmares were based. But this was different. Those dreams had been about what her existence could mean to him; and worry about what the future held for her.

But last night had been different. Last night they had shared a dream.

And that had never occurred before.

His fingernails cut into his palm as he fought the urge to go to her; to see if the dream had affected her as virulently as it had him. He'd never felt such a longing before. Not for a person at least. His hand rose again, as if of its own volition. It took everything he had not to open the door. Instead, he stood there, palm pressed against the wood, body quivering with a need he could barely contain.

Merda. This wouldn't do. It wasn't just that he couldn't go in there. He couldn't stay here. Not while he felt like this. Not where he could give himself away at any moment and allow her further inside than she already was. He couldn't stay here where Vincente Solari's too acute stare would see something that could not be allowed to come into being.

He was a fool. Standing here like this where someone could find him at any moment ...

He shook his head. Dawn was but a breath away and with the dawn the Cousins would be up and preparing for the day. He supposed he could say he was guarding Ardenne's door if found here by one of them. Although they'd be right in questioning that lie—the Cousins' compound was in the safest place she could be aside from Lord Hei's castle in the mountains.

He paced away from the door, only to return seconds later, the sound of her desperate whispers too loud in his ears to ignore. He couldn't go in, and he shouldn't stay, but Lord help him, he couldn't make himself walk away.

Would he ever be able to walk away again? After the dream last night, he was uncertain.

He'd bitten her in the dream, tasted her blood. He'd called it ambrosia, and it was. Food of the Gods, transformative to all others, a siren's call to all but a few, and dangerous to all. Then he'd fed her his blood, his deepest fears brought to life, and just like the prophecy had predicted, she'd become sighted. The look on her face had almost been worth it, but then Anita had come to spoil the moment, just as she had always come to spoil everything since he'd turned her and brought danger to them all.

Damn Anita to hell. She'd obviously found a way in. Through his vulnerability? Or because Ardenne's mind was left open after what he'd done last night? Or maybe a bond was created with her too at the moment of Ardenne's birth? He didn't know. But he would shore up the weakened sections of his psyche and make certain *she* didn't find entrance once more. She could never be allowed access to Ardenne again.

His lips curled as he thought about what could have happened last night. Anita threw out the word 'truth' like a tasty morsel, wishing Ardenne to gobble it up. But Ardenne was smarter than that. So, Anita had taken over the dream instead and brought death to him there.

It should have been impossible for her to take such control; a fact he couldn't let her know or take advantage of again. Not that he was afraid of the Dark Brethren and Wild she'd conjured from the depths of her subconscious. No. But he was afraid of what lies she might spin for Ardenne and how someone so open and trusting might believe them. Especially when she found out the identity of the voice in her mind.

No. That could never happen. Anita could never meet her—not even in dreams. He could stop a real-life meet, but a dream one where Ardenne listened to Anita's insanity? He shuddered.

There was only one thing to do. He would hunt that insane vampire-witch down and he would do to her what she'd done to him in the dream last night. Make certain she was ash on the wind. For Ardenne's safety, for the safety of everyone he loved, this must be done.

Hei would grieve, but he would understand if it was done to protect Ardenne.

Ardenne's safety was their greatest priority after all.

But if he had to do this, it meant he had to leave. Now. There was no other choice. He would be back, however. There was no choice in that either. Not after what had happened last night.

Hand on the door, he whispered, "Be safe." Then he turned and left before he could change his mind.

Whether he could stay away for a few days, a few weeks, or a few months, he had no idea. He supposed he would find out just how strong his will could be.

CHAPTER 13
TRIAL

The One must send the assassin with cold love in his heart.
It must be he and no other.
The One will know who he is.
Extract from The Middleton Manifesto, Prophecy 23, Book 2

Ardenne lifted her hand, about to knock on Sarita's door when she realized her Companion was on the phone having—if the furtive, slightly angry tone of her voice was anything to go by—a very private conversation. She was about to turn away, but then she heard her name mentioned, and without thinking, leaned closer to the closed door.

"Do you not think Ardenne is ready?" a deep, cultured English-accented voice asked quietly. She could hear the voice as clearly as Sarita's, although it did hold the slightly echoing quality voices on the other end of phones had to Ardenne's acute hearing.

"Carrington ... you know it's not that. She's ready. Ardenne might be a little naïve about the ways of the world—no wonder given how isolated they kept her—but she's thirsty for knowledge. Not that it matters if she's ready or not. Her power is pushing to get out of her."

"You're worried."

"Of course I'm worried," Sarita snapped. "You would be too if you met her. While she's a little impulsive, stubborn, and impatient at times, she's also kind and intelligent and generous with her affection once it's earned. Everyone here loves her already. As do I. So I don't want anything bad to happen to her."

"You're worried about her power? Its potential?"

"Not really."

"So ... You're worried that the kind of thirst she has for knowledge could lead to dark as well as light."

"Yes. No. I don't know." Sarita made a hissing sound of impatience. "No. What I'm really worried about is that her kind of thirst to want to know everything, to be everything she can, could soon kill her lovely naiveté."

"She can't stay naïve if she's to stay safe."

"I know. I know it's an impossible wish. I just wish I wasn't party to that side of her being destroyed."

Carrington chuckled. "So dramatic."

"Don't laugh at me, Carry."

"I'm not." Sarita made a snorting sound of disbelief. "Okay, maybe I am. But I don't mean to." He sighed then said more quietly so even with her excellent hearing, Ardenne had to strain to hear. "You know this is where your destiny has led you."

"I'm aware," Sarita said, sounding anything but happy about it. "I just don't understand how my destiny could have led me to working with that man again. Why him? Why does it have to be him?"

"Sasha Piven is the best we have. Surely you want Ardenne to be trained by the best."

"Of course I do. But Piven ..." She made a sound of disgust. "The man's a pustule on the boil of the lowest humanity has to offer."

Ardenne pushed her hand against her mouth, trying hard not to laugh and give away the fact she was listening in. But honestly, what did they expect when nobody ever told her anything?

Carrington obviously found Sarita's insult amusing too because he chuckled again, a warm, rich sound. "You do have a way with insults."

"It's the truth. The man is a psychopath."

"I know you've had your problems with him in the past, Sarita, but he's hardly a psychopath. He's one of my best friends and confidants. Besides, my mother wouldn't have taken him under her wing if she thought him a psychopath. She trained him especially in her techniques because of his unique skills. Like her, he is a master at identifying Potentials. You know that, given he identified you."

"Don't remind me."

"You wouldn't be as strong as you are now if not for Piven."

"His techniques are abhorrent."

"I think that's an over-exaggeration."

Sarita snorted. "I don't think you see him clearly. You were brought up to treat him like a brother, but do you even remember that he was a trained assassin? That he used his skills in telekinesis to kill people?"

"He had no choice about that, as you well know. You, more than any other, should understand that you can't be held responsible for what people made you into when you were a child. Besides, he hasn't been that for a long time."

Ardenne went still, breath held. The bit about Piven being an assassin had shocked her, but that last part ... what had happened to Sarita as a child? Now she desperately wanted to ask, to understand and empathize as a friend would, but she couldn't, because that would give away that she'd been eavesdropping.

She should move away, but she couldn't make herself. Not when the conversation was so interesting and there was the possibility she could find out things to help her today in her meeting with this Piven person.

She leaned in closer to the door, cheek against the wood now.

Sarita was saying, "Even when he's wearing that bloody immaculate Italian suit of his, he exudes menace. If you took his telekinesis away he's still one of the most dangerous men I've ever met. There is so much darkness in him still. I sense it every time he gets near me. And his urge to kill ... it's like a scab I know he'll have to pick at some stage in the future. I just don't understand why you trust him like you do."

There was a loud sigh. "I'm well aware of your feelings on this matter, Sarita." Carrington's voice suddenly had a harder edge to it, like he was now talking to a subordinate. "But I'm not going to have this conversation with you again. Ardenne is a Potential. An important one. Perhaps the most important. And we must be sure she is the one spoken of in The Middleton Manifesto."

Ardenne frowned. The Middleton Manifesto? What was that?

"So," Carrington continued. "You will work with Piven as I have decreed, is that clear?"

"It's clear." Sarita didn't sound happy about complying, but there was also a tone of acceptance that overrode the disgust in her voice. Then her tone changed to something warmer as she said, "I wish you could be the one to come, Carry."

"I wish that too, Sarita, but you know I can't chance being seen by those who would intuit too much by my presence. Not until we are certain."

So she wasn't going to meet the mysterious Carrington today. Just this Piven person Sarita didn't like.

Sarita said, "I have to go now. I'll call you after the meeting to let you know how it went."

"Good. Piven will make his own report of course."

"Of course. I hope to see you soon, Carry."

"Me too. Bye, love."

There was a sound as if Sarita was putting on a jacket and then footsteps neared the door.

Ardenne took a step back and knocked on the door before Sarita could get there.

The door opened a second later. "Ari? What are you doing here?"

She smiled and held out her hand. "Master Solari called up to say the car is ready and waiting for us."

"Oh. Okay." Sarita stepped out of her room and closed the door before placing Ardenne's hand on her elbow. Ardenne didn't need that kind of guidance, which Sarita knew, but Master Solari had told them it was a good idea for her to do things other visually impaired people would do when they were out and about in public so people wouldn't start to guess that she was anything other than human. "Let's go."

Half an hour later—after an uncomfortable journey in the car where Sarita and Master Solari sat in utter silence as if they'd had an argument—the car pulled up outside a building in the middle of *Firenze* and the door opened.

"Sarita, take Ardenne inside. I want to give the driver instructions for when to pick us up."

"Okay." Sarita ushered Ardenne from the car. Their feet slapped on the pavement and then onto the softness of a thick carpet. Someone said, *"Buongiorno signorina,"* and there was a sound that told Ardenne the hotel doors were being opened.

As they entered, Sarita leaned in, lips close to Ardenne's ear and whispered, "I wanted to tell you this in the car, but couldn't in front of Vincente. Mr. Piven is Carrington's envoy. He's here to administer the Trial. And you need to know he's dangerous."

"He is?" Ardenne was pleased that she sounded so surprised.

"Of course. Anyone with the amount of power he can wield always will be. But don't worry. I know you can manage him. Just remember what you felt on the train when you defended against the vampire. But most of all, be careful not to get impatient or lose your temper—he will take advantage of it."

Ardenne wanted to ask her more, but the distinctive sound of

Master Solari's footsteps came up behind them and Sarita straightened.

"Right, ladies. Let's go in."

They walked inside and were ushered through to the tearoom of the *Grande Palazzo Albergo* by a soft-spoken waiter.

Obviously Piven was already there because Sarita stiffened beside her then shuddered. Ardenne squeezed her arm but didn't ask if she was okay because she knew her friend wasn't. And now she knew why. As they drew closer, Ardenne could feel something ... not right about the man in front of her. He didn't feel evil or anything so simple. It was more that he felt ... big. Like the cavern of the room they were in wasn't enough to hold someone like him.

"Piven," Vincente hailed him. "Thank you for coming." The slide of skin against skin as they obviously shook.

"When I heard who the job was for, I had to come."

Sarita made a slight hissing sound.

Ardenne jolted. Not because of Sarita's reaction. No, she jolted because that voice! It wasn't at all what she'd been expecting. It was soft and cultured like Carrington's had been except with a slight twist to it, almost as if English wasn't his first language.

"I'm glad you did," Master Solari said, his smile obvious in his voice. "I want the best to teach Ardenne. You know Sarita of course."

"Of course."

Sarita stiffened even further if that were at all possible.

"Now, now, Sarita. Be nice," Mr. Piven said. "I only wish to shake your hand."

"You wish more than that, you snake. And you can take your hand back because I'm not touching you. I learned my lesson last time."

"I thought Carrington told you to be nice."

"I don't do everything Carrington wishes of me."

"More's the pity."

Master Solari sighed loudly. "Honestly, you two. People are beginning to take note."

"Quite right. Perhaps we should concentrate on why we're here." She barely heard him move but knew he had because his presence pushed into her. "This must be Ardenne."

"Yes, I am."

Ardenne tried to mask the tension playing her nerves like a master at his violin as she extended her hand. As soon as he grasped it, Ardenne knew why Sarita thought him so dangerous.

Vibrations emanated from him, indicating power and darkness and secrets beyond comprehension. Something ... his power? ... was coming off him like waves. No, not waves. Hands. With fingers that stroked her as if trying to feel out the shape of her. Almost like what she did when she felt someone's face to get a picture of them in her mind.

Except, this felt very different from that. Her touch was objective and kindly inquisitive. At least, that's what she intended. This was ... unpleasant. It didn't just content itself with feeling the shape of her face. It pushed inside her mind.

She gasped, even though the sensation was more surprising than painful. It was a pressure that couldn't be pushed away like she'd pushed aside Sarita and the vampire on the train.

She felt something stir inside, a response to the unspoken question put to her by the searching presence.

Her mind responded to the challenge, leaping at the pressure to tangle with it. As her thought touched the pressure, reality changed around her.

She no longer stood in the hotel dining room.

It was dark, as everything always was, but there was no sound, no scent. Then a light flared to life and Ardenne *saw* a man standing in front of her.

She closed her eyes. Hope fluttered in her chest like a caged butterfly. But when she opened them again, the man still stood there. A man wearing a smart tailored suit, his silky silver-white hair cut short with military precision. A smile tilted one side of his full mouth, while green eyes watched her with an expression that could only be called avaricious.

"*I can see you.*"

"*Of course you can.*"

His cultured tones gave her the clue as to who he was. "*Mr. Piven?*"

He nodded.

"*But this isn't like how I saw on the train.*" It was just like in her dream of Gabriel.

"*No. We're in a space between time, connected through your mind. In this place, mystical energies are equalized. The mistake in your blood, the thing that makes you blind, is canceled out here.*"

"*What mistake?*"

He waved his hand. "*Let's not get caught up with trivialities.*"

Trivialities! The fact she could see with her own eyes was hardly trivial! The man was not only dangerous he was unfeeling.

"*You're right. I am,*" he said, reading her mind. "*I don't care how seeing me makes you feel. I'm here to administer the Trial, to see if you're worthy to be trained. Nothing more.*"

Sarita was right. The man was an ass! But showing her anger would gain her no answers, so she swallowed it down and asked, "*The Trial? Sarita mentioned it.*"

"*I'm sure she did.*"

"*But she didn't mention why it's necessary. You already know I have power. Why not just train me?*"

His lips quirked. "*What happened on your journey to Firenze tells us you have some talent but it doesn't tell us exactly what that entails or where your strengths truly lie. Now, let's start with something simple.*" He tapped his lip. "*You thought of Gabriel a moment ago. Show him to me.*"

Ardenne gaped at him. "*How did you know that?*"

He rolled his eyes and spoke slowly as if to someone incredibly stupid. "*We are connected to this place through your mind so I can hear your thoughts as loud as my own. It's how we're communicating now. Haven't you noticed you're not actually speaking with your mouth?*"

She blinked. No, she hadn't noticed.

"Now stop quibbling about unimportant details and show me what I ask, otherwise I will report back to Carrington that you aren't worth our time."

Reining in her anger as Sarita had warned her to do, she closed her eyes, concentrating on the strongest image of Gabriel she had. The one she'd 'seen' on the train. Sweat prickled her brow and she thought for a moment she wasn't going to be able to do it, that she'd fail. Then his heavenly face—what she thought was his heavenly face—formed a vivid picture in her mind.

"Good. Strong projection."

Uncertain what he meant, she opened her eyes and was shocked to see the image of Gabriel standing in front of her.

It wavered for a moment before coming back into focus. Then he smiled at her as he'd done in her dream.

"My, my. This is quite remarkable. Although I never thought him quite so pretty. Or quite so well built."

"You know Gabriel?"

"The Lonely Angel? Yes, we've met."

A shudder, like ice shearing off a glacier, sliced through Ardenne at the tone in his voice. The image of Gabriel disappeared, sucked back inside her, almost as if she was trying to protect him from the predatory gleam in Mr. Piven's eyes. Before she could shrink from it, Mr. Piven straightened, his gaze returning to the cooled disinterest of earlier.

"Now, show me something else. How about the Tea Room?"

Ardenne swallowed hard, confused by the sudden change of topic. *"Of this hotel?"*

"Of course."

Ardenne frowned. *"But I haven't been here before and nobody has described it to me so I can't create a mind-map."*

Mr. Piven rolled his eyes. *"You can see with more than your eyes. I've already told you we know what you did on the train."*

"*But ... I've only ever used a vampire's eyes to see and there isn't one at the hotel.*"

His nostrils flared briefly before he said, "*Then how do you explain that stunning image of Gabriel? Who was with you when you gained that image?*"

"*Sarita.*" The name shuddered out of her as hope fluttered in her chest again. "*So, I can do this with anyone?*"

"*Of course. You are an empath in the full sense of the word.*"

"*An empath?*" What did that mean?

He sighed and looked around as if to ask the empty air 'Am I talking to myself?'

"*Yes, girl, you are an empath. You feel what others feel, think what they think, see what they see. You can read the images out of people's minds. How else do you explain all you've accomplished despite the fact you're blind?*"

Ardenne stiffened. "*I always thought I've accomplished all I have because I'm intelligent and determined. And because I had a good enough imagination to shape people's descriptions into images in my mind.*" That had to be it. It couldn't have been because she actually saw through people's eyes because Lord Hei would have known. Did he know? No, he couldn't. He wouldn't do that to her. Wouldn't keep such a truth from her. Piven was wrong.

He smiled. "*Such fatiguing naiveté.*" He waved his hand in a brushing motion. "*Now, read the images out of my mind to show me the tea room. I need to see how much I will have to work with.*"

If she hadn't been pre-warned by Sarita, she would have lost her temper then and called him the bastard he truly was. But she had been warned so she held onto her emotions and endeavored to do what he'd requested.

She thought about the feeling that had rocked through her when she'd entered the minds of the vampire on the train and the ones on the streets of *Firenze* and tried to recapture it.

A tight pressure caught at her mind, like pushing through deep water. She fought it, lungs bursting with the effort and then she was through, something buoyant breaking the surface.

A picture clarified in her mind.

Concentrating on it, she smiled as tables and chairs appeared around them where there had only been dark. The tables were covered in crisp white tablecloths, set with sparkling crystal, fine china, and sterling silver cutlery. The chairs had rounded backs, the arches carved and beautifully polished, the seats covered in brocade—little flowers in greens and russets and browns—the names of the colors pulled out of his mind along with the images.

The floor shifted and changed, and plush carpet appeared there, billowing in waves to finally settle underneath them. A fine wool carpet woven into checks made up of rich burgundy and deepest turquoise.

Hungry to see more, she turned slowly.

Miniature copies of famous statues by Michelangelo, Ammannati and Cellini—the names supplied from Mr. Piven's mind again—flanked the windows and doors. Walls appeared, covered in striped wallpaper in cream and pinks and burgundy. Heavy porcelain vases with ornate handles stood in the corners of the room, a bowery of flowers exploding from them. Chandeliers hung from the ceiling, glistening in the light, sending little rainfalls of rainbow colors over everything.

"Good. You do have talent. Sarita tells me you channeled the vampire's power to kick him away. Show me."

"How? There's no vampire here."

"You should be able to show me by moving whatever you set your sights on. I'll give you some incentive, shall I?"

Suddenly one of the vases was hurtling toward her. She ducked and it smashed against the wall behind her.

"You move quickly. Which is good. But that's not what I had in mind. Shall we try again?"

"Wait!" she said, as another vase lifted, shoving her hands up in front of her.

The vase stopped moving and Mr. Piven turned to her, brow raised. *"Good."*

Ardenne stared at the hovering vase. *"I'm not doing that. Am I?"*

"Well, I certainly didn't stop it." He let the vase drop to the floor and then another one lifted. *"This time, don't just stop it. Push it away as you did the vampire on the train."*

"I don't know how."

"Pull the how out of my mind like you pulled the names of the colors and the artists. You let your instincts guide you in that. Let them guide you in this as well."

He didn't give her time to take that in, just threw the vase at her with his mind. She lifted her hands as she'd done the first time, willing it to stop. The vase halted in mid-air. *"Good. Now think about it smashing against the wall over there,"* he said. *"Use the information in my mind to show you how to do it."*

She reached into his mind, saw how he used his power—visualizing what he wanted then using the vastness of magical energy inside him to make it happen. She mirrored his experience and a second later, the vase smashed against the far wall.

"Not bad. Now, try this."

He led her through several exercises, each designed to test her, each increasingly more difficult. Ardenne couldn't shake the feeling he wanted her to fail. And for each task, she had to press into his mind to scavenge for knowledge that would help her to succeed.

The contact with his mind sickened her. There was darkness inside him that made her tremble and a strong sense that he was allowing her inside only because it amused him. If he wanted to, he could shove her out or damage her in a way from which she would never recover.

But for some reason, he didn't. He held that viciousness back. She wondered at the power he held reined in. Would she ever have the power to match it? Power to match Gabriel? So she could stand beside him, his equal, as she'd done in the dream?

She hoped so.

"That's enough," he said, then disappeared.

Around her, everything became pitch black, as if he'd taken the light with him. Dread crept up her chest and her breath caught in her throat as she tamped down the panic of being left in this awful blank place with no way of escaping. She didn't know how to get out of here without his help. *"Come back!"*

A shadow flickered in the corner of her eye and then he stood beside her.

Shock ricocheted across his narrow face. *"How did you do that?"* He grasped her shoulders, fingers pinching.

She shook her head, vibrating with fear. *"I … I don't know."*

"No one has ever called me back. No one has ever been able to except …" He stopped, visibly shaken, his fingers bruising her flesh. *"No. You're not your mother."*

"My mother? You knew my mother?" She had no idea how he could. Before her death, Tara Bartolli had never left *Casa Cinque.*

He shook his head, ignoring her question. *"I need to see Carrington."*

He began to fade away. *"Wait! How do I get out of here?"*

"Think of Sarita. She's your anchor. Take yourself back to reality and kindly let me stay there this time. Oh, and by the way, only a second has passed in real time. Give nothing away."

Too excited to be angry with his impatience, Ardenne closed her eyes and willed herself back to Sarita. She heard the change, knew by the velvet darkness behind her eyes that she was back in the tea room. But after all she'd just been through, only one thought entered her mind: Had Mr. Piven told the truth? Could she use anyone's eyes to see? Could she do so now without anyone being the wiser?

She opened her eyes and practiced first on Mr. Piven. That connection was easy, though disturbing. With the incautious eyes of a newborn wanting to see too much, she popped into Master Solari's mind then Sarita's. She tried someone nearby, then another person. It was difficult at first, but as she moved around, it became easy, like breathing.

Despite Mr. Piven's sense of urgency in the Trial, he now seemed completely unconcerned as he took a seat at the table beside Master Solari and discussed her training over cappuccino and *torta*.

It gave Ardenne time to explore with this new knowledge of power.

The first thing that struck her was the difference in everyone's perceptions.

Sarita looked at everything with the hunger of a starving person, as if afraid everything good was about to be taken away.

Ardenne frowned. Maybe that had to do with Mr. Piven's presence. Her friend was certainly worried about him. And rightly so given all she'd felt inside him.

Her thoughts slipped back to him and what being in his mind was like, and suddenly, she was there again, looking out of his eyes.

His perception was sharp, but flattened, as if everything bored him except when he looked at Ardenne or Sarita.

Masking a grimace and a shudder, she slipped out and into Master Solari's mind again. His perception was the opposite of Mr. Piven's, full of warmth and excitement at what life brought. He looked at Sarita with unmasked affection, so proud of his beautiful niece. Ardenne agreed with him regarding Sarita being beautiful. With her short, choppy, urchin hair, golden brown eyes, and a lovely smile widening her generous mouth, she was just as Ardenne had imagined.

She realized she didn't have to 'imagine' again and almost laughed out loud at the thought. She could now 'see' the world as others did. Just like she'd seen Gabriel. Seen out of his eyes last night on the hill when he'd used his powers to topple her into his memory.

Remembering the darkness, the terror, the passion, she shivered.

"Are you cold, Ardenne?"

She shook her head, shoving all thoughts of Gabriel aside and skipped from person to person to 'see'. Conversation swirled around her until she heard Piven say, "Well, I think that's all I need. I imagine you want Ardenne's training to begin immediately?"

"It is a priority," Master Solari said.

"Have Sarita bring her to my studio tomorrow, promptly at nine and we'll get started."

"That's wonderful, isn't it, Sarita?"

Sarita nodded, her expression saying how far from wonderful she thought it.

She'd said he was dangerous but right now, Ardenne didn't care. He'd taught her so much already.

No matter the cost, she wanted to learn more.

CHAPTER 14

THE COVEN

Her sight is gone but her talents lend her vision. It is a wonder and a burden to see with others' eyes. This I know. For her burden is mine.
Extract from Mary Middleton's Diary, June 6, 1534

"Gabriel? No, he can't come with us. He's gone."

"Gone?" Ardenne paused, the spoonful of cereal halfway to her lips as Master Solari's words stabbed through her. "What do you mean gone?"

"He's gone hunting. Plenty of Wild and Dark Brethren around at this time of the year." Master Solari patted her on the shoulder. "No need to worry though. You're perfectly safe here, otherwise Gabriel wouldn't have left."

"He's not staying to train me alongside Mr. Piven?" For some reason, despite Gabriel telling her he was leaving when they were on the hill overlooking *Firenze,* she'd not allowed herself to believe it was true. He had to stay here to train her. He had to.

"Piven is perfectly capable of training you without Gabriel's assistance. He is one of the best the Middleton Coven has to offer.

His talents don't only lie in the specialist training you need; he is also an expert at all forms of martial arts. I've never seen anyone better—except Gabriel. Now, there's a match I'd like to see. Not that I'm likely to." He sighed. "Oh well. Special things ahead for you, Ardenne. You're a very lucky girl. You will be in very good hands. Speaking of which ..." He stood, his chair legs making a screeching noise as they dragged across the tiles. "You better get a hurry on, or you'll be late."

He came to stand beside her, his large hand curving over her shoulder, giving it a light squeeze. He gave her an avuncular kiss on the top of the head and then left the room in the same way he always did—with a great amount of energy and gusto.

Ardenne swallowed hard and dropped her spoon in her cereal. She was no longer hungry.

She forced her mind to the day ahead.

She was so nervous. Would she have been so nervous if she'd known she was a witch all her life? Would that have made the idea of the training ahead seem less stressful? She had a feeling it might have.

She wished she knew for certain why they'd kept it from her. Sarita said she didn't know why, other than it was probably because it was dangerous being a witch among vampires.

"*I know that more than others,*" Sarita had said to her. "*My association with the coven has had to be kept secret from all but the Cousins because others can't know that Lord Hei has had an association with the Middleton family for centuries.*"

"*But why? Why is it like that?*"

"*There are certain covens who would come after us simply because of our association with vampires—for them, it is sacrilege that a witch would use their powers in the service of them. But for you, the Wild and Dark Brethren are also a risk in a way they aren't for me. I'm too low a cog in the wheels of the machine for them to take notice of, but they wouldn't stop in their efforts to get to you if they knew Lord Hei had a witch as Prime. Apart from the fact vampires and witches have been mortal enemies for centuries, they quite simply wouldn't countenance Lord Hei having that kind of advantage."*

Everything Sarita had said made sense, and Ardenne had tried not to let the secrecy of it all matter. She could get angry about it, or she could just get on with her training and try to be more than anyone ever imagined.

Be more than Gabriel thought she could be.

Damn it! Why did he have to slip back into her thoughts again?

"Good morning, Ari."

She jumped as Sarita dropped a kiss on her cheek.

Sarita laughed lightly. "Sorry, I didn't mean to scare you."

"You didn't scare me. I was just lost in thought."

"I can see that." The chair scraped a little as she took a seat. "Is that apple and rhubarb compote? Ooh, I'll have to thank Chef later. He knows I love apple and rhubarb with my cereal." The jingle of spoon against pot as Sarita helped herself, rang in the air. "Are you going to finish your breakfast, Ari? You know you should have a good breakfast. Piven is going to work you hard."

Ardenne picked up her spoon again, toyed with it. "Did you know Gabriel has left?"

"Yes."

"He didn't say goodbye."

"Did you expect him to?"

"I ... no ... I ... When will he be back?"

"I don't know. Gabriel is a law unto himself."

"But he's my Guardian."

"Yes. But tracking down the Wild who attacked the train and finding out how they knew you were on it is more important than staying here where you are guarded by the Cousins."

"The train? That was weeks ago."

"He's apparently got a new lead."

Ardenne didn't believe that. It was just an excuse so he could get away from her. He regretted showing her his past, sharing himself with her. Now he was shunning her. And for what? Because he was ashamed? Worried that he'd done the wrong thing to share what he had?

Anger a rising buzz under her skin, she said, "What if more Wild or Dark Brethren are close by and come for me here? Who's going to protect us?"

Sarita laid her hand over Ardenne's, stopping her from drumming the spoon on the table. "Is that what this is about? You're worried about being attacked again?" She gripped Ardenne's hand. "You don't have to worry about that. We're capable of protecting ourselves. All the Cousins are fully trained, and I'm not the only witch among them with abilities that can be used to protect you. Besides, Lord Hei is sending Corinna. She'll be here later today. Now, finish your breakfast. We need to get going."

"I'm not hungry." Ardenne pushed her chair back and stood. "I'll finish getting ready then meet you at the car."

"Ari—"

Ardenne rushed away, ignoring Sarita's call. After all, what more was there to say? Gabriel had left her again and he probably wasn't ever going to come back if he could help it.

She battled with her anger, her disappointment as she put on her sneakers, cleaned her teeth, and brushed her hair. It annoyed her further that she couldn't even explain to herself why she was so angry and disappointed. Gabriel had never promised her anything. Just because she'd thought they'd had a special moment on the hill overlooking *Firenze* didn't mean it was special for him. In fact, for him, obviously, it meant the opposite.

He was gone and who knew when he might be back? It could be years. Probably would be years given his record.

Some Guardian!

She pulled her laces tight. They snapped in her hand. "Crap!" Kicking off her old runners, she grabbed the new pair she'd bought with Sarita last week. Thankfully she had these, as trying to find a new shoelace and stringing it would definitely make her late.

Being gentler this time, she tied her laces and stood up. She had to pull herself together. Prepare herself. Mr. Piven wasn't going to be easy to deal with. She needed to be mentally present, or he would make her suffer.

Grabbing her backpack, she headed downstairs and outside to the car.

Sarita was already there. Alone.

"Is Master Solari not coming?"

"No. He's got things to do this morning. But we'll be fine. Bruno is ex-special services and Paulo's car is like a tank."

Ardenne nodded and hopped in. The engine revved and they were off.

She tried to center her mind as they drove; tried to enjoy the sounds and scents wafting in the car from outside. Tried to be excited that her training began today. Tried to enjoy the character of *Firenze* as they drove through her labyrinthine streets, but today's journey wasn't like the other ones she'd made. She'd lost something and she was damned if she understood exactly what it was. Except she knew it was wrapped up in what had happened between her and Gabriel on that hill above *Firenze*.

"Ardenne, we're here."

Ardenne started and fumbled for a moment, trying to focus. She slipped into Sarita's mind to see where 'here' was.

To their left, the *Arno* wended its way under the Florentine bridges. To their right stood a traditional *Firenze* building, its yellow facade faded and crumbling, but like an old lady who clings to memories of youth, it held onto grace by its wrinkled fingertips, loving the morning shadows that hid the worst of times' ravages.

Sarita made her wait for Paulo and Bruno to exit the car and check out the area before she let Ardenne push open her door. Together, they walked inside, Paulo in front, Bruno behind, and ascended the steep stairs.

The scent of wood polish and the dusky pungency of old mold hung in the air and increased her feeling of loss, the echo of their footsteps an empty ache in her chest. She sighed and mentally berated herself. *Get over it, Ardenne. He's gone. This is exciting, so be excited.*

She pulled back her shoulders and lifted her head. She was going to meet Mr. Piven with a smile on her face, head held high.

On the third floor, Sarita pushed open a set of double doors. They walked into a room set up for training in all forms of martial arts.

Mr. Piven stood behind a desk in the nearest corner. "You can go. She's safe in this building," he said, indicating Paulo and Bruno. They both nodded and left. Ardenne heard the heavy clunk of their boots echo through the stairwell as they descended.

"You can go too," he said, gesturing to Sarita. "I'll call you when we're done."

Ardenne felt hostility shudder through her friend as she said, "I'm not going anywhere."

"You'll go if I tell you to go."

"Relax, Sasha. I want Sarita here."

Sarita gasped and turned as another man entered the room behind them. Tall, slim but well-muscled, he was dressed casually in a loose wool knit gray top and jeans. He looked like a scholar, his face pale and drawn. His hair was a chestnut brown—the color she picked out of Sarita's mind—and cut short. He was handsome. Not Gabriel handsome, but an earthy handsomeness, with lovely golden eyes tilted at an exotic angle.

"Carrington? You said you weren't coming yet."

This was Carrington? Did this mean he was sure? And what was he sure about? Her?

She wanted to ask but the turmoil of emotions tumbling around her friend's mind at the sight of this man were too overwhelming— exquisite happiness mixed with anger.

"Surprise," he said, smiling wide.

Sarita ran into his arms.

Ardenne fell out of her Companion's mind, but not before she'd felt that moment of contact, body to body, mouth to mouth.

Oh! She should have picked up on this when she'd overheard

their call. The way Sarita had called him Carry; the gentleness in his voice when he'd spoken to her had been more than the affection of a boss to a subordinate. It had told her they were a couple if she'd only chosen to listen.

Her lips tingled from the remembered sensation of being in Sarita's mind when they began to kiss. She touched the back of her hand to her lips, sucked in a breath. Heat raced through her, chased by a curious, needy sensation that raised the hairs on her arms. An image of Gabriel appeared in her mind. His lips widened in a smile, teeth glistening in the light, eyes burning with a fire she wished was real. Ardenne thought she might faint from the heat, the jittery awareness rushing through her body.

"Touching," Mr. Piven drawled. "But do you think we can get on with things? We're here to begin the girl's training."

"First things first, Sasha." Carrington's voice was a little different from when she'd heard it on the phone; more like a warm caress from a good friend.

Ardenne couldn't help but like him. Especially given the feelings emanating from Sarita. It was strange realizing she'd always been able to read other people's emotions, she'd just never known that's what she was doing—it gave her quite a heads-up.

She slipped back into Sarita's mind as Carrington's large warm hand surrounded hers and shook. "I couldn't wait to come and meet you after what Sarita told us, but I have to say I'm even more impressed to meet someone who could actually disconcert Sasha."

"Mr. Piven's first name is Sasha?"

"Piven to you. You can drop the Mr."

His killing tone made it clear she'd suffer if she laughed. "Of course, Piven." She didn't think she could call him Sasha without laughing. It was just such an impossible name for a man like him.

"Sasha, are you able to give us a few moments?"

Piven sighed. "If I must."

"You must."

"Don't do it for my benefit," Sarita snapped.

"I wouldn't do anything for your benefit. I've got a few things to organize anyway that would be better done without sticky ears around."

"I'll let you know when we need you," Carrington said.

"Very well."

The door clicked closed and he was gone. He moved so quietly, Ardenne couldn't even hear the click of his shoes on the wooden stairs outside the door.

Tension strung the air as she turned her attention back to Carrington and Sarita.

"You didn't have to do that for me," Sarita said quietly.

"Yes, I did, Sari." He brushed the hair away from Sarita's face, cupping her cheeks in his warm hands. "Besides, I did it as much for Sasha. You two could kill each other with looks alone."

Sarita snorted. "I'm not that bad. I just don't see why you had to send him."

"You know why. He's the only one I fully trust with Ardenne."

Ardenne frowned at that. "Why? Why am I so special?"

"Because you're Lord Hei's prodigy, that's why."

She laughed at that. "I wouldn't call myself that."

"What else would you call yourself?"

She shrugged and changed the topic. She didn't want to talk about herself. "How does Master Solari seem to know Piven so well? And why has he been sent to teach me?"

"I think Sarita has already told you that the coven have been working with Lord Hei for years against our mutual enemies. Sasha has built a relationship with Vincente Solari over the years to help train his men in areas they usually don't cover."

"Wet work," Sarita snarled.

"Some. When necessary."

"Magic?" Ardenne asked.

"No. Although, he is adept. Except for a few, like my Sarita ..." His voice warmed at her name, "... most of them have no magic. Unlike the Bartolli though, they do need to know how to work and fight with those who do. And so people like Sasha are sent to train them."

Ardenne frowned. "So, Piven will teach me magic and wet work?" She wasn't sure what wet work was, but it didn't sound good.

"No, he will not train you to be an assassin. He will train you to defend yourself and attack, both with magic and physically as necessary. He is our most accomplished technician of all magical forms as well as a most accomplished master in the arts of self-defense. You are very lucky."

"Or very unlucky."

Carrington turned amused eyes on Sarita. "I know you don't like Sasha, my love, but you can't deny his talent."

"His talent is why I don't like him." She leaned forward, her voice a harsh whisper. "I don't trust him."

"But I do. And that will have to be good enough. Right?"

Ardenne frowned, searching his face through Sarita's eyes. "What are you talking about?" She hoped to draw them out, to share more of what she'd overheard yesterday so she wouldn't have to pretend.

But Carrington's gaze went steely as he said, "That's unimportant. What is important is that before you begin your training, I need to show you something. I need you to see the results of what Piven can do for you so you trust him and don't question his intentions."

"And if I question?"

"Questioning him will be questioning me and Lord Hei. You don't know me yet, so I wouldn't expect you to follow me as Sarita and Piven do, but what it comes down to is, do you trust Lord Hei?"

She crossed her arms, fingers digging into her skin. Did she trust Lord Hei? A month ago, the answer would have been unequivocally yes. But now ... Now that she'd found out that she'd been lied to all her life, that nothing was truly as she'd been brought up to believe, that to learn, she must participate in the lie to most of her family back home—the yes didn't come quite as easily. Except ...

She wanted to learn. She longed for knowledge and to learn more of the truth. There was much they were keeping from her. What she'd learned wasn't even the tip of the iceberg. It was but a snowflake lying at the top of it.

Trust and truth. They kind of went hand in hand. She'd had a taste of both in the last month as she'd learned more about the truth of the world she lived in, trust that she could handle it finally being given to her. It was freeing even though she knew so much was still being kept back from her. But she wanted to know it all and the only way for that to happen was to learn from Piven. If that meant doing everything he said without question ... "I agree to your terms. When do we start?"

Carrington laughed. "You're exactly like your mother."

Before Ardenne could ask how he'd known Tara Bartolli, he placed his hands on her face, fingertips pressing into her skin, just like Gabriel had done.

"Enter my mind."

Knowing this was the first test of the unquestioning agreement she'd just made, Ardenne slipped into Carrington's mind to see a war of emotion rage across Sarita's face, tinged with concern. Then Carrington closed his eyes, his fingers firming. "A memory was given to me. I want you to see. Watch. Listen. Learn."

Blackness greeted her. And just like the other night with Gabriel, images began to flicker past, lightning fast. She was pulled, and then fell, but knowing what was happening this time, she didn't panic.

However, instead of slipping into the memory with a gentle slide, she collided with it, slamming into another's consciousness, another's sight, with a force that caused pain. The pain lasted a bare moment and when it was gone, she gasped. She'd been in this mind before, just the other night.

This was Gabriel's memory. But how?

"It doesn't matter how. Watch. Listen. Learn."

CHAPTER 15
THE PAST

I have only one lesson on the importance of history and it is this:
The past is just as important as the future.
This I have to remind myself as I lose hours, days, weeks, to the
visions of the future that plague my very existence. For, the only
way to truly understand the future possibilities I see is to learn all I
can about what has already passed. It is incumbent on us to learn
all we can of history and to never forget.
So while you study the visions of the future I see, make sure you do
not ignore the past. It will be to your detriment if you do.
Extract from The Middleton Manifesto, Section on History,
Lesson 1

Questions were pushed aside as Ardenne concentrated on the scene before her. The dark of night draped the landscape—the moonlight obscured by silver-tinged black clouds lent no light to what she was seeing. Yet despite the lack of illumination, Ardenne could see as if it were day.

No. Clearer than day.

A dark alley spread out below her, a narrow canyon between towering walls of brick and steel and concrete. She saw every inch, every scratch and lump in the brick and concrete, every mark in the surface of the steel and glass.

Everything was beautiful. More than beautiful. Breathtaking. Extraordinary. None of those words quite expressed the exquisiteness of what she was seeing; how she was seeing.

This was vampire sight.

No, not just any vampire. It was Gabriel's vampire sight. She knew from the feel of it, the texture, the emotion that lay behind it, because she'd experienced it with him in the memories he'd already shared with her.

How could he function when he saw things like this? All she wanted to do was stay here and *look*.

Longing stirred inside her. If only ...

But no. Even if she could gain sight, it would never be *this*.

Jealousy's clawlike fingers gripped her, but before she could sink into its green haze, a sound caught her attention.

A woman stumbled along the alley, bare feet tripping on the uneven paving stones. Her tight scarlet dress and stockings were ripped, one of her sleeves missing. Strands of her hair stuck up and hung down in uneven tumbling clumps. She steadied herself on the wall then lurched forward, leaving a dark smear behind.

Blood—red, dark. Gabriel gasped, a violent, *needful* hunger roaring to life inside him. But before it could take hold, he clamped down on it and forced himself to still and simply watch.

The woman's breath hiccupped in frightened gasps. Clouds shifted. Moonlight draped her in a silver glow. Her gaze darted up, nostrils flared. A red river marred the pale skin of her brow, her cheek.

Whimpering, she stumbled forward, bouncing off the walls, the dumpster, a car.

Glancing back, eyes wide, her dilated pupils searched the darkness. She stumbled forward, tripped on scattered garbage. Air exploded from her lungs as she hit the pavement.

Ardenne felt her pain, smelled her fear.

The woman's breath backed up in her throat as the sound of footsteps echoed along the alley.

"No!" A tortured whisper. A plea.

Ardenne could feel Gabriel tamping down the instinct to save in the same way he tamped down his hunger. He was here simply to watch.

She couldn't understand his attitude. The woman needed his help. Why wasn't he moving? Wasn't that their main tenant? To save the humans from all paranormal threats, especially of the vampiric kind? But no matter how much she wanted him to go to the woman's aid, he stayed where he was. Watching.

Shadows grew large on the wall. Four figures slipped from the darkness, fingers extended, nails like talons, heads shaved, fangs bared, faces covered with tattoos.

Dark Brethren. She knew they were because they matched Gabriel's description to perfection.

They were hunting the injured woman.

Fury ripped through her; why was Gabriel still holding back? His hunger had roared to the fore again, as did his need to save, but he remained where he was.

What the fuck? Couldn't he see she was about to die?

The Dark Brethren were almost upon the woman when she sprang to her feet, the cry on her lips no longer one of fear. Spinning, she loosed something from one hand then the other, flashes of silver too fast to make out.

Two of the Dark Brethren flew backward, landing with a thud.

Screams erupted. Their bodies jerked with spasms before exploding in bright flame that flared and died in a moment, leaving only ash and a puddle of molten glistening silver.

The remaining Dark Brethren screeched, razor-like teeth flashing in the low light, then leaped toward the now-grinning woman.

She dove sideways. Her roundhouse kick whipped through the air, connecting with one of the Brethren. He flew back into his brother. In the blink of an eye, they were up.

So was the woman.

Power exuded from her. Despite obvious injuries, she was strong, determined.

A silver streak spun from her hand again. It caught one of the Brethren mid-leap, flinging him back. He crunched against the wall like a rag doll, falling to twitch and spasm then burst into flames. The last Brethren halted mid-stride, weighing his options. Then he leaped up, almost too fast to be seen.

A sword appeared in the woman's hand—where it had come from, Ardenne couldn't see. It arched through the air, decapitating the vampire as he sailed overhead. There were two sickening thumps.

The woman wiped the sword on her torn dress, barely panting—Ardenne was more breathless—a satisfied smile curling her lips.

"Anita! What the hell do you think you're doing? I told you to wait."

The woman spun to face a man who appeared in the alley behind her. "I didn't. So kill me."

"That's not funny."

"Sorry." She didn't sound sorry at all. But she did pout, the pout of a woman determined to get her way. "Come on, S. Help me clean up this mess. I can't do it by myself. I need you."

His pose made Ardenne think of the way Sarita felt about Carrington. But Anita didn't return his longing. She smiled at him, a crooked I'm-sorry-but-don't-expect-too-much smile. He moved forward, muttering under his breath. His pale hair glinted silver in the moonlight, a brilliant flare against his pitch-black attire.

"For Christ's sake, Anita. Four of them? Did you realize there was four of them before you sprung your trap?"

"No. It was a bit of a surprise. But I handled it."

He sighed. "We were going to go after these together." His gaze roamed over her again. "Your brother is going to kill me."

"Not if you don't tell him."

He lifted his face from the carnage and Ardenne gasped as moonlight showed her his features.

Piven!

A younger Piven. Although not too young. There was no roundness of youth to his features. He was a man. Danger emanated from him like steam off a hot pavement. Darkness lurked in the depths of his green eyes—that Gabriel could see quite clearly. Whatever had made him that way had already touched his life.

He focused those green eyes on Anita, all signs of desire gone, anger flickering in their depths.

"It's not my job to nursemaid you."

"I didn't ask you to," Anita snapped, all pretense of sweet-talk gone. "Now stop blathering and help me clean this up."

Muttering under his breath, Piven waved her aside and, using his telekinesis, he lifted the body parts and dropped them onto the pile of ashes. Then he drove the same pale silver liquid she'd used to kill the others deep into the lumps of flesh. A bright, hot flash and the last Dark Brethren was gone.

Anita stepped back, wiping blood from her brow. "I don't suppose you could heal this?"

Piven gave her a long-suffering sigh, but after a moment, relented. He brushed a hand over her brow, then one over the wound on her side, the gesture loving, intimate. "You did this to yourself?"

"Helpless woman. The scent of blood—how could they resist?" She grinned.

Cocky, breathtaking, alive. Gabriel approved.

Piven shook his head. "Why I taught you how to fight, I'll never know."

"Because if you didn't, I'd go out hunting anyway. I'd already be dead."

He reached out and pulled her to him, brushing his hand over her dark hair, possessive. "Don't say that. Don't ever say that."

Pulling away, she smiled, patting his arm. "Hey, S. Come on. Don't go all mushy on me."

"I'm not. It's just that I lo—"

"No. Don't say it." Anita put her fingers to his lips. "We both know that's not on the cards. There's no point in ruining a beautiful friendship over something not meant to be. I love you, but as a friend. You need to be content with that."

He nodded slowly. "I am." Ardenne's heart went out to him in that moment. "But only because no other man will touch you either. The prophecy is clear." Her heart slammed back into her chest at the glint in his eyes as he said those words.

Anita frowned. "You know how that part of that particular prophecy upsets me."

Piven smiled knowingly. "You're not upset—not really."

"Yes, I am."

His smile saddened. "No. I know you, Anita. You don't want to give yourself to anyone. Not even someone who has always been there for you; even going up against my conscience—"

"You mean my brother!"

He glared at her but carried on as if she hadn't spoken. "... my conscience to champion you and your abilities."

"And I have thanked you for that, over and over."

"But you don't truly appreciate it, do you? And you have no idea of what it does to me when you—" He waved his hand at the alley where carnage had reigned only minutes before. Then he shook his head, turned, and began to walk away.

"Come on, S," she said. "Don't be like that." She grabbed his arm.

For a moment it looked like he'd shrug her off, but then he stopped, acceptance dulling his eyes as she said, "Pretty please with a cherry on top?"

He rolled his eyes and threw his hands in the air, an almost smile twitching at the corner of his lips. "I can never stay cross with you."

"I know." Her smile was quick, mischievous.

"You're a demon."

"No. I kill demons."

"Yes, you do. I'm half afraid that one day you'll see the demon that's deep inside me and do what you were born to do."

"I would never hurt you. Not my precious Sasha. You know how much you mean to me. How much I rely on you."

His mouth flickered into a smile and he nodded then looked down at their clenched hands.

Ardenne shivered. Their silence, the way he looked at Anita, unsettled her, but she had no clue why.

Anita broke the tableau. Looking up at Piven, she flashed him a smile. "Show me how to retrieve the Silver Fire? There's only a little left and my brother mustn't know I stole it."

Piven shook his head. "I have no idea why I allowed you to talk me into using it."

"Because you knew I was right."

He rolled his eyes. "What if I teach you the extraction technique and something happens—we can't replace it as you well know. Mary Middleton took the knowledge of how to make it with her."

"Unbelievable, right? What was she thinking?" she said, sounding like she was mimicking him as she led him forward to the pile of ash that had been a Dark Brethren only moments before. "To let one of our greatest weapons against the vampire plague disappear with the mists of time? I ..." She shook her head, striking a stiff pose that looked comically like the one Piven held. "Words escape me." Then she laughed, nudging his arm and waggling her brows. "We'll just have to find the secret."

"Yes, and while we're at it we'll discover how to turn coal to gold."

"Pessimistic much?" She snorted. "Come on, Mr. Grumpy. Just show me. Nothing bad will happen."

"How do you know?"

"Because you're you and I'm me and together we're going to rule the world!" She laughed again as he grumbled something but then moved to show her exactly how to get the Silver Fire out of the pile of ash.

"*She is magnificent, isn't she?*" Gabriel's rich, slightly accented voice whispered in the air.

"*More than magnificent.*" A deeper voice, just as beautiful, answered. A voice she knew as well as Gabriel's.

Lord Hei.

He must have asked Gabriel to give Carrington this memory. But why?

"*She's ... dangerous.*" There was a slight pause and then he said, "*You were right about her, Gabriel. We cannot allow these killings to ruin our plans. Nor can we allow her to be hurt in her endeavors. She is talented and Piven has trained her well but she's ...*"

"*Overconfident. She's bound to make a mistake at some stage.*"

"*Exactly. Which makes it even more dangerous for everyone. Especially if she is, as you rightly suspect, a Huntress.*" He cursed under his breath. "*I must talk to Carrington as soon as possible about bringing her to us for testing.*"

"*You want me to stay and ensure she gets into no lasting danger until she can be sent to us for the right training?*"

Lord Hei's chuckle rang softly in the air around them. "*Do not worry, my son. I am not tying you to watch this witch or to train her. I will send someone else to take on the role of her Guardian until she is ready to be sent to me. Which, given how progressed I think she is, will have to be soon. But until I talk to Carrington about her, you must stay. I feel there is something about her other than the obvious ... she must stay safe.*"

"*Yes, my Sire.*"

Movement at his side and then, "*Also, try and learn more about this Silver Fire. I never knew such a weapon existed. It seems Mary kept more secrets than I knew.*"

"*Your will.*"

Gabriel turned from the scene below.

But before she could journey with him, another presence

slammed into her, knocking her out of the memory and away from the beauty of Gabriel's sight.

Swirling black and sparks of white surrounded her as she gasped for breath.

"What? Where am I?"

"I'm sorry that hurt, but I needed to talk to you." The familiar feminine voice rang in her ears, the voice from her dreams. *"They will use you as they used me. Remember this. Remember it well."*

"Who are you?"

"All in good time, my darling. All in good time."

Ardenne turned around, spinning in the darkness, searching. She had to know. Had to find out. *"Where are you?"*

"Ardenne!" Carrington's voice stopped her cold. *"Come back to me, now."* His command pulled her through the darkness, away from the other, terrifyingly familiar presence and into the light of his sight.

"No!" she cried out, but it was too late. The presence was gone and, in its place, a stabbing pain as all she'd seen surged through her. She pulled out of Carrington's mind, but it made no difference.

Sarita grabbed her arm as she staggered, lowering her into a chair.

"Here, let me help." She put her hands on Ardenne, in much the same way Carrington had, but rather than falling into a memory, the images softened, and the pain slipped away.

"Better?"

Breath slicing her lungs, Ardenne nodded. "Better."

"I'm sorry to cause you pain," Carrington said. There was something of grief in his voice which indicated the pain she'd felt might have been his.

"Why did you show me that? It wasn't just about Piven's ability to teach me, was it?"

"Not entirely."

Ardenne slipped into Sarita's mind, needing to see his face.

"Sari," Carrington said. "Would you be so kind as to look at me? I think our young pupil here would like to see my expression."

Sarita turned abruptly to face him. "See your expression? What do you mean?"

Chuckling, Carrington patted Sarita's hand but never moved his gaze from Ardenne's face. "A light touch. You were right, Piven."

Piven was back?

"I'm never wrong."

Sarita frowned. "What are you talking about?"

Carrington turned to Sarita and cupped her cheek in his pale hand. Ardenne felt the contact like water sizzling on a hot plate.

"Sari, my love. What occurred with Ardenne on the train was not an anomaly when she used the vampire's eyes to see. She's an empath. She can slip into any of our minds and see. She's probably done it for years without realizing."

The shock on Sarita's face was replaced with a happy welling of tears. "Oh, by the Goddess! You can see! That's ... amazing. I never guessed. What's it like?"

Ardenne screwed up her mouth, touched by her friend's excitement. "It's like ... I can only see what you're looking at. If I'm interested in something else, then it's bad luck. Also, people see things so differently. If there are many people in a room, I can skip between them and see the same thing in a different way each time. It's confusing."

"What an incredible talent!"

"Oh, for fuck's sake! She's talented, you're talented, we're all talented. Can we get on with why we're here?"

"Now, now, Sasha," Carrington broke in. "No need to get snippy. Ardenne is incredibly gifted as you well know."

"A gift is nothing without the ability to use it."

"Which is why we're here. And I think Ardenne has proven that she's willing to learn how to use her many gifts."

"Gifts? I thought I only had one."

"Oh no, my dear. Being an empath is but one of many gifts Sasha identified. Your ability to amplify and transfer the gifts of others and use them for yourself is one of the most impressive I've heard of.

Your intelligence, strength of will and character are also gifts. And that nifty trick you used pulling Sasha to you against his will ... I'm not sure what that was or how you did it. Maybe it has something to do with the vampiric blood that runs in your veins."

Ardenne frowned. "I don't have vampiric blood in my veins. I've not blood-bonded with Lord Hei yet." She slapped her hand over her mouth as she realized what she'd just said.

Carrington touched her shoulder. "I know of the ceremony. You give nothing away. Lord Hei and I have a long history. How do you think I got access to Gabriel's memory? So, don't worry. Besides, I didn't mean—" He shook his head. "Never mind. That's something for later. What is important is the reason I showed you that memory."

"But why did you want Gabriel's memory?"

"Because it's the pivotal memory; the one that changed everything for my sister."

"Your sister?"

Sarita grasped his hand as he nodded. "Anita was my sister. And this brings me to the other reason I showed you this memory." He shook his head and whispered hoarsely, "She died. She died because she was driven. Because after witnessing the murder of our father, and the slow, sad death of our mother, she lusted for revenge. It made her incautious."

Ardenne couldn't stand looking at him as he told her this and slid out of Sarita's mind.

"I showed you this memory because I wanted you to see that, for all the power I think you might hold, you'll never succeed in learning all you must if you let emotion sway you. Anita was one of the most talented witches of our time. And yet, because she allowed revenge to become her reason for learning, in the end, all she learned was how to die. She let emotions rule rather than serve her—you saw that here—and they led to her death."

He stepped forward, crouched in front of her and took her hand in his. "Look at me." She obeyed and slipped into Sarita's mind.

"You must never forget the woman you saw in this memory. There are things you will learn, truths that have been kept from you and some that must still be kept from you—"

She opened her mouth to protest, but he squeezed her hand, shook his head, and continued. "They must still be kept from you until the right time. However, these truths will make it difficult at times to see past the now and understand the whole. Piven can help you to keep your emotions in check if you follow his training, but that isn't always enough. It wasn't for Anita. Because she lacked trust and questioned when she should have just listened. This is why I give you this memory. If you remember her, what she was, what she became, you will learn from her mistakes and not repeat them. I won't sanction your training if you do not promise me this."

Ardenne frowned. How could she make the same mistakes as a woman she'd never met? But she'd seen what Anita could do and knew how good Piven's training could be. If she learned from him and learned well, she would be one step closer to being Gabriel's equal.

"I'll remember. I promise."

"Good. Now I want to hear about what you've been learning so far and then Piven and I will map out your training regimen this afternoon."

"I won't be doing any training today?"

"Your training will start in full tomorrow. For now, take a seat and we'll talk."

Gabriel stood in the shadows of the bridge, watching as Sarita guided Ardenne out of the old, yellowing building hours later. He'd intended to leave. He had. But he had to stay just to make sure her meeting with Piven and Carrington went well. Had to make sure she was okay after seeing what they had shown her.

Looking up, he saw Carrington standing at the window. The

leader of the Middleton Coven shifted his focus from Ardenne and Sarita, his gaze unerringly finding Gabriel in the shadows.

With a small gesture of his hand, he indicated things had gone as planned.

Gabriel closed his eyes for a moment. He should be relieved. But the hot, roiling sensation inside him didn't allow relief. Since taking Ardenne to the hill where he'd died, showing her that memory, relief had been in short supply. He'd intended to frighten her, to make her give up whatever demon had made her follow the Wild that night. But even though she'd been frightened—the scent of her fear had been a bitter note on the clear, perfumed air of the hill—he'd seen that look of determination come over her face.

He'd erred, once again, in his dealings with her. It was the goddamned bond. It tore his determination and good sense to shreds. He wished he could be rid of it, but nothing he'd tried had worked. It was still there, gnawing away at his soul, worse than ever, making him behave as he'd never done before.

He should leave now, but he wanted to watch her for just a few seconds more. Make certain she was okay. As Sarita chatted to her, and the driver opened the car door, Ardenne hesitated.

"What is it?" he heard Sarita ask.

Ardenne turned, head cocked. "Can you look over there, Sarita?"

She pointed right at him. Sarita turned her head. He moved and was over the other side of the river before her eyes locked on the shadows he'd been hiding in.

"There's nothing there."

Ardenne nodded, her voice tight as she said, "I must have been mistaken. I'm tired. Can we go home?"

"Sure."

They were in the car and driving away before Gabriel dared breathe again.

She could sense him! Lord's Blood, she could sense him.

He had to go, just like he'd told Vincente he would. Her ability to sense him now made it damned obvious he couldn't stay another day. Because if she could sense him with such ease, would she be able to get into his mind more than she'd already done?

That couldn't be allowed. Certainly not now. No matter how much he'd hunted and fed over the last few days, he hadn't been able to fully lock the knowledge of what he must keep from her behind the door in his mind. He couldn't get the scent of her sweet blood out of his nose. He could barely stop himself from following them now.

When he'd told Vincente he wouldn't help train her, he had intended to stick around, hunt the area, see if he could pick up signs of Anita nearby—she would eventually come here—but just stay out of Ardenne's way, keep his distance, pretend he wasn't around. However, he couldn't even do that.

She was becoming a drug, an addiction.

He had to go cold turkey.

Clenching his fingers, he forced himself to breathe deep, filling his senses with the dank smell of moss and mold that clung to the rocks and houses by the river. It made no difference. The drive to follow her was overwhelming. He could feel through the bond a mix of emotions from her, a cocktail of confusion, wonder and hurt. It pulled at him.

He clenched his fingers tighter until the scent of his own blood stung the air. But the pain as his fingernails sliced into his skin wasn't enough.

He leaped over the river—so distracted, he didn't even check if anyone was watching—and raced away from *Firenze*. Away from Ardenne, determined this time to leave.

He had to keep her safe. But not just from himself. From the woman who had made it impossible for him to live his life the way he'd always lived it ever since she'd given birth in that tiny cabin in Switzerland.

Anita.

She was at the heart of so much.

He could no longer wait for Anita to come to them. He would hunt her down. And when he did, she would die. And then he would get back to what he did best: hunting the pestilence that threatened to destroy everything he'd ever loved.

He wasn't the Lonely Angel as people called him. He was an avenging one. And nothing and no one could be allowed to get in his way.

THE BLOOD OF TREESER

CHAPTER 16
TRAINING

*Violence is at her core, in her blood. It is carried in her flesh
memory from both her father and her mother. It marred her birth
and will mark her out as a target for others to find. But she can be
trained. She must be trained. It is essential if she is to survive.*
Extract from Mary Middleton's Diary, June 30, 1534

The next day, Piven alone was waiting for them at the door
at the front of the building when they arrived. According to
Sarita, Carrington had headed to Prague where he was
having a meeting with another large coven—apparently part of his
job was regular face to face meetings with all the major covens of the
world.

Ardenne watched Piven through Sarita's eyes as the car pulled up
outside the building. Despite her friend's jaundiced view of the man,
he still cut an impressive figure.

Today he was wearing all black—not the karate Gi of a Dan, but
cargo pants and a t-shirt. The muscles of his arms bulged out of his t-
shirt as he stood leaning nonchalantly against the door waiting, one
foot crossed over the other. It was difficult to tell what age he was

but given what she'd seen in the vision Carrington had shown her, he was obviously older than both Anita and Carrington, so he had to be in his late forties. Maybe even in his fifties.

She hoped she was as fit and ageless when she was that age.

Piven jerked his head at Sarita as she got out of the car. "Why are you here? I was told you had duties to attend to for Vincente today."

"Part of those duties is to see Ardenne to and from her training every day," Sarita said as she rounded the car to stand beside Corinna—who had appeared that morning ready to take up her responsibility as Ardenne's Guardian—as the vampire opened Ardenne's door so she could get out.

Piven snorted and pushed away from the door. "Fine. Time to stop the hand holding though. You can go as soon as you've put Ardenne's things inside," he said to Corinna as she closed the door behind Ardenne.

"I've been instructed to stay close and maintain a safe perimeter."

"Whose instructions?"

"Gabriel's."

Piven sighed heavily. "We'll be heading out soon, so just do a general sweep of the area if you must but otherwise stay clear." He turned to face Sarita, dismissing Corinna. Ardenne gaped at him. It was true Corinna was unlikely to hurt him or take offense given she was one of Lord Hei's sirelings, but she was still a vampire soldier and not someone to be dismissed so rudely. But before Ardenne could say anything, Corinna stuck her tongue out at Piven's back, pulled a funny face—which made Ardenne giggle—then sauntered off inside with Ardenne's workout bag slung over her shoulder, dark ringlets bobbing around her head and hips swaying as if she didn't have a care in the world.

Ardenne admired her attitude.

Piven's voice pulled her attention back to him. "Time to say goodbye and go."

"I'll head up with Ardenne first if that's okay with you," Sarita said, obviously biting back the words she wanted to say for Ardenne's sake.

"Ardenne isn't going upstairs. We're going for a run."

"A run?" Ardenne asked, surprised.

"Yes. A run. You've got runners and your workout gear on. You're ready to start. So let's start. I can't teach you anything if you have no stamina."

"What about her magical training? You'll need me to help with that at some stage."

Piven rolled his eyes. "I suppose it will be necessary."

"Well, unless you've suddenly become proficient at the healing arts and herbology, you will need me."

"I was thinking more about that other little talent you have that allows you to see through walls. That came in handy in Prague all those years ago, didn't it?"

The tension in the air as Sarita stiffened was like an acrid taste on Ardenne's tongue. "You know I don't like to talk about that," she ground out.

Piven didn't seem to notice there was anything wrong. He simply shrugged and said, "Well, if you want to be useful to Ardenne, you're going to have to. But not right now. We need to start her physical training first. She's too soft and weak. I need to toughen her up. So if you wouldn't mind?" He gestured back toward the car.

Ardenne could feel Sarita fight with herself for a moment, but then she leaned over to give Ardenne a kiss on the cheek. "Just call if it becomes too much."

"I will," Ardenne said, knowing she would do no such thing.

Ardenne let go of Sarita's eyesight as the car pulled away and turned back to Piven, shifting uncertainly from foot to foot. "So, a run?"

"Yes. I know you've been doing workouts and basic fight training, but it has barely touched on where you need to be with your fitness to do the things I will expect you to accomplish. So we will start with working on your stamina. To that end, we will have a run every morning."

"How far?"

"Until I'm satisfied."

That was fine by Ardenne. She'd run a lot in the mountainous safe area around *Casa Cinque*. It was one of her favorite things to do with Papa when the weather was good. When it wasn't, she used the treadmill in the gym Lord Hei had built for his people to use.

She soon discovered Piven's runs weren't anything like the running she'd done before. They were full-on marathons. Not only that, but he also insisted she use her powers to see through his eyes as they ran—when he talked about stamina, he'd meant both physical and magical.

For the first hour she managed it easily even though it made her uncomfortable to be in his mind for that long. There was something oily and toxic in his mind, reaching out to wrap nasty tendrils around her emotions. It made it difficult to stay focused, to stay positive. But he had told her to do it, so she did.

After an hour though it became a different thing entirely. Both mental and physical muscles began to ache. She settled into the physical ache—her runs with Papa were often a couple of hours—but she wasn't used to the mental ache and her mind began to feel foggy like it did when she became too tired.

She kept pushing though.

The second hour ticked into the third and he kept running.

She knew he was tiring too—her empathy could feel the pull—but he ignored the sensation and kept running. Gritting her teeth together, she did too, even when her muscles started to burn and her feet throbbed with a sharp tearing that meant she had blisters—goddamned stupid new running shoes! But worst of all, it was getting harder to keep the connection with his mind as strong as she'd like. She was certain he could feel her slipping because those tendrils wrapped more tightly around her, sinking in further, making her wince.

She kept going. She couldn't be as weak and soft as he thought her.

A half hour later it was too difficult to ignore the agony in her body with Piven's pounding at her too. She pulled out of his mind and swapped back to using her radar senses.

Piven noticed right away. "Get back in my mind."

"I can't," she wheezed between gasping breaths.

"We haven't even done four hours. You need to do better than this."

She managed to run using her radar for another half hour, the sun beating mercilessly down on her head before her rubbery legs gave way and she collapsed onto the grassy hilltop they were running across.

Piven's shadow covered her a few moments later. The asshole was barely panting. "You can rest for twenty minutes, then we'll head back. Here." He handed her a bottle. She drank gratefully, surprised to find it was salty and sweet and had a zing that spoke of magic.

"What is this?"

"Something special I concocted. You should feel better shortly."

Five minutes later, she was surprised to find out that was true. Maybe he didn't need Sarita's help with potions and healing after all if he could concoct something like this. Her muscles still felt a little watery, but they didn't buckle and protest when she eased to her feet.

"You need to stretch to stop lactic acid build-up. And finish that drink. It won't work properly unless you do."

His tone made her want to snarl at him, but remembering her promise to Carrington, and to herself, she swallowed the rest of the strange tasting liquid as she went through a series of stretches her papa had taught her.

"At least you know how to stretch properly. That's something."

Once she'd finished the drink, he took the bottle from her, commanded her back into his mind and began to run again. By the time they got back to the training building it was well after lunch. He allowed her to stop long enough to eat the high carb, high protein lunch Sarita had packed for her. Then, when she was finished, he made her run up and down the stairs until her feet were throbbing, bloody pulps from all the blisters and her calf muscles were one big cramp.

"Sarita will be able to heal your aches and pains tonight, but you need better training shoes," he said before dismissing her for the day.

She managed to make it to the car without any help but by the time they got back to the compound, she could barely walk. Sarita and Corinna helped her out of the car, but when she almost collapsed trying to take a step, Corinna swept her into her arms and carried her to the healer's room.

"Place her on the healing bed," Sarita said. Ardenne was too exhausted to try to see through either of their sights, and just lay back on the bed, thankful to be lying down.

Sarita carefully pulled Ardenne's runners off. "That bastard," she swore under her breath. "I'm going to give him a piece of my mind for this."

"You know that will change nothing," Corinna said, "Except to maybe make him go harder on Ardenne just to piss you off."

Sarita said nothing for a moment, then sighed heavily. "We'll go shopping for better runners than this as soon as we can," she said to Ardenne as she placed her hands over Ardenne's bloody and swollen feet to begin the healing. "Corinna, could you fill that foot bath with warm water and put some lavender and rosemary oil in the water? After I've done the healing on these, Ardenne will need to soak her feet while I take care of her legs."

The warmth of the healing was so lovely that Ardenne drifted off into an exhausted sleep, only waking groggily when Sarita raised the bed so she was sitting up and could put her feet in the foot bath Corinna had brought over.

Sarita then continued the process up Ardenne's legs before

wiping her feet off and lowering the bed again. "Roll over, Ari, and I'll do some work on your back."

Ardenne sighed as the warmth sank into the aching muscles of her back and then drifted off to sleep again.

"Ari. Wake up. You need to get in the shower."

Ardenne pulled herself off the table and staggered into the bathroom. Everything felt so much better, but exhaustion pulled at her, making movement and thinking very hard.

"I'll rub some ointment into your legs and feet once you're out of the shower," Sarita said. "Then we'll get you into bed."

"What about dinner?" Despite the exhaustion, she was starving.

"I'll bring a tray up. You can eat in your room."

Sounded good.

Thanks to Sarita's healing, she was able to shower and get into her pajamas without wincing. Sarita wasn't in her room, so she flopped on the bed and lay back, enjoying the quiet and stillness, her muscles relaxing into the soft quilt.

She closed her eyes, enjoying the familiar purple darkness. She liked being able to see with other people's eyes, but it had been utterly exhausting being in Piven's mind all day, not to mention having to deal with the precise way he looked at the world. Nothing escaped him. His eyes were constantly darting around, taking in the most minuscule of details and behind all that, she could feel his brain ticking over constantly, never at rest. It had been exhausting. She didn't know how he dealt with being like that without exploding. Although, he probably didn't know any different.

It was nice to be back in her own mind though, not having to cope with the stress of his sight and emotions, and those strange, awful tentacles that pulled and pushed constantly, threatening to burrow deep if she didn't hold strong against them. She massaged her head. Her mind felt bruised.

She hoped she wouldn't have to be in his mind for so long every day—she wasn't sure how she was going to cope if she did.

She sighed, relaxing a little more as her thoughts drifted away. The darkness deepened and she fell into it.

It surrounded her. Lush and warm. A friend. Then she noticed a pinprick of light in the distance. It was getting larger and larger, and she realized she was running toward it.

"Come to me, my darling. Come to me."

The voice pulled at her, urging her on even though she was so tired.

"I have so much to tell you. So much to share. All you have to do is come to me."

Yes. She did want to know. She wanted to find out everything. "I'm comi—"

"Chef has made your favorite lasagna, Ari."

Sarita's voice pulled Ardenne violently backward out of the dream. In the distance she heard someone scream in rage. She sat up abruptly as she came jarringly awake, her hand to her chest, heart hammering like she'd been running a race. She gasped in a breath, and another.

"Ari, are you alright?"

There was a dip in the side of the bed as Sarita sat beside her.

"I'm fine. I just fell asleep. You startled me."

"Out of a bad dream by the looks of things."

Ardenne frowned. "No, it wasn't a bad dream. I was running toward someone for some reason." She couldn't remember more of it than that. Just the urge to find someone. To go somewhere. The sense that it was important.

Sarita chuckled. "It's not surprising you're dreaming about running given what you did today. But here, eat this. You need carbs and meat. Once you're done, you can go back to sleep. You obviously need it."

"Yes, I do."

She wolfed down the lasagna, barely tasting it, skolled the salty herbal water Sarita handed her and then lay down while Sarita completed the healing session from earlier with a final check of what she'd done.

She was asleep before Sarita finished.

She woke up the next morning a little disappointed that the dream hadn't continued. She was curious about what she'd been running toward.

Who she'd been running toward.

Training was a repeat of the day before leaving her as exhausted, her body as wrecked as the first day, necessitating another long healing session with Sarita afterwards.

Sarita did have words with Piven after that, but it made no difference, as Corinna had said. He just pushed her harder the next day and the day after that and the day after that until one day bled into another in an endless stream of running and exhaustion and pain followed by long healing sessions and her falling into bed after eating dinner, into dreamless slumber.

She had thought she was getting used to it, until Piven began to push her even harder, taking her for even longer runs on tougher terrain. It got so bad, one day, she collapsed and vomited all over the rocks they were running through. Piven had had to carry her back, his contempt a heavy blanket over her even though he didn't say a word.

He was barely even puffing when they got back and he simply handed her over to Corinna with a, "Don't be late tomorrow," then stalked inside.

Corinna carried her to the car and thankfully didn't say anything as they drove back to the Cousins' compound. Sarita, who'd been sent off on some tasks, so hadn't been with Corinna, met them when they arrived, and apart from a soft, "Someone needs to tear that bastard's balls off for this," she simply bade Corinna to take Ardenne to the healing room and followed.

After the healing and a long shower, Ardenne entered her bedroom to find Sarita already there with dinner. She ate in silence and then let her friend tuck her in.

Before her friend could bid her good night, Ardenne said softly, "I don't think I can keep going like this." Her voice wobbled, and she pressed her fingers against her closed eyes, trying to stop the threatening tears.

Sarita sighed and sat down on the edge of the bed, taking Ardenne's hand in hers. "Then tell him."

"How will me talking to him make any difference when he doesn't take any notice of you or Corinna? And I promised Carrington I'd do what Piven instructed, no questions. Besides, Piven says until my stamina is acceptable, there's no point teaching me anything else."

"I'll have a talk with Master Solari then."

"No, Sarita. You can't. I don't want him to know I'm not coping."

Sarita gripped her hand more tightly. "But something has to be done. Pushing you physically is one thing, but you shouldn't be so exhausted you can't stand. Or pushed so far you vomit and cry."

Ardenne swiped at the tears that she hadn't even noticed were wetting her cheeks—she was too exhausted to feel them. "I just need to sleep."

Sarita kissed her forehead then left her to rest.

She had no idea if her friend had spoken with Master Solari or not, but if she had, nothing changed. In fact, if anything, it got worse. So bad that she cried every night in the shower—the only place in the house she could be certain nobody could see or hear her weakness—and didn't come out until all evidence was washed away.

The torture continued, but she wouldn't let Piven see her distress and made certain not to complain to anyone else either, especially Sarita. Not that Sarita couldn't feel her pain every time she healed her, but she pushed harder so that she never collapsed or threw up again or needed to be carried by anyone.

Then one day, at the end of July, she realized she'd made it all the way back to the training compound without stopping, maintaining contact with Piven's mind the entire way without the need for his tentacles to tighten on her to keep her there.

A six-hour round trip with no stop.

She wanted to jump for joy but instead could only tremble with jubilation at her achievement.

"Good," was all Piven said. "Now we can move on to the next thing."

"Fighting?"

"In your dreams."

"Training my magic then?"

He snorted. "No. You're not ready yet. Besides, Sarita's shield is holding strong, so there's no rush."

No rush? She felt like she was about to explode with the need to explore what magic she could do. But she kept that sentiment inside her like she kept everything else and just nodded.

The next day he proceeded to make her run endless flights of stairs. Up and down and up and down winding, narrow tower stairs using his sight at first and then only her other senses. They ran every morning and did stairs in the afternoons. Some days Piven mixed it up and there was a combination of running and stairs throughout the day.

They kept this up as summer heat turned the rolling green of the surrounding hills brown and humidity increased so that it felt at times like the air was pressing in on her. The only concessions to the weather was that Piven had her carry an extra bottle of water and had them start earlier in the mornings before the heat of the day became too much and they were finished their run by mid-morning. And he added obstacle courses to the regime in the afternoons—sometimes outside, but mostly inside.

"I see no reason to baby her just because the weather is hot and humid," he told both Sarita and Corinna when they separately voiced their concerns despite Ardenne's pleas to not say anything. "Are you telling me the Wild or Dark Brethren won't attack just because it's too hot? Besides, Ardenne doesn't seem to mind, do you, Ardenne?"

She shook her head, too exhausted and thirsty to make her mouth work.

Days of this merged into weeks, the obstacle courses increasingly more difficult. She had to climb and swing and crawl and hop and leap, balancing on precarious planks unknown distances from the floor, ducking objects being flung at her, or worse, sections suddenly falling away. To begin with, she was allowed to use Piven's sight, then when she became better at navigating through the courses, he made her go without that help and use only her radar senses.

There were times Ardenne wanted to scream obscenities at him as he ordered her to accomplish more and more difficult tasks, but she clamped her jaw shut and continued.

Each night she fell into bed exhausted and slept without dreaming. That was the only bright spark in all of this—the fact she wasn't dreaming of Gabriel or that voice that pulled at her so enticingly. Although, she didn't make it through every day without thinking of Gabriel. Thoughts of him would slip in at the most unfortunate moments, usually causing her to make a mistake and have to start a course again after Piven had berated her for her clumsiness and stupidity.

She *was* clumsy in comparison to him. He never seemed to tire regardless of what they were doing. He was relentless, pushing constantly, never saying anything nice. She longed for one compliment, one encouraging word, but she got nothing from him. Sarita and Corinna gave her plenty, even Master Solari said how well she was doing, but it didn't seem to matter. All she wanted was for Piven to let her know in some way that she was accomplishing his training regimen, to ask how far along she was, to know when she might move onto fight training or, even more importantly, her magical training, so that she could do more than slip in and out of other people's minds and use their sight. But he never gave her anything other than a, "Right then, let's move onto the next thing."

She kept reminding herself of her promise, of her determination to become as good a fighter against their enemies as Anita. As

Gabriel. But there were times when Ardenne couldn't help but wonder how she was going to see it through. She felt like she was going to burst open with frustration—the only thing stopping her from doing that was exhaustion. She had no energy for anything but to get through each day and onto the next.

The only light in the dark of her training—aside from not dreaming of Gabriel—was that at the start of September, her one day off a week from Piven's training to spend time with the Masters teaching her about the cults and Lord Hei's history with the Cousins and the coven became two days. She spent the second day 'off' with Master Solari and Corinna, going on excursions into the countryside. They went to nearby towns where he'd introduce her to people who were friends to him and the Cousins and ran their various business interests. There were vintners and artists, weapons makers and farmers, businessmen who worked the stock markets, teachers who taught the next generation, and families. So many families. She had no idea so many people worked for Lord Hei out in the world. Some who knew what he was, some who were kept in the dark.

Those days were what kept her going because the training with Piven certainly didn't. They'd run. He'd create new obstacle courses every week for her, challenging her balance, her strength, her stamina, and her ability to use other people's perceptions to guide her even when they were standing far away. He said he was reshaping her, like Professor Higgins did to Eliza Doolittle in Pygmalion. Except rather than creating a lady, he was creating a warrior.

A warrior. Ardenne tried to armor herself with the idea every time she faltered, except with all the leaping and flipping and twisting she was supposed to do with her body, she felt like she was training to be a gymnast rather than a warrior. She wanted to be a warrior more than anything she'd ever wanted in her life, but she never expected it to be this grueling, or to experience this level of fatigue and frustration every single day.

All her energies went into not breaking. Ardenne was certain that's what Piven was trying to make her do—to say she couldn't do it. To prove him right. But she would never do that. Couldn't do that.

So, she kept going, doing everything he told her without so much as an outward sign of resistance. Inside her head was another matter. She screamed at him, calling him all sorts of names. She'd put Sarita to shame with the number of epithets she thought up to say to him. It helped to make dealing with the slave driver easier, creating conversations in her mind where she told him just what she thought of him and his endless, painful training methods.

In her mind, she ranted and raved and questioned and denied, while outwardly she gritted her teeth and continued to do as he instructed.

At night, exhausted, she'd fall into her bed and into a deep sleep, too exhausted any more to even bother crying.

She wasn't sure she had any more tears in her.

CHAPTER 17
RESPITE

I have learned through the years to treasure the times spent in celebration with family and friends. Holydays are particular gifts —for no matter what other dark things are going on around us, we can find light in the time spent together. Always find the things that bring light to your life. It will not only help you to navigate through the dark, it will help you to define it, to fight it. There is perhaps no more important a lesson I can give you than that.
Extract from The Middleton Manifesto, Section on Choices, Lesson 2

Ardenne ran through the outskirts of *Firenze* as she did every day with Piven, but today there was something different. Decorations had sprung up everywhere overnight draped over ancient stone, tinsel and holly and mistletoe all declaring one thing: Christmas was a month away.

Even though Piven didn't look at the decorations with anything but a sense of frustration at the silliness of it all, Ardenne couldn't help but feel a small spark of delight. Christmas was one of her favorite times of the year. But more than that, she'd been told that morning that she was to have a week off over Christmas to enjoy the celebrations and spend more time with Master Solari.

She couldn't wait. She missed the snow that would have blanketed the ground at home by this time of the year, but at least it was cooler, which made things more bearable.

Joy filled her at the thought that her favorite time of year was just around the corner and that joy seemed to make her perform better than ever. She ran and flipped and swung and leaped through the obstacle course—the most difficult yet—as if she were born to it. The thought of Christmas was like a beam of sunlight inside her, pushing away all the darkness that came with being in Piven's mind.

"That wasn't half bad," Piven said, his tone full of incredulity. "What's gotten into you?"

She just laughed and said, "Christmas is coming."

"Don't expect me to give in to Christmas cheer."

Ardenne laughed at that too. She didn't even care when, over the weeks leading up to Christmas, Piven wouldn't let Sarita pick her up early so she could do Christmas shopping or go to any of the celebrations that were occurring all over *Firenze*. "Do that ridiculous stuff on your time," he told her. "It's bad enough you've got a week off over Christmas. You'll become weak and sloppy and we'll have to start all over again."

Despite Piven being a Scrooge, she did manage to squeeze in some time on the days she spent with Master Solari and Corinna to shop for gifts for everyone here and at home. She took particular care to buy the right gifts for Papa, Mia and Lord Hei—gifts that could be sent via Master Solari's courier.

Buying them gifts made her realize it had been months since she'd truly missed them. She'd been too damned exhausted to miss anything. Master Solari had told her she was allowed to call them on Christmas Day—the first call home she'd been allowed since arriving in *Firenze*. Excitement thrilling through her, she spent a little more time choosing their gifts, wanting them to be just right.

She also bought the perfect gifts for Sarita, Corinna, Master

Solari and Chef Romano, and despite his bah-humbug attitude, she even bought a little something for Piven.

And for Gabriel.

Not that she'd be able to give it to him. Master Solari had no expectation of his return any time soon, although, when pressed, he did let slip that Gabriel would be back at some stage. Even though she knew she couldn't give him his gift at Christmas, when she saw through Corinna's eyes the bronze carving of the ancient tree on the hill—its leaves created so they looked like they'd been caught in the act of moving in an unseen, whispering wind—she had to buy it for him. It reminded her of their night on the hill, his loneliness, the ancient stoicism of him. His secrets.

She bought a special box to put it in and wrapped it in plain gold paper with a silver bow and a sprig of holly and placed it under the tree.

She knew it was foolish, but having it there seemed the right thing to do.

Her sense of Christmas joy didn't abate no matter what Piven put her through, and before she knew it, it was Christmas Eve and the Cousins' traditional gathering.

It was a fun evening with food and drinks and all the people who worked on the estate there, chatting and celebrating.

She went to bed happy and full, and not a little tipsy, having imbibed a few glasses of delicious Prosecco.

She flopped into bed, her head barely hitting the pillow before she was fast asleep.

Gabriel appeared in her dream. Despite the fact she was annoyed at him, she couldn't help smiling at him—it had been so long since she'd dreamed at all, let alone dreamed of him. She walked toward him, holding out her hands. And miracle of miracles, he took them.

"Ardenne," he whispered in that melodic deep husky voice of his. "How are you here?"

"It's my dream. Of course I'm here." She tipped her head, her smile widening. "It's Christmas Eve."

"I know."

Of course he did. He'd know what she knew because he was a figment of her imagination. But despite knowing that she said, "I bought you a Christmas present."

His brows rose. "You did?"

She nodded.

"I've got you one too."

Before she could respond, the voice sounded in her mind: *"Get away from her. You do not belong here. She is not yours."*

Gabriel let go of her hands. His smile disappeared, his expression turning to menace as he looked around them. "She is not yours," he said to the empty air. "She doesn't belong to anyone. And you will get her over my dead body."

"As you wish."

Before Ardenne could do anything, Wild and Dark Brethren descended and they fought, but there were too many and soon he was torn apart and there was nothing she could do because she couldn't move. Couldn't see. Her field of vision was covered in darkness streaked with blood red. Violence and terror stabbed through her out of the red and the dark.

She jerked awake on a sob. Tears streamed down her face and a horrible ache clutched at her heart.

"Shit! Shit!" She buried her face in her hands. Deep, jagged sobs tore at her throat and chest, sawing on the air. She couldn't stop. Couldn't stop. There didn't seem to be enough tears. Enough grief. Not for what she'd seen. Not for what she'd felt in that moment Gabriel had been torn apart.

It happened every time he and the voice noticed each other in her dreams and she couldn't seem to stop it. Not months ago and not now.

But there had to be a way. It was her dream. Surely she could control her own dream? Sarita or Piven might know of some magical way, but she couldn't ask them. That would mean admitting to seeing Gabriel in her dreams like he was real. And it would mean admitting to hearing voices.

No, not voices. A voice. The same voice.

And she couldn't admit to that. She could barely admit it to herself for fear of what it might mean.

Finally, exhaustion took her over, the sobbing quieted, and fists clenched against her aching chest, she fell into the dark velvet of sleep again.

She woke to the sound of a bird chirping in the tree outside her window. The sound caught at her, the music of it lifting the ache in her heart. How a bird happened to be on her windowsill in the middle of winter, she didn't know, but she was happy about it. She'd slept, mercifully without any more horrible dreams, and even though the memory of the dream she'd had during the night and the desolation it had left in its wake was still a throb on her soul, she couldn't help but feel revived from the undisturbed few hours of sleep she'd had and the happy music of the bird welcoming the coming day.

Things didn't seem so bad. Especially with a week off from the torture she endured with Piven stretching out in front of her.

It was Christmas Day and she wasn't going to think of things that made her feel bad. Nothing was going to ruin her joy on this day. Even though it was her first Christmas away from home, she was determined to have the most wonderful day.

She hopped out of bed and went to have a shower to wash away all the bad of the night before.

Half an hour later, feeling rejuvenated by the hot shower and dressed in the dress Sarita had helped her buy for the occasion, she headed out of her room.

"Merry Christmas!" Sarita sang at her as she left her room, enveloping her in a warm hug. "Let's go down and see what's under the Christmas tree, shall we? I think a little elf was very busy last night."

She wasn't wrong. There were piles of gifts under the Christmas tree and plenty of people to share them with—and plenty of people to allow her to share their sight so she could take in every aspect of it. All the Cousins who'd been at the party last night were there as well as some others who'd arrived early that morning. Some had cups of steaming hot chocolate wrapped in their hands, the scent of cocoa, nutmeg, and cinnamon wafting warmly on the air; others were munching on little pastries, courtesy of Chef Romano and his team. She was embraced by so many people, and wished *Buono Natale* and Merry Christmas, her mind began to spin dizzily.

Before she could get to the tree though and give out the gifts she'd bought, she was called away to take a phone call from Papa, Mia and Lord Hei. They wished her a Merry Christmas, even Mia sounding happy to talk to her and saying she missed her.

The call made her laugh and cry, and after a long goodbye, she returned to the room with the others.

They were all opening their gifts and through Sarita's eyes, she saw the joy of giving and receiving for the first time in her life. She'd felt it many times over the years at *Casa Cinque*, but had never been witness to what people's faces looked like in this moment. She didn't think there could be a better gift.

She was wrong.

Sarita pulled her over to the pile of gifts that were for her. Surrounded by laughter and gasps of surprise as others also tore open paper and oohed and aahed over their gifts, she gave out the gifts she'd bought others before settling down to open her own.

Very soon she had a pile of torn paper in front of her and things to treasure. A new watch from Papa which spoke the time and kept track of her vitals while she trained, a set of fantasy books by Ardenne's favorite author that Lord Hei had ordered specially for her in braille, and a soft scarf from Mia in swirling sunset shades and startling slashes of emerald green throughout. If someone had described it to her, she couldn't have pictured it, but through Sarita's eyes, she saw the strange beauty of it and how striking the colors looked against her dark hair and pale skin.

Corinna gave her a set of throwing knives, the handles carved with swirling bronze in the pale wood. She whispered to Ardenne that if Piven didn't start teaching her how to fight with a knife soon, she would teach her herself. Ardenne held that promise to her heart and gave Corinna a big hug.

Matteus had sent her a beautiful book that was an illustrated history of Leonardo DaVinci and his inventions and artwork. There was braille for her to read, but she'd need someone else's eyes to see the drawings. It was a gift that came from conversations they'd had about the man and she loved it.

There was a package that, even before she opened it, she knew were the special mini whiskey-current cakes that Chef at *Casa Cinque* knew she loved, the scent of the cakes whispering to her even through their packaging. And her aunts, uncles, and cousins had banded together to buy her a new laptop with braille keys with all the software she'd need already loaded.

Master Solari handed her a gift he said was from him and the other Cousins at *Palazzo Maimoona*—a beautifully carved bow and arrow set made from the lightest and most flexible metal that warmed to her touch when she picked it up. She wondered when she'd have a chance to learn to use it. Perhaps Master Solari would teach her if Piven wouldn't?

This gift and the one Corinna had given her, gave her hope that her training would change after the break.

Sarita appeared behind her and she turned to look up. "I wanted to give this to you myself." She handed Ardenne the oblong package and, as Ardenne unwrapped it carefully, she said, "It's a book on herb craft that has been kept in my family for centuries."

Ardenne gasped as she pulled it from the wrapping and opened it. The paper was thick, old, and yellowed in the earlier entries, with the latter ones on the smoother, white paper used now. "I can't accept this," she said, using Master Solari's eyes to look at Sarita. "This is a family heirloom."

Sarita pushed it back into her lap. "You are family. I'm supposed to hand it on to someone I'm training, someone I love. That's you. You must accept it. And together, we can make new entries."

She hugged it to her chest, tears pricking her eyes. "Thank you," she whispered.

Sarita pulled her into a hug. Ardenne held her fiercely. "It is, and will continue to be, my absolute pleasure."

A choked laugh in her throat, Ardenne pulled away. Sniffling, she wiped her eyes and pulled out of Master Solari's mind. She didn't want to be in anyone's head right now. She wanted to fill herself with her own emotions, uncluttered by anyone else's. "We better get all this paper cleared up." She could hear others were already taking care of their own mess of torn paper and pile of gifts.

"What about these gifts here?"

She didn't have to use anyone's eyesight to know what Corinna was pointing at. "One of them is for Piven. Just leave it there. I'll give it to him when I see him."

"You bought a gift for Piven? I hope it's something he's allergic to."

Ardenne chuckled at Sarita's suggestion. "You wish."

"What about the other one?"

"Don't touch that!" she cried out as Corinna reached to pick it up.

"Why? Is it for Piven too?"

"No." She lowered her head so her hair swung forward, covering her face. "It's for Gabriel."

Sarita brushed Ardenne's hair back from her face. "You know he isn't coming back any time soon, right?"

Ardenne shifted away, letting the hair fall back to hide her face. "I know. It just felt right to buy him a present."

"I can find out where he is and send it to him," Corinna suggested.

Ardenne shook her head. "No. I'll keep it and give it to him when he comes back."

"Ari." Sarita's hand landed on hers, stopping her harried motions as she scooped up the torn Christmas paper.

Ardenne lifted her face. "It's fine, Sarita. I knew he wouldn't be here. It's just, when I saw the carving of the tree in that shop where we went to buy Master Solari's gift, I thought it was something Gabriel would like. So I bought it. I knew he wouldn't be here. I'm not disappointed or anything. And I'll give it to him the next time I see him. Whenever that is. It's fine."

"If you're sure?"

"I'm sure."

She pulled away from Sarita's gentle grasp and ignored the sensation of everyone looking at her as she continued to clear away the paper. They could think whatever they liked. She knew the truth. She'd bought Gabriel a present just like she'd bought everyone else one—because it was a time for giving and she thought he might like it. There was nothing more to it than that.

The doorbell rang. "I wonder who that can be?" Corinna said as she took the pile of paper out of Ardenne's arms and stuffed it into a big plastic bag.

"Whoever it is, they're in time to help with the clean-up," Sarita said.

"Ah good. You're all finished. I timed it perfectly."

Ardenne's head snapped up at the sound of Piven's voice. "What are you doing here? We don't have training today."

He chuckled. "No. Although, if I had my way, we'd at least go for a run. But I was invited."

"And you came anyway?" Sarita snorted. "I didn't think Christmas would be your thing."

"For your information, I enjoy Christmas. I just don't like all the sappiness."

"What's that?"

Ardenne slipped into Corinna's eyes to see there was a wrapped present in his hands.

"It's a gift."

"You know, you're not supposed to buy gifts for yourself, Piven," Sarita said.

His mouth twitched. "It's not for me. It's for Ardenne." He held it out to her.

"Ardenne? You bought a present for Ardenne?" Sarita said as if it were the most implausible thing she'd ever heard.

An uncomfortable expression crossed his face so quickly, Ardenne wasn't sure she'd seen it, because he smiled and said, "Yes. Is there something wrong with that?"

"No. I just ..." Sarita waved her hands and then dropped them to her side with a gesture that indicated she was lost for words.

An uneasy silence followed, broken by Corinna. "Ardenne bought you a gift as well."

"You did?" Piven asked.

"Yes."

"Why?"

"Why did you buy a gift for me?" she asked him.

He seemed unable or unwilling to answer—and so was she. Corinna picked up the gift and handed it to her. Uncertain how he would react, Ardenne shoved it at him. He took it and held out the box he was holding—it was square and heavy.

"Thanks."

"Thanks."

It was one of the most awkward gift-giving moments she'd ever experienced.

Finally, Piven coughed. "Yes, well. I'll leave you to it. I need to speak with Master Solari."

"I think he's in his study," Sarita said.

"Good." He turned to leave but then paused at the door. "Merry Christmas, Ardenne."

"Merry Christmas, Piven. And thank you for this." She nodded at the present in her arms.

"Make sure you read them." Then he was gone.

"That was strange." Sarita drew her down onto the couch. "I've never known Piven to give a gift before. What is it?"

She tore the paper off and opened the box. "It's a set of books." She ran her hand across the cover of the top one. There was a slight tingling in her fingertips. Magic. "It's written in braille as well as English."

Sarita took one of the others from her. "They're books of magic." She opened it up. "Goddess! He must have had them specially made for you. I've never seen books on magic with braille." She laughed. "Trust Piven to give you homework for a Christmas present."

Ardenne knew that's what they were, but she was also strangely touched. She'd never thought to have her very own set of magical texts like Sarita had. Despite being homework, she treasured their thoughtfulness.

"What's that?"

She moved into Sarita's vision and saw there was an inscription written inside the front cover of the book she'd opened. She read it out loud. "Remember, trust is earned with unhidden truth. Huh."

"That's a strange thing for Piven to write."

"It's not his writing," Sarita said.

"Even stranger," Corinna mused. "They must be second hand."

"They don't look second hand. Perhaps I should check them out before you read them," Sarita said.

Ardenne pulled them away from her. "Check them for what? Magic? They're books on magic. I can feel the impact of the spells and histories already sparking in my fingers. Besides, Piven gave them to me. It's not like he's going to give me something that could harm me."

"I'm not so sure about that."

"That's just your dislike of him talking. What do you think, Corinna?"

The vampire tipped her head, considering for a moment. "I can't smell anything wrong with them. All I smell is Piven and another scent I don't recognize—probably the person who wrote them? I don't think there's anything to worry about, Sarita."

"See!" Ardenne said, opening the first one. "You're not taking them away. Piven said I had to read them, so I'm going to read them. Starting now."

Sarita made a harrumphing sound, but she left Ardenne to it while she and Corinna finished tidying up.

Ardenne spent an hour pouring over the first book—it was filled with histories of different covens and witching families, and the famous spells they'd created. It was fascinating.

Before she knew it, she was being called by Master Solari to join him on his traditional walk in the garden and surrounding hills.

Reluctantly, she put the books aside. "Is Piven joining us?"

"No, he had some things to discuss with Master Ricardo." Master Ricardo was the Cousins' weapons maker. A whippet thin man with arms as strong as the metals he worked with, Ardenne had met him several times with Master Solari. He was a man of few words unless the subject was weapons. Then he was full of information and knowledge. Piven and he would probably chew each other's ears off.

Ardenne and Sarita pulled their coats, gloves, hats, and scarves on and joined Master Solari at the back door. *"Andiamo!"* he said, setting out into the crisp, cold day.

Their boots crunched on the frost that still covered the ground, the sound echoing in the silence and, despite her longing to get back to the books Piven had given her, she enjoyed the quiet crispness of the winter air.

As they stepped back into the warmth of the *palazzo*, Sarita rushed past her, clapping her hands together. "Brr, it's so cold out there."

Ardenne hadn't really minded the cold. In fact, she kind of wanted to stay out there. Her heart throbbed with a strange ache, and she rubbed her chest. She hadn't realized how much she'd missed that cold mountain air scent of Gab ... of home. Yes, it was home she missed.

She removed her coat, gloves, scarf, and hat and followed Sarita and Master Solari back into the house. She breathed in appreciatively. The house was full of the scent of baking meats and vegetables and spiced puddings.

"Chef Romano is outdoing himself," Master Solari commented.

"Mmm." Sarita breathed in deeply. "It's making me hungry."

Ardenne's stomach rumbled. She laughed, pressing her hand against it. "Me too."

"Then, let's go eat."

Sarita and Master Solari whisked her into the dining room where she was assailed with sounds and scents and greetings from those she hadn't seen yet.

Giving herself over to the warmth and love in the room, she bounced around various people's minds taking in the sights. Everyone saw the room so differently. Some focused on the lovely table decorations, others the candles creating a softly lit glow to the wood paneling in the room, some the food—the pile of mince tarts and *panetone* on spectacular display on the sideboard and the dishes that were being brought out of the kitchen piled with meats and vegetables—and others were focused on the people around them.

The room was soon full of the laughter and joy of the morning as they all stuffed themselves silly on ham and baked turkey and pork with all the trimmings. Even Piven laughed and joked with people, especially Master Ricardo. It was strange to see Piven laugh. She didn't think she'd ever heard him truly laugh before—the sarcastic laugh he used at Sarita's barbs didn't count. His laughter made him seem human, almost boyish, and she realized just how handsome he was. At least, Corinna certainly thought so.

Traditional English plum pudding with custard and brandy butter was served alongside the *panetone* and *biscotti*. There was *Prosecco* and *Moscato* and white and red wines to drink alongside spiced warm cider, mulled wine, and mineral water.

Ardenne was feeling very full and a little lightheaded when they returned to the lounge room where she collapsed on the sofa. "I don't think I'll ever eat again," she groaned.

"I know what you mean," Sarita said, patting her stomach.

"Oh, look, Ardenne. There's another Christmas present here for you. You must have missed it before."

CHAPTER 18
GIFT

The sword of life
The sword of blood
The sword of strife
The sword of love
The sword to bring eternal doom
The sword cut from a mother's womb.
Extract from Mary Middleton's Diary, December 25, 1565

Sarita looked up so Ardenne could see where Corinna was pointing. A long package sat in the place where Gabriel's gift had been. "Gabriel's present is gone." She turned to Master Solari who she knew from Corinna's sight, was standing behind her. "Has Gabriel come back?"

Master Solari looked mystified. "Not that I know of. Corinna, did he say anything to you?"

The vampire shook her head. "He didn't mention it at all. Although, I thought I scented him out in the woods earlier, but when he didn't make himself known, I thought I was mistaken."

"Apparently not," Master Solari sighed. "I wonder why he didn't come and tell us he was here. It's not like him at all."

That surprised Ardenne as it sounded exactly like the vampire she'd come to know—mysteriously keeping himself apart from anything normal or anyone he might come to care about, or who might care about him.

Sarita picked up the long gift and handed it to her. "Open it. It must be from Gabriel if he took your gift."

Ardenne's fingers curled around the long, rectangular box, her heart fluttering strangely in her chest. She longed to open it, to find out what it was, but at the same time, she didn't want to. Not in front of everyone.

"Go on. Open it."

"Here's the card," Corinna said, handing her the envelope. "It fell off when Sarita picked it up. It's definitely Gabriel's writing," she said, pointing to the name scrawled on the front of the smooth, white paper.

Ardenne's fingers shook as she pulled the card from the envelope. "Here." Sarita sat next to her. "Use my eyes."

Ardenne,

It is tradition for a Guardian to give his trainee something they can use in their training. And so I give this to you. It is a Katana. Lord Hei gifted it to me centuries ago and now I gift it to you.

Like all unique swords it has a name: Seer's Blood.

It is a spirit-blade. A soul sword.

Piven will be able to train you in its use and Master Ricardo in its care. Take good care of it. It is ever hungry for blood, but I hope you never have to truly whet its appetite.

Ardenne tore open the paper and lifted the lid from the box.

Nestled inside was a beautiful Japanese sword in its scabbard. Lord Hei had a sword like this in his office. He'd allowed her to get a mind-picture by picking it up and touching the handle—or *tsuka*—and the scabbard—or *saya*—but never the blade. She'd learned about different weapons with him and her papa, as did all the Bartolli Family children, but she had never used one before. And she'd never actually seen one with her sight—or borrowed sight.

It was beautiful. More beautiful than she'd imagined.

The white rayskin that protected the wood core sparkled through the overlapping patterns of the dark suede *tsuka-ito* that was wrapped around the *tsuka* to give it extra grip. Patterns could be seen embedded in the rayskin, swirling veins of rich amber that ran from the ornamental *fuchi* that sat just above the *tsuba*—the hand guard—to the tip of the *tsuka*. The same swirling veins were also on the *saya*. Against the dark, lacquered surface they looked like blood. In among the swirls, runes were embedded in the wood, so dark she almost missed them. She was familiar with a few runic characters, but none of these were those, so she couldn't read what they said.

"By The First. He gave you Seer's Blood!" Corinna exclaimed.

"It's beautiful," Sarita said, her voice awestruck. "Look at the design on the *tsuba*. Are those wings?"

"Yes, they are," Corinna said. "The sword maker was inspired by Lord Hei—he said he looked like an avenging angel. He also included the wing designs on the *fuchi* and the *mekugi*—the peg that's embedded through the *tsuka* to hold it all together."

"It's just ... I've never seen anything like it," Sarita said, her voice full of awe. Ardenne knew how she felt. The blade ... it was more than beautiful. It was perfection.

"I've heard of this blade but never seen it," Master Solari said from behind her. "Unsheath it, girl. Let's see it."

Ardenne swallowed hard, and trying to settle her shaking hands, lifted the sword from the box. It was lighter than she expected, the *tsuka* warm to her touch.

Holding it carefully in front of her, she pulled the *ha*—the blade —from its *saya*.

Gleaming, steel slid out with a hiss. She was surprised to see that there were runes carved into the blade near the *tsuka*—the same runes that were on the scabbard. *Katana* could often have patterns and ornamentation in or added to the metal of the sword, particularly near the *fuchi* and *tsuba* to express the beliefs and nature of the swordman, but runes were unheard of. "What do the runes mean?"

"It says, 'Seer's Blood; Demons' death: Angel's undoing.'"

"Angel's undoing? What does that mean?"

"Nobody knows, Ardenne," Master Solari said. "It's a mystery. The maker was as much witch as sword master. The story goes he told Lord Hei that when he placed it in the hands of its new owner, the sword would name itself and announce its purpose. The moment Gabriel unsheathed it, the sword glowed golden as the words etched themselves where you see them now and a voice whispered the name in his mind."

Ardenne didn't know what to say. The sword was so beautiful. And centuries old. "Why would he give it to me?"

"He said it in the card," Sarita said. "It's tradition."

Ardenne nodded, even though she didn't agree. He could have given her anything else—a book, a weapon he'd had made for her— and yet he'd given her a precious gift that Lord Hei had commissioned for him centuries ago. A weapon with a story and a mystery behind it. A sword that Gabriel had most likely used to slay many of their enemies. A sword he hoped she never had to use.

A sword called Seer's Blood.

Was he mocking her?

She gritted her teeth, her fingers tightening on the *tsuka*. She wanted to be angry with him for leaving this for her and not being here to answer her questions. But she couldn't. Because she was so overawed by the gift, by the fact it felt so right in her hands, as if it had been made for her.

It might not have spoken to her as it had reportedly spoken to Gabriel, but she could clearly hear something coming from it. The living hum of it as she held it was pure intent, the song it sang a promise of what it would do when she used it; when it finally sliced through the air, it would find the blood that was its succor, its redemption.

The sword was alive, and it was hers.

Staring down at it she bit her lip. Whatever his reason for giving her this, she didn't care. She was going to be worthy of such a gift. She'd make certain of it. And the next time she saw him, she'd thank him by showing him just how proficient she was so he'd know that despite his wish, she would use it.

Seer's Blood would sing once more as it took out their enemies. It wouldn't be angel's undoing, it would be demons' death. It would never go hungry. She'd make certain of it.

Gabriel pulled back from the window. She had his gift.

He should never have come back, should never have succumbed to giving her something that could be his destruction, but the sword's need had become too great, matching his own, and he'd made the journey. Given to her what he'd hoped he'd never have to give. If only Hei had listened to him, none of this would be necessary.

But that was a ship long sailed and here he was, watching the awe on her face as she lifted his sword and angled it, her head tilted a little as if she was listening to the soul in the sword.

He wondered what it was telling her. Or if she could even hear it yet. After it had announced its name to him, it had taken him a while to understand the murmurs in his mind every time he held it. But once he did, there was no separating them in a fight and it had served him well.

Now it would serve Ardenne. It would keep her safe as it had kept him safe. Probably better. Because the truth was, Seer's Blood had never truly been meant for him. He had simply been the custodian until it ended up in the hands of the person it had been meant for.

Ardenne.

He knew he should stay and train her in its use, but he couldn't do that. The very fact he had come back here when he'd sworn not to until Anita was no longer a threat, spoke volumes for how little control he had where Ardenne was concerned. So, no, he couldn't stay and train her to use Seer's Blood. He had to trust that Piven would make certain she learned how to use it properly. The man was supposed to be a master in all sorts of weaponry. Although, he'd probably never held a sword like Seer's Blood before.

Most soul swords were lost to the myths of time. But a man like Piven, even if he couldn't feel its life, couldn't hear it speaking to him, would know the lore. He would be able to teach Ardenne all she needed to know to wield it.

His fingers tightened on the box in his hands, reminding him of its presence. He hadn't been able to stop himself from picking it up when he'd seen his name on the card.

She'd bought him a present for Christmas. She'd told him in the dream but somehow he hadn't believed it until he saw it. He knew the gift was from Ardenne without even opening the card. Her scent was all over it.

He should never have picked it up. Should have spurned it. Leaving the gift there beside the one he'd left for her would have been a clear message. But he could no more have left behind her gift to him than he could change what he was.

She'd thought of him, and the knowledge of that warmed him.

He shouldn't open it. Should throw it away. That would be sensible.

Yet ... His fingers tightened around the box, and he held it closer to his chest. He wanted it more than anything he'd ever wanted before. He wanted to tear the card open, read the words she'd written to him, savor them, then open the gift, careful not to tear the paper she'd wrapped it in.

But he couldn't do that now. Certainly not here. If he did, he would not be able to stop himself from going inside and thanking her. And while keeping the gift was an act of foolishness, going inside to thank her for it would be an even bigger mistake. One he knew neither of them would recover from. Not until she was fully trained and didn't think of him as something to look up to; to try to be like.

He should never be an example or mentor for anyone, let alone her.

He took off through the orchard and into the surrounding hills. He'd intended to head north then east, to where he'd last caught scent of Anita before the dream of Ardenne had drawn him back here, interrupting his hunt.

But instead of his intended direction, he headed toward the safe house just north of Assisi. A few hours' drive from *Palazzo Maimoona*, it took him only a quarter of an hour before he was running up the drive that led to what looked like an old, crumbling villa. Of course it wasn't crumbling at all. On the inside it was in pristine condition, most of it kept exactly as it had been when he'd bought it two centuries ago. It had been a base for him on and off since then. A place he could come to be alone.

And tonight, he wanted to be alone as he unwrapped Ardenne's gift to him.

Settling in front of the cold fireplace, he didn't even bother turning on the light. He didn't need it with his vampire sight. Carefully, he opened the envelope and read her simple scrawled message. Given the large script, the deep indentations and the fingerprint marks and smudges, she must have written it without the use of another's eyesight, feeling each letter as she pressed it into the thick paper of the card.

Gabriel.

I saw this and thought of you.
I hope you like it.
Buono Natale.

Ardenne

Setting the card aside, his heart thumping harder and faster than usual, he opened the gift, folded the untorn paper, and put it next to the card. Then he lifted the lid.

Inside was a lump of plastic bubble wrap. He lifted the lump from the box and placed the packaging reverently on the floor next to him. As if he held a precious child, he unwound the gift from the bubble wrap. And gasped at the perfect, simple beauty of what she'd bought him.

It was a carved tree, its exquisite boughs twisted and smooth, lifting to the heavens as if in supplication, its branches and lime-colored leaves stretching out to shelter any who came within its shade.

Tears pricked his eyes and he blinked.

How had she picked this? Why? It was almost an exact replica of the tree on the hill where he'd taken Ardenne and revealed the horror of his making to her. He'd thought he'd scared her that night, had made the place terrible for her; made it impossible for her to know how precious that place was to him despite the pain of some memories.

He loved that spot on the hill. Had returned there many a time to sit under that tree and contemplate his human life, his vampire existence. Things never seemed so sad there. Never so endless. The shade of the tree offered him hope. It offered him succor. It whispered to him of a higher purpose. It reminded him of the God he'd once worshipped and believed in with all his heart when he was human, and the reason for that belief.

It reminded him of who he was in the deepest, most hidden part of his soul.

And she'd gifted him a slice of that peaceful place that he could carry with him.

He swallowed hard. She would not have given him a gift that meant pain. So, she had to have guessed how much he loved it there. How much it meant to him.

Hands trembling, he placed the tree on the table next to him before he could drop it. He had to thank her. There was only one way to do that without going to her in person.

He'd been fighting the dreams ever since they'd begun to infiltrate his mind. They were a sign of the bond he wished he could refuse. But tonight, for the first time, he'd make use of that connection.

Just this once. And never again. Once he'd thanked her, he could go back to his task and know that he owed her nothing more than to keep her safe from what was planning and scheming to come for her.

He waited until night had deepened, then closing his eyes, he wandered into the darkness of his mind and found the thread that was the bond. Taking a deep breath, he reached out a mental hand to it. The song of it stilled the pounding of his heart, settled the breath rattling in his throat.

Home, it sang. Belong.

No. Never home. Never belong. But tonight, it could be used to thank.

Giving over to its pull, he let it take him and flew through the bright landscape of the astral to her.

ARDENNE DIDN'T THINK she'd ever go to sleep. Her mind was spinning, so full of the day and the questions it had brought. But eventually, the pull of exhaustion had its way and she finally succumbed.

She fell into a familiar scene, of her and Gabriel standing on the hill. Except, this time, she was holding Seer's Blood in her hand.

He looked down at it. "She looks good with you."

She knew it was what her mind wanted to hear him say, even so, it felt good to hear him say it. "Thank you for the gift of her. But why did you give it?"

"She belongs to you. She's been singing it to me since your birth. Can you not hear her?"

Ardenne could. She still couldn't understand the words it sung, but she felt the intent. Seer's Blood was hers. Even so ... "Why would you give me such a gift when you don't think I can succeed?"

"I never said you wouldn't succeed. If you took my words that way, I am sorry. I meant that I wished there was no necessity to have you trained. Or at least, to have it put off until you were older or more prepared." His smile was sad as he looked at her with eyes shaded by history. "I think you can succeed at whatever you set your mind on."

His words jolted inside her, making her heart race even as she knew they were not truly his words. Simply what her mind longed to hear him say. If only it was true. "I know you, the real you, would never say that."

He sighed. "Maybe not. But not because I don't believe in you, but because I can't ever say those words out loud to you. It would be far too dangerous if I did."

"Then it's lucky this is only a dream."

He smiled that sad smile again. It clutched at her heart.

"I know you don't believe this is real, and that's as it should be, but I hope you take these words to heart. You are more than capable, and fearless enough, to do everything you set your mind to. It frightens me just how capable and fearless you are. And because of that, what I wish is that you learn to set your mind on the correct things."

"Correct to who? You?"

"No. You."

"What do you mean?"

"Never make big decisions to please others. The only person you should ever make big decisions for is you; if they feel right to you. I hope one day you'll understand that everything I do is to make sure you will learn that most important of lessons; a lesson it took me too long to learn. You will save yourself worlds of pain if you can."

She opened her mouth to ask him what he meant, but he held up his hand again. "I don't have long here with you and I didn't come to talk about that. I came to thank you for your gift." He held up the carved tree. "It is beautiful. I will treasure it always."

She trembled and Seer's Blood vibrated in her hand, its song one of sad longing and hope that reflected his words and wrapped around her heart. "I'm so happy you like it."

"I more than like it. It is perfect."

There was so much to say to that, but all she could manage was, "Good."

There was a noise in the distance, and he turned his head, nostrils twitching as he scented the air. Then his lips curled into the vicious smile of a hunter. "They're coming." He looked down at the sword in her hand. "Maybe things will turn out differently this time now you've got that. Let's fight."

"I don't know how."

"Seer's Blood will guide you. Besides, it's your dream. You can do whatever you want in it."

"You would trust me to fight with Seer's Blood at your side?"

"Always."

She readied herself alongside him, Seer's Blood lifted in a way that felt right as the Wild and Dark Brethren tore up the hill toward them.

Their war cries turned to terror and pain as Seer's Blood showed her the way, singing its song of death in her hand. They fought until there were no more attackers left and for the first time ever in her dreams, Gabriel wasn't overwhelmed by them and destroyed.

Panting, he turned to her, a wild look of joy in his eyes. "Beautiful," he whispered.

She looked down at the sword that was humming happily in her hand. "Yes, she is."

"Not her. You."

She caught a look in his eyes that so shocked her, she woke up with a start.

Her sight was gone. The world was its usual purpling dark. The house was silent. She should feel alone and frightened like she always felt when she woke suddenly from a dream in the middle of the night. But she didn't. The thrill of Seer's Blood singing in her hand as she fought side by side with Gabriel still thrummed through her. The look on Gabriel's face made her tingle with secret expectation.

It might have all been a figment of her imagination, but that didn't matter. For the first time in a long time she didn't wonder if she could do this. In her mind, she knew she could. Her subconscious mind had said as much to her with Gabriel's face, his voice.

She was ready.

A smile of triumphant expectation settled on her lips. When she returned to her training next week with Piven, things were going to change.

CHAPTER 19
MIND GAMES

Seer's Blood is in her veins
Seer's Blood to take the reins
Seer's Blood turns you insane
Unless you are the Seer.
Extract from The Middleton Manifesto, Prophecy 34, Book 1

The next week was full of spending time with Master Ricardo to learn how to look after Seer's Blood and trialing different scabbard mounts to see what worked for her best. She ended up deciding on the specially designed back-mounted scabbard—not fully traditional, but it felt right reaching for it over her left shoulder to whip it out and was more balanced for maneuverability.

She expected to go back to her training on New Years Day, so wanting a good night's sleep, had decided not to join in with the other's New Years Eve celebration plans. But Piven was unexpectedly called away and wasn't due back until late on the first, which meant training wouldn't start back until the second.

Suddenly free, she decided to join Sarita, Corinna, Master Solari, and some of the others. They planned to drive into *Firenze* to join in the festival there.

Ardenne had more fun than she expected. They danced among the crowds in the *piazzas*, eating pizza and lasagna at Petra's, laughing as the bistro owner teased and flirted with Master Solari who'd joined them, and finally standing with everyone to watch the fireworks bring the New Year in.

She'd never seen fireworks before, and it was fun seeing the bursts of starlight in the sky from many people's perspectives.

She was so tired when she got home that she fell into bed and straight into sleep without preparing her mind for the dream to help bring it on—as she'd done every night since Christmas Day, wanting to relive that moment spent in it fighting with Gabriel.

Even so, before she knew it, she was standing on the hill. However, it wasn't the same as it had been before. The brightness of her usual dream vision darkened as she turned to see there was no Gabriel, no Wild, no Dark Brethren. She wasn't even holding Seer's Blood.

She was all alone.

She began to tremble as clouds swept overhead, dimming the light further until the darkness was so thick it was almost like being blind. But this darkness wasn't like the purple dark she lived in every day. It was deeply red, like blood. She shivered as it glowed around her and felt nothing but loss and interminable cold.

Then the voice began to whisper in her ear.

"Come to me. Find me. I am waiting for you." The words shuddered through her. She wanted to deny them, given the cold, terrifying dark that accompanied them, but she couldn't. They were far too enticing for that.

"Don't deny me. I have so much to tell you," the voice continued. *"So much they are keeping from you. He might have given you Seer's Blood, but there is so much he is keeping from you. They are all keeping from you, and the sword alone won't help you find the truth."*

"What truth?"

"Everything you always wanted to know."

"Tell me, tell me now." The idea of not knowing was suddenly as terrible as the blood-red dark.

"It's not safe to tell you here. He's in here with us, too close because of the damned bond despite my efforts to keep him away. But all you must do is find me. Come to me and I will tell you all."

"Where are you?"

"Find me. Search for me."

"I don't know how."

"Read the books. They will help you."

"The books?" An image appeared in her mind. "The ones Piven gave to me?"

"They weren't from him."

"Who were they from?" Her voice echoed in the dark. "Who were they from?" she screamed again, but there was no answer. The voice was gone, and she realized she was once more in the purple dark of her blindness.

She sat up, supremely disappointed to be awake.

A bird chirped outside her window, singing the same song it had sung to her on Christmas Day. Except, this time it was New Year's Day. Her last day of rest before training restarted.

Tomorrow, everything would be different. She was going to be more in charge of her destiny. The thought had her pushing aside the frustration of the dream. She hopped out of bed with a smile on her face.

Everyone was tired from their late night, so nobody really noticed how she couldn't stay still, especially given they were exclaiming over the fact it had snowed heavily overnight—snow was a rarity in *Firenze* and its surrounds.

Thankfully, after breakfast, Corinna dragged them all out to have a snowball fight with some children from the nearby village where she was able to run off some of her excess energy. Master Solari was a particularly good shot, catching several of the combatants, including her, in the face. It made her laugh and try to figure out how to get him back with the best viewpoint perspective.

Wet and cold and panting, they all finally trooped inside to dry off and eat some lunch. Ardenne was finally able to settle, even though excitement and trepidation surged through her at the thought of tomorrow.

She spent the rest of the day curled up in front of the fire listening to music, and, remembering what the voice had told her in her dream, she started to read her new magic books. But she wasn't able to stick to that for long because Seer's Blood was calling to her, so she picked it up and decided to give it a polish.

And as she did, she tried not to think about the argument she knew she was going to have with Piven tomorrow about training her to use it.

~

"Are you ready to run?" Piven asked as soon as she entered the training room. She could tell he hadn't even turned to face her.

"No." She stopped herself from reaching up to fiddle with the harness that allowed her to wear Seers Blood strapped to her back.

He sighed. "I told Vincente it was a mistake to let you have so much time off. You got lazy."

"I'm not lazy."

"Then get ready."

"No."

"What do you mean, no?" Whatever sounded like a book thumped on his desk. "Well, well. What do we have here? Look at you all dressed up like a Samurai ready for business. You look ridiculous."

Squaring her jaw, she pulled her shoulders back and stared straight ahead. "I don't want to just run and work on my stamina and agility anymore. I want to start training."

"We are training."

"No. I want to start training with weapons. You know Gabriel gave me Seer's Blood. I want to learn how to fight with it."

"You do, do you?"

She flinched at his tone. She couldn't help it. The build-up over the last week, thinking of this moment, how important it was, made her nerves jump and spasm. Shaking, she tried to keep her voice even as she answered him. "Yes. And don't act like what I'm asking is unreasonable. Gabriel wouldn't have given the sword to me if he didn't think I was ready."

"You think so?"

"Yes."

"But he's not here, is he?"

Tears pricked her eyes at that blunt statement, but she wouldn't let them out. Wrapping her hand around the sword's *tsuka*, the leather strapping warm under her hand, she pulled it out of its scabbard, the song of it making her heart beat faster. "No, he's not. But I know I'm capable of this. You've been getting me ready. The training, it's all been leading to this."

"How do you know?"

"The moves you've made me practice, the stamina and muscle strengthening exercises, the endless obstacle courses encouraging acrobatics, flexibility, balance, poise, and quick thinking. It's all for a purpose. *This* purpose."

"Really?"

His incredulous drawl just ratcheted up her anger and desperation. "Yes, you bastard. Really. I've seen it in my dreams. Seer's Blood sings in my hand as I cut down the Wild and Dark Brethren. Together we move like fire and water." She wouldn't admit to doing so beside Gabriel; shouldn't have even admitted that much. Knew it as soon as she said it and the nasty pause that followed. "We are one," she said, breaking the horrible silence.

"You're dreaming about fighting? Who are you fighting with?" If avaricious interest had a tone, she'd just heard it.

"Nobody," she said, too quickly. She knew he'd heard it, but she wasn't about to give more away. She had to calm down, steady her trembling. Even so, her words came out far too breathy, pleading. "I know I'm ready. Gabriel said in his card that you would be able to train me in how to use Seer's Blood. Was he wrong?"

"No. He wasn't wrong. I'm one of the best swordsmen you're likely to meet."

"Then you'll start my weapons training?"

"No. Not yet."

"What?"

"You heard me. Now, enough of this nonsense. Put that stupid sword down, take off that harness and get your coat back on. We're going for a run."

Incredulous, she stared into the purple dark. She thought she'd had him with the dreams. With the knowledge of what her training had been leading to. He'd seemed interested. But now, she heard him turning from her, shuffling papers before closing a drawer and moving toward the door.

He might be done with the conversation but she wasn't.

"I want to learn how to use my sword!"

"It's not your sword."

"Yes, it is. It sings to me. It wants me to use it."

"Then it's going to be disappointed. You're not ready."

"Yes, I am," she shouted over the sound of Seer's Blood's pleading, over the rushing noise of wind in her head. Her fingers tightened around the *tsuka*. "I'm ready, you fucking bastard!"

"I'll say when you're ready."

His tone, that calm tone in the face of her anger, tipped her over the edge. "You will teach me what I want to know."

"No."

Screaming a sound that echoed the song in her head, she flung her arms out. Power surged through her, burning through veins and tendons, searing nerves and muscles. It cascaded out of her fingertips, a wave of noise like a surging gust of wind. There was a deafening woof.

The windows blew out; the sound of exploding glass a glory in her mind.

Piven laughed, a joyful sound, and began to clap. "Well, well, well. What do we have here?"

His laughter brought her back from the edge. The power fell away as quickly as it had come, leaving her panting and shaking, Seer's Blood still clenched in her hand, silent. Oh, no. Had she hurt anyone? She ran to the window, wishing that Sarita was here so she could use her eyesight. "Is anyone down there? Are you hurt?"

Silence greeted her cry, broken by Piven's applause and laughter behind her. "Oh, my dear. Nobody is here but me. Nobody here to see how magnificent you can be. You know, I thought the possibility of you was never going to turn up."

She turned to face him. "You're happy I did that?"

"Of course I am. You showed your true self to me. I couldn't be more delighted. I was beginning to think you would never show me what you're made of. Now we can begin."

She gaped at him. She could smell blood in the air. His blood. She'd hurt him with her burst of uncontrolled power, but he didn't seem to care. "You're going to train me to use Seer's Blood?"

"Oh, I'm going to train you to use more than that." He rubbed his hands together, the sound grating on her still aggravated nerves. "Finally!" She could tell he was grinning. "You show some spine. Given who your parents are, I had to figure there was some in there somewhere. Your mother would be proud today. I think you'd even give Anita a run for her money."

It still seemed strange that he knew her mother, but she'd given up asking him about that. He would never answer her. Instead, she concentrated on the latter part of what he'd said. "You think I can be as good as Anita?"

"Perhaps. With time. But only if you do exactly what I say. Anita was brilliant, a true Huntress, but she lacked discipline. I won't allow you to repeat that mistake. Do you understand?"

"Whatever you say." She gestured to her sword. "Where do we start?"

"We start with you putting Seer's Blood away."

Her grip tightened on the sword. "But you said—"

"I said I'd train you, but even the most accomplished don't start at the top. We'll begin with the poles and work our way up to practice swords. That way, you'll learn how to fight and move regardless of the length of your enemy's weapon or the weight of yours. You won't always have Seer's Blood to hand. So go put it away."

She wanted to argue, but what he said made sense. As she walked to the corner she removed the halter and unhooked the scabbard. She sheathed Seer's Blood and placed it on an empty sword block she knew was there, then hung the halter on a hook to its left.

Behind her, she heard Piven pace toward the weapons wall. He began to talk, but his voice was so low, she knew he wasn't talking to her.

"So, poles to begin with." He slid something from the wall. "But I think we need to work on throwing knives and stars. Yes, they'll be good weapons for her and will work well with her speed and agility. But there needs to be something else as well. A bow and arrow?"

"Master Solari and the Cousins gave me a bow and arrow set for Christmas. And I was given a crossbow before I left *Casa Cinque* as well."

"I want you to bring all the weapons you've been given here. But for now, we'll use the training ones." She slipped into his mind. He was running his hand over a crossbow.

"You'll train me to use the crossbow?"

"Yes. I'll have to devise special moving targets for you after we're done with stationary ones." He rubbed his hands together. "This is going to be fun." He spun to face her again, the poles in his hand whipping out, buzzing on the air. She could feel the satisfaction inside him alongside the usual roil of heavy darkness that she'd never got used to. She pulled out of his mind. She'd only go back in if he demanded it of her.

He turned and walked back toward her. "Here, take this." He thrust one of the poles into her hand. "I want you to use your senses first, so don't go into my mind to see what you're doing." That was fine by her. "I want you to feel the length of it, its weight, what happens when you hold it in different places regarding both its balance and yours. Yes, that's right."

She felt the pole, its circumference, the heft in its weight, ran her hand along its length. It had been hand-carved—there were notches where the knife had carved in a little deeper, dents that hadn't been sanded and polished out, the flow of the woodgrain. It had age, this pole. Knowledge of being used.

"You feel it?"

She nodded.

He began to walk around her. "Now, I want you to hold it and move through the first *kata* in the discipline of karate. I know you learned multiple *katas* for multiple disciplines as part of your physical fitness regime at *Casa Cinque* and that you've kept them up while here, so I expect perfection."

She began to do what he asked, moving through the basic pattern that had become second nature over the years. The pole felt a little strange in her hand and she faltered.

"Start again. And this time, hold it against your arm as if it's part of you."

"But if I hold it against my arm, I'll hit myself on some of the movements."

"Not if you move your grip and the pole to accommodate your movements. The pole should be fluid in your hand, an extension of your arm, moving out, up and over as the need requires."

"How do I know what that is?"

"You'll know instinctively, or you'll learn through pain."

"Excellent. More pain," she grumbled, but took position in the first stance, holding the pole as he suggested. "Like this?"

"Almost." He adjusted her grip. "Now begin."

She made it through more of the pattern this time before she caught her foot on the pole and it smacked into her head. She stumbled sidewards, letting the pole go to catch her balance. It cluttered loudly on the floor and she rubbed her head. "Ow."

"Do it again." His voice held as little sympathy for her as it always did, but for some reason, she didn't find it as abrasive as usual. Finally, she felt like she was being taught something tangibly useful.

After a bit of scrabbling around—she didn't want to use Piven's sight to find it and she hadn't listened to where it had fallen and rolled to—she found the pole and began again only to falter at the same spot.

Piven's aggravated sigh was almost as loud as the pole smacking into her head. "You're thinking too hard. You're not letting the pole be part of you."

"Yes, I am."

"If you were truly thinking it was your arm, you wouldn't hit yourself with it."

"You make it sound so easy."

"It is. Here, let me show you." He moved behind her, positioning himself at her back, his front touching her ever so lightly as he aligned his arms with hers, covering her hands. The power in him pushed at her and she had to stop herself from jerking away. "We'll move through the movement together and I will show you what I am talking about."

She shifted on the balls of her feet and forced herself to breathe. She wouldn't be able to do this if she didn't relax. But it was difficult to relax with Piven's breath brushing across her ear, the power of him burning through the thin t-shirt she wore.

"Hold your hand over mine so you feel my grip on the pole. Good. Now center yourself, breathe deep, and run through the *kata* in your mind." His voice was a rumble in her ear and through her chest. "You've been taught to visualize, so do that now. Then, as you start, sync the visual with the movement. Begin."

She began, sure that his proximity would affect the smoothness of the movement, but he moved in sync with her, his hand flexing under hers as he rolled the pole up and over, through fingers, along his arm, over his shoulders, out in front of him, across his back and even through their legs. It was one of the most remarkable things she'd ever experienced.

They came to the end of the pattern, not faltering once, the pole held once again along their arms.

"Now, do you understand?"

"Yes," she breathed.

He put the pole in her hand. "Concentrate on where the pole fits in your hand. Let it move with you, not as a rigid piece of wood, but as fluid as skin and bone and ligament. Do you feel it?"

"Yes."

"Now try it by yourself."

She did exactly what he said, allowing herself to sink into the feeling of what his movements had been like. She was a little jerky to begin with, but as she moved, the flow began, the connectedness between her and the pole. Piven was right. It wasn't something separate from her, it was a part of her.

When she finished the first pattern, she couldn't help but break into a smile. "I did it!"

"Don't get too excited. That is the simplest *kata*. Let's move through the first ten and see how you go."

Creating the same sensation between mind, body, and pole, she executed each pattern without a flaw.

"That wasn't horrible," Piven said after she rose from the last position and bowed. "You need to work on the transitions between your extended positions and turns. You're letting the pole tug you off balance, when it should help your balance if you're holding it right." He took her hands. "Here and here."

She nodded, picturing in her mind what he meant. "Like this." She executed one of the more difficult extension movements, flipping into a rotating scissor kick and ending up in ready position.

"Yes. Exactly like that. But now you need to do it at speed."

Her muscles were heavy with the strain of completing so many patterns one after the other with the extra weight of the fighting pole in her hands, but she didn't say anything. Piven clapped out the fast rhythm he wanted, and she bowed and took up first position.

"Begin."

He made her run the series of *kata* twice more and then he gave her a different fighting pole, this one heavier, thicker, and weighted at the end with sharp points. "Now, do the same with this."

The pole felt alien in her hands after the first one, but she knew she had to treat them the same. So, she ran her hands over the pole, learning its length, the mars in its surface, the sharpness of the points at the end, and when she was certain she could envision it in her mind, she began.

She cut herself, just the slightest nick on her back, in the twisting leap in the ninth *kata*. But even though it stung as sweat dripped into the cut, she didn't stop. She made herself continue, determined to learn from the mistake. She'd dropped her concentration for one moment and let the pole become unbalanced in her hand as she transitioned the movement from front to back. She wouldn't do that again.

And she didn't, even though Piven made her run the *katas* three more times with that pole and again with two shorter ones that had a grip on the end like a sword and were used one in each hand.

By the time Sarita arrived to pick her up, she was dripping with sweat, exhausted, but exhilarated. For the first time, she felt like a fighter, like she could really do what she saw herself doing in her dreams. She'd told herself over and over she had to learn to be a fighter, but there had always been a niggling doubt at the back of her mind that whispered she could never be accomplished at it. That her blindness *would* be a hindrance. But this day's training had cut that nasty whisper into tiny pieces and blew them away with the wind whistling around the eaves.

Even though she was tired, she grinned at Sarita as her friend entered the room and said, "Look what I can do." She broke into the last and hardest of the *katas*, accomplishing the acrobatic movements with athletic grace.

"You've learned all that today? That's amazing."

"Not so amazing, given the work we've already put in. I would expect her to be at least as competent in this as she was today. We will see how she goes tomorrow when we spar."

"You're teaching me to spar tomorrow?"

"Yes. Hand-to-hand at first and then with the weapons."

"Excellent." She pumped air.

"Don't get too excited. You'll spend much of the time on your back on the mat," Piven warned. "And I want you to keep reading the books I gave you. They'll help you to open your mind to using more than just your senses. When you're out there, your senses can be affected by fear and other emotions, but if you've got powers to add to the mix, you're less likely to make a mistake."

Ardenne nodded, eager to get stuck into this more exciting part of her training. She was so glad Gabriel had given her Seer's Blood, because without the impetus the sword had given her to push Piven to leap her training forward, she'd still be stuck running, doing obstacle courses and acrobatics. The gift was more than just a sword; it was turning out to be a gift of confidence that the future she longed for—and had thought was never coming—was within reach.

For the first time in a long time, she felt truly positive about the future and her place in it.

Dutifully, she got home that night and after dinner, sat down and continued reading through the first volume of magic. The spells and cantrips and exercises to calm the mind were interesting, but they just made her wonder when she'd get a chance to put them into play.

She didn't last long with her reading though, tiredness overwhelming her and she trudged up to bed.

She fell asleep quickly and found herself standing on the hill again, even though she hadn't called the dream to her. Although, like last night, this wasn't her usual dream.

The usual calm was gone, wind blowing wildly around her, lightning flashing in the distance. She turned to see Gabriel standing a few paces away. He was shouting at her, but she couldn't hear what he was saying above the wind. All she could hear was the roll of thunder, the clap as the lightning zipped across the sky and then the whisper of the voice.

"This is only the beginning. Come find me and I will show you so much more. I will show you everything you'll need to follow your destiny."

CHAPTER 20
TRUTH'S END

Extract from The Middleton Manifesto, Prophecy 45, Book 1

Ardenne woke the next morning, thoughts of her destiny swirling in her head, feeling she could do anything.

She came down with an abrupt thump though when she turned up for her training. They went for their usual run in the morning and then Piven began to teach her hand-to-hand combat. To begin with they simply used the movements from the *katas* of different martial arts, Piven doing opposite actions so that her movements were blocks and attacks.

Then Piven moved to free-sparring.

He moved so fast, she couldn't keep up, even when she pushed into his mind and tried to feel and see what he was going to do. Somehow, he always caught her, and she ended up face down on the mat, Piven's foot at her neck, her arm twisted up painfully behind her, or flat on her back with Piven's forearm crushing her windpipe.

"How do you keep doing that?" she asked, rubbing at her throat as she pushed herself up from the mat when he stepped back.

"I am at one with myself and my surrounds. My powers and my senses are not separate entities. They are one."

"You're so fast. I can't keep up with where you are. Can't you slow down while I learn?"

"The Wild and Dark Brethren will be faster than I am. You must learn to keep up."

"But I don't even know how to use my powers properly yet, so how can I become one with them? I need to learn to use my magic just like you use yours."

"You know enough. The problem here is not what you do or don't know, but what you think you *should* know. You're thinking too much. You have all the skills necessary to be able to match me at this level."

"At this level? You mean you're going easy on me?" All her confidence from yesterday evaporated beneath the heat of anger that flared. "Are you trying to make me feel bad, or is that just a special talent you have for being an absolute asshole?"

"Now you sound like Sarita."

"Yeah, well, now I'm getting an appreciation for why Sarita feels the way she does." She folded her arms, hiding her trembling palms under her armpits. "You're having fun at my expense, aren't you?"

"No. I can assure you, this isn't fun for me. But it is necessary. For both of us."

"Well, I've had enough for today. I obviously don't know enough about my magic to help me and if you're not going to teach me, I'll get Sarita to ask Carrington to send me someone else."

He was suddenly there before her, his fingers wrapped around her shoulders, his breath a brush of coolness over her heated face. "There is no one else who is capable of teaching you. I am the only chance you've got now that Gabriel has abrogated his duties. You cannot have full access to your powers yet."

"What do you mean?"

"It is good that Sarita has a shield around your powers, keeping them in check, as they're too powerful, too dangerous, until you learn to control yourself. Control of your body and your mental capacity. Control of your emotions."

She couldn't believe what she was hearing. "My power isn't dangerous."

"Yes, it is. You could destroy this building, hurt your friends, bring *Firenze* to ruins with just a little uncontrolled lash of temper. Remember what you did to the windows when you became angry with me. Witches who have just reached their majority are always a danger, but those who have been brought up in ignorance of their inheritance ... Well, the Great Fire of London wasn't caused by a spark from Thomas Farriner's bakery oven."

"The Great Fire of London was caused by a witch?" She shook her head. "Scratch answering that and answer this instead: There have been others like me before now?"

"A few. Not often. But history is riddled with disasters that were started by a witch losing control of herself."

"Why hasn't anyone told me this?"

He let go of her and she could hear him begin to pace. "Because they cosset you."

"*You* don't."

"No. But they made me agree to keep some things from you if I wanted the job."

"You want to be here? I thought Carrington made you."

"I am where my destiny demands I be."

She paused, thinking about what he was telling her. "What things are you keeping from me?"

"That I can't say. There are always things that should be kept until a person's knowledge allows them to understand and act on that knowledge in an appropriate manner. But I promise that at the right time I will share with you all I know, despite what others may think in opposition."

"Why? Why do the others not want me to know about my magic?"

"They are afraid."

"Of me?"

"Of destiny." He stepped forward as she began to tremble and grasped her shoulders again. "Never be afraid of destiny. It does you no good. You have too much of your mother in you to let the idea of destiny get on top of you."

Her senses sharpened even further as she realized that he wasn't talking about Tara Bartolli as she'd thought. He was talking about her birth mother. Knew her birth mother.

She had so many questions to ask him, but all that came out was, "I'm like my mother?"

"Yes. In some ways. In the not good ways. And if you think I'm going to be drawn into a discussion about your mother, you're wrong. But there is one thing I will tell you. Those books I gave you were your mother's. She left them for me to give to you."

"She had magic books written in braille?"

"Of course not. I had the braille added so you wouldn't have to rely on anyone else's sight to learn. And learn you must if you want to come to an understanding and control of your powers. You need to read them, need to memorize the cantrips and lessons they hold within. They helped your mother. I know they will help you, too."

Ardenne didn't notice when he let go of her shoulders, her thoughts lost in the notion of the magic books having belonged to her birth mother. It was the only thing she had that was her mother's and it felt like a gift from her. They were special to her before now, but she would treasure them even more so.

"Enough talk. Let's continue with hand-to-hand."

Her muscles protested angrily as she settled herself into the ready position.

He came at her so suddenly, she barely had a chance to move

before she was flat on her back again. Swearing, she pushed to her knees. "I'd be able to do it if you let me use your eyesight."

"You need to be able to do this without relying on other people's sight. As you well know, it's a flawed tool. You will always be better off if you learn to use both your natural abilities and your magical ones."

"But I already know how to get around perfectly well without sight."

"You don't know how to fight using only your other senses. You need to be able to use everything individually as well as all together. In a fight, it's even more important that you listen, to feel the wind of movement." He began to circle her. "The vibrations of feet through the floor, the warmth of body heat, to sense the emotions in your opponent. All those things will give you what you need to defend yourself from an attack without ever entering someone's mind and using their sight."

"I thought you were teaching me to use my sight to help me. I thought that's what all that running while in your mind was about."

"The running was to strengthen your physical and magical stamina. Now, we must strengthen all other aspects. Because if you end up in a fight and there is nobody's vision you can slip into aside from your opponent, that could end in your death."

"But, if I can get in their head, I can feel what their next move might be and use that."

"And if they know you can do that and use it against you?" He sighed. "You cannot have a weakness, Ardenne."

She hated the fact he had a point. "Okay."

"But this is not the only weakness you own. Right now, your biggest weakness is that you think you are less because you are blind."

How did he know that? "I bet most blind people feel that way when faced with learning things like this."

"Met many blind people?"

"I live among vampires, what do you think?"

He made a sound that almost sounded like a chuckle. "Exactly." His voice sobered. "I was trained by a blind monk, and he was one of the most lethal men I have ever known. He made me train with a blindfold on, and I can tell you that was much harder for me than it is for you. I didn't have your heightened senses. But he made it so I could fight just as well blindfolded as sighted. So, stop whining about what you don't have and concentrate on what you do. Now, get ready."

"I wasn't whining," she muttered, settling down into the more balanced fighting stance, feet planted firmly into the mat, the right one forward, knees bent. She raised her hands to protect her head, took a deep breath and nodded, indicating she was ready.

She breathed in, smelled the faint dryness of dust and chalk, but nothing else. Piven didn't smell like anything—not soap or shampoo or aftershave or sweat. Scent-wise, it was as if he wasn't there. So she listened.

She could barely hear him breathe, let alone move. The only sign he had moved was the slight vibration through the mat just before his palm smacked into her chest. She stumbled and his foot hooked behind her legs. The smarting pain as the flat of his foot caught her low in the calf and tipped her up was nothing to the pain that slammed through her as she hit the floor.

She opened her mouth to try to suck air into her protesting lungs, but all that happened was a rattling, sucking sound. She tried again, but there was nothing. She couldn't catch her breath.

Fighting panic, she rolled onto her side, gasping. She tried to summon healing warmth to the palm she was rubbing over her chest as Sarita had shown her in their lessons, but it wouldn't come, trapped behind panic. She gasped—a long, ugly sound. Tears stung her eyes. Blood pounded in her head. Her mouth worked, trying to pull in much needed oxygen; a gasping rattle.

"You fucking bastard! What did you do to her?" Sarita's voice was like a whisper through the roaring of blood in Ardenne's ears.

"I taught her a lesson she needed to learn."

"She can't breathe!" Hands rubbed along her back, warm, soothing the ache there.

"She'll be fine in a moment. She's just winded."

"Just winded, my ass! Look at her. Why aren't you helping?"

"She needs to learn to help herself. Babying her is what got her winded."

"Hitting her square in the chest and then landing her on her back was what got her winded, you ass!"

"No. Not training her until she is almost too old to be trained properly is what got her winded. If I'd had her ten years ago to train as I'd suggested, she'd have landed me on my back today instead of the other way around. I thought after what happened with her mother, after she got her proper training almost too late, everyone would have been keen to ensure this one wouldn't go through the same. If Hei and all his people hadn't been so busy coddling her, I'd have a warrior to spar with instead of this sack of unfit lard lying on the floor gasping like a guppy out of water."

Ardenne rolled over onto her back. "I'm fine," she managed to wheeze out, thanks to Sarita's ministrations. She began to push herself to a sitting position.

"Easy." Sarita reached to help her, but Ardenne shrugged her help off and rocked back and forth taking in big lungfuls of air. It still felt like she couldn't quite get a good breath.

"Here." Sarita began to rub her back.

Ardenne winced.

Sarita lifted the t-shirt up and gasped. "Her back is black and blue!"

"I'm fine," she said, shrugging away and standing up. "I'll just go and change and get my stuff." She grabbed her bag and stalked off to the little bathroom on the far right of the room. Using her radar senses, she found the basin and splashed water on her face. Still dripping, she pulled her sweat-soaked yoga top and pants off, wincing at the pull on her sore muscles. She'd have to have a long soak when she got home. She knew Sarita would want to heal her, but she couldn't let her. Not anymore. Piven was right. She'd been coddled. It was going to stop.

She wiped the sweat from her skin and pulled another, warmer top from her bag, the soft merino wool a lovely caress against her skin as she put it on, then shimmied into her jeans. After putting her boots on, she shoved the sweaty clothes into her bag and was about to open the door when she heard the tight voices. Hand pressed against the door, she listened.

"And so was yours when you learned to fight. She'll be fine. Stop cosseting her. You're not doing her any favors by fully healing her every night," he said, echoing her thoughts of moments before. "She won't learn to get up even when things are broken if you keep it up."

"Just because I can't stand her being in pain doesn't mean I'm cosseting her."

Piven chuckled. "You're like a tiger with its cub. But a tiger eventually stops the cosseting and lets the cub experience the harsh reality of the world. You need to do the same for Ardenne or ..."

"Or what?"

"She'll end up just like her mother—in a position where she can't stand up for herself. She might as well be dead."

"I don't know what you're talking about."

"Yes, you do."

There was taut silence and then steps approached the bathroom.

"Ardenne. Are you dressed yet?" Sarita called out. She was almost at the door.

Despite the fact her mind spun with what she'd just heard—her mother was trained almost too late and because of that she'd what? Died?

The door opened. "You ready to go?"

Ardenne pulled a smile onto her face. "Yep. Ready and willing. See you tomorrow, Piven."

"Tomorrow."

She could feel his eyes on her as she crossed the room at Sarita's side. She wondered if he knew she'd been listening.

THE NEXT DAY she walked in fully intending to ask Piven about what he'd said about her mother, but didn't get the chance. The moment she walked in the door he announced, "We're working on knives today, but first, a run."

After that, she didn't have time to think about what she'd overheard. The morning progressed as usual with a long run, obstacle courses and then some practice with the fighting sticks. After lunch, they moved over to the back wall where he kept the weapons.

"I've set up some targets here." He allowed her to see them in his mind before telling her she couldn't use his sight again today.

He gave her a set of different sized and balanced knives and taught her how to throw each of them. This teaching required him to touch her again, just like he'd done when he was showing her how to work with the staff because once again, he didn't want her to use his sight.

"Your body is another instrument. You need to have complete control over it. If we let you rely entirely on your powers, you will be at a disadvantage. The Dark Brethren and the Wild won't use only one of their vampiric powers against you. They will use them all. You must do the same. And each one cannot be reliant on the others. They must be a strength in and of themselves."

She threw knives until her wrists ached, but she began to get good at it quickly through Piven's strict tutelage. Most of them struck the target point in, although from the occasional thunk, she knew she'd hit the wood beside the target.

"You need to work on your accuracy," was all Piven said at the end of the session.

"I know." She smiled.

"And read those magic books. I know you haven't been reading them every night like I told you to."

"Yes, I have." She turned away, not wanting him to see her blush at the lie.

"Don't lie to me. I know you haven't. Your mind is still too weak."

"I've just been really tired."

"Tired or not, you must read them."

"I will."

And she did.

The next day, she did better. She felt stronger despite being bruised and sore. But she still wasn't hitting the targets with any regularity.

The days progressed and so did she, although too slowly according to Piven. "Your mother was already proficient after a few days."

She wanted to point out that her mother could see the targets, but he'd just claim she was complaining again, so she held her tongue.

Each night, she dreamed, sometimes vividly, sometimes like it was in a fog. But each night the voice grew stronger and stronger, so much so, that she wasn't at all surprised when she began to hear it during her training. She supposed she should be worried about that, but the voice didn't seem to want to do anything but encourage her.

"Well done, Ardenne. You are doing better than Piven is letting on. It won't be long now before he lets you start your sword training."

Ardenne smiled every time she heard it. She longed to learn how to use Seer's Blood. Every time she picked it up, it sang its longing to her; its hunger. It wanted. She knew how that felt.

Despite the voice's encouragement, it took her over a week to finally hit every target dead center regardless of the knife she threw.

"He's sure to teach you swordplay now."

But he didn't. Piven made her swap to left-handed knife throwing. She tried not to be annoyed, not to allow the hope the voice had given to drive her disappointment. This was Piven. He never did what she expected.

He drilled her and drilled her on left-handed knife throwing. It took her slightly longer to master the left, but finally, she was able to do it.

When she showed Sarita the next day, her friend was suitably impressed. "That's amazing. And you're not even using mine or Piven's sight to do it?"

"No. Piven wanted me to be able to do it without using my magic."

"Well, I must give you your due, Piven. You're a good teacher despite being a total ass."

He snorted. "I'll be happy when she's able to hit a moving target without fail with both her left and right arms. The enemy will never stand still to let her throw at them."

"You could encourage her, Piven. Let her have today's accolades."

"Accolades won't keep her alive. Killing accuracy will."

His lack of enthusiasm hurt, but at the same time, it made her even more determined to do the very thing he set before her. Especially given Sarita was backing up what the voice said to her: that she was doing well. That she was ready. She simply had to show him how ready she was.

As he did every day before she left, he reminded her to read the books he'd given her. "Practice the meditation cantrip and the one for calming the mind and extending the senses. Your senses are good, but going into battle, you don't want to rely on what is normal. You want something more. You want to be better."

Yes. She did. She wanted to be better than anything they thought she could be. She wanted to be better than Anita and Piven.

"And Gabriel."

She instinctively went to deny what the voice said, but then she stopped herself. The voice was right. She did want to be better than Gabriel. She knew she was probably setting herself an impossible task, but it was something to aim at.

And her aim was getting pretty good.

The days raced by even though there was a predictability in the routine Piven set. At times she was frustrated with the monotony of it, but the voice and Sarita were encouraging and the cantrips in the magic books were making her stronger, more certain of herself, feeling more like she could do anything, be anything.

She tried to tell Piven, but he never seemed to hear her. He just kept on with the routine occasionally throwing a phrase at her that sounded like something you'd read in a fortune cookie.

"The concrete must be set before you can build on the foundation."

"Rome wasn't built in a day."

"Something isn't truly learned until it is felt in every fiber of your being."

And her favorite: "Remember the three Ps, Ardenne. Patience, practice, and practicality. Those will see you through. And if they don't, return to practice. That's what we're doing."

Each time he said one of them, the voice snorted in her mind and made some quip Ardenne struggled not to laugh at.

She knew the voice was her subconscious getting stronger because of the meditations and cantrips in the magic books she was practicing and reading every night, but sometimes it didn't seem like her at all. And sometimes—just sometimes—she wished it wasn't becoming so loud, because despite its encouragement, it sometimes came at the most inopportune moment, breaking her concentration and making her miss a step or fumble with a throw, which always made Piven tutt and say, "More practice," and he'd take her back a step.

She tried not to let it get to her, but it was frustrating.

Every day, they'd run, then do obstacle courses, followed by the martial arts patterns, slow and fast. Then in the afternoon, they'd spend time on the fighting poles, sparring and working on her technique for an hour, then he'd switch to knives.

He'd set up a series of targets on pulleys that could be moved back and forth and side to side. She was terrible at hitting the moving targets.

"Not terrible."

"Yes, terrible," she told herself. To Piven, she said, "I can't do it.

I'm not hearing what you want me to. Why can't I use your eyesight? That would be easier."

"Easier, but not better. Now, try again."

She continued to be terrible at it. The encouragement of the voice and Sarita and everyone else just made the failure worse, and Piven still wouldn't let her use his sight. She'd tried—oh, how she'd tried. But he hadn't let her in, no matter how sneakily she edged in, and he didn't allow anyone to come into the room while they were practicing so she couldn't use their eyesight.

She tried to hit a target doing it his way. And tried. And told herself she should be able to do this. That they were all expecting her to do this. It was keeping her up at night. She worried about the failure like a frayed thread, and the worrying made it worse until after more than a week of trying, she finally broke.

"I can't do it," she said, throwing her last knife down where it clanged and skittered across the floor rather than sticking in point first. "It's useless. I'm useless." She knew she was acting like a spoiled toddler, but she couldn't seem to help it.

Piven greeted her outburst with silence. Then she heard him pick up the knives that were on the floor or stuck into the wall, having missed their moving targets after which he came to stand in front of her.

"The problem here is you're not truly listening. Try again."

"I am listening," she said, thumping her foot on the floor. "But the sounds aren't giving me a proper indication. I can't make out where the noise is coming from until it's a second too late. A second late will get me killed."

"Yes, it will. But that's not what I meant. You're listening too hard with your usual hearing. You need to reach past that."

"I don't know how."

Silence again, and then, "Come."

He took her hand and pulled her toward the door.

"Where are we going?"

"You'll see."

He took her downstairs and then outside and over to his car.

"An outing?" Corinna asked as she slid into the back seat.

"Yes. We'll be spending time outside every day now. But I'll need you to keep your distance. I don't want you making a noise that will distract Ardenne. At least not until I say."

"You're the boss."

"Yes. I am."

He drove them up into the hills far from the noise of the city. He stopped the car at the end of a dirt track and then made Ardenne track further up into the hills until they entered a small clearing.

"Stop using Corinna's eyesight now and sit down, there."

She saw where he was pointing before she slipped out of Corinna's mind and sat where he pointed. Corinna slipped away.

"Now, I want you to listen. Calm your breathing, steady your heartbeat, sink into your mind using the cantrip in the first book. Make your body null and void."

She did as he asked, settling into herself. The scratchy feel of the grass under her fell away, as did the weak warmth of the early spring sun softly heating her skin until she was nothing. She was nowhere.

"Good." Piven's voice came from a long way away. "Now stretch outside yourself and listen. There are sounds all around you, things we never hear until we are completely quiet. Can you hear them?"

Yes. Yes, she could. So much noise. Too much. She winced.

"Filter it out, let them in only as you need them. Now, tell me each individual thing you hear."

CHAPTER 21
SOUL HEARING

Listen and hear far past the fear
Listen and see what can truly be
Listen and feel everything that's real
Uncover the soul of our life's ultimate goal:
She must survive!
Extract from The Middleton Manifesto, Prophecy 16, Book 1

It took a moment before Ardenne could pull individual sounds out of the melee, but then one came to her, the soft susurration of the breeze in the trees, followed by another, the scamper of little feet in the undergrowth. The trickle of water running down a rockface rose to her, coming from her far right, while the song of the birds as they hopped from tree to tree were all around her. One took flight on the wind, its wings beating a happy song as it soared higher and higher behind her.

There was more, so much more, and by the time she had finished telling him, tracking others down, some of them to their source, twilight was folding in on the land, bringing with it a different range of sounds.

They returned to the hills the next day and the day after. When she had mastery over all the sounds of nature and could describe where they were without fault, he changed the drills, making them about her sense of smell. Then he made them about the vibrations she felt through the earth and the air. This was trickier out in the open than it was inside a room, but after some frustrating, and painful, mistakes, she managed it. She even found the softly ticking clock he'd hidden in the forest.

She had begun to look forward to their outings when he changed things again.

"Right, enough sensory drills. You know what's needed. Now throw the knives and find your targets."

He made her try to hit a moving target again, using her hearing, the vibrations in the air, scenting the wood, and dried paint smell of the targets. She began to throw them with more consistency, hitting nine out of ten. He then made her start throwing dummy knives at him. He was harder to track than the targets he'd rigged because he was much better at moving without affecting the air around him. But after weeks, she realized she could feel the vibration of him through the floor, could smell the faint scent of lemony soap he used on his skin that hadn't been perceptible to her at first and now was as distinctive as wild jasmine. At first, she could only hit him if he kept on a straight line, but after a few weeks, she managed to hit him eight out of ten times when he swung and leaped around her in unpredictable patterns.

"Better," was all the praise he gave.

That night, she dreamed about her training. Gabriel was there, smiling proudly in the background. "You are a marvel, Ardenne."

She glowed under his praise.

"You may not be like me, needing Hei to complete your training, but Gabriel should be there to train you. He may be an utter bastard but he is the only one who can truly teach you how to use your sword. And you should be learning how to use it. You can only save me in the future if you know how to use it."

She frowned as the voice whispered to her through the dream. Save her? Why did the voice need saving? And in the future?

"What is it?" Gabriel asked as he took her hands. "Are you not happy with your progress?"

She shook her head clear of the voice's strange words. She might not understand what the voice meant, but one thing she did agree with. "I should be learning how to use Seer's Blood. You should be here to teach me."

He smiled at her sadly, his fingers tightening around hers. "I wish that was possible. But Piven will teach you when you're ready."

"She's ready now, you traitorous bastard!" the voice shrieked.

Gabriel jerked, his fingernails slicing into Ardenne's skin.

She awoke with a gasp, jolting upright, cradling her hand. She could still feel the sudden slice of Gabriel's fingernails across her skin, smell the tang of her blood, but as she rubbed her fingers over the soreness, she felt nothing but smooth skin.

"It was just a dream. No matter how real it felt," she whispered. The voice was just her frustration given voice. And Gabriel ...

Well, she didn't want to think why he was there or why his smile was so precious and his touch even more so.

It took her hours to settle back to sleep, so that the next day when she arrived expecting to continue training as they had been, she was surprised when Piven handed her a crossbow—smaller than the one she'd been given which she'd brought in months ago along with the other weapons she'd been given.

"Aren't we running?"

"Now it's time to learn something else. Something different."

"What about my sword?"

"No. Not yet."

"This is too cautious, even for him. I need you to learn. Tell him you need to learn." The voice was almost a shout in her mind. She winced.

"What is it?"

If she didn't know better, she would think Piven was worried. "Nothing," she began to say and then stopped herself. No. It wasn't nothing. "Actually, I really feel like I need to learn how to use my sword."

"I think differently. And guess whose opinion matters more?"

Normally she would have left it there, but today, she couldn't. Both the voice, and what Gabriel had said were warring inside her. She touched her brow. "It's worrying at me that I haven't learned to use it yet."

"There's nothing to worry about. Now, we need to get to what I've planned for today."

He began to talk about the crossbow he'd pulled off the wall and she knew it was pointless to argue further. He wouldn't listen.

"This is an ultra-light pistol grip, which means it can be fired with one hand. It generally is a better option to take into a fight because you don't have both hands tied up and you can use it as a weapon as well if they come close. Feel it, the tensile strength of the firing wire. This is it loose, now feel the difference when I've set it for firing." He went on about the speed it fired at, then handed her a bolt. "These are blunt tipped with a hooked barb on the underside so they punch a hole in your target, rather than slice right in. It won't kill the Wild or Dark Brethren, but it will knock them back a few paces and tear out a large chunk of flesh if they rip it out. Like any living thing, they weaken with lack of blood, so make sure you hit them near a major artery."

She tried to keep up but was distracted by her thoughts and the voice that kept whispering in her mind that she'd be better learning how to use her sword. She tried to block the voice out, but didn't really know what she was doing, as nobody had taught her how to do that yet.

Just another thing she wasn't being taught.

After she'd managed to load the crossbow within the time he allotted as acceptable, he taught her how to stand and aim.

"Now, stand firm and fire."

She did and almost dropped the crossbow when the kickback hurt her already aching wrist.

"Terrible. Try again."

She fumbled loading the arrow and then when she set it off, her arm jumped again with the kickback, sending the bolt to the right. It hurt her wrist and forearm even worse than throwing the knives did.

"Hold your wrist firm, not stiff."

Ardenne couldn't see the difference, but she bit her lip, trying to do what he told her. After half an hour, the crossbow, even though he said it was a light one, felt like a lump of concrete at the end of her arm. Her tendons trembled with the effort of holding steady as she turned and shot at the target. As it kicked back, something twanged in her forearm, pain shooting up to her shoulder. She dropped the crossbow to grab her arm, registering the loud snap and glistening tinkle of breaking glass. She'd broken a window with her arrow. "Fuck!" Her chest felt tight, her nerves jangly, wound up. Fury bubbled under her skin, driven by anger at Piven, at the voice that pushed and pushed and wouldn't stop. Why couldn't she even control her own subconscious thoughts?

It was stupid. She was stupid. They were all stupid.

"This is ridiculous. Why can't we learn swordplay? That would be easier."

"No. There's a progression we must follow. You might not understand my reasons, or even comprehend I might have them, but I do. We will learn this first." He stepped toward her, pulled her back to the firing line. "You lost control of your crossbow and shot wide."

"You don't have to tell me I shot wide. I can hear I shot wide."

"You locked your wrist and elbow. I told you, firm, not stiff."

"I don't know the bloody difference!" Tears stung her eyes and she blinked them back.

"Obviously not. Shall I show you?"

"My arm hurts."

"You need to rise above the pain. If you get hurt in the middle of a fight, you can't let pain stop you. You must fight on. Use the other arm if necessary. Switch to another weapon."

Anger a hot flare in her chest and mind, she grabbed three

knives from the table at her side and threw them, one, two, three, into the target. She knew they'd hit without using Piven's eyes to see.

"Good. Now try the crossbow again."

She did but holding it steady sent a hot arc of pain up her arm from her wrist. "I can't do it."

"Poles," was all he said, throwing her a pole. She fumbled it, hitting herself in the head, but managed to hold off his attack, using her left hand to brace the impact of his blows on her aching right arm. She knew she'd pulled a tendon or something, but Piven didn't let up and it was little point asking him to. Hot tears stung her eyes, fury tightened her chest, making her gasp for breath, making it harder to concentrate. Even so, she held her own—just—and almost sobbed in relief when he stepped away.

"Crossbow."

She picked it up and tried to hold it in front of her, but her wrist couldn't bear the weight. "I can't do it," she said, a sob in her voice she hated.

"Try your other arm. You should be learning to be ambidextrous anyway. Most of all, don't stop. If you're out there you can never stop."

She tried her left arm, but the bolts went wide, nowhere near her target.

"Come on, Ardenne. Concentrate. You should be able to do this. Your mother was a crack shot."

Again with a comment about her mother. "I'm not my mother."

"No, you're not."

Her fingers itched to pick up a knife and throw it at him, but the voice broke through the angry maelstrom in her mind and said, "*Get your sword.*"

"*I don't know how to use it,*" she answered back in her mind.

"*You know enough about sparring from the work you've done with the fighting poles. Besides, your sword will tell you what to do. Don't get angry. It won't do you any good. Show him your resolve. He won't stop if you don't. He's a relentless prick."* The words were harsh, but there was a note of appreciative warmth in them.

"You know Piven?" Stupid question really, given the voice was her subconscious talking to her.

"I'm not your subconscious. And in answer to your question, he trained me too."

Piven clicked his fingers in front of her face. "Earth to Ardenne. Don't just stand there, get another weapon."

"Your sword. Get your sword."

Before she could stop herself, she raced to where she placed Seer's Blood every morning and swept it out of the scabbard. It was light in her hands after the crossbow, the blade singing to her as she swung around. Holding it made her forget what the voice wanted—or even what the voice might be. All she knew was that the blade was hers and she needed to use it. Now.

She held it up in front of her. "I've been dreaming of using this. Of slicing through the cults who are attacking me and G ... those fighting with me." She'd almost said Gabriel's name but had pulled back just in time.

There was a strange pause before he said, "Those are ... dreams. You're not up to using it in reality yet."

"I think I am." And so saying, she darted toward him, light on her feet just like he'd trained her. Seer's Blood sang in her mind, a joyful song that swept into her muscles and bones. Pain faded; exhaustion left as adrenaline surged to the fore bringing with it untold energy. So much energy. Her limbs buzzed with it. And all around her, the song. A song that had her spinning through the air, bringing the blade down through where Piven had been standing only moments before. The song lit her up, showing in her mind an image of Piven racing for the wall mounts where he kept his swords.

She was no longer Ardenne. She was Seer's Blood. And she was hungry.

She leaped after him, bringing Seer's Blood up in a block as Piven swung to meet her with his blade. The impact jarred up her arms, but the song in her blood and muscles and bones didn't care about her sore wrist and arm. It just urged her to hold it in a two-handed grip and meet him blow for blow.

They twisted and turned, the loud clang of metal-on-metal ringing through the air. She felt a slice in her shoulder, the sting only an echo in the back of her mind, the scent of the blood driving her on.

Faster and faster she moved, getting closer and closer to striking Piven.

His power sizzled in the air, against her skin, but he was no match for her despite him using it. No match to Seer's Blood in the hands of the one who was meant to be hers. They were together at last, doing what they were always meant to do.

They shared blows over and over, the power of them zinging up her arms, and with each one, she learned more, heard more, felt more. Piven was obviously defending, not trying to attack at all, but trying to disarm her or knock her out.

A voice screamed at the back of her mind to stop; that Piven wasn't the enemy. But another, louder voice told her anyone who stopped her from doing what she must *was* the enemy.

She spun as he riposted a jabbing move designed to slap her wrist and disable her, swapping the sword to her other hand. Piven's sword tip sliced her skin, but she didn't worry. It was barely a paper cut. She could do more damage. She brought Seer's Blood up and around. There was a tearing sound and Piven jumped back. Seer's Blood sang her a song of the long gash it had made down his forearm.

Seer's Blood sang a song of blood in her head. *Blood. Blood. I want the blood. I want to drink it in, revel in it. More. More.*

Ardenne let out a cry, pressing her attack.

"Ardenne. Ardenne, stop! What are you doing?"

She became aware that someone else had entered the room. She altered her stance so she could face them too.

Sarita, the voice in the back of her mind—her voice—whimpered. *She's not a threat.*

And yet, the thing inside her didn't see the witch that way. Everything was a threat ... except for the one wielding the sword and the power it contained inside: the living soul now meshed with her, guiding her. They were no longer two beings. They were one.

She raised the sword, ready to attack.

CHAPTER 22

FINDING POWER

Training does not give all the answers she seeks
But training is important, for danger still peeks
Ever closer if she does not find
A way to make the sword to her bind
Forever to give its loyalty so it heeds
Her will, her power, so she never bleeds.

Her blood is the death-nell
Or maybe it's his hell.
Extract from The Middleton Manifesto, Prophecy 11, Book 1

"Ardenne. Put down the sword," the one called Sarita demanded, as if she truly thought they might take heed of her. She lifted the sword higher.

"Why are you attacking Piven?" the witch asked, taking a tentative step forward. "Whatever he's done, you can't attack him with that sword."

"She can't hear you. No!" Piven threw out his hand, but it was too late, Sarita had got too close. She had her hand outstretched as if to take the sword.

Ardenne lifted it up and brought it down in a wide arc, designed to take off a head, the pathetic voice that was once her screaming and screaming at them to stop. But they couldn't. Not now. Not with the berserker need for blood thrumming in their veins.

Sarita leaped sideways as Piven threw all his power against Ardenne, managing to make the sword shift from its direction, but it still sliced Sarita across the shoulder. A cry of surprise left the witch's lips, followed by a grunt as she hit the floor and rolled.

But they couldn't worry about her now. The greater danger stood before them.

Piven.

They leaped toward him and engaged, the clang of swords ringing in the air.

Behind them, they were aware of the witch rolling to her knees, pushing to her feet.

"Ardenne, stop!"

They glanced at her, pushed into the witch's mind, not caring that they made her wince in pain. Then they were looking at their face. They were smiling, their eyes impossibly wide. And there was no color there, only black.

They felt Piven move behind them and tore out of the witch's mind to deal with him, defending from his sword blow easily before going on the attack, forcing him back.

Sarita gasped. "Her eyes are black, Piven."

"Of course they're black. She's been possessed." His voice was punctuated by the blows he fended off, tight with the exertion of using an incredible amount of his powers. Although not his telekinesis. Curious. They smiled wider.

"Possessed?"

"Stop asking inane questions and help me."

"Can't you stop her?"

They understood the witch's confusion. Piven was far and away above Ardenne in skill with any weapon. But he was no match for them together, meshed as one.

"Not if I don't want to kill her. You must hold her still."

Sarita didn't move for long seconds, as if what he asked had frozen her in place. "I-I can't do that."

"Of course you can."

"Not unless I have to."

"Believe me. You have to. I can't use my telekinesis on her while using it to keep up with her in this fight. I could accidentally make her brain bleed. You have to do it."

They spun in the opposite direction from where they'd been going—taking advantage of his distraction—and almost sliced him through the back.

He grunted as he blocked the attack. "Hurry! Use the power. We need its violence, its wildness. Don't hold back."

They understood his urgency. They had cornered him, their blows getting closer and closer to hitting him.

"Don't hurt Ardenne," the witch pleaded—and some part of them knew she wasn't talking to Piven. "Just hold her still."

Then power like they'd never experienced before hit them.

They stopped mid-spin and flew backward to slam against the wall by the door. They snarled and spat, trying to fight free of the thing holding them frozen against the wall. But it was useless. They couldn't move.

They screamed their rage.

"Oh, Goddess. I'm hurting her."

"No, you're not. She just doesn't like it."

"Are you sure?"

"Does it matter when this is the only way? Just hold her there, while I try to disarm her."

"Disarm her?"

"Yes. I've got to get her to let go of the sword. It's the problem."

The sword? No. He couldn't take the sword from them! It was part of them.

They tried to fight against the thing holding them, but all it did was suck on their energy, making them weaker as it strengthened.

"I should be able to wrench it from her now I'm not fighting for my life."

Then suddenly, his power yanked on the sword in their hand.

They screamed, and then they were in Sarita's mind, then Piven's then back to Sarita's, bouncing between them, unable to stop shifting between perceptions. In those minds they could see their knuckles shining through their skin, so white they were almost silver, as they held onto the sword.

"Fuck, it's strong."

In the moments they were in Sarita's mind, they could see that Piven stood there, one hand out, his entire body trembling with effort, his jaw clenched tight.

"She's not letting go."

"No shit, Sherlock."

Piven held out his other hand, and with a shout, pulled back with his arms.

The sword was wrenched from Ardenne's hand and flew across the room to Piven.

Ardenne let out a piercing cry like a limb had been severed—no, not completely severed. Only partially severed. She could still feel the soul. It still whispered in her mind. She had to get to it. Had to. She struggled against the power holding her against the wall.

Piven caught the sword that flew toward him, his eyes snapping open and flaring black for a moment before returning to normal. "Holy crap. The power in this thing. Why bloody Gabriel gave it to her in the first place is beyond me. He should have known better." He placed it on the bench behind him.

"He wouldn't if he'd known this would happen. He also probably thought you would have taught her to shield by now. Goddess knows I thought you would have so I could give up my burden of shielding her from the world."

"Is poor baby exhausted from shielding her?" Piven drawled.

Sarita wiped at the sweat beading her brow, her hand trembling. "Shut up and do something productive. I can't hold her for much longer and she's not calming down."

Ardenne kicked and struggled against the magical binding, starting to shout at the witches before her, the words in a language she'd never spoken or even heard of before. And from the shock she felt in Sarita—she was still somehow in her mind—the witch had never heard it before either.

Sarita whipped around to look at her.

The part of her that was still Ardenne was shocked by what she saw—the wildness in her aura and the black that had covered her usually moon-colored eyes, a light sparking in their depths.

"Do you think she can see us?"

"I don't think she sees anything but the fight and the blood."

"What do you mean?"

"She's connected with the soul of this sword still."

"Isn't that what you're supposed to do with a soul sword?"

"Not like this. Not this deeply."

Just then Seer's Blood began to vibrate against the bench, emitting a keening sound that grew higher and higher.

The thing that had been inside her, that was being pulled out of her now the sword was gone from her touch, didn't want to go. It grabbed on with claws, gaining strength as the noise grew higher and louder.

Ardenne began to vibrate against the wall, her hands and heels and head slamming against the plaster. Little chunks of wall rained down around her.

It hurt. It hurt. Please stop. Please stop.

"What the hell!" Sarita's hands clamped around Ardenne, but she got bucked off as the thing that had connected with Ardenne tried to gain full control again.

"Fuck."

"Don't be a pussy. Use your power," Piven snarled at her.

"It could hurt her."

"This will hurt her more!"

Magic curled around her and tightened like cords, binding her, trying to still her.

Ardenne cried out as pain lashed through her, the keening cry of the sword now a shriek. Piven slapped his hands to his ears and she felt Sarita wince, the power pull back a little.

"Don't stop," Piven yelled.

The power tightened. She screamed again as the thing inside her fought back.

Sarita grunted. "She's frothing at the mouth. There's blood in it."

"It doesn't matter. Keep going or we'll never get her back."

The awful power tightened again. She struggled against it, claws in her mind swiping at the cords that were bound around her and were trying to push into her mind.

"Do something, Piven. I can't hold her tighter without hurting her more."

Through Sarita's eyes she saw Piven's lips thinning and then he flicked his fingers.

Ardenne made a sound as power smacked her in the head, a blow that knocked her nearly unconscious.

And in that moment, Piven's power got in, slicing the connection between her and the sword. The screaming in her mind echoed away in the distance leaving nothing but a ringing in her ears made worse by the silence that had suddenly fallen on the room.

The sword was gone from her mind.

Slowly, trembling, Sarita let go of the power holding Ardenne to the wall and with Piven's power helping, gently lowered her to the floor where she slumped in a tangled heap.

And as Sarita and Piven edged toward her, cautiously, her sight dimmed until unconsciousness reached up to swallow her.

~

ARDENNE WOKE GROGGILY to a bird cheeping at her window. She couldn't remember how she got in bed or why she felt like she'd been trampled in the running of the bulls in *Pamplona*. She groaned as she sat up, head pounding. Nausea welled and she raced to the bathroom.

When the heaving finished she was too weak to get to her feet and make her way back to bed. Every muscle ached and trembled. Sweat stung her brow and lip. Her stomach roiled even though it was empty, and the air burned in her lungs. Sobbing quietly, she lay on the floor. The tiles were blessedly cool against her hot, aching face.

She would have stayed there forever if Sarita hadn't come.

Rushing into the bathroom, she raced to Ardenne's side. "Oh, Ari. Why didn't you call me?"

Ardenne tried to shake her head, but the pain increased. "Couldn't. Too sick," she managed to mutter through the pounding. She'd not had a migraine for years and had forgotten how bad they were.

"Let's get you back to bed. You're freezing."

Really? She didn't feel freezing. She felt hot. So hot. Maybe she had a fever, not a migraine.

Sarita hooked her arm under Ardenne's shoulders and carefully pulled her upright. Ardenne's legs buckled as the pain in her head increased. With a grunt, Sarita swung Ardenne into her arms and carried her carefully to the bed.

"You're so strong," she managed to whisper.

"Years of training." Sarita lowered her onto her bed.

Ardenne sank into the cool sheets with a grateful sigh.

"Here. I brought this for you to drink. It will help you sleep, and when you wake you'll feel much better."

She helped Ardenne sit up enough to drink the bitter liquid. After settling her again, she kissed Ardenne on the forehead. "Sleep."

The heaviness of sleep settled over Ardenne before she could ask Sarita what was wrong with her.

In sleep, she found herself in a darkened tunnel. It was blessedly quiet, the ground beneath her soft, yet cool. Trembling, she sank into the softness, wanting to pull it around her and never rise again. She drifted for endless moments until she became aware of a change.

Voices called to her from afar.

Gabriel.

And the other one.

She didn't move from where she was huddled in the dark. She didn't want to face him or the voice from her subconscious. She particularly didn't want him to find her like this. Didn't want him to know what had happened.

But what had happened?

Something terrible. Something she couldn't remember. Or didn't want to remember? The last clear memory she had was Piven challenging her. She remembered running to pick up Seer's Blood to spite him. Then …

Nothing.

A big blank.

She shuddered in the dark, whimpering.

"Ardenne? Are you okay?"

It was a faint echo, the voice from her subconscious, and it hurt her head. "Go away," she hissed.

"I need to make sure you aren't hurt. I was so worried. I tried to help. I wanted to help. But they've kept you from me for so long. The connection isn't strong enough so I couldn't help you control it. I'm so sorry, Ardenne. Ardenne?"

Control it? Control what? And why was her subconscious talking about being kept away from her? It was almost like it was someone else talking to her. "Who are you?"

"I can't tell you that now. Not yet. But soon." The voice sounded closer. *"Right now, you are more important. I was wrong to make you use the sword. You can't pick it up again. Not until you've learned to shield yourself. You can't let it control you like it did."*

"Control me?" But as she asked the questions, an image of her with black eyes, hair whipping in the wind, Seer's Blood a crimson blaze in her hand as she swept it down, down, toward someone.

She whimpered and burrowed further away from the image.

"It's okay, Ardenne. It wasn't your fault."

Ardenne covered her ears. "I don't want to know. I don't want to know." The voice kept talking, but she wouldn't listen, willing it and the memories it brought far away until she was alone again.

She drifted there for what seemed an age but might only have been an instant. She became aware of footsteps coming close. Soft, careful footsteps of someone approaching an injured animal. "Ardenne?"

A gentle voice. *His* voice.

She smiled. The sound of his voice soothed her in a way the other didn't. He never wanted anything from her. He never berated her in her dreams or was insistent like the voice was. Right now, she needed his calm.

"Gabriel." She turned toward the sound of him, eyes still closed. "Everything hurts."

"I know."

"I'm so tired. What's wrong with me?"

Cold hands touched her, the scent of mountain air curled around her. "It's all right, Ardenne. You're all right now. Nothing's going to hurt you. You're safe."

She shook her head. It was so difficult to believe when she felt like this. Like something inside her had changed in a way that scared her to death. She didn't want to face it.

The cold hands moved from her shoulder, ever so gentle, to brush her hair away from her face. "You did change, Ardenne. But it's not your fault. It's nobody's fault but mine. I should have waited to give you the sword. Nobody blames you."

There was something to blame her for?

"This will pass and you will be yourself. You *must* be yourself."

He sounded so sad. So desperate. She opened her eyes, looked up into the face that always made her feel that if there was a God, surely this was his work. Gabriel. His Lonely Angel.

"So, you came to make sure I am alright?"

"Of course I came. I will always come when you are troubled." He smiled wryly. "Or when you are in trouble."

Her heart lurched at his words, his smile. If only this wasn't a dream.

He helped her sit up, his arm staying around her as he supported her against his chest. The touch made her stomach muscles curl and her breath falter. But even in her dream she couldn't let him see it. She took a steadying breath and tried to concentrate on what he'd said. Frowning, she asked, "Something happened?"

He nodded.

"I don't remember. I don't remember why I feel so lost. So ... ashamed."

The smile faded. "I wish you never had to remember, but that's not up to me. Besides, there's no need to feel ashamed. You didn't do anything wrong. It wasn't you. You are not to blame." He looked over his shoulder, then back at her. "Ardenne?"

She looked into his lovely face. "Gabriel." She touched his cheek, couldn't stop herself. "So beautiful."

His expression changed for a split second, reminding her of what longing felt like, but then it was gone, and his expression was simply concerned. "I have to go."

"No!"

"Yes. Besides, it's time you wake up. You must not get lost in the dreams, Ardenne. Promise me you will never get lost in the dreams."

"I promise."

"Make sure Piven helps you strengthen your mind against intrusion. Make sure he helps you learn to shield and to control your magic. It will be much better when you do."

"I can't make Piven do anything."

"I think after what happened, you will find he will do this." He cupped her face, the cold of his hands burning her skin in a way that didn't feel like pain. "Remember when we watched Anne of Green Gables when you were little?"

She nodded. She did. They'd watched it together after her uncle was killed, before his funeral, to keep her away from the horrible grief of her aunts and cousins. She hadn't been able to see what was going on in the series, but it hadn't mattered. Gabriel explained it all and the dialogue said so much. She'd wanted to be Anne after that, partly because she'd enjoyed the series and partly because Gabriel had watched it with her, spending time with a little girl who should have been below his notice.

"Remember the phrase she said that captured your attention?"

"Tomorrow is a new day, with no mistakes in it."

"Yes. Remember that." His lips touched hers, a brief caress that shattered something deep inside her, and then he was gone.

She woke up, fingers touching lips that still burned from a caress that wasn't real.

"Oh." The breathy sound vibrated in the quiet morning air. The bird outside her window chirruped as if to greet her. She smiled at the friendly sound and then touched her head. It no longer throbbed sickeningly. In fact, she felt better than she had in ages. It must have been what Sarita gave her to drink. And the sleep.

And the lovely dream of Gabriel where they didn't fight to save his life. Where he'd shown he cared. Been so gentle. Kissed her goodbye.

She touched her lips again. "Tomorrow is a new day, with no mistakes in it," she said into the empty quiet of the room. Those words had always brought her comfort and hope.

Why did they make her ache a little now?

Her door opened. She knew it was Sarita before her friend spoke. "Good morning, Sarita."

"You're awake. How are you feeling?"

"You don't have to whisper. I'm better now." She touched her head. "I haven't had a migraine like that in years. It must have come on really quickly. I can't remember anything other than feeling strange when Piven was drilling me, pushing me to be better at the crossbow."

Sarita gently sat on the bed at her side. "Do you remember anything after that?"

"Not really. I think I picked up Seer's Blood. It was singing to me, like when I picked it up on Christmas Day, but then it got so loud, and I couldn't think and then ... oh." Memories lurched sickeningly in her mind.

"And then what?"

She rubbed her brow, the memories swirling in a murky mist. "I don't know. It's all such a muddle. I think the migraine must have struck then."

"Yes."

"Were you there when it happened?"

There was a brief pause before Sarita answered. "I came in just after. It had already hit you by then. I helped Piven settle you and then we brought you back here."

"How long have I been asleep?"

"Two days."

What! "I've never had a migraine last that long."

"No, I don't imagine you have. Piven thinks it might have something to do with your magic bursting out of you. It's been pushing against the shield I created with the blood promise for the last month, but it burst out at your training two days ago. That's what caused the migraine."

"Will it happen again?" She hoped not. She might not be able to remember much of what had happened, but she remembered the pain.

"No. Both Piven and I are shielding you now to keep you hidden from others, but he realizes it is time to train you how to maintain the shield yourself. And to help you funnel your power more positively so that it doesn't have that backlash effect on you again."

She sat up. "He's going to start training me to use all my powers?"

"Yes."

She clasped her hands together. "Are you sure?"

Sarita laughed. "Yes, I'm sure. Now, if you feel up to it, go have a shower and then come downstairs for breakfast. We'll go for a walk after."

"What about training today?"

"You have the day off. We want to make sure the migraine is completely gone before you start back with Piven."

"I don't want to wait."

"You have no choice. Doctor's orders. Well, Lord Hei's orders."

"Lord Hei knows about the migraine?"

"Of course. He and Tomas were worried when Master Solari called. In fact, Tomas was ready to leave *Casa Cinque* and fly down here."

"He can't do that!" Ardenne was horrified. She loved her papa, but she didn't want him interfering in her training. No other Bartolli Prime had ever been visited by family while training. It wasn't done.

Sarita's hand on hers made her realize she was worrying them so hard the knuckles popped. "Don't worry. Vincente talked him out of it, with Lord Hei's help. But he wants you to call as soon as you are up to it."

Ardenne sighed. "I'll do it after breakfast."

It was lovely to hear Papa's voice, even though she was a little annoyed at his overreaction to the migraine. It wasn't like she was going to die or anything.

Finally, she managed to convince him she was fine and that she just wanted to get back into her training, but it was still a while before he let her go. "Be careful, Ardenne. I don't want you in danger again."

She snorted. "I was hardly in danger, Papa."

He sounded so careful when he said, "Even so. Just take care."

"I promise."

The day after that dragged by. She wasn't allowed to do much of anything except read her magic books. She wasn't even able to oil

Seer's Blood, as apparently when the migraine had kicked in so suddenly, she'd fallen on it and the blade had snapped out of the hilt. Master Ricardo was currently endeavoring to fix it.

"Oh God! I can't believe I damaged it. What's Gabriel going to say when he hears I destroyed such a precious sword? It's irreplaceable."

"You are the one who is irreplaceable. I think Gabriel will simply be happy that you didn't hurt yourself with it."

She hoped Sarita was right, although she couldn't quite make herself believe it. "Not that Piven's ever going to let me touch it again, right? He'll say I'm too clumsy or something."

Sarita patted her hands. "He won't say that. I think he's planning on starting your sword training soon. But with wooden swords, not real ones. You need to learn the basics first."

"Right." But something inside her cried at the thought. She didn't want to use another sword. She wanted to use Seer's Blood. She just hoped she hadn't damaged it for good.

Rather than think about that though, she concentrated on the fact that tomorrow she would start her magical training.

She couldn't wait.

CHAPTER 23
DARK LIGHTS

One is for life, Two is for pain
Three is for passion, Four is for gain
Five cries the tears of eternal rain
As he struggles to hold all together again
For the One who is coming to remain sane
She must survive their deadly game
Where hate and love together reign
And Dark Lights swallow all in savage flame.
Extract from The Middleton Manifesto, Prophecy 18, Book 1

"Very good. Very good," Piven said as she came to the end of her obstacle course. "But enough of that today. It's time to start working on other aspects of your powers."

Ardenne's heart leaped in her chest. She'd begun to doubt what Sarita had said because when she'd arrived today, Piven had continued her training as per usual. "So, you'll start my magical training today?"

"Yes. It's become apparent that it's a necessity. We can't have what happened the other day happening again."

Gabriel's words in her dream echoed back to her. He'd said this would happen. Was this some hint of prescience, or just her subconscious mind seeing things she missed?

"Why are you frowning? I thought you'd be happy about this."

"No. I mean yes, I am happy. I was just thinking of the migraine," she said. "I don't really want another one like that again."

"Believe me, none of us want that to happen again. I'm going to do everything I can to make certain of it." Piven sounded full of deep sincerity.

"Thank you." Her lips trembled.

"No need for maudlin thanks." She heard him turn and stalk over to his desk. "Let's get started. Now, while you've been strengthening certain aspects of your powers by being in my mind and the mind of others, there's much more to your powers than that. We need to build up those mental muscles further. Teach you how to control the power more effectively so that you can use it to do other things outside your own mind."

"Sounds good to me."

"It might sound that way now, but I'll be surprised if you say that by the end of the day."

That sounded ominous. And challenging. Ardenne smiled.

"You'll find once you open the door to your power, you'll never stop learning about it."

"I love learning."

"You have no choice even if you did mind. If you want to learn about your powers now, you must learn theory and concepts quickly. If you've been reading the books I gave you and doing the exercises, then that will help, but the practical is something else and there are many paths you can follow, many types of power and magical forms. You will have a natural proclivity for certain types of magics as we all do. And while you can, and will, learn about the others, they will never come as easily as those that are natural to you. In fact, some you will not be able to manage at all."

"That makes sense."

"We are also going to have to spend a lot of time in each other's minds."

"Haven't we already done that?"

"This will be different. Deeper. It won't be fun or comfortable, particularly as you are so untrained. But if you do your homework, and more importantly, do as I say and learn from my example, then you should pick up how to strengthen and defend your mind quickly."

"Good."

There was the scraping sound of a chair being pulled out. "Sit." She did. Rather than sitting too, he began to pace, as he always did when he lectured her. "You've started your weapons training, but those are physical weapons. That is all very good, but they are simply tools. They can break or be taken away from you in the midst of battle. The powers in your mind can never be taken as long as you learn to block outside intrusion."

"What do you mean?"

"You need to learn how to block your mind to others as much as you need to learn to punch through any kind of block and get into someone else's mind. It's something not everyone is capable of, but given your particular skill set, I think you will prove adept with time and practice. You must also learn how to manipulate and work in the Gray."

"The Gray?"

"Yes. That place between time and space I used when I tested you. That place is what those in the coven call Aether or Ether. Some even call it the Void. But I call it the Gray."

"Why do you call it that?"

"Because of the color the mind perceives when there."

"Is it dangerous?"

"Oh yes. It takes a lot of effort to enter the Gray and learn how to use it safely, for if you ever lose yourself there, you will die. One cannot live without their soul."

Ardenne gulped.

"It might interest you to know that you already have some affinity with the Gray."

"How?"

"You mentioned the dreams you've been having. The ones of seeing you with Seer's Blood cutting through the enemy cults."

"I did?"

"Yes. Before the migraine. They are not dreams. They are visions."

"How do you know that?"

"Because others have seen this too."

Ardenne swallowed. Hard. "Who?"

"That isn't important. What is important is that this means you are already communicating with the universe or another mind. And what's most important now, before you lose yourself to these visions you see, is to train you how to control them, how to interpret them."

"But what does this have to do with the Gray?"

"Everything. Visions travel along the same astral planes as the Gray. Sometimes they even kiss up against each other, intermingle. When they do this, that is where the past, the present, and the future collide. It's what happens when prophecy is made."

She shifted in her chair uncomfortable, shivering. "Prophecy? You think my dreams have something to do with telling the future?" She hoped not. Because in so many of her dreams she was somehow responsible for Gabriel's death.

"Maybe. But the future is rarely ever set, and what is seen in prophecy can often be changed."

"How?" She leaned forward a little. If she was having visions of the future, she was very interested in how to prevent the bad futures from coming into being.

"Through choice. You must listen properly to what these visions are telling you. See outside them to the whole. Once you understand this, you can begin to shape what others have foretold.

Very few manage this, but then again, many don't have your skills. If you work hard, you will be able to change what you see. But you must have strength of will beyond what is normal. You must be able to not only see but understand what the universe is telling you."

She didn't respond. The truth was probably written all over her face, in her shaking limbs. Finally she whispered, "I want that. I don't want what I've seen come to pass."

"Hardly anyone ever does. But in studying this path, you will find that things are never as simple as they seem." His chair creaked as he sat.

"I understand."

"Do you? You'd be truly remarkable if you did."

She ignored the part of herself that whimpered at his doubt—the part that agreed with him—and crossed her arms. "Okay. I get it. It's going to be difficult, and I won't like a lot of it, but I need to learn it. So, come on. Teach me how to enter this Gray and use it if that's what's going to help."

"It's only one of the things that's going to help. I have been teaching you about your most powerful tool already. Your ability to enter another's mind. At the moment you're just a passive user, but in time, I can help you strengthen it until you can manipulate and affect what another is doing."

Ardenne frowned. "You mean I can force someone to do what I want?" She wasn't sure if that was good or bad.

"More than that. But we'll discuss this later. For now, we need to start on simpler things."

"Like the Gray."

"Oh, the Gray isn't simple. No, I'm not starting you with the Gray. First, you must enter my mind."

"Okay." That shouldn't be too hard given she'd done that nearly every day for the past ten months.

Centering herself once again, she took a grasp on her empathy and reached out toward his mind only to hit a barrier and be shoved back into her own mind. "Ow!" She rubbed her head, the ringing in her ears high-pitched and painful. "What the hell was that?"

"That's my shield. It's what I'm going to teach you."

Despite the tingling pain in her head, she couldn't help but smile. "Really? You're going to teach me that?"

"Of course. You don't defend yourself by tickling your opponent. You need something that's strong enough to hurt. Pain is one of life's great motivators."

"So I'm learning."

"Yes. Now, try again. Get into my mind."

She took a breath and tried again, a little more cautious this time. But even though she didn't go barreling into his mind, she was still knocked back, a sensation like an electric shock making her nerves twitch so badly she almost fell off the chair. "What the hell was that? I thought you said I could get in this time."

"No. I said you *had* to get into my mind."

"How am I supposed to do that when you keep repelling me with different levels of pain?"

"Ah, now that is the trick, isn't it?"

"Are you kidding me? Is this a test?"

"Of course it is. The most important kind. Because, if you can learn to overcome this kind of pain to get through the shield I've put in place, then you'll learn what you need to create one of your own far more effectively than if I taught you step-by-step. As I said, pain is a great motivator. It's also one of the world's best teachers."

"There are other ways of teaching," she grumbled.

"Yes, there are, but they're much slower and are to do with worlds that aren't as deadly as the one you wish entry into. If you wish to play in the big leagues, Ms Bartolli, you will need to learn to face the pain and take it."

Ardenne gritted her teeth but nodded. She'd dealt with physical pain. This couldn't be worse. And if she mastered it, she'd finally have what she longed for—control.

By the hour's end she had blood pouring from her nose and ears and felt like her brain and nerves were pummeled black and blue even though Piven had never laid a hand on her.

"Again."

"I can't," she panted, wondering if she was going to pass out. She'd been driven off the chair and onto her knees.

"Do you think if I were one of the Wild or Dark Brethren that you would be able to stop to get your breath back? Do you think they would care you're tired and bloody? Your condition would just encourage them to more violence. Use your mind, Ms Bartolli. Think your way through this."

"I am."

"You're doing it wrong."

"If I'm doing it wrong, it's because you're a lousy teacher," she yelled.

Piven chuckled. "Am I? Then how come you're ready to fight again?"

Ardenne's lips trembled as she bit back the words struggling to get out. He was right, damn him. He'd made her angry and the anger had energized her, bringing her to her feet. Without warning, she shoved out of her mind and at him, but this time, just before he shoved her out, she saw something she hadn't seen before.

A crack in his shield. A way in. Had that been there before and she just hadn't noticed it, or had her pummeling at him for an hour made a dent? She didn't know, but knowing didn't matter. Trying to think of a way she could use it did.

He was right about that, damn him. She hadn't been using her mind in the right way. She'd just been going at him like a bull in a china shop. She couldn't use brute force against those who were stronger than her. No. She had to be smart. So, if she couldn't use brute force, then she had to be sneaky.

Balling her fists, ignoring the fresh blood running from her nose because of the latest failed assault, she took a deep breath. Then, a growl in her throat, she pushed out, as if she was going to try the same thing yet again. However, this time, she sent a little tendril of herself sideways, hidden in the major assault she pummeled Piven with, feeling for the crack.

There!

She slipped into it and was inside. Inside the dark, broiling insanity-making intensity that was his mind. Swallowing hard, she pushed forward into his sight at the same time she backed off her assault on his shields and staggered as she captured his eyes.

She looked at herself standing there, trembling, dark red blood marring her pale, golden skin, her moon-like eyes glowing in the near dark of the room.

"Again," Piven said, his tone tight. She realized then this was costing him a little something too.

"There's no need," she said, a smile starting to bloom on her face.

"Why? Don't tell me you've had enough of getting your ass whipped?"

The smile grew on her pale face, her eyes twinkling with triumph. "No."

"No? So you're not giving up?"

"I don't have to. I'm already in." She lifted her hand and waved at him.

His shock ricocheted through her as he realized she spoke the truth. Then the shock changed, became a caress against the part of her mind that was now inside his. She shuddered.

"How did you manage it?"

She told him.

"Good. Remember what you learned today. Every shield has a weakness. You've just got to find it and be clever enough to figure out how to twist it to your advantage."

"That sounds Machiavellian."

"Machiavelli was a great thinker. You would do well to be like him." He moved toward her, his gaze raking over her as she stood there trembling, yet triumphant. "Let's see how long you can stay in my mind now you're in. We'll go for a run, and I want you to use my sight to lead."

"What?" She was exhausted and almost ready to drop and he wanted to go for a run?

"Persistence and stamina. They're key in using magic and in fighting. Let's go."

She wanted to tell him to go fuck himself because she didn't have to prove anything right now given her success at the task he'd set her. He was just being cruel. But she didn't say it. Instead, she took the lead, wanting to prove to herself she could push beyond endurance and be okay.

She was Ardenne Bartolli, chosen by Lord Hei to become his Prime after her papa. She was a secret witch with untapped powers she was now learning. She was training to be a great warrior. All of this while being blind in a sighted world full of creatures who were more than human, and she didn't need a single one of them to help her get around. She was strong. She was resourceful. She was smart. She had Seer's Blood, the powerful sword that Gabriel trusted her to learn to use. She wanted to be worthy of the sword. She wanted to belong to it as much as it belonged to her.

She could do this.

No.

She *would* do this.

CHAPTER 24
KILLING PAIN

Today I had a vision which I thought I might never arise from. It speared through my soul and into my heart. I saw love. Terrible, horrifying, wonderful love. A love that would last forever. One that could end us all with its killing pain.
Extract from Mary Middleton's Diary, April 1, 1534

Gabriel shook his head as he moved through the damp, cold caves, cursing the pain pushing through his skull. It had been a constant this last week as he tracked Anita through the Siberian wilderness, and he could have done without it. He'd already followed some false leads, too easily fooled because he was distracted by the pain and what it meant. He needed to concentrate now, entering what he believed was the place Anita was holed up.

There would be booby traps. He had to have his wits about him.

The darkness closed in around him as he moved away from the light coming in through the entrance where the sun glinted harshly off the snow that still blanketed the mountains here all year around. Not that he had a problem with the dark.

Strong scents assaulted him—wet clay, the minerals of the water leaching through the rocks, the pungency of the moss carpeting the walls and floor. And yet, through all the muddle of scents, he could swear he smelled the scent of blood lighting the air.

His fangs slid out further as he breathed in, trying to catch the scent again. There it was. Stronger than ever. Definitely blood. But not just any blood. *Her* blood.

Impossible! She was far away training with Piven. Vincente assured him that she had recovered well after the incident with Seer's Blood. Piven reported improved skills with the weapons, her fighting, and her control over her magic.

So, why the fuck was he smelling her blood? Feeling pain?

The pain had to be a trick. Anita had probably encouraged some of her insane followers to put some kind of spell on these caves—as if the cold and isolation of the furthest reaches of the Siberian Alps wouldn't be enough to stop anyone from delving further into them. He half laughed at her crazy paranoia. Although he supposed she was right in one respect given he'd found her caves.

He shook his head. It pounded harder at the movement.

Hell! He rubbed his fingertips against his brow, trying to massage the agony away. Whatever this spell was, it had to be strong magic to get through a vampire's defenses, especially one as old as he. Anita had never done anything by halves. Her Huntress heritage was partly to blame, even though all those magics were torn away from her when he'd saved her life by making her into a vampire.

Still, to do this ... She must be running through her Romani witches at a great rate if she was using magic like this as a permanent thing. And it was permanent. He'd felt it long before he'd arrived.

A well of sadness filled his chest. At one time, Anita would have done anything to protect those with magical powers. She'd been the fiercest Huntress that they'd ever seen, her powers a bright sun in the dark of the hunt, taking down all those who meant to cause innocent humans and witches harm.

Now look at what she'd become.

She probably fed from them, filling them with the bliss of her venom and tricking them into giving their lives for her worthless cause. She'd once been so single-minded in her desire to destroy those responsible for the attack on her coven, her home, and her parents' deaths. Now, all she seemed to concentrate on was chasing prophecy, wreaking havoc and mayhem as a consequence, careless of who she hurt in the process. It was like the Huntress powers had taken her down like they'd feared before she'd mastered them.

Except, it couldn't be that causing her actions, because the Huntress had been burned out of her when he'd fed her his blood. A witches magic never survived the change.

But regardless of why she was like this, she had to die.

Even his Sire knew it was time. Gabriel's lips quirked into a cynical smile. Hei hadn't exactly given him the thumbs up, but he hadn't stopped him. Killing Anita was the only way to protect Ardenne given what happened on the train on the way to *Firenze* and her interference in Ardenne's dreams. As long as she was alive, she wouldn't stop trying to fulfill the prophecy she thought she was part of.

She couldn't be allowed anywhere near Ardenne ever again.

There was a shift of movement in the air before him. Three scythes lashed out of the wall at different heights—aimed to take a person's head off and chop them into little pieces. He leaped out of the way, but not fast enough. The top one caught his shoulder, the bright bloom of his blood staining the air with its tantalizing scent.

Fanculo! "Concentrate, Gabriel. Stop thinking about Ardenne." It was difficult though with the pain—pain he now realized wasn't created by some spell, because as he moved deeper into the mountain, the pain was dulling a little.

So where was it coming from?

He sucked in a breath. No. It couldn't be.

But it was, because when he looked he saw clearly it was coming through the bond with Ardenne. As was the scent of her blood in his mind.

What the hell was Piven doing to her that was causing her such agony?

He would have to go back to *Firenze* and find out. He didn't have a choice. Vincente obviously wasn't telling him the entire story, and Ardenne was giving nothing away in her dreams.

But first, he would take care of Anita.

Pulling his mind forcefully back to the task, he moved more carefully down the tunnel that led deeper into the mountain, certain that the first booby trap was one of many. His wound was already healing, but he couldn't afford to be caught off guard like that again.

He moved, silent and careful, listening, scenting, feeling for vibrations in the stone around him. Nothing. He began to frown. He should have come across another trap by now. But that wasn't the only thing of concern. He couldn't hear any sounds that would indicate Anita and her people were here.

Maybe that was the magic he felt. He could have walked right past a concealed entrance. Although, he didn't think he had. Magic left a distinct impression in the air, making his skin prickle as though lightning was collecting near. He'd felt nothing like that.

Only the most subtle of magics could sneak under his notice, and he was certain Anita didn't have anyone capable of such things. So, either they weren't here, and his information was wrong, or they were hiding in some cave deep in the mountains still out of range of his hearing and sense of smell.

He continued on.

Deep in the mountain he came across an obvious trap—a pit filled with stakes. He jumped over it easily. Not much later, he rolled out of the way as a barbed net fell from the ceiling followed by a rain of spears that shot out of the wall, the tips filled with holy water. He laughed at its crudeness. They would only work on the Wild. The Dark Brethren and Lord Hei's sirelings were from different blood stock and weren't affected by such mundane things as holy water.

Why would Anita be expecting the Wild down here? Was it because they'd found out she'd betrayed them at the train? Maybe he could use that to his advantage. Except for the fact he'd already killed all the Wild in the area on his way here. Their blood still coursed through his veins. It had helped temporarily with the pain, which was a dull throb now, almost like it was being dulled by the mountain of earth above him. Or perhaps it was because he was truly on the hunt now, his nature surging to the fore and pushing all else aside in its animalistic need to bring down its intended prey.

Growling low in his throat, he sped up. Finally, he came across signs that people had been here. Footprints in the dirt. Many footprints, entering from a tunnel to the left and continuing down the tunnel he traveled.

Hunger and expectation dried his throat, made his skin tingle. He sped down the tunnel, silent as only a vampire could be.

He had her. She couldn't escape now.

The sound ahead changed, and he slowed down. There was still no sign or scent of humans here, but there was something different up ahead. Cautiously, he crept forward and soon found himself in a cavernous space. Phosphorescent veins of some kind of moss ran up the walls, lighting the area in an eerie green glow. Evidence of fires and places where people had laid mats down to sleep, the smell of stale cooking, the pungency of human waste wafting from another cave on the far side of the cavern, told him there had been a camp of some sort here not long ago. A day, maybe two.

He'd missed them.

"*Fanculo!*"

He knew this had been Anita's camp. He could smell the faint scent of her in the air, like a taunt. It was stronger to one side, near a fire pit. The area around the fire was bare and the coals cold. He kicked at the remnants. Something hit the far wall with a dull slap that did not sound like charred wood. Gabriel bent to pick it up.

A piece of parchment with writing on it so faded he could hardly read it. He was about to drop it when his fingers ran across something strange. There were little raised lumps underneath the indecipherable words. Evenly spaced lumps clustered together in such a way they could only be one thing.

Braille.

There was braille on this ancient piece of parchment.

There could only be one reason Anita had something written in braille that she'd tried to destroy rather than chance it fall into his hands.

Ardenne.

Ice ran through Gabriel, chilling his skin. His fingers ran along the sentence fragment on the parchment, his lips moving as he read.

'... *her blood, hides the sign, of First's hidden codes, forced to al ...*'

He frowned. It was a fragment of Middleton prophecy. He knew it as certainly as he knew the scent of his own blood, the cadence of Mary's writing unmistakable. But he'd never read it before, and he'd read all her works. How could this be?

That thought was taken over by an even more disturbing one. The only reason Anita would have this unknown prophecy printed in braille was so she could give it to Ardenne to read.

Sire's Blood! That could never happen.

He had to get back to *Firenze* now. Ardenne was in more danger than even he'd imagined, and he'd let himself be led away from her so easily. The fucking bitch had been taunting him, playing with him, just so she could get closer to Ardenne.

His fingers tightened on the old piece of parchment. The edges crumbled away. Magic sparked across his fingers. Cursing, he dropped it and watched as it burst into flame.

He tried to stamp out the flames before it was lost. He had to take this back to Vincente. He'd done more research into Mary's work than any other outside a Middleton Coven Librarian. He might be able to shed light on what it meant and why Anita would want to give it to Ardenne. But the flame continued to engulf the parchment. "No. No."

"You can't stop it."

Gabriel spun around to see a man at the entrance of the small cave opposite. He was filthy, covered in mud and what could only be excrement. The man had used the pungent scents to hide his presence. But why? And why had he been left behind alive? It was not like Anita to give him a prisoner.

As if he'd read Gabriel's mind, the man said, "I asked my Lady to leave me behind. I didn't want to hold her up and I thought I could be a good distraction. Stop you from chasing after her immediately."

Gabriel growled, the hunting instinct alive in him, heightened by his worry for Ardenne and the fresh danger Anita posed.

This man was one of hers. And now, in her place, he was going to die.

Gabriel leaped toward the man. The man raised his hand and Gabriel hit a wall of air. Magic skittered along his skin, holding him in place.

"You cannot get to me," the man said, his voice husky with lack of use. "Not yet. Not until Anita has gotten far enough away."

Gabriel almost laughed at his hubris. The man was powerful. But not powerful enough. Gabriel wasn't made quite like his brothers and sisters. Magic didn't affect him in quite the same way.

He pressed forward, his actions slow as if he were in turbulent water. The man trembled. Gabriel moved a step closer. Then another. His fangs bit against his lower lip as he pushed forward with every fiber of his being, with sheer force of will. Tendons tightened, close to snapping, in his neck, along his shoulders, through his chest and arms, down his legs. He was strong. Stronger than this Romani covered in filth. Another step. Another.

The man trembled harder, clutched at the wall as if it were the only thing holding him upright. Gabriel was now close enough to see the stress and pain in the man's eyes. Close enough to notice the pallor of his skin beneath the muck on his face, neck and arms, the deep purple bruises under his eyes. Close enough to smell something under the miasma of dank earth and shit. Something biting. Rotting.

He knew that smell.

This man was being eaten away by cancer. He was dying.

He faltered, horrified at what he'd been about to do. What he'd done already. He didn't kill humans or witches. He didn't feed on them.

His fangs retracted as disgust rose over him. He stopped moving. "I won't hurt you," he said, his voice gentle. "I just want to help."

The man laughed, his trembles now a bone shattering shaking. "She said you'd play games. Said you'd say anything to get me on your side. But you don't understand. I don't care what you do to me. My time is almost up. My mind is almost gone. This is all I've got left. This moment, holding you here, allowing my Lady to escape. My last action, saving her." His face lit up as he mentioned Anita.

"It doesn't have to be your last action. Maybe I can help you. The cancer might not be too far gone."

The man cackled, his grip on the wall desperate, the power holding Gabriel slipping, fading, fizzing to nothing. The man didn't seem to notice, his hand held out in front of him as if he were still in control of the spell. "Nothing can help me. Except being turned into a vampire, which is the last thing I want. So I stayed. She didn't want me to, wanted to ease my suffering. But this was the only way to let her get away in time to do what she must."

Gabriel didn't move closer. He stayed where he was, unwilling to frighten this obviously sick and unstable man even further. "And what is that? What must she do?"

The man's mouth opened and closed. "I ... I ..." He made a strangled sound and fell to his knees, eyes bulging as if he was choking. He fell forward, heaving in harsh breaths.

"Here, let me help you up."

Before Gabriel could touch him, the man yelped, "No!" and tried to scrabble backward, but he had been through too much. Too ill, too weak from using a power he should never have used in his state, he collapsed.

"You must realize you're too weak to do whatever Anita wanted you to do. Let me help."

"No." Nostrils flaring, eyes wide, every muscle trembling, the man shoved away Gabriel's offer. Rolling over, he pushed himself up, and then using the wall, managed to make it to his feet. He fumbled something out of his jacket pocket. "It's time for you to die."

Gabriel swore. The man held a vile of Silver Fire. Anita must have stolen some from the coven. An alchemical substance Mary Middleton had created to help in the fight against the Wild and Dark Brethren, the chemical composition and spells used to make it had been lost with her. The small amount left was held by the coven, tightly guarded. Or so they thought. The stuff, while deadly to Wild and Dark Brethren, couldn't kill him or any of Hei's sirelings. It hurt like hell though, burning like acid through skin and bone.

He held his hands up. "You don't have to use that. I won't hurt you."

The man was shaking. "I said I'd do it. For her. I gave my vow." His thumb moved over the stopper at the top. The way he was shaking, he'd spill it over himself first. While Silver Fire had been created to eat through vampire flesh and turn it to flames and their bones to ash, it could still do damage to human skin.

He didn't want this man more damaged than he already was. He couldn't believe Anita had been this cruel. Tears fell down the man's face now, pain and fear and the torment making their scent so terribly bitter. "You are not a killer."

"Not like you. But I can do this. I'll die knowing I've gotten rid of my beloved Lady's greatest tormentor. Her greatest enemy."

"The Silver Fire won't kill me. But it will hurt you."

"I don't care. I don't care." He pulled himself to his knees, his shaking fingers edging toward the top of the vile to pry it off.

"I won't let you hurt yourself." Before the man could flinch, Gabriel moved, taking the vile of Silver Fire from his shaking fingers.

The man let out a harsh cry and collapsed onto the floor. "I'm so sorry, my Lady. I failed you. I failed." He moved.

Gabriel saw a flash of silver. "No!" He smacked the knife the man was about to plunge into his own chest out of his hands. "No more. Anita will not have your life too. She's not worth it."

"She's worth everything," the man blubbered.

Gabriel wanted to harden his heart, but he couldn't. He'd never been able to turn his back on suffering and the thought he would be adding to it was a bitter one. There was only one thing he could do with this man.

He had to get him back to *Firenze*, to be cared for in his last days if he truly couldn't be saved. He could take him to *Casa Cinque,* which was closer, but he also needed to know if there was anything useful the man could tell them about Anita and her plans. Piven was the only witch he knew who would be able to go into the man's diseased brain and pull out whatever information might still be there without hurting him. However, he couldn't carry him there all the way against his will.

There was only one way he could do that.

He never liked using compulsion or his venom against others— taking someone's will was not something he relished doing. But there was no choice if he was to help this man.

He pressed his finger against his fang, extracting venom, grabbed the man's head, tipped it up. The man opened his mouth to protest and when he did, Gabriel pushed his finger with the venom into the man's mouth. The man gagged, trying not to swallow as he realized what the sweetness in his mouth was, fear written clearly in his tear-stained eyes. Satisfied all the venom was off his finger, Gabriel forced the man's mouth closed and held him until he swallowed reflexively, once, twice.

Gabriel let him go, his stomach roiling with revulsion over the necessity of what he'd just done.

With a cry, the man rolled over, tried to spit it out.

"It's too late, my friend," Gabriel said softly. He watched as the man tried to force himself to vomit by sticking two filthy fingers in his mouth. "It's already in your system. It seeps through the muscle wall and into the veins and never makes it to the stomach. You can vomit all you like, but it's too late. In a few seconds you will be mine as you were hers."

The man turned to him, tears streaming from his eyes, snot dripping from his nose, mixing with the mud and shit already on his face. "My Lady never forced venom onto us," he screamed at Gabriel. "She loves us. She would never do such a foul th—"

His words stopped, the echo of them fading away as all the anger and fear and stress disappeared. His face took on an expression of rapturous bliss as he looked up at Gabriel. "Oh," he breathed. "You are an angel." He was trembling now, but for a completely different reason.

Cursing at the effect of his venom, Gabriel put his hand under the man's arm. "Here, let me help you up." The scent of the man was almost overwhelming. "You can't come with me smelling like that."

"There is a warm pool through there." He pointed to the tunnel Gabriel had come down. "Do you want me to bathe?"

"I think that would be a good idea. Do you have any spare clothes?"

"Yes, my Lord."

"I will help you bathe and change. After that we will depart."

The man's goofy smile shone from his dirty face as he rose to his feet. "Your will, my Lord. My Angel."

"Don't call me that." He let go of the man. He took a step, stumbled. Gabriel grabbed him before he could fall.

"Thank you, my Lord."

"I said, don't call me that. Call me Gabriel."

"The angel Gabriel." He giggled. "They say you are the deathly angel. But I welcome you, my Lord. I am ready, my Angel. My Gabriel."

Gabriel tensed his jaw. He hated this part. "I am not an angel or your Lord. I'm just a vampire, plain and simple."

"There is nothing plain or simple about you my L ... Gabriel."

Gabriel swallowed down the bile that was suddenly in his throat. He hated that the enraptured could often see through to the truth. It was one of the other reasons he disliked using his venom for this purpose. "I'm sorry I had to do this to you. I'm sure you've been abused enough."

"Oh, I don't mind. The pain has gone away. It's blissful without the pain." He frowned for a moment. "Besides, my Lady never abused us. She loves us."

Gabriel didn't bother arguing with him—there was no point with the enraptured. Anita had obviously used her venom on the man, despite what he said. Luckily, Gabriel's venom was more powerful and could override her influence—mostly. "Do you remember your name?"

"Filippo. My name is Filippo."

"Well, Filippo. Let's get you cleaned up. Then we will head to *Firenze*, to people who will be able to help you."

And who would hopefully be able to give him the information he needed to finally capture Anita. He would also finally be able to get to what was causing Ardenne's pain and put a stop to it.

CHAPTER 25
QUESTIONS

In birth there is pain. In death there is pain. What lies in-between? Love, friendship, family. They make the in-between flourish with joy, despite the pain ahead and behind. They are the water and bread of our lives. They are a panacea for what ails us.
Despite knowing this, what I truly desire, what makes life shine with a bright light and lifts it above birth and death and the pain that lies in-between, is the eternal quest for something more. To find the answers to the four most important questions in the universe:
How? What? Where? Why?
Extract from The Middleton Manifesto, Section on Pain, Lesson 6

Ardenne couldn't shake the feeling something was wrong. She'd caught Master Solari and Sarita deep in conversation several times in the last few days, the conversations always snapping to a stop when they realized she was near. They both denied it though when she confronted them, and after that, she didn't catch them at it again, but still, it bothered her.

And it wasn't only them. Corinna and Piven seemed to be tense around her too. And they watched her even more closely than usual —something she noticed when she was using their eyes. It was like they were waiting for her to explode. The thing was, she didn't feel like she was going to explode. She felt strong. In control.

Except for in her dream-visions.

She tried to use what she was learning to stop her dream-visions, to shape them. But Gabriel barely ever came to her even though she called for him, and the voice she'd once thought her subconscious, but was now realizing was something else entirely, hadn't visited her since just after her migraine. It had come to find out how she was, to tell her she must find 'her', that she had so much to learn still and Piven and the others weren't going to let her learn any of it. *"They haven't even told you about Mary Middleton. About her prophecies and wha—"*

The voice had cut off, and no matter how she'd tried, Ardenne had failed to call it back.

"Penny for them?"

Ardenne started as Sarita's voice broke the silence. "What?"

"You look deep in thought. Want to tell me what's up?"

Ardenne shifted in her car seat. "Nothing. I just feel ... I don't know. Restless."

Sarita patted her leg. "What you need is a night out. Some good food, good wine, and maybe some dancing. How does that sound?"

Ardenne shrugged. "I'm a little tired." She wanted to get home and go to bed as soon as she could, to sink into her dreams and try to reach the voice again. She wanted to know what it was going to tell her.

"Oh, come on. We haven't been to Petra's for ages. And I know for a fact she's made *panna cotta* today."

"Really?" *Panna cotta.* She loved that particular creamy, custardy dessert. Especially Petra's with the berry coulis she served it with. "Okay. Maybe pizza and *panna cotta* would be good."

"Terrific. Corinna, let's go to Petra's."

They had a fun night, and Sarita even got her to agree to go dancing at a nightclub. When they finally got home, it was late, and she was ready to fall into bed. Despite the delicious pizza, mouth-watering *panna cotta*—she had two serves—and more *Prosecco* than was good for her, sleep wouldn't come.

After lying there for what seemed like hours, Ardenne sat up. "This is ridiculous." She might as well do something positive. Piven had finally begun to teach her swordplay. It might only be with wooden swords, but she didn't mind that so much now. Master Ricardo had finally fixed Seer's Blood and given it back to her, but she was afraid to pick it up. Afraid it would no longer sing to her after she'd broken it.

Trying not to think about that, she dressed in some workout gear and headed downstairs to the ballroom.

It had been set up as a sparring and exercise space for the Cousins living in and around *Palazzo Maimoona*. She'd used it several times with Sarita to practice Tai Chi and meditation in preparation for her lessons on healing, but never for sparring.

It was a large, echoing space with soft wood floorboards and walls covered in fresco-style paintings that helped invite the outside indoors. She loved to go there and look at the scenes through Sarita's eyes whenever they had a spare moment. She could stare at them for hours. Frescoes of rolling hills with a storm billowing on the horizon; fields and orchards sprawling down to an ancient township captured at dawn; a boiling sun sinking into roiling ocean waves viewed from cliffs. It was so peaceful and evocative to look at them through Sarita's eyes, she could almost smell the scents of the trees and the ocean, hear the rolling thunder over the plains, the sound of the waves crashing against rock, the tweet of the birds peeking out of the trees, the sound of the crickets in the waving fronds of wheat.

The artist had put some of his or her soul into those paintings and through Sarita's perspective, she could see someone who understood the secret wisdom of nature and longed, as she did, to be outside and running free.

She wished she could sit and let their peace sink into her now, but with nobody up at this time of night, she'd just have to be content with the memory of them as she worked out. Rather than going the long way round through the hall, she cut through the morning room. It had a secret door hidden in the wood paneling that accessed the ballroom directly.

She stopped for a moment to rub her toes in the soft weave of the morning room carpet, glorying in the soft sensation. She took a deep breath, scenting the slight sweetness of beeswax polish and the faded scent of dried rose petals that had become so familiar in her time here. It was strange to think of how frightened, how lost and yet determined she'd been when she first got here eleven months ago. She was no longer that same girl. She was strong and powerful and determined more than ever to succeed where others thought she would fail.

She was almost at the door of the ballroom when she became aware of the sound of fighting. She stopped, stock still, heart squeezing tight in her chest.

Who could be fighting in the ballroom? Her fingers tightened on the heavily carved wooden door to drag it open, but just before she pulled, laughter broke out. The sound brought her to a dead halt.

"I don't think baiting him like that is a good idea, Piven." It was Master Solari. "He's likely to take your head off given the mood he's in."

"He couldn't take my head off even if he tried," Piven said, a little breathless.

"You think so?"

She slapped her hand over her mouth to cover her gasp.

Gabriel! He was back.

She wanted to rush in there, demand him to tell her where he'd been. Why he'd left. Why he hadn't given Seer's Blood to her himself. And to ask if he'd liked the present she'd given him.

Her hand was on the door. She meant to push it open. Wanted to. But something stopped her. Made her move closer to the gap created by the partially open door. She knew she should either tell them she was here or go back to her room, but she couldn't make herself move away or move forward. She'd just watch for a little while. There was no crime against watching. Or listening.

She slipped into Master Solari's mind.

Gabriel didn't look as ethereal through Master Solari's mind as he looked in her dreams, but he was still more beautiful than any one person had a right to be. There was also a little something different about him since she'd seen him on the train through Sarita's eyes. He was in his usual black, his auburn hair a little longer and wilder, his face more alive with emotion, like in her dreams, a smile curling on his lips, enticing, animalistic. He raised his hands, flexed his fingers in a 'come on' gesture, poised on the balls of his feet.

Piven held a staff, the ends sharpened metal points, and began to circle Gabriel, the staff spinning so fast it made a whooping sound.

"Aren't you going to let him pick up his staff?" Master Solari said, sounding amused.

"If he wants his staff, he can get it." Then moving faster than she thought humanly possible, Piven swung.

Gabriel slid sideways, his body bending back in defiance of gravity to avoid the strike. As Piven brought the staff back up and around, Gabriel recovered, flipped over Piven's shoulder. Still moving, Piven spun in a circle, the staff twisting and slicing in a wide arc as he went. There was the sound of tearing, the slight sting of copper as the tip of Piven's staff found its target. Gabriel landed a little heavily, going down into a crouched position, his hands catching his fall.

"Oh-ho. Moving a bit slow today, Gabriel," Master Solari commented. "He's disarmed you and got in the first touch. Have we finally found you a worthy sparring partner?"

Gabriel looked up from his crouched position, a grin on his face. "I think Piven is fighting with more weapons than just that staff in his hand."

"Are you saying I'm cheating?"

Gabriel pushed to his feet. "Not at all. I bowed to Vincente's request for me to make it fair and have not used my vampire speed. But now I know we're using everything at our disposal, I won't hold back either."

Piven exposed his teeth in a shark-like grin. "Good."

Ardenne watched, heart in her mouth, as Gabriel and Piven clashed.

The lessons Piven was giving her suddenly made sense. He didn't try to do what Gabriel was doing—he couldn't. He wasn't a vampire. He was a witch with skills all his own that he used in concert with his fighting skills. She began to see now why he pushed her and was so brutal with his training. He wanted her to see the truth about who she was. She wasn't a vampire, but she wasn't just a blind witch either. She was powerful in ways others weren't because of her lack of sight. Her powers, her blindness—and therefore her ability to use other people's sight—the fighting skills she'd learned, they all added together to give her strengths and individuality that no one else had.

With the proper training, she could match even Gabriel as Piven did.

For a moment, she lost herself in the thought, imagining a time when they would fight, side by side, taking on the evil of the Wild and Dark Brethren as a team. The image was so enticing she slid out of Master Solari's mind and fell into the pictures conjured by her thoughts.

As she could in her dreams, she smelled the blood and sweat, heard the blows and grunts of pain and terror of their enemies, the grateful cries of those they saved, felt the grit of the smoke in her throat from the burning fires, Gabriel's hand on her shoulder as she turned to face him. There was a look in his eyes that made her tremble. A different kind of fire chased over her skin, pooling deep in her gut as he leaned close, his gaze on her lips, his hands sliding up to cup her face, to claim her as she longed to claim him, everything arrowing down to one touch, the mingling of their names on each other's lips as—

Something thunked into the other side of the door, the impact slamming the door closed and jarring Ardenne from her imaginings with a violence that hurt.

She blinked, uncertain where she was or what she was doing there. She looked down, wondering why she was standing in the morning room in her workout gear trembling, a strange tingling between her legs, in her breasts, on her lips.

She reached up and touched them, surprised at how sensitive they felt. Where had the smoke gone? The scent of blood and sweat and ... passion? The air here was clear, like the fresh bite of mountain air and there was no evidence of a battle or ... Gabriel?

She gasped. Gabriel. He'd been with her. He'd fought with her, held her, had been about to ...

A sharp laugh broke across her thoughts. Then there was a burst of applause. "Good move, Gabriel." That was Piven's voice.

Another laugh. Gabriel. "You too. You almost got me with that last move."

"I don't think I've ever seen a better match." Master Solari's jovial voice.

Their voices pulled her back from the abyss of the vision. She dug her feet into the familiarly plush carpet again, pressed her nails into her skin forcing herself to feel the physical.

She had come perilously close to losing herself in the dream scape, to falling into the Gray. She'd learned a lot from Piven in the last month about the Gray. He'd warned her about the dangers involved if she was to lose herself to the visions that skated along the edges of that dangerous, nebulous place. She would die.

She pinched her skin harder. She could never let that happen. Not even to have a vision like the one she'd just had.

The undeniable sound of steps drew near on the other side of the door, the click-clack of leather sole on wood floors, bringing her thoughts firmly back to the present. It sounded like someone was heading right toward her. She was about to be discovered.

Turning, she raced across the room to squeeze in between a large, overstuffed couch and the wall. Then she slipped into Master Solari's eyesight once again. He was standing at the door she'd been hiding behind, but he didn't open it. Instead, he reached for the fighting pole that was wedged firmly in the wood. With a grunt, he pulled it out, the door vibrating on its hinges. He peered at the large gash that now separated one of the carved nymph faces in the dark wood from the nymph's body. "Humph. I'll have to get Alberto in to fix that. He won't be happy."

"I'll take care of it," Piven said as he finished wiping his face with a handkerchief he'd pulled from his pocket. He stared at the door and Ardenne could feel Master Solari's eyes widen as the wood began to melt back together. A few moments later, the nymph was whole, the polished wood gleaming in the light.

"That's remarkable."

Piven waved away Master Solari's comment. "When you've learned how to kill people by moving the cells of their bodies around, mending a door is child's play."

"I suppose it is," Master Solari said, sounding less amused. He moved away from the door to the other side of the room and poured himself a glass of wine. Ardenne slipped out from her hiding spot and back over to the door so she could hear better. The voices were a little more muffled now the door was closed, but given her hearing was so acute, she could hear them if they didn't mumble.

"So, now you've had time to de-stress and unwind, Gabriel," Master Solari said after taking a sip of wine, "Maybe you can answer some questions."

Gabriel placed his fighting pole back on the rack with the other weapons before he turned, his expression grim. "First I'd like to know why Ardenne has been hurting so badly. Why I can smell her blood everywhere I go?"

What? Gabriel could sense her pain? How? Unfortunately, nobody thought this strange. In fact Piven simply snorted and said, "I should have known you'd sense that. It's nothing to worry about though." He waved his hand nonchalantly. "I've been teaching her to shield her mind. It's difficult work."

"Does it have to hurt her so badly?"

"Only if you want her to be truly strong and proficient at doing it regardless of what is going on around her."

Gabriel made a harrumphing sound.

"Surely you've sensed things have been getting better for her over the last few weeks?"

"It's the only reason I didn't tear your head off when I got here."

Piven laughed. "I'd like to see you try."

Gabriel took a step toward him, a growl erupting from his throat.

Master Solari stepped between them, hands raised. "Enough posturing. Now I want my question answered. Gabriel, are you going to tell us what the hell you're doing back here with one of that woman's minions?"

"There is nowhere else to take him." He sighed. "He's dying. It took me weeks longer than it should have to get him back here he was so weak. I frequently had to stop for days to let him rest. Even when I carried him the movement took too much out of him."

"Then why did you persist in bringing him here?" Piven asked.

"For information. And, if we can't help him, he deserves to die in comfort at least."

"But do you think it wise to bring her minion back here? Especially at this time? Surely you should have taken him to Lord Hei?"

Ardenne frowned. A minion? Whose minion? Surely Gabriel wouldn't have brought one of those foolish humans back here who served the Wild or Dark Brethren?

Gabriel picked up something from a side table. "I know the timing could be better, but I needed someone who could get into Filippo's mind and find out what he knows about why she sent those Wild to attack Ardenne. I mean, what's the ultimate plan? Why involve the Wild, who are just as likely to torture and kill her as hand her over to that vampire-witch?"

Ardenne jerked in surprise. Vampire-witch? She'd never heard of such a thing. Was this a new player? And if so, why would she be interested in capturing the next Bartolli Prime?

She listened more intently, not wanting to miss a thing.

"She's come too close to taking Ardenne twice now and we need to know what else she plans."

"I thought that would be obvious, given she's Ardenne's mother."

The words were like a bomb exploding inside her head and she clutched it, staggering back from the door.

She couldn't have heard right. Her mother—her birth mother—was dead. That's what she'd always been told. But then again, she'd not been told she was a witch and had gotten the powers from her mother either. Maybe the story of her parents being killed by Dark Brethren was nothing more than a convenient lie to cover up a truth they didn't feel her capable of dealing with.

It seemed, given what she'd just heard, that was true. Her mother wasn't dead. She'd been turned into a vampire.

Breath a dry burn in her throat, a roar in her ears, she staggered again as the world seemed to pitch around her. She managed to catch hold of the little table next to the door to steady herself even though the world was swirling around her.

Her lungs ached as she gulped in air that sawed down her throat like jagged ice. She felt like she was about to pass out. But she couldn't. She had to hear what else they said, had to confirm if what she'd heard was true or not.

She stumbled back to the door, catching herself on the door jamb, and leaned carefully against the door. Fingers digging into the wood, she tried to hear past the roar in her ears. She'd already missed too much of the conversation and it took her even more precious time to pick up the thread.

"... and I thought, given Piven was here, he might be able to use his talents to go into the Romani's mind and find out whatever we need."

Her mind roared and she could barely hear. She needed to see.

That would help her concentrate better. Grappling for control, she shoved her mind through the door and into the room, grabbing for Master Solari's sight. She slammed into it so hard she was surprised he didn't feel her, but she heard Piven say, "I'll have to see him before I know if it's possible. Where is he?"

"In one of the rooms in the old dungeons," Master Solari said. "The ones we use for excess guest accommodation when everyone is here. They're secure enough, although from the look of him when you brought him in, he's not going anywhere."

"I'll go find him then." Piven went to move, but Gabriel put out his hand to stop him.

"He needs rest first."

"And I should probably send in Sarita to see what she can do for him in the morning," Master Solari said.

Piven rolled his eyes. "I don't know why you'd bother. We all know she can't save him if he's as bad as you say. Nothing can. Cancer is one of those things that trumps magic."

"Yes, but Vincente is right. We can at least make him comfortable before you force your way into his mind. He might have worked for the enemy, but he is a witch. We are supposed to save witches."

"Fine, fine," Piven said, waving his hands. "But you'll have trouble getting Sarita on board with this. You know how she feels about these things."

"Carrington will make her."

Master Solari chuckled. "If you think that, you don't know women very well." He waved his hand. "I will speak to her and bring Carrington in if need be. In the meantime, both of you should go bathe then get some rest. You'll have a busy day tomorrow."

Piven inclined his head. "Of course. I'll bid you both adieu for tonight."

Ardenne's heart thumped as she heard his footsteps coming closer. Her legs were still shaking too much to carry her anywhere. *Please don't come through this door. Please.*

Thankfully, someone must have been listening to her plea

because he headed toward the main doors to the ballroom and left via the hallway. Ardenne sucked in a relieved breath.

Gabriel started to leave too, turning to the balcony doors.

"A word, Gabriel."

Gabriel turned, brow raised. "I need to feed."

"There's blood in the fridge behind the bar. The kind you need."

Gabriel nodded and headed to the fridge. He lifted the bag he pulled out, tore open the top and held it to his lips. His brow creased as if he found it distasteful.

"It's fresh."

"It's not that. It's colder than I like." He took another pull, eyes closing, throat working.

"Do you need us to get more of that for you? After that bag's gone, I've only got animal blood."

Ardenne frowned. What other kind of blood would he drink?

Gabriel swallowed, his throat moving, eyes closed, a look of pleasure creeping onto his face as if he were drinking the most wonderful nectar. He squeezed the bag empty and licked his lips. "No. Animal blood will do for now. I don't plan to stay for long."

Ardenne wished she could see Master Solari's expression because something about it made Gabriel look away. "Don't," he said softly.

"Don't what?" Master Solari asked equally softly.

Ardenne pressed closer to the door.

"Don't go on about the need for me to stay. I've heard all the arguments before. You know why I can't."

"You're not being fair to either of you."

"That's for me to decide."

"What about Ardenne?"

"What about her? She's better off without me here."

What? Was that why he stayed away? Why would he think that? Ardenne rubbed her chest at the ache his words caused.

"I don't think you can truly believe that, given you are unable to stay away."

Gabriel looked away, his jaw tightening. "I have to check on her."

When he looked up the expression in his eyes was that of someone in excruciating pain. "But I can't give in to more than that. I can't."

"You're leaving again then."

No! He couldn't leave. Not when he'd just got here. Not before she could show him what she'd learned, talk to him, try to make him see that he had to stay.

She was about to push through the door, give away that she'd been listening when Gabriel said, "Not immediately. I think Anita's heading here. I think she's going to make a move on Ardenne again."

Anita? Carrington's sister was called Anita. But she was dead. Or so she'd been told.

"Yes. Anita is less likely to try something with you here."

"I know. But it won't stop her for long." He paused, a troubled expression crossing his face. "I think we need to tell Ardenne."

Master Solari sighed. "I know your opinion on this, but Lord Hei hasn't changed his mind."

"I understand that, but ... Anita has been contacting her through her dreams."

"You know this for certain?"

Gabriel shook his head as he dropped the empty blood bag in a bin in the corner. "I'm not the only one in her dreams. There is another voice there too. She never shows herself, but she certainly doesn't like me being anywhere near Ardenne."

Ardenne had to slap her hand over her mouth to stop from gasping. Gabriel. In her dreams? Did that mean that he saw what she saw? Cheeks flaming, she leaned her forehead against the door. He'd have to know how she'd started to feel about him. Please don't let him truly be in those dream-visions.

"... then it might be her. We need to talk to Piven about this," she heard Master Solari say through the roar in her ears.

"I intend to."

"That must be very difficult for you."

"What? Telling Piven? Hardly."

"No. Being in Ardenne's dreams. Given the bond and your feelings ... It must be excruciating."

A bond? What bond? She shared a bond with Gabriel? How? Why?

Mind swirling with questions, she watched Gabriel through Master Solari's eyes and listened to this conversation they never meant her to hear.

Gabriel's lips thinned, his expression tightening. "I don't want to talk about it."

Master Solari let out a little huff of breath. "No. I can imagine not. But you should talk about it with someone. Things like this are never good if kept bottled up. My door is always open—"

"I'm fine," Gabriel said, waving his hand dismissively.

"Is that why you gave her that sword at Christmas? Because you're fine?"

"The sword is hers. It was always meant to go to her. I was just its guardian."

"Hmm." Master Solari didn't seem convinced. Despite her confusion, Ardenne wasn't either. "Whatever your intention, you made things far more complicated by giving it to her. She's working herself to the bone to learn to use it as soon as she can."

Gabriel shifted, looking away. "She needs to learn to use it."

"*You* should be teaching her."

"I can't do that."

Master Solari made a hissing sound. "I don't know why you would do that to yourself. Or to her."

"I'm doing nothing to her. She doesn't feel anything for me. The bond doesn't create feelings, just obligation on my end. And it's best it stays that way. You know that as well as I."

Master Solari breathed deeply, a sad sound. "I used to think that. Now ..." He shook his head. "I'm not so sure."

Gabriel's head snapped up, eyes burning. "Why do you say that? What's happened? Has she had another incident? I thought that's why Piven was teaching her to shield so it doesn't happen again."

Incident? What incident?

"No. There's not been another incident. I was merely talking about how she's doing generally. You'd be amazed what she's accomplished in the last eleven months. She's thrown herself into her training and her studies—has time for nothing else."

"Well ... that's good, isn't it?"

"I'm not sure she's doing it for the reasons we think."

"What does Sarita say?"

"Nothing to me. She cannot betray her trust by spilling her emotions to mere males like you and me." He chuckled softly. "If you spent more time with people, you'd remember that."

"You know I can't do that."

Master Solari sighed again. "Actually, Gabriel, I don't understand why you punish yourself this way. If I had my chance to find fulfillment and happiness again, I'd take it, no questions asked. I don't know why you fight against it so hard."

"I fight it because it's not my choice. I never wanted this. Any of this. If I could get rid of the burden of it, I'd never look back."

Ardenne bit her knuckle to suppress the sob wrenching to get out. *She* was the burden he was talking about. And the bond he'd mentioned ... a bond with her ... He didn't want it. Didn't want her.

Tears stung her eyes.

"You will do what you must."

"As I have always done," Gabriel said firmly.

"Yes, as you've always done." He paused. "You are not to blame for what happened to Ardenne's mother." Then, without another word, Master Solari walked out.

Ardenne swiped at the tears coursing down her cheeks, letting go of Master Solari's vision now that she could no longer see Gabriel, returning to the familiar dark of her own sightless eyes. She stood there, knuckles pressed to her lips, hardly breathing. After a long pause, she heard the balcony door of the ballroom open, and knew Gabriel had fled through it.

CHAPTER 26
SIMPLE TRUTH

*Simple truth. Is there such a thing? I am uncertain I will ever find
it if there is.*

*Truth has layers that bely it being a simple thing. It has depths
colored by motivation, by emotion, by a human's very existence.
For what is truth to one, is lies to another. What can be shared
openly between some, must be kept from others.*

*Moreover, the reasons for holding onto a truth and keeping it secret
may not be nefarious. Holding onto that truth might be the thing
that saves the world.*

*I cannot say what will be best for the future. So much of what I see
is illusion and whirling tendrils of possibility in the Void. However,
what I see tells me that trying to keep the simple truth from being
understood could destroy the world.*

**Extract from The Middleton Manifesto, Section On Truth & Lies,
Lesson 1**

Ardenne leaned against the door, legs trembling. What she'd heard ... it was too much to take in, to think about. It made her numb, her mind and body shutting out all thought, all feeling, submerged in the tsunami of information she'd just overheard. It was too much of a jumble. But she couldn't stay here. She had to move.

But where to? Nowhere felt right. There was an explosion of something about to go off inside her and nowhere felt safe. If she fell apart, Sarita would know, and she'd make Ardenne tell her what was going on. But how could she explain? How did she tell her friend she'd overheard things they never meant for her to hear; things that meant they had all been lying to her about more than the fact she held magical powers inside her.

If she was to believe what she'd heard—and right now, there was no reason not to—her mother was alive and coming after her. And Gabriel was bonded to her in some way but hated it.

At least the latter explained his behavior to her; but then again, it didn't, because he had come to her in her dreams—it had actually been him and not her imagination! What's more he behaved differently there.

And what had he done to her mother that he felt so guilty about?

More importantly, why hadn't they told her the truth? Why keep this from her? How dare they keep this information from her?

Energy flamed through her body. She pushed away from the door and started across the room, determined to find one of them and demand the truth.

Truth from liars. The voice had told her they lied. Was this what it meant? The voice that, from what Gabriel had admitted, was someone called Anita. Which was Carrington's sister's name. Was that a coincidence? Anita had been a witch and they said her mother was a witch.

Was this Anita her mother?

The thought brought her to a standstill, trembling hand to her lips.

By The First! Was the voice her mother trying to get through to her?

If it was, that meant she couldn't ask any of them about it. Gabriel had said that he wanted to stop the voice from coming to her.

No. She couldn't let that happen. She might have mixed feelings about the voice—it confused her, and it wanted to kill Gabriel—but it also wanted to tell her the truth. She couldn't allow them to get rid of it. Especially if it was her mother. But how could she find that out without giving away the voice was coming to her all the time now, not only in her dreams?

The prisoner.

Gabriel had said he was a minion to this vampire-witch, Anita, who could be her mother. The prisoner had been brought back here because of what he might know. She had to find him. She had to get him to tell her before Piven got into his mind and took it all.

Slipping out of the room, she made her way quickly down the now empty hallway toward the kitchen. She'd been shown through all of the *palazzo* when she arrived so knew where the dungeons were. Most of the old cells had been converted into accommodation or were used as storerooms and behind a hidden door was another section where the security control room was for the *palazzo* and its grounds.

She'd never thought back then that they might actually be used as cells to keep prisoners in, but now she had to wonder how many had been kept there at one time or another. Lord Hei, despite how gentle and kind he was, had enemies; he was unforgiving to those enemies.

She swallowed hard, wondering who else might be down there.

Fear and anger bubbled together inside her, pulling on her power. She couldn't let it. Couldn't lose control now. She'd need it to help her get into the prisoner's mind.

She just hoped she'd have time before someone came down and discovered she was there.

She shook her head, flexed her tingling fingers at her side.

Hurry. She had to hurry.

Cool air pimpled her skin as she opened the door to the wine cellar and moved through it as silently as Piven had taught her. She ran over to the secret door into the dungeons. Slipping through the door, she closed it with a quiet click and then made her way down the stairs, hand trailing on the rough stone wall as she wound down into the cool damp earth under the *palazzo*.

The dungeons had once been natural caverns underground. Over the years, they'd been expanded and shored up, but even through the scents of concrete and wood, she could smell the muddy coolness of the earth still damp and chilled from the recent winter.

The stairs spilled out onto a long corridor. Along the corridor, doors were spaced evenly left and right. Which one could the prisoner be in?

She remembered that the first few were larger rooms, two cells having been joined together to create a meeting space on one side and a communal bathing area on the other. She slipped past them, knowing he wouldn't be in one of those. The next couple were storerooms, so she skipped those. But he could be in any of the others. She'd have to check in each room.

What if his room was locked? She hadn't thought of that before.

Shit!

She couldn't let that stop her though.

She kept going, moving from door to door, listening for signs of life behind them. When she reached the third door on the right she knew before she even opened it that he was in there by the smell of sickness emanating from under the door.

She opened the door slowly.

The sick scent of him—sweat and a bittersweet smell, like rotting flesh—as well as an antiseptic smell hit her strongly and she had to swallow down the bile that rose to her throat. There was a faint clicking sound—something mechanical and yet fluid. An IV?— coming from beside where she could sense the bed was.

She faltered, no longer secure in her idea to question the man, to push into his mind if she couldn't get anything out of him verbally.

She shouldn't do this. It was wrong. It was wrong for Piven to do it. The man was ill. They could kill him. She'd have to find out about the voice and her mother some other way. Have to make them see they couldn't use this man to get the information they wanted out of him. It was cruel. Awful. Monstrous. They weren't supposed to be the monsters.

She began to back out of the room.

"Oh, you've come. She said you'd come. Don't go."

She stopped. There was a rustling noise, like he was sitting up in bed.

"She said she'd talk to you. Send you to me." His voice was tired and a little husky, but he didn't sound sick.

"Nobody sent me."

"Oh, have they blocked you from hearing her?"

"No. They don't know I hear her at all." That wasn't exactly true given what she'd overheard Gabriel saying, but it would do. "Who are you?" She moved closer until she was at the end of the bed.

"My name is Filippo Gruerta. And I am your mother's humble servant."

"My mother!" So, it was true. Her mother was alive.

"Yes, your mother. You look so much like her, it's impossible to miss."

Ardenne's mind whirled. There were so many questions she wanted to ask, but one came to the fore. "Is my mother a vampire-witch?"

"Yes. She was once a witch, as you are. Now she's a vampire. She's been coming to you in your dreams."

"I didn't know she was my mother. She never said."

"Oh, how she wanted to tell you. She longed to—" He coughed, the sound an ugly wheeze.

"Are you okay?"

"Water," he managed to gasp.

"Where?"

"On the bedside table. I'm too weak to pick up the jug."

She managed to find it and poured him a glass, then carefully held the straw to his lips so he could sip. Once he finished, he lay back with a sigh.

"Thank you," he said as she returned the cup to the bedside table.

"Are you okay to talk to me?"

"Yes. I want to." He took in some deep, rattling breaths, then said, "Your mother ... She longed to share the truth of who she was with you, but knew it was so very dangerous to give away too much too soon. That was one of the reasons she left me." He took in a few more rattling breaths before continuing. "She knew the Lonely Angel wouldn't leave me to die alone. Knew he'd bring me here. Of course, I didn't let on to him that little fact." He sounded so pleased with himself. "I have a message for you."

"A message?"

"Yes. She wanted me to—" His voice cut off as he cleared his throat. "More water, please."

She set the straw to his lips again. He drank slowly, then finally sank back into his pillows. "Is that better?"

"Thank you. They have me on a drip with medication for the pain, but I'm still so terribly thirsty."

"They shouldn't have left you like this. It's cruel."

"Oh, the Lonely Angel would never be cruel."

"What do you mean?"

"My Lady said he had too much heart to ever be like other vampires. I know it's true. He was so kind, so gentle, bringing me here. I'd already be dead if not for him."

"I'm sorry you're sick."

"Oh, don't be. It is my time. And it meant I got to meet my Lord."

Ardenne frowned. "Your Lord?" Was he a religious man?

"Yes, the Lonely Angel, Gabriel. So lost and alone, and yet so wonderful and kind. If he wasn't, I would not be able to give you your mother's message."

She was so confused as to why he was talking about Gabriel like that. But there were more important things to ask him about. Like … "Her message?"

"Yes. She wanted you to know … she wanted you to know …" Filippo faltered, the words stuttering out of his mouth as if something blocked them. "I … she said … wanted me to …"

"Wanted you to what?"

"I don't … I can't …" He cried out like he was in pain. "I'm sorry … it's gone … it's gone." He began to sob, racking sobs that turned into gasping, chest rattling coughs.

Ardenne tried to soothe him, but he wouldn't be soothed.

"Stupid … stupid … it's eaten too much … I can't remember … I can't remember … I've failed my Lady … I've failed."

"No. Please don't think that. Don't cry." She grabbed him, held him still against her chest as he sobbed, stroking his hair while he shook and moaned. "There has to be a way you can tell me."

He stopped moaning and shifted his head so she knew he was looking up at her. "Go into my mind. You can go into my mind. I know you can do it. My Lady said you were being trained."

"No. I can't. You're very ill. I could hurt you."

"I don't care. You must do it. Please. Please. You must do it before they come and remove it themselves."

She didn't know what to do, didn't know what to say except, "Yes," so as to stop his pleading.

His breath hitched as he asked, "Promise?"

She didn't want to. Didn't want to do something that could hurt this sick man. But his fingers tightened on her arms, showing his determination, his need, to fulfill his promise.

"You have to promise."

"I promise." The words were torn out of her, but she had no other choice. She couldn't let him die in such a state without doing the thing he'd put his life in jeopardy for.

He relaxed his grip and pulled away. "Thank you. Thank you." He lay back down against the pillow.

She felt nauseous. Nauseated from the sick smell of him, but mostly from what had been done to him, how he had been used by her mother and by Gabriel, how he would be used by Piven and the others to gather information, how he would be used by her as she went into his mind searching for her mother's message. She held her hand against her mouth, swallowing down the bile that burned her throat.

She didn't want to do this but ... he wanted her to. Needed her to. And she couldn't deny him.

She'd done a little bit of this kind of thing with Piven and Sarita, going into their minds and trying to find a memory. It wasn't quite like mindreading, as she didn't hear their thoughts. It was more about accessing past visuals and expanding that to see and hear the memory. It was a new skill, but she had enough confidence in her ability that she'd come down here thinking about using it. It didn't hurt the person, unless they were blocking, and then it could hurt quite a bit.

Which was her worry with Filippo. The cancer in his brain was blocking the memory and digging through that block to find the memory could hurt.

She remembered something Lord Hei had told her a few years ago when they were discussing their enemies and how they must always cling to their ideals.

"We do not act like our enemies, Ardenne. We hunt and kill them, but it is done humanely and with mercy and only because it saves human lives. The Wild and Dark Brethren are horrifying, but they cannot help being what they are. However," he'd taken her chin in his hand, his voice soft, but firm. *"I never take what we do lightly and the only reason we do what we do is because the Wild and Dark Brethren cannot be rehabilitated. If they could, I would spend every single last waking moment of my life doing just that."*

"You don't like killing them?"

"We should never enjoy taking a life, Ardenne. We should never enjoy hurting another. We should always be cognizant of our actions and what they mean to us and others. An eye for an eye is not the way to live. The ends rarely ever justify the means."

The memory of what he'd said clung to her. He was right, so how could she do this? "It's going to hurt you. There must be another way to find out what my mother told you." She tried to think past the surging panic. "She's been coming into my dreams—you said that she had—and sometimes I think she's even been able to talk to me when I'm awake. If she can do that, why can't she tell me what she wants to say herself?"

"Your dreams are being watched."

"Piven?"

"Probably. But I meant my Lord, Gabriel. He has been there too, has he not?"

Yes. She knew now that was true. "But—"

"You promised. You can't break your promise. There isn't another way."

The desperation in his voice was too much for her to deny. "I know," she whispered.

"You'll do it?"

"I'll do it." Taking a deep breath, she took his face in her trembling hands, her fingers cupping the back of his head. She could do it without touching him, but it was easier this way. "Are you ready?"

"I am, Ardenne."

Closing her eyes, she breathed deeply and then sank into her mind. Past the ramble of thoughts, deep into that place where it was quiet and velvet dark. Where her powers were seated, a spark in a silent, roiling sea. Tapping into that spark, she wrapped it around herself, made her conscious the center, and then she moved out, through her touch, through her senses to Filippo, his mind, his essence, and as gently as she could, she ventured into his mind.

It was worse in there than she thought it would be. Flashes of thoughts and visuals moved in a scrambled, turbulent mess, his neurons sparking in an unsyncopated flurry of sound and color as they tried to find other paths to travel to continue vital functions. The cancer loomed over all of it, a mass of flesh-eating flesh, gnawing into his mind like a pack of wild dogs gnawing on a bone.

The pain of it was excruciating and she was only feeling it second hand. She couldn't believe he'd managed to talk to her as sanely as he had.

There were no more memories where the cancer was. That part of his mind was dead. But there were others, trapped by the tendrils of cancer that hadn't quite taken over yet. They were the block. The memory of her mother's message had to lie there.

She tried to move forward, into that part of his mind, but the block pushed her back. It was different to the magical block Piven and Sarita had used to keep her out of their minds in the training. This was thicker, harder, and seemingly had no end. It was tied into his mind and there was no loose thread to pull on, no chink in the block. If she tried to break through by force, she'd kill him.

"You promised."

His voice in her mind was like a shout in a roiling sea.

She couldn't give up. He wasn't going to let her. And she couldn't let his last act become a failure. She must find a way of retrieving this memory.

There was no other option.

CHAPTER 27
GUT FEELING

I feel my end coming upon me soon, but there is one thing I need to share with you.
Our magic can give us so much, yet it can take more from us than we ever care to give. This I have learned hard and learned well. If I wish for anything, I wish for those who follow after me to know this too: Magic will be our undoing if we do not take care.
Extract from The Middleton Manifesto, Section on Magic, Lesson 100

Gabriel was restless when he returned from his check of the perimeter. There was still no sign of Anita and that made him nervous. What could she be up to? She had to be somewhere close, ready to jump at any opportunity that got her access to Ardenne. The only problem was, he had no idea what that might be. Her mind was truly Machiavellian.

Although that shouldn't be surprising given she was trained by Piven.

Adrenaline pumped through him, making his nerves twitch.

Something was about to happen. Something dangerous for all of them. He just knew it.

He sighed. He felt too edgy to go to the room Vincente had assigned for him. He'd be too tempted to slip down the hall to Ardenne's room and check on her.

He might as well go and check on Filippo and ensure he was as comfortable as possible.

He jogged through the quiet *palazzo* and into the kitchen. Nobody would be up for hours, and the sound of silence echoed around him, ringing in his ears. It was a strange thing, silence; it was too full of the hidden for him to ever be comfortable in it.

He sped up, eager to get to somewhere the silence wasn't so heavy. As he reached out to push open the door into the wine cellar, a scent hit him and he stopped.

A chill chased over him.

Ardenne had been here! And not long ago. The scent was still warm. Maybe she'd come down to the kitchen to get something to eat. But if that was the case, why was her scent centered here? There was only the wine cellar through here and beyond that ... the entry to the stairs that led to the dungeons.

The chill expanded.

No. She couldn't be in the dungeons. There would be no reason for her to be there. Not unless the feeling he'd had earlier in the ballroom had been correct and she *had* been nearby. If she'd come down to work out, which was highly likely, she could have been just outside the door—and would have overheard what they'd been talking about.

Fanculo!

Shoving the door open, he raced through the cellar, smashed through the door to the dungeon, and raced down the dungeon hallway. Her scent was stronger here and getting stronger with every step.

Merda e fanculo.

She was with Filippo and The First only knew what the sick man was telling her.

He was in Filippo's room a breath later and … stopped dead, breath in his throat, shivers cascading over him as the magic in the room electrified his skin.

"Ardenne, no."

She was grasping Filippo's head, her eyes closed, face pale, a deep frown furrowing her brow. Filippo writhed on the bed, his mouth open on a silent scream, veins popping from his skin like angry red-blue welts as Ardenne pushed her way into his mind.

Sire's Blood! What had happened to make her do such a thing? What had she overheard? By the looks of him, Filippo's heart was about to explode with the exertion of what she was doing. And if he died …

He wanted to tear her away from the sick man, but if she was too deep, he could damage her mind permanently. However, if Filippo died while she was in here—and it looked like that was a definite possibility—that would be bad.

Very bad.

There wasn't time to track down Piven and get him to pull her out in a way that was safe. He'd have to try to coax her out himself.

Grasping a hold of her shoulders, he shook her gently. "Ardenne. Ardenne, you must come out. Come out now."

No response. Not that he'd expected anything. It was obvious she was in too deep. He called her name louder. She didn't even twitch.

Maybe something else would work.

He grasped her head, tipped her face up to his, pressed his lips against her brow, her closed eyes, her cheek. "Ardenne, please come back to me."

If she didn't come out now of her own accord, there was only one option, and The First help him, he'd never wanted to do this again; never wanted to enter her mind like he'd done on the hill. It was bad enough being pulled into her dreams. And this time it would be worse because he'd have to engage the bond. He'd have to make the connection between them as strong as possible so that he could pull her out if she didn't want to come.

"Don't make me do this," he whispered into her ear. But she didn't respond.

Resigned, he held her close—the closer he could get physically the better as it would help both of them when he got her out—and reached out with his mind to deliberately engage the bond.

He flew through the velvet dark of the bond—shot with the vibrant emerald and turquoise and amber that was Ardenne. It was different from when he went to her in the dreamscape—something that happened without his will or hers, and for the first time, he was able to take in the true beauty of the bond and the mind it connected him to. It was so alive, so strong, just as she was. He could get lost in the song of joy that broke through him at the acceptance of this essential connection. But even before he could grasp hold of that thought and deny it, he broke into the chaos of Filippo's damaged mind and landed beside the avatar Ardenne had given herself in this place.

She was reaching out to touch a tendril of something that throbbed and writhed as it wrapped itself in and around a flickering visual in Filippo's mind; a memory. Before he could think about what he was doing, he grabbed her arm and pulled her away.

She swung around, ready to fight him, but seeing him, her eyes widened, mouth popping open on a gasp. "Gabriel."

"You can't touch that, Ardenne."

"Gabriel," she repeated, reaching up to touch his face. "You can't be here. It's not really you."

She thought he was a memory Filippo had conjured. He was almost tempted to let her think that but knew she wouldn't listen to him if he did. She had to know he was real.

Grasping her hand in his, he pulled it to his chest. "I'm real, Ardenne. I'm real."

"But how? How can you be here?"

"Because *you* are. Because it's not safe. You're in danger."

She frowned at him. "You're lying. You just don't want me to find what Filippo must tell me."

"He can't tell you anything, can't you see that?" She pressed her lips together, tried to shrug away from him, but he couldn't let go of her. "You must come with me now. You have no idea what it will do to you if you get caught up in this diseased mind. You should never have forced your way in."

She shook her head. "I didn't have a choice. I don't want to hurt him, but it was the only way. He insisted." Her face clouded. "He has a message to give me from my mother. Why didn't you tell me my mother was alive?"

Accusation was a bitter lash in her voice, marking him with guilt for the lie told. But he didn't back down. Didn't flinch. "It was safer that way. Your mother is dangerous."

"Not to me. She can't be dangerous to me."

He growled low in his throat, stifled by all the things he wanted to tell her; all the things he must keep hidden. But she wouldn't believe another lie. "There is so much you need to be told, Ardenne, and I promise, I will tell you, but not here. Not in this place. Filippo is dying and if he dies while you're here, you might never find your way out. He is too weak to take the pain of what you're doing. You're killing him."

She blanched and for the first time seemed uncertain. "But he needs to tell me. He made me promise I wouldn't let him die without telling me."

"We'll find another way, Ardenne. But you can't be responsible for his death. Not like this. I won't let you have that blackness mar your soul. Neither would Filippo. And despite how dangerous she is, neither would your mother."

She glared up at him, tears in eyes that were no longer white, but a brilliant blue just like her father's, just like in the dreams. "I don't want to hurt him."

"Then leave with me now."

She looked back at the flickering memory that was nearly

completely covered by the tendrils that represented the cancer eating at Filippo's mind. Loss and longing reflected on her expressive face and then there was a flash of determination as she tore herself from his grasp. "I promised," she said, then leaped toward the disappearing memory.

He tried to grab her, but he was too late. Before he could do more than grasp her trailing arm, her hand sank into the flashing swirl of color and sound and she gasped as the memory merged with her mind, echoing in her eyes. "Mother?" she whispered, but the whisper turned into a scream as a tendril of the cancer wrapped around her hand and began to pulse up her arm.

Gabriel tried to pull her away, his arms wrapped around her body.

"It burns! It burns," she screamed.

Gabriel let go of her and tore at the tendril, ignoring the burn of it, flicking it away before it could grasp a hold of him too.

"It hurts. It hurts. It's killing him," she screamed as torn bits of the tendril kept a hold of her, trying to pull her in.

Then with a final tear, he had her free, and, wrapping her in his arms, he spun away. Grasping a hold of the bond within both their minds, he tore his way out of Filippo's mind.

He came back to his body with a thump and staggered, almost dropping Ardenne who had gone limp in his arms. He looked down at her glacial eyes, staring past him as if she was looking at something he couldn't see. Her lips were moving, but no sound came from them and then she cried out, "Mother, don't go," and passed out in his arms.

"Ardenne." He patted her face, shaking her a little, but she lolled in his arms. She should have come back with him when he pulled her out, should have been awake now. Her face was pasty white, but her chest rose steadily. Thank The First! She had simply fallen unconscious.

He glanced at Filippo. For a moment, he thought that his last desperate act had killed the poor man, but then Filippo's eyes fluttered open and reaching out toward Ardenne, he whispered, "Thank you," before falling unconscious.

The scent of stale sweat, blood, and urine was heavy in the air. He had to get Ardenne out of here. This wasn't a place she should be. Picking her up, he cradled her against his chest and strode out the door and down the hall. He made his way upstairs, through the cellar and kitchen and up to her room.

Even if he hadn't known it was her room, he would have known he was in the right place the moment he pushed through the door. The white walls were devoid of any paintings or posters. Instead, bookshelves lined the walls, crammed with books and little knick-knacks from her visits to *Firenze*. Brocade curtains hung open at the windows and an armchair stood nestled in the corner between the far bookshelf and the window. A side table took up another corner where weapons were laid out and there were flowers, scented roses and jasmine, in a bright yellow vase on the table by the window. All the furniture featured carvings that would come alive under her touch.

There were no side-table lamps to turn on, just the overhead light, which he left off. He didn't need the light either. He knew he should place her on the bed, but for some reason, couldn't make himself let go of her yet. So he strode to the armchair and sat, holding her in his arms.

She should have woken up by now. She'd been unconscious too long. Holding her face in his hand, he said, "Ardenne, wake up." She didn't move. "You're safe now, Ardenne. You need to come back to me now."

Nothing.

She remained limp in his arms.

Had he hurt her when he'd pulled her out? Traumatized her somehow? Sire's Blood, that couldn't be true. He shifted her in his lap, stroking her hair back from her face. "Ardenne. I'm sorry I had to pull you out like that, but I had no choice. It was dangerous. But you're safe now. Safe in your room. Come back. Come back to me now. Please."

He never pleaded for anything anymore, but he pleaded for this. Pleaded for her to simply be unconscious because the magic had exhausted her, not because he'd torn her out of there and hurt her.

He never wanted to be responsible for hurting her. It was one of the reasons he'd stayed away so long because he could never trust himself. Not fully.

He still couldn't trust himself. He should leave her be; go fetch Sarita. But he couldn't. He had to make sure she was okay.

He held her against his chest, whispered in her ear. "I promised I'd tell you about your mother, but you must come back to me. Come back, Ardenne. Come back." He kissed the top of her head rocking a little as he pleaded with her to wake up, more desperate with each second. He needed her to look at him with those beautiful eyes once again. He'd even be happy if she looked at him with hatred or condemnation. If only she'd wake up.

He leaned her back a little so he could cup her precious face in his hand, needing to feel her skin against his, willing her to wake up. And then, even though he knew he shouldn't, he couldn't stop himself from leaning down to kiss her brow, her cheeks, her eyelids, whispering between kisses that he needed her to wake up.

A VOICE WAS CALLING to Ardenne, calling to her, but she didn't take any notice of it. She had to concentrate on the memory of her mother. The one she'd collected from Filippo.

It was damaged. She couldn't see her mother clearly. But she could hear stuttered fragments of the message.

"I love you, my precious one. I never ... to leave you. I've been kept ... against my will. You can't believe ... tell you. Only I ... the truth. Not ... your father and ... with Gabriel. They don't want ... know

… and dangerous … think you … are weak. Come to me. You … find me. I will … Manifesto. You must … for you to … only truth. Find me."

That was it. Like a telephone call interrupted by static. She could hardly make sense of it. How could her mother have relied on a sick man to get her a message of such import? Filippo had been prepared to give up his life to pass this on to her and this was all she had to show for his sacrifice!

Oh, shit! Filippo. Had she killed him with her selfish act? She didn't want to think it true, but she'd heard his piercing cry as Gabriel had pulled her out of his mind. She needed to know. Needed to find out, but couldn't seem to pull herself out of this place she was in. It was so cold here. So nothing.

"Ardenne. You must wake up now." The voice echoed through the nothing space.

She knew that voice. It was Gabriel. He sounded so far away. And upset. Desperate.

"Gabriel," she called out, except there was no sound, as if her voice was stuck in her throat. Or that there was no sound here. Except, why could she hear Gabriel? Was his voice all in her head?

"Please. Come back to me. I couldn't bear it if I'd hurt you. Wake up."

His voice sounded so real, even though she couldn't see him. Couldn't feel him like she could in the dream, but she could smell him. His cool, fresh mountain air scent which reminded her so of home.

She wrapped the scent around her cold limbs, warming herself, and followed the sound of his voice.

So sad. So sorry. So desperate.

She had to tell him she was fine. Had to let him know he hadn't hurt her, that she'd found what she wanted. She had to ask him about Filippo. Ask him to fulfill his promise and tell her about her mother.

Although, her mother said she couldn't trust him. So would he tell her what he knew? Or would he lie to her still? She had to find out. Had to know whom she could trust.

She followed the sound of his voice, his scent becoming stronger and stronger as she rose out of the nothing she was in and into the velvet dark she knew so well.

She was being rocked in someone's arms, her face cradled in gentle hands as something soft and moist brushed over her cheeks, her nose, her brow. Like when Papa had kissed her all over her face to make her giggle when she was little—except, there was nothing paternal about the feeling flowing through her as those lips continued to move softly against her skin, the kisses scattered between pleading words.

Pleading words said in a voice that never failed to touch her deep inside.

Gabriel's voice.

It flowed all around her. As warming as the arms that held her.

Arms that, given how close that voice was, had to be Gabriel's.

Gabriel was holding her! Which meant ... Gabriel was kissing her face.

Was this a dream?

Her eyes fluttered. The velvet dark remained the same as she opened her eyes. Which meant ... it wasn't a dream—for she had always been able to see in those dreams of Gabriel.

Wishing she could see him with all her soul, she reached up to do the next best thing—touch his face. But her arm was too heavy to lift. "Gabriel," she whispered, her voice hoarse.

"Ardenne! Ardenne, you came back to me."

The words were said against her cheek in a rush of relief as he held her tight. She shifted her head slightly.

Their lips met.

Ardenne sucked in a shocked breath. "Gabriel."

He lifted away for one electric moment and then his fingers firmed in her hair and with a guttural growl of her name, his lips came back down on hers.

In the space of one breath she went from feeling numb to exhilaratingly alive. A current of heat and thick, weighted desire flooded from the point of contact to encompass her entire body, beating back her hurts, blanking her mind until all she could do was breathe in Gabriel.

Feel Gabriel.

Kiss Gabriel.

Her hands wound in his hair as his mouth continued to devour hers. This was no gentle first-time kiss, but oh, she didn't care. Didn't care. Wanted more. His tongue swept over her bottom lip right before he sucked it into his mouth. She groaned, opening her mouth and his tongue swept inside, tasting, twining with hers in a delicious dance.

She'd thought he smelled good, but his scent was nothing compared to the taste of him. Vibrant and alive like a mouthful of *limoncello* imbibed on a sunny day at the sea and yet sweet and bubbly like a fine *Moscato* drunk by a roaring fire in the middle of a winter in the mountains. His touch was cool and yet heated; a zinging warmth that sang through her body, pulsed through her veins, and centered in a throbbing mass deep inside.

Wet warmth pooled between her thighs, and she clenched them together at the same time she wanted to part them, open herself even more to him, invite him in. Deep inside her.

Deeper than he already was.

She clutched at his head, his shoulders, fingers tracing the muscles in his arms, his chest and back up to his jaw as he continued to invade her mouth. Such a sweet invasion, his tongue tangling with hers.

Emboldened, she stroked his tongue with hers, then delved inside his mouth, sweeping it over his lower lip before sucking that full lip into her mouth just as he'd done to her.

He growled, a growl so low she barely heard it, could truly only feel it vibrate through her. Smiling, she repeated her action wanting desperately to feel that vibration once again. It felt so good, heating all the parts of her that she hadn't realized had been cold and lonely for so long.

He growled, clutching her closer. "You bewitch me," he breathed before blazing a trail of hot, wet kisses across her jaw and down her neck.

She clenched one hand in his hair and the other raced down his neck to chase across the muscled planes of his shoulders.

He trembled under her touch but he didn't stop what he was doing. His lips brushed over her thumping pulse, once, twice. "Smell so good," he groaned. "I've never smelled anything better."

Ardenne knew what he meant. She had never come across a scent that did what his did to her. She breathed him in as he suckled at her neck, his pointed eye-teeth scraping her skin but never biting. Although she could tell he wanted to by the way his trembling increased, an indication of not just violent passion but the hold he had on himself.

He was holding back.

The knowledge was a stab to her heart.

She didn't want him to hold back. She wanted to feel his teeth sink into her skin, feel the movement of his throat as he drank from her, taking in the thing that gave them both life. She wanted to tell him he could drink from her, take what he so obviously wanted. She would give him anything, especially if it meant he'd press closer; be closer in every way imaginable.

But she couldn't get the words out, her breath a catch in her throat as she desperately tried to drag air into her lungs.

As if he could sense her need to be closer, his mouth opened— hot and insistent—on her neck as he pulled her tight against his body. Her breasts crushed against the hard, unyielding mass of muscle that was his chest.

But it wasn't enough. Not nearly enough.

She wanted to move, to straddle him, to press closer, to take his mouth with hers again, to feel the hardness of his erection against her core, not pressing into her side as it was right now. She wanted to rock against that hard length, against him, until, until ...

"Can't you sleep again, Ari ... Gabriel! Oh, I'm so sorry. I ... I d-didn't know you were here."

CHAPTER 28
VOICES

The voices! The voices! Why can they not leave me alone? If I cannot gain control of them, how will I ever be able to help her understand her destiny?
Will I ever even know her to tell her how much I care?
Extract from Mary Middleton's Diary, May 5, 1534

Gabriel moved so fast Ardenne was left clutching air as, head spinning, she found herself seated on the chair by herself, Gabriel now far across the room. He stood still, so still. She only knew he was there because he was panting, just as she was.

"I ... I didn't mean. I'm sorry ... I should have knocked. I didn't think ... I heard a noise and thought ..." Sarita cleared her throat. "I was just coming in to check Ari was fine. I didn't realize anyone was here with her. I ... I thought you were down with the patient, Gabriel."

"I was," he said, his voice so raw it was almost unrecognizable. "Ardenne was there. I brought her back up here."

"Oh. Okay." Sarita was obviously trying to make sense of that. Of how that had led to this. To what she had walked in on—Ardenne and Gabriel kissing.

Oh, hell! Ardenne had been about to crawl on top of him, straddle him, devour him while he devoured her. If Sarita hadn't interrupted, she knew that's exactly what would have happened.

How it could have happened, she wasn't clear. This wasn't her dream. This was real life. And Gabriel didn't want her in real life. He'd made that abundantly clear repeatedly, to her and to others. And yet, he'd saved her from making a terrible mistake, brought her back from the nothingness where she'd been trapped with his desperation to keep her safe and kissed her into a raging torrent of passion when she'd come back to him as he'd begged her to do.

That didn't sound like the Gabriel she knew at all.

"I ... um ..." Sarita cleared her throat. "What was Ari doing down with the prisoner?"

"She'd obviously overheard Piven, Vincente and me talking about her mother. She went down to see him to find out what he knew, seeing none of us had ever told her the truth."

His voice was flat, the passionate husk turned to cold steel. Almost accusatory.

She slipped into Sarita's eyes to see his face, to see how he looked.

His voice might be cold, but his expression as he tried not to look at Ardenne was anything but. He looked like he was burning with a fever, eyes bright, fangs extended, lips plump and glistening. His hands were clenched by his side, the muscles she'd gripped only moments ago now tight cords as he trembled. He looked like he was fighting some terrible inner demon.

If it was anything like the need roaring and alive in her, a need to get up and race across the room to him right now, she knew why he was trembling. She couldn't make her breath calm down. Her skin ached. Her nipples were so tight they hurt. And that place between her legs, it was curled so tight with longing, she thought she might be sick from it. She began to shiver with the agony of loss that suddenly swept through her, because as she watched Gabriel through Sarita's eyes, it became apparent he wouldn't come back to her. Not now.

Perhaps not ever.

"Ari, are you okay?"

She shook her head, unable to make her mouth work. There were no words for how she felt, no sound but a keening that rose in her chest, pressing to get out. But she couldn't let it out. Not with Gabriel standing there. She couldn't let him see how devastated she was over the loss of him. Over the loss of what they'd almost done. What, going by the hard steel of his features, would never have a chance of happening again.

"I should go," Gabriel said, his voice not so cold, not so certain.

"Yes. Perhaps you should," Sarita said, walking toward Ardenne. Ardenne couldn't stand the sight of herself through Sarita's eyes. She looked as awful as she felt. Passion still burned through her veins, but unfulfilled, it left nothing but devastation in its wake.

Horrible, aching loneliness, worse than anything she'd ever felt before.

Gabriel still hadn't gone. She didn't know why. She wished he would.

Turning her face in his direction, she said the only word she could manage. "Go." He still didn't move. "Go!" she screamed.

The door slammed shut in the wake of his leaving.

Tears burned behind Ardenne's eyes but wouldn't fall. She pulled her feet up onto the armchair, wrapped her arms around her legs and buried her face in her knees.

"Ari." Sarita's arm slipped around her back. "Ari, what happened?"

Ardenne couldn't speak for long moments, but Sarita waited, ever patient. Finally, she managed, "I don't want to talk about it."

"But you and Gabriel?"

"I don't want to talk about it. It was a mistake. It will never happen again."

"But, Ari, I saw you. Such passion. It's rare. The way you feel … the way he feels … how can you be so certain nothing will come of it?"

She looked up, swallowed hard, his taste a bittersweet reminder of loss on her lips. "He will make certain of it." Her chin wobbled.

"Oh, Ari. I'm so sorry."

Hot breath heaved in and out of her chest as her eyes burned, the velvet black of sightlessness a relief for the first time in her life. She didn't want to see the pity in Sarita's eyes. It was bad enough hearing it in her voice. "I'll be fine. It was nothing. Just something stupid that happened in the moment."

"How can you say that?"

"Because I have to. Because if I let myself think about it in any other way, it will tear …" She couldn't finish that thought. Shook her head. Swallowed down the grief that seemed absurd given they'd only shared one kiss. She had to think of something else. Her mind instantly flipped to what she was doing before Gabriel found her. It snapped her out of her self-pity, her head jerking up. "Sari … I think … I think I did something bad. Downstairs. I think I might have hurt Filippo. Can we go down to check?"

"I don't know if that's a good idea, Ari."

"I need to know he's okay."

"Gabriel might be there. And Piven."

Crap! She sucked on her lip, thinking. She really wanted to see Filippo with her own eyes—well, through Sarita's eyes—to make sure he was okay. She wanted to talk to him if possible—she still had so many questions—but it was difficult enough to even think Gabriel might be around, let alone that she'd be in the same room with him.

And Piven. She didn't want to face Piven after what she'd done to Filippo. She really wasn't in the mood for that particular lecture. Particularly as it would include the fact she'd needed Gabriel to pull her out. She didn't want to think about how he'd managed to do that. Didn't want to think about him at all. Her hands twisted in her lap as she trembled.

"Ari?" Sarita's grip on her hands stopped their twisting.

"I'm fine. I'll be fine. I just need to know I haven't hurt Filippo. Can you go down for me? To see? Tell him I'm sorry. Look after him. Please."

Sarita squeezed her hand. "I'll see what I can do." She leaned forward and kissed Ardenne's cheek. "Everything will be okay. I promise. We'll sort this out."

"I don't want anything sorted out. Not about ... that. Just check on Filippo. Please."

Sarita sighed heavily but stood up. "Try and get some sleep."

A hysterical bubble of laughter escaped Ardenne's lips. She didn't think she'd ever sleep again. Not if it meant seeing Gabriel in her dreams.

Sarita left and finally she was alone.

She bit her lip. She didn't really want to be alone. Her thoughts were too loud and too difficult to manage. They shouted at her, wanting her to think about the very thing that caused joy and agony in one breath. No. She couldn't. She couldn't. She'd have to go downstairs and see if she could find someone. Maybe go for a run. Corinna should be around. She'd go with her, for sure.

She stood up, stumbled, her legs still trembling with adrenaline and emotions she couldn't get a handle on. She caught herself on the window ledge, bumping her head against the window frame. "Shit!" She hit the wall with her fist, the ache in her hand a welcome relief from the ache in her heart. She hit it again, and again and ...

"Ardenne! Ardenne! Help me."

Ardenne's hand stopped in mid-air as the voice she now knew was her mother's, rang in her ears. She turned around, almost expecting her mother to be there behind her, but she could sense nobody there. She was still alone. "Mother?"

"Yes. Yes, it's me. Ardenne, I'm so sorry. I wanted to come to you, to help you. They've captured me. They're going to torture me."

"Who? Who's captured you?" Her mother's voice ... it trembled. Like she was frightened; so different from the confident, sometimes angry voice she was used to hearing. Her heart began to pound in her chest when there was no answer. "Mother? Mother!"

"*I'm here. They've fed from me and I'm weak.*"

"Who? Who has fed from you?"

"*Dark Brethren.*"

Dark Brethren! No.

"*They took me just outside Firenze. There were too many. I couldn't fight them off. They want to know about my family, about Lord Hei. About who made me. I can't. I can't tell them. You must come. I have no one else who can rescue me.*"

"Piven ..."

"*No. You can't tell him. Or anyone else. They won't come and they'll stop you and then the Dark Brethren will get what they want. We can't let them know. They'll use my knowledge against Lord Hei. They want to wage a war and if they know what I know, they might very well win it.*"

Ardenne sucked in a breath, shaking. She hadn't finished her training. She didn't know if she could do it.

"*You can. I know you can. I've seen you. And you've got Seer's Blood. You know how to block better now. It won't take you over again. Not like it did.*"

"It didn't take me over," she said, a sick lurch pulling at her stomach.

"*They lied about that too? Goddamn them. Don't they realize what they're playing with? I can't believe they're still lying to you. Come save me, and I'll make sure the lying stops. Please, Ardenne. I need you. You are the only one who can save me.*"

Ardenne had so many questions about what her mother just said, but only one was important right now. "Where have they taken you?"

"*Their base is an old church in the hills to the east about thirty minutes from the Cousins' compound. It was part of an old monastery but is now mostly a ruin.*"

"I know where that is." Master Solari had pointed it out on one of their excursions. "But how do I get there?" She couldn't drive.

"Go to the farm to the east of the palazzo. The farmer there works for the Cousins. Tell him you are on a secret mission and must get to the monastery church tonight to pass the test. He's used to these requests. He'll take you."

She had no idea how her mother knew all of that—maybe she'd known Papa or other Bartollis and they'd told her. It made sense, given she'd been adopted by them. Her mother must have been a close friend or something. "Okay. I'll come."

"Bring your weapons. Especially Seer's Blood. It will show you what to do to defeat the Dark Brethren here."

"I'll come. I promise."

"Thank you. Thank you, precious girl. I knew you wouldn't let me dow — No, no. They're coming. They're coming!"

"Mother? Mother!"

Silence greeted her.

"No. No!" Ardenne dove deep into that part of her mind that her mother used to communicate with her, reaching for her power in a way she'd never done before, desperate to get her mother to reply. But before she could do more than gather it, her mother cried out, *"No. I don't know anything. I don't know anything. Please, don't—"*

A high-pitched scream of such agony rang through Ardenne's head, making her blood chill.

"Mama?" she gasped. "Mama!"

No response.

Sire's Blood! What were they doing to her?

She had to go. She had to save her mother now.

CHAPTER 29

FATE BEGINS

Once the Blind One begins to see, her path will be inextricably drawn into the arms of Fate. There is no turning from this path once she has stepped upon it, but more than this, I do not know. Fruitlessly I have searched, trying to find a way to help, but my visions will not show me more than I have already seen. I think this is in part due to the influences of others around her, whether they will teach her what they must despite everything. All any of us can do is pray she is strong enough to hold steady and stay her course. To do otherwise would spell disaster for those of us who can track our blood back to The First.

Extract from Mary Middleton's Diary, August 8, 1534

The truck pulled to a halt at the bottom of the hill below the ruins of the old monastery. Through the farmer's eyes Ardenne could hardly see anything. It was a moonless night, the clouds hanging low and dark over the landscape, full of the coming storm. He'd turned his lights off when he'd turned onto this old road—she'd explained as part of her training, they needed to be stealthy—but there was a glow up on the hill, a fire perhaps, that allowed her to pinpoint where she was headed.

Wind buffeted the truck, thankfully covering the noise of their driving. The air was getting heavier, threatening rain. And there was an acrid scent that meant there would be thunder and lightning.

She only hoped she'd be able to get inside the church before the storm hit in full, because it was going to be harder to fight if she was wet.

The farmer pulled the truck to a stop and looked up at the hill before them.

"There it is. You can just make out the tower in the old church. The back of it abuts the monastery wall but there is only access from the front or side."

Shit. That wasn't good news. She hadn't brought anything for scaling walls.

"I haven't been here for years," the farmer continued, seemingly oblivious to her distress. "But the last time I was, the wall had come down just left of the back wall of the church. I doubt anyone has bothered to fix it. You could gain access through there with little trouble."

"Thank you, *Signori*. That's very helpful."

"Anything I can do to give you a little advantage. I'd like to see someone best one of their tests the first time." She heard the smile in his voice.

Moonlight took that moment to shine through the clouds allowing her to see what he was talking about. She also saw lines of an old, overgrown orchard marching up the hill before her. It would be good cover. If she skirted around the base of the hill under cover of the orchard then up the hill, she'd be able to go over the section of broken wall just next to the church and maybe, just maybe, slip inside without being seen.

It was a plan.

She hopped out of the truck, closing the door quietly, and then went around to her weapons bag. She put on the specially designed cross halter that allowed for ease of movement as well as quick access to the blade and fighting sticks on her back with places in the front to slip throwing knives into.

She placed Seer's Blood in its sheath at her back as well as a set of short fighting sticks in theirs. She pulled out a dozen small knives and put them in the pockets on her pants legs and in her vest as well as the front of the halter. She wished she'd become fully proficient with the crossbow, because that would have come in handy too to take some of the enemy down without getting too close, but she would just have to manage this with close contact. If she could be stealthy enough, she might even be able to take a few of them out before they knew she was here.

She picked up the dozen glass vials each filled with a flammable liquid the Cousins used to set their enemies on fire. All the Bartolli were given these vials because after beheading a vampire, fire was the only way to make sure they stayed dead.

Piven had told her once of a fight he'd been in where the Dark Brethren he'd beheaded had pulled itself back together as he faced another and attacked him from behind. It was a lesson he never forgot—the scar that ran from armpit to waist a constant reminder.

"Never think you've killed them until they are ashes at your feet."

In her lessons with Master Solari over the last few months she had learned much about the cults they fought against. One of the most important was that they all hunted by scent. She bent over and scraped up a handful of mud from the side of the road and wiped it on the exposed skin of her face, neck, and hands. They wouldn't be able to smell her coming now. They'd think she was just a part of the countryside.

Her hands shook and she wiped the excess mud off on her pants. She wished she could fit a few more knives and a full-sized fighting pole into her clothing, but there wasn't room.

"It will be fine," she whispered to herself. "I can do this."

Seer's Blood sang a song of agreement and longing to her. Her mother was right. The sword would be able to help her. She just had to let it.

And remember everything she'd ever been taught.

She turned back to the farmer who was watching her from the cab of the truck. "Thank you for bringing me here. I must go alone now."

"You will be fine. Master Solari talks highly of you, and I have heard Mr. Piven is a fine teacher. I expect you will do better in this test than others before you."

She blinked hard as tears stung her eyes. She'd not been expecting encouragement at this point and felt horrible for lying. But she had to. There was no choice. "Thank you, *Signori* Caletto. I hope so."

He patted her shoulder. "They won't be expecting you to come this way. You were smart to ask me to bring you here. Only I know this back road. No one else ever uses it."

She hadn't known that. It made her feel a little more hopeful that the Dark Brethren wouldn't be keeping a watch out this way. "That's great. Thanks."

"Good luck."

She nodded. She would need it.

He turned the truck around and drove away, the low hum of the engine and crunch of tires on the hard-packed road covered by the sound of the lonely wind whistling through the trees. Now she was thankful for the coming storm. If it had been a still, quiet night, she knew the Dark Brethren would already be all over her.

Heaving a sigh and trying not to feel utterly alone and out of her depth, she turned and began to jog around the base of the hill to the point she'd seen in the farmer's eyes. The tree branches swayed heavily in the increasingly wild wind, the noise making it difficult at first to fully discern her surroundings, but she wasn't Piven's student for nothing. He had drilled her senses until they were more finely honed than she'd ever dreamed they could be. She just had to trust in them.

She reached the point she'd seen in the farmer's eyes and began her trek up the hill toward the part of crumbling wall next to the church.

As she drew closer to her goal, shivers prickled across her skin. Not because of the cold wind. Or for fear of discovery—she knew the Dark Brethren would soon sense her presence. No. She was afraid of failing.

Failing was not an option. She had to save her mother.

She shook off the fear and concentrated on moving steadily forward, her steps quiet and sure.

She was almost at the wall when a strong scent washed over her. That had to be the Dark Brethren. She almost gagged. It was hideously strong, redolent of violence and blood. Not clean, coppery blood. No. It was more like the putrid stench you'd smell from a wound that had got infected, mixed with the acrid smell of fear-laced sweat. Unlike the scent of the Wild, it made her want to run, to hide, to curl into a ball and wish herself into oblivion. The Wild's scent enticed and seduced. The Dark Brethren's scent was fear incarnate. It reeked of death.

A scream sang through the night.

She froze.

Her mother. What were they doing to her?

Another scream. It sent shivers icing over her skin and sank dread deep into her heart. She was about to race forward when the scream sounded again, and she realized it was coming from behind her.

She spun, sent out magical feelers for any presence and came up against something not human. An animal. A bird. No. An owl. Another scream. The owl was calling to the night. Not her mother being tortured again at all.

Letting out the breath she didn't know she was holding, she took a step forward, but her legs were trembling so hard she stumbled over the smashed stone in front of her, landing hard on her knee on a sharp rock. The scent of her blood stung the air. Shit. Shit. The Dark

Brethren would smell her and be on her in a second. She scrabbled around and found a handful of wet dank smelling leaves and mud and quickly lathered that over the tear in her fighting pants where the sharp edge of stone had cut through the material and skin.

Was it enough? Had she acted quickly enough? Hand on Seer's Blood's hilt, she stood silent, waiting for Brethren to descend on her.

Everything was quiet; the only sound the wind whistling around the ruined building in front of her and through the branches of the trees behind her.

Layered over that, singing only to her, was Seer's Blood's song. With her hand on the hilt, she heard it louder than before, pushing her forward, filling her with confidence and certainty.

"*Move. Move,*" it seemed to urge. "*We are more than capable of dealing with the Brethren scum.*"

Yes. She knew they were. All doubt faded in the beauty of the song filling her mind. Of the need to seek out the enemy and turn them to ash.

Rocks and broken stone lay before her, a vivid imprint of them stamped in her mind through scent and the sound of the wind as it tumbled around and through them. She raced silently forward, the sting in her knee forgotten in the beauty of needful song as her hand curled around Seer's Blood, holding it out in front of her, ready to feed.

So far she'd been lucky, but she knew that wouldn't last if the Brethren were close by. And she knew they were. Their proximity caused a throb of stinging pressure under her skin. At least, that's what she assumed it was as she'd never felt its like before.

Their stench grew with every step she took.

Finally she was through the crumbled section of wall and skirted around a curved wall of the church—the apse—to where the transept must be. If this church had been constructed as the churches in its time had been, there would be a side door into the transept. She soon found one, but quickly felt it was nailed shut with bands of steel across it.

That wasn't going to be an entry point for her. She would have to go around the front.

She skirted the long wall that ran down the length of the nave and came to the edge that led around to the main entrance. Sound and scent told her in front of her lay an open space, a small *piazza* between the monastery buildings and the church. Torn plastic sheets flapped in the wind, making a hollow slapping sound against the skeletal stones. The tang of rust and dirt and brick dust scented the air.

Laughter, thick and hard, drifted from the church. The Dark Brethren were having fun whatever they were doing. A sharp cry told her they hadn't finished torturing her mother. Prickles of worry skated across her skin as she sent out her thoughts, searching for feeling.

Heated rage greeted her probing, surging over her, through her, making her shudder. If she hadn't known before there were Dark Brethren here, she couldn't have mistaken their presence now. She'd been told about the madness of their bloodlust, but she'd never imagined it would be so all encompassing, eating away any shred of humanity they might have once had.

They were animals. Worse. They loved to torture before they killed—it was fun to them to experience another's pain; as much food to them as the blood was, sadism at the heart of their nature.

Putting up blocks against the worst of the sensation, she searched for any sign her mother was here.

There! The fast-paced patter of an adrenalized heart. Curious. It beat like Gabriel's did. It had to have something to do with their making. But that heartbeat couldn't belong to anyone else. And it proved her mother was still alive.

Not conscious though. She didn't answer as Ardenne called to her with their mind-link. Hell. What had they done to her?

Changing the direction of her search, she sought eyes to see through.

Contact.

Her stomach swirled in unpleasant waves. The Dark Brethren's mind was as different from the Wilds' minds she'd been in as those minds were different from Corinna and Gabriel's. Nausea overwhelmed her at the direct contact, so much more potent than the gentle touch she'd used to search for her mother.

Images swam in her mind, painful in their intensity, infused with a red haze of blood at the heart of their violence. Struggling, she held back the piercingly ugly thoughts and feelings of the mind she was in.

Only the eyes. I just need the eyes.

She sucked in a sharp breath, letting the images settle, allowing herself time to adjust.

The red haze stopped pulsing. She could see out of his eyes.

The vampire was standing in the left transept looking at a group of other Dark Brethren. One of them was talking, gesticulating wildly, his eyes mad with hunger and violence. There was more laughter, and the one whose eyes she was using laughed too, but kept watching his Brethren, eyes shifting from one to the next like he was waiting for an attack.

She counted nine as he looked around. Including the one whose eyes she was using that meant there were ...

Ten.

Ardenne's breath caught in her throat. Ten! Holy crap.

How was she to kill ten of them?

She swallowed hard, trying to stop her heart from beating faster in reaction to her surprise.

Her mother never mentioned that many. It was highly unusual for Dark Brethren to travel in packs that large. It was even unusual for the Wild to travel in such a large group. Six was usually the largest for the Wild; for the Dark Brethren it was more likely to be three or four. Unlike the Wild, they didn't travel in mated pairs or link up with other mated pairs to have regular orgies.

Panic began to rise inside her, her fingers spasming on Seer's Blood's hilt. The sword's song changed, became soothing, stroking through her veins, dampening the panic, assuring her it would be fine.

"We can take care of ten. There are ways. We will figure it out. Simply look around."

Yes. Piven always said to use what was around her, whether the lay of the land, the buildings, even rocks and dirt and plants could be used to help win a fight. Except the Dark Brethren whose eyes she was using was only looking at the group he talked with.

"Push further into his mind. Force him to do your bidding."

Seer's Blood was right, but she hesitated, sick at the thought of going deeper. But she didn't have a choice. She needed to know the lay of the land in the church; needed to know if there were more of them she wasn't sensing and where all of them were. She still wasn't good at reading a mind's direct thoughts, but when she went deep enough, she could read emotion—to the point where it almost swamped her—and could tap into images from a person's memories. Piven had said she could make someone do her bidding as well. They hadn't started those lessons, but she realized after he said it that she had, on occasion, made the person whose mind she was in look where she wanted them to. She hadn't meant to do it—didn't like to think of herself as some kind of puppet master forcing others to obey her commands—and it had only happened when she was fully entwined with them and their emotions, but she had done it.

So she could do it now. For a few minutes at least.

Hopefully, that would be long enough because the emotions she was already getting from it were horrific.

Steeling herself, she dove deeper into its mind, twining with its emotions, grasping for control. She was expecting to have a fight—that its mind would be trained to repel intrusion, like Corinna's and Gabriel's—but she slipped further inside without coming across any kind of barrier. She supposed the Dark Brethren didn't have to worry about shielding their minds from others, given most mind readers wouldn't even think to try what she was doing. They'd be too frightened if they ever got this close.

Bile rose in her throat, but she swallowed it down. She didn't have a choice. This had to be done.

She slid forward into the maelstrom of violent chaos in the mind she was in, and then, surprisingly, there was a click as she grabbed a hold of his mind through his emotions and forced him to look around the church.

Pews lay in a pile of splinters. A broken crucifix sprawled drunkenly across the pile. Obscenities were smeared in blood on the walls of the nave. Something that looked like it had once been an altar now lay smashed in three pieces against the far transept wall. He'd thrown it there. She could feel his pleasure as he looked at his work. His eyes continued to move around to the middle of the church, to where the altar once stood.

There was a cage with thick bars covered in red she knew wasn't rust.

Inside the cage was a woman.

Her clothes were dirty and ripped, black hair blanketed her face in a thick, knotted tangle. Through the vampire's mind she could smell the woman's blood. Strangely, he didn't find it appetizing. Had he fed enough already? Although, from what she knew of Dark Brethren, that was hard to believe.

It was clear they'd tortured her. She'd heard them begin that torture before her mother was torn from her mind back at the *palazzo.*

I'll make them pay, Ardenne vowed to herself.

Anger burned inside her. Seer's Blood sang in her hand, pushing into her mind, making her want to round the corner, smash through the door and tear through every single one of them until the floor ran crimson with their blood.

She took a step forward ...

Then stopped herself. Her mother said Seer's Blood had taken her over, and even though she couldn't remember that happening—didn't want to remember because that memory held fear and horror in it—she felt it was true. If she let it take over her now and not just guide her, she might not survive.

Even if she did, she might not remember she was here to save her mother and not just kill Dark Brethren.

Thankful for Piven's harsh training for the first time, she quickly built a block around her mind, forcing Seer's Blood to the periphery where it could not control her. The sword keened in her hand, but she stroked it, now the one to soothe. "Not yet," she whispered to it. "Soon. We must be smart about this." Running in there unprepared could get her killed and her mother with her. She needed a plan.

Pushing down the heat of anger inside and maintaining control over Seer's Blood so it didn't take her over, she took tighter control of the Dark Brethren's mind and made him look around some more.

There were few places to bunker down and nowhere to hide. No chance of an ambush. No place to fall back to. Except …

The windows.

When the sun rose in a few hours, she could smash through the window opposite where the majority of the Dark Brethren congregated, letting the sun in. Not that the sun could kill them. But it would hurt enough to give her the upper hand for a moment. For some reason nobody had explained to her, Dark Brethren and Wild were affected by the sun. Lord Hei's children were the only ones it didn't truly affect. Maybe it had something to do with their diet? Not that it mattered why right now. Only that it was a tool she could use. If she could let the sun in, it would distract the Dark Brethren long enough to allow her to kill at least half of them with no worry.

She made the vampire look up.

Damn.

The lead-stained glass windows were all boarded up. It would be too difficult to break through them without giving herself away. So much for that idea.

She couldn't fight them in there. She'd lose under those conditions, no matter how good she might become with Seer's Blood's help. If she couldn't fight them in there, then there was only one option, and it wasn't running away.

Piven had told her in one of his many lectures during their runs that a direct assault is not usually the best form of attack unless you have superior numbers. *"Lay a trap. Smarter is often better than more force. Break the enemy up, draw them apart, take them on in smaller numbers. Use everything at your disposal. Magic, speed, stamina, fighting skill, smarts. Everything."*

She still didn't know how to use her magic in an offensive manner. All she could do was what she was doing right now. But alongside her fighting skills, her speed, her stamina, and Seer's Blood's help, what she could use would have to do.

She grasped for the vampires' memories, trying to make him think about when he'd arrived here. What the church and *piazza* looked like from the outside. A flurry of memories followed, what they'd done in getting here, the people they'd slaughtered, tortured, fed on. There were bodies in a pile in a nearby building. A pile of parts. Vomit flew up from her stomach and into her mouth, but she slapped her hand over her lips, forcing herself to swallow it down. She couldn't vomit here. They'd smell it. Know she was here.

She concentrated on finding the memories she needed of the outside of the church, looking for the best place for her attack. Finding it, she knew exactly what to do, her plan clear, clean steps in her mind.

She had to draw them out a few at a time.

If she perched on the cupola above the main door, she'd be able to do just that and maintain the upper hand.

She thrust Seer's Blood into its sheath and ran to the stairs, using the balcony of stone on the near side to help pull herself up. Then, when she was in position, Seer's Blood singing a song of exultation and killing in her mind, she pulled her sword off her back and made a whimpering, helpless sound.

A moment later, two Brethren slid out the door, their footsteps cautious. They glanced around, searching for the source of the noise.

But they couldn't see her. Ardenne held her breath, fighting the nausea caused by the intense feeling of being in their minds.

They moved further into the *piazza*.

She vaulted off the cupola. Seer's Blood sliced out in a wide arc and their heads fell to the ground with a sickening wet crack. Landing nimbly, she kicked the heads away, doused the bodies with the flammable mix that instantly turned to flame when it hit their bodies. They went up with a whump—the Brethren inside had to have heard it.

She stepped back, another vial of fluid in her hand.

Wind gusted in the *piazza*, buffeting the heat of the flames against her as she waited for more to come out, to see what had happened to their comrades. Thunder rumbled in the distance. The storm was picking up. She hoped the rain would hold off for a little while longer. She didn't need it to come and douse the flames she needed to help kill the Brethren.

Two more Brethren rushed out the door. Her sword's song turned to wild laughter and Ardenne laughed with it, pushing into their minds to use their eyes.

Their disdain washed over her as they glared at her across the flames. They saw her as weak; an easy snack. They leaped over the low flames eating at their compatriots' bodies. As they did, she threw the second vial. Flame whooshed, high and strong and hot. With a scream, the two new vampires went up in flames along with their decapitated brothers.

"Four down, six to go," Seer's Blood sang to her.

She laughed at the joy in that countdown, tightened her grip, and continued.

CHAPTER 30

FIGHT

Drills are some of the most important tools for teaching both internal and external witches. Because drills teach patience and patience leads to control.
If you wish to be a witch that helps in the fight against the cults, then you must be a witch who has absolute control over your magic. Because to be without control is to fall into the kind of destructive chaos that drives the cults.
Extract from The Middleton Manifesto, Section on Magic, Lesson 38

Using sound and scent, Ardenne leaped to the scaffolding on the left-hand side of the door, the wind blowing the acrid scent of burning flesh and the flammable liquid to her. She was surprised the stench didn't make her dry retch. Maybe the adrenaline racing through her counteracted the effects.

Beneath her, four Brethren sped out into the *piazza*, narrowly avoiding the pyre blackening the cobblestones. Four perspectives swam in her mind, almost overwhelming her as they breathed in the violence like a fine perfume, eyes wild, bloodlust rising. The smoke and acrid fumes helped mask her but even so, these wouldn't fall as easily as the first lot. They were fully warned now.

But with Seer's Blood guiding her, she knew they would fall.

She couldn't let them close though—they were too strong. Her only hope lay in subterfuge and guile. Searching their minds, she found one with a slice of power. Strange. She didn't know vampires had access to magical powers. She thought the vampiric conversion wiped all magic away—a question to delve into another time.

The one with the slice of power was well-muscled and tall. The others looked at him with the kind of whipped reverence a mistreated dog gives its master.

The Leader.

"Use his power," Seer's Blood sang to her. *"Go into his mind and take what you need. You know you can."*

The sword was right. She'd done it the day Piven had tested her when she'd brought him back into the testing space. He'd told her later it was a quirk of her empathic power, the one that allowed her to use someone's eyesight, which allowed her also to use any part of that person's mind, including their power, if it was seated in the mind. But, apart from that one time with Piven, she'd never done it again. She wasn't sure if she could.

"You must."

The sword was right. And if she was going to do it, she had to do it now. Gritting her teeth, she pushed inside his mind, past where she collected eyesight, into the core of his being, the seat of his power. Despite the fact she'd now been in the minds of his comrades already, his violence repelled her. The rage filling him was deeper and more heavily seated in who he was. He was a violent murderer long before he became a Dark Brethren. He'd used his magic to murder and steal. She touched that power now, felt it thrill through her.

It felt wrong, using it this way, but she had to. Had to tap into this Brethren's strange magic, use it to strengthen herself against the others, to help her move faster, be stronger. She sunk her mental hand into it and pulled.

The Leader staggered and glanced around, disoriented, uncertain what had happened. His uncertainty made him angrier than he already was. But he still didn't know what she'd done, that she now had his strength and speed thrumming inside her.

Seer's Blood sang a song of expectation, its satisfaction thrilled through her along with the Leader's magic. She smiled, drew on the power of her sword to give her the skill she needed to fight, and then leaped.

Landing a kick to the stomach of the closest Brethren, she sent him stumbling back, straight into the fire. His howl of agony and fury was cut off as she swung her sword, decapitating him in the flames. Still spinning, she sliced the one who pounced toward her across the stomach, then rolled away. She was dead if they backed her into the doorway—there were still two inside from what she'd seen through the eyes of the first mind she'd entered.

A roar of rage sounded. Through the eyes of Stomach Wound she saw Leader leap over the dying fire toward her. Instinct kicked in and she pulled on another aspect of his power, holding him over the flames. Sweat broke out all over her body—telekinesis was harder than it looked—as she fumbled to grab another vial. She threw it just as she lost control of Leader, slipping out of his mind. The fire blazed. Screaming, jeans on fire, Leader landed and came at her, despite the blaze racing up his legs.

The other two vampires circled the fire, Stomach Wound able to move but hampered by his injury. His mind gave her the best vantage point.

The wind buffeted her as she drew a dagger and threw, catching Leader in the jugular. He tore it out, eyes blazing, and threw it back. Ardenne spun sideways but the knife grazed her arm. The cut burned more than a knife cut should, the pain a surge through her veins.

Heart pounding, she honed the rush of adrenaline and, with another vial in her hand, jumped as if to push Leader into the fire, but changed direction at the last moment and, using the last of his powers that she still held onto, pushed him back with her mind. He stumbled and before he could right himself, she threw the vial at him. He exploded in a bright flash that blinded Stomach Wound.

Ardenne rolled and gained her feet, Seer's Blood's song filling her mind, helping her to ignore the pain in her arm and the burning heat on her face. Spinning, she faced the two remaining Brethren, surprised the two inside hadn't come to help finish her off. *Thank the Lord for small mercies.*

Stomach Wound held his guts, hissing and growling, circling her, as did the other one. She saw herself through their eyes. Smelled her bloody wound, heard her heart pound hard and strong, sensed her weakness now she no longer had Leader's power to pull on. Using his power had taken something out of her. They howled with excitement. The deaths of their brothers fanned the flames of bloodlust now centered entirely on her.

The wind keened through the *piazza*, pushing at her, but she stood firm, knife and sword in hand, waiting. She wouldn't give in. She'd never give in. She had to save her mother.

Stomach Wound crouched.

A shadow knocked him sideways. Stomach Wound's fear stabbed into her as he was slammed against the church wall—his fear and her shock holding her in place as much as it did him. He hovered there, the fearful part of his mind contemplating escape as he watched the Shadow turn to fight his comrade. The Shadow was good. His comrade was going to lose. Stomach Wound smiled, turning to face Ardenne. While the Shadow was busy, Stomach Wound would have himself a little snack.

He dove for her. Ardenne threw the knife at him and then dropped and rolled. She heard the knife clang to the pavement just before his fist contacted her temple. Her head rang with the blow. Seer's Blood slipped in her hand, its angry scream a visceral pulse in her head. Senses in shambles, it took a moment to reclaim her hold on Stomach Wound's eyes, surprised he wasn't on top of her.

Blinded—he was blinded by the flames! They scorched him. They burned.

The Shadow had flung him into the fire.

Ardenne wrenched from his mind, yet not fast enough. Her skin felt on fire as if the wind-whipped flames burned her too. She groaned in pain.

The sound made the Shadow turn. He stalked toward her, footsteps drowned by the howl of the wind. The echo of pain fled as she scrabbled away from him, gaining her feet. She had no idea who he was or what he wanted. He could be another Brethren even though he'd killed the others instead of attacking her. They were known to war against each other, except ... they seemed to be working together to hold her mother for some reason.

So, if he wasn't Brethren, who was he?

She took in a breath, trying to find his scent, but the acrid smell of burning flesh clung to her nostrils, making it impossible to figure out who it might be. So she tried to press into his mind.

Violent bloodlust poured into her like venom, stabbing her mind. Crying out, she dropped Seer's Blood and pressed her hands to her head. It was a mistake—she knew it was a mistake. She had to fight, to defend, but it hurt. It hurt!

Fear reared, choking her. Then he was there, standing in front of her, his presence pushing into her in a way that made her gasp.

She knew he was reaching for her and yet she couldn't move. Couldn't do anything but wait for the death coming her way.

The Shadow grabbed her. "Are you insane, Ardenne?"

The voice. It was dearer to her than any voice she'd ever heard and yet, it was one that had also caused her so much pain.

Gabriel.

Relief shuddered through her followed quickly by panic. What was he doing here? How had he found her? She didn't want to see him. Didn't want him to be here. He'd stop her.

Her heart beat fast enough for two hearts as she fought against panic. "Let me go." Her voice was a shrill gasp. His grip tightened. She twisted. "Let me go."

"I can't. I can't." There was a clap of thunder above their heads. The wind whipped her hair across her face. With the sound of a rushing train, rain gushed over them. It hit the cobbles so loudly, she barely heard him say, "I have to get you out of here."

"No! No." She couldn't let him do that. "My m ..." No. She couldn't tell him it was her mother. Water poured down her face, into her mouth, she swallowed, needing it to wet her parched, smokey throat. "There is a woman. They've got a woman. Inside the church. I came to save her."

"How did you know that? Why didn't you tell someone?"

"I ..." She shook, still trying to twist out of his grip. She didn't want him to touch her. His cold hands were a hot brand through her wet top as he held her arms. It was too much. Too much. "Please. Let me go. I don't want you to touch me."

His grip loosened as she heard his sharp intake of breath, but he didn't let her go. "I don't care what you want right now. I must get you to somewhere safe. *Merda!* If I hadn't felt the bond screaming at me, I don't know what would have happened tonight." He pulled her against his chest, his lips pressed to her hair. "You have no idea how afra ... how worried I was, Ardenne."

The last was said under his breath, but Ardenne heard and wished that she could see his face. He sounded so angry. And his words made no sense. He spoke of the bond—although she still didn't know what it was or what it meant. If it was supposed to keep them together, it hadn't worked—it had caused her only pain—so she wasn't very impressed with whatever it was. And what else had he said? Had he said ... She gasped. "You were afraid for me? But why? How did you know what I was doing?"

His grip spasmed on her arms. "Because I can sense you through the bond. I could feel your fear, your panic, your worry."

She bristled. Sure, she'd felt that, but it wasn't all she'd felt. She couldn't stop herself from saying proudly, "Could you also feel how well I was doing? I killed eight Dark Brethren."

"*Cavolo*, Ardenne. That's not the point." A little shake. "You shouldn't be here. Shouldn't have put yourself in this kind of danger. You have no idea—"

"Of course I have no idea. None of you ever tell me the truth about anything." Her voice rose above the sound of the rain and the wind, but she didn't care. She was so furious. With Gabriel. With the Cousins. With Lord Hei and Tomas. With the world. "If you don't tell me the truth, then what choice do I have but to go out and search for it myself?"

"We're only trying to keep you safe."

"Safe from what?"

"From those who would harm you."

"But why am I in more danger than anyone else? Is it because I am blind? Is it because you think it makes me incapable of—"

"No. Never. Never think you are less because of that."

Confusion shoved through her, causing hot tears to prick her eyes. "But you said—"

"I know what you think I said, but I assure you, I know you are capable of anything you set your mind to. And already you are almost as good a fighter as Piven, especially with Seer's Blood in your hand."

"Then it doesn't make sense. I want you to tell me. Tell me!" Her voice rang in the *piazza*, bouncing off the cobbles and stone walls, a lonely, aching sound in the sudden stillness—the rain had stopped as suddenly as it had started, the wind dying with it.

Gabriel didn't answer her. He just stood there, hands moving up and down her arms, as if warming her. His fingers brushed over the cut where the knife had caught her. She winced.

"You're injured." His voice sounded raw as he took in a shuddering breath. The hairs on her arms rose. "Were you bitten?"

She shook her head, tried to pull away, but his hands tightened, pulled her closer.

Too close.

The heat of her anger softened, turned molten in her veins. But she needed to make him stop. She couldn't take his rejection again. "Stop it, Gabriel. I'm fine."

"You're injured." He breathed in, nose running along her arm.

Hating the way his closeness made her tremble, she struggled against his hold. "It's nothing. Just a knife wound. I swear. Let me go!"

He tore at her sleeve. Dipping his head, he licked the already coagulating blood.

"Gabriel," she gasped, the intimacy of his lick darting all the way to her core, hot and molten.

Ignoring her, he licked again. "There's vampire blood here."

"God no! Will I have to suck out the vampire blood? I don't know if I could stand it. Her blood's sweet. So sweet."

His lips whispered over her skin as the strange words whispered in her mind. Whose voice was that? It sounded like Gabriel. But it couldn't be because that would mean ... A sigh of longing mixed with confusion shuddered out of her.

"Did any vampire blood get in?" His voice was broken, husky.

"Not enough to matter," she muttered.

"Thank The First."

His hold gentled, fingers moving in hypnotic circles. "I couldn't have stood it if anything happened to you, Ardenne. The First forgive me ... I shouldn't have left you like I did earlier." His head dropped, forehead resting against hers.

Fire chased the tingles across her skin as his fingers traced patterns up and down her arms. Ardenne held her breath, waiting for him to push away, to say something sharp and biting again.

He didn't. He just held her in front of him, breath a whisper on her face.

The gentleness confused her. Even with his mind blocked, the feelings emanating from him were more than mere worry. And those words she'd heard before ... None of it made sense.

He'd always acted as if she was a burden, clearly wanting to get as far away from her as possible. And here she was, stupid again, building fantasies that were so far from true, they were laughable. Humiliation flushed her face.

Cool fingers trembled over the heat on her cheek. "Ardenne ... You can't understand the consequences of putting yourself in such danger. Don't do that to me again."

His tension, his worry, washed over her. Without thinking, she slipped into his mind trying to understand their source.

And saw herself through his eyes.

Breath caught in her throat as she saw what he saw. Felt what he felt.

Her heart-shaped face, pale and glowing in the moonlight, lips trembling, brow furrowed in confused passion, was beautiful to him. Even blood-smeared, singed, her wet hair plastered to her skin, she was beautiful to him.

His gaze roamed over her face then settled on her eyes.

He was lost in her eyes. So pale a blue like the heart of a glacier but not cold. Never cold. He was so afraid of those eyes and what they could see. She felt his fear. It trembled there, on the surface, smothering what lay beneath.

Through his eyes, she saw understanding dawn on her face.

"Gabriel?" she said, the sound husky and raw.

"No, Ardenne. Don't."

She wanted to go deeper, to feel more, but there was a door there, blocking so much. However, what she could see, what she could feel, she'd always thought it impossible. Just something from her dreams. Impossible dreams.

"Gabriel." She lifted her hand, brushed his cheek, thumb tracing over his lips. "Gabriel."

He stilled like a deer coming upon a wolf. How strange to think she was now the wolf.

She stood on tiptoes and slowly, so slowly, pressed her lips against his.

He stiffened, fingers tightening on her arms as if to push her away. But he didn't.

She swept her tongue over his lips, asking, enticing.

His resistance was in every trembling part of him, but she could feel his control slipping ... slipping.

With a groan he crushed her to him.

Their mouths meshed, lips, teeth, tongue, as if he was trying to taste all of her at once. And she opened to him, sharing all she was, hearing his thoughts, feeling his emotions as if they were her own.

Senses heightened by the fight, she became lost as her passion mingled with his.

She heard one part of his mind fighting everything this kiss made him feel, shouting at him to hold onto his vow as he'd once held onto his priestly vows. But the other part of his mind was too strong. It had been suppressed for too long, and the worry, the relief, the scent of the fight on her, the sweetness of her blood on his tongue, the trembling of her skin every time he touched her, was too much.

Too much of everything he'd ever wanted.

If there was a heaven and it had a taste, he was sure this would be it. He couldn't hold back.

Pulling her closer, his moan joined hers as the flame raced through her, into him and back to her as if they were one. As if they felt the same.

"*Let her go.*"

The voice in her mind was Gabriel, telling himself what he should do.

Using that same part of her mind she said back to him, "*No! Don't let me go.*"

He acquiesced to her demand. His fingers wound through her hair, dislodging her wet ponytail, tipping her face so he could take the kiss deeper, glutting on her taste, her scent, the very essence of who she was. "*This can't last.*" His voice again. But still, he didn't stop.

Reveling in her power, she let his emotions sweep her away.

One hand dropped down her back, urging her closer. His fingers tightened, digging into a wound she hadn't noticed.

With a gasp, Ardenne tore her lips from his, sanity returning.

What the hell had just happened? It was like she'd been taken over.

Frightened, she pulled away from him, but not enough. Still inside his mind, she saw herself as his gaze swept over her face. In his eyes she was the most hypnotic combination—the one thing he knew he couldn't have and yet he wanted to feast on her and never stop.

"Gabriel? What are you doing?"

He took a step, a low growl in his throat. She stumbled back, heart thumping painfully in her chest. Was he going to feed on her? He couldn't. Could he?

He took another step toward her as the sliding click of his teeth descending sounded.

Oh Lord! He could.

She wanted to run but couldn't move. His scent overwhelmed her as he came to stand so close, she could feel the cold of his skin seeping into her warmth. His sweet breath brushed over her face.

"Don't run," he said, his voice so low and rough she could barely make out the words. "If you run, I may not be able to stop from hunting you down."

Trembling—not entirely from fear—she stared up at where she thought his eyes might be and whispered, "I won't run."

An enraged shriek pierced the night, coming from behind them. An answering cry rang out from the deserted monastery buildings to their left.

Gabriel pushed Ardenne behind him and turned to face the Dark Brethren who had just run out of the church. There were more footsteps coming from the left—two or three more of them.

"Stay here," he ordered her and then he was gone.

"Fuck that." She picked up Seer's Blood, took a step to follow him, but then stopped. The Dark Brethren who'd been in the church were fighting Gabriel. He'd make short work of them and be able to deal with the couple who were running this way.

Her mother was now in the church alone and Gabriel would be occupied long enough for Ardenne to free her and get her out of there and toward safety.

Turning, she raced to the porch, slipping on the wet cobblestones, and tripping up the stairs. Hands in front of her, she smacked into one of the stone pillars that made up the porch but didn't stop.

She had to get inside before Gabriel was finished taking care of the Dark Brethren. Had to get to her mother.

CHAPTER 31
REVELATIONS

Relationships lost, once profound
Have come to be buried under the ground
From underground, truth comes to light
Carried by mother's fiendish delight
Three times three times three times three
Our daughter is made, so mote it be.
Extract from The Middleton Manifesto, Incantations, Verse 24,
Book 1

Ardenne entered the shadowed quiet of the church. Old scents of dust and incense and candle wax lay under the brighter smell of blood.

"Mother?"

There was a rustle and then the voice she'd always heard in her dreams, English-private-school and polished, rang out in the quiet. "Ardenne? You're here. You came."

She raced forward, fingers curling around the bars of the cage. "Mother. What have they done to you?"

"I'm fine. Or I will be when you get me out of here."

Ardenne's hands raced over the bars of the cage, feeling for the opening, found the lock. Her fingers clutched around Seer's Blood which was still in her hand. She lifted it to strike against the lock.

"No! This metal is designed to stop the strength of a vampire. You will only damage your blade."

"Then how?"

"They left keys. Over there on the ledge of that window. Use my eyes to see it."

Ardenne slipped into her mother's mind, surprised at how familiar and warm it was. She saw where her mother indicated and, shoving Seer's Blood into its sheath, raced over to grab the keys. The key trembled in her hand as she returned and reached for the lock, clanging against the metal. Her mother's cool hands against hers stopped their shaking, helped her to insert and turn the key. There was a loud clank, and then she pushed the door open and rushed out to wrap Ardenne's shivering frame in surprisingly strong arms.

"Oh, my darling girl. My darling girl. Never did I think to hold you in my arms again."

Ardenne clung to her mother, sobs ratcheting up from deep inside her. "I thought you were dead. I didn't know. I didn't know."

"Shh." Gentle hands brushing over her hair, lifting her face, thumbs brushing away the tears she hadn't even known she was crying. "I know. None of it's your fault. They are the liars. And they will pay for it."

Ardenne shuddered at the hatred in her mother's voice. Her fingers wound around her mother's wrist, feeling the steel strength of the bones and sinew. And the blood. "You're hurt." Her hands rushed over her mother's arms, her shoulders, feeling the open gashes, the swelling, the stickiness of blood everywhere. "What did they do to you?"

"Nothing that a little blood won't fix."

"I don't have any blood with me. I didn't think. I'm so sorry. But I can get you to a farm or the Cousins' compound. They'll have supplies there and—"

"No," she said, interrupting Ardenne's hurried words. She pulled Ardenne close, breathed her in, nose to skin. "So fresh. So young and vulnerable. Yet full of determination, like laced steel. You are so like me, my precious girl. Your blood is all I need."

Before she could even process the words, her mother's teeth sank into the soft flesh of her neck.

Shock and vampire venom kept her immobile as her mother began to suck.

Then slowly, realization struck. Her mother was feeding on her!

She had known she was a vampire, given what she'd overheard, but she'd thought she must be one of Lord Hei's sirelings, and they didn't drink from humans. Aside from the fact they preferred to exist on animal blood, feeding from humans was forbidden. Their venom alone acted like a drug, addicting those bitten.

"Lord Hei didn't make me. Another betrayal made me. Making me something ... other." Her mother's voice rang in her ears. *"But none of that matters. Only the truth of who I am matters right now. Let me show you the truth."*

Images, vivid and wild, were suddenly spinning through her head, then everything fell away to focus on one image in particular: A teenage girl was laughing with a young Carrington, a man and a woman at their side looking fondly down at their bent heads as they shared a joke.

She knew that girl. It was Anita, Carrington's sister.

But why would her mother have this image in her head? It didn't make sense.

Unless she *was* Carrington's sister, Anita. She'd wondered if the Anita they'd talked about as being her mother was Carrington's sister and yet it seemed too fantastical to be true. Too strange that they'd show Anita to her in a vision while trying to hide the fact she was her mother.

"Yes. Yes. Now you are seeing the breadth of lies. I am Anita Middleton. They have shown you some of me, but not all of me."

The image shifted; Anita as she was forced to watch her father fed on by Dark Brethren, forced to watch him being turned; Anita unable to move as he stalked toward her, intending to feed on her; a scream of despair and desperation from her mother as she arrived, blowing apart the vampires who'd made her father before, with grief-fueled rage, killing the thing wearing her beloved husband's face, too late to save him or most of the others in their coven either; Anita as she fought alongside Sasha Piven, learning all he could teach, hatred and revenge always on her mind; Anita, surrounded by vampires, desperately fighting with all the tools in her arsenal even while knowing it wouldn't be enough; Anita waking in a stranger's arms and knowing instantaneous love stronger than her will to deny.

Ardenne's head spun with the confusing array of emotions, coming to rest on the final image, the one where all she could see was the eyes of the one who had saved her mother, and the overwhelming emotions looking into his eyes made Anita feel.

She understood those emotions, had felt them when Gabriel held her.

Through Anita's eyes she looked up at the stranger, his face hidden in shadow, the eyes of a vampire glowing in the dark. Ice blue with a pinpoint of fire in their depths.

Anita, who spent all her time and energy hating and killing vampires, had fallen in love with one!

Then the final image shifted. Anita looked down at the baby in her arms, love and desperation flooding through her for her little girl with eyes the color of glacial ice.

Ardenne cried out against this proof of what she was being told.

Anita, Carrington's sister, the woman they had said died because she allowed grief and revenge and willfulness to color her existence, was her mother.

But that couldn't be true. It couldn't be. They would have told her. Wouldn't have kept that from her. What would be the reason?

"Oh, so many. They are keeping more than that from you too."

"No. No," she sobbed, too lost in denial to realize Anita had stopped feeding. That she no longer heard that mellifluous voice in her head.

"Yes. And now you've seen this truth, let me show you more."

Something dark and thick and wet touched her lips. The compulsion to lap it up overwhelmed. But she couldn't. She knew it was Anita's blood. She couldn't drink vampire blood. Not after being bitten. The combination of venom and blood could turn her.

"It will be different for you, Ardenne. Don't deny what you want. Drink, my precious girl."

The faint whisper in her ear faded, washed away by the all-consuming need welling inside. A need fueled by the drugging tendencies of the venom in her skin, in her blood, spreading. Slowly spreading. Driving her will away, driving the turmoil of her thoughts and what she'd been told far away so she couldn't remember what she was so upset about. All that was left was compliancy.

And need.

Her tongue darted out. The taste was sharp and sweet and thick. Ambrosia.

With a growl, Ardenne latched on and began to suck.

Anita gasped. "Drink. Know the truth. Become one with me. Let me give you back your sight."

"No!" Strength returned at those cruel last words. Her sight? Nobody could give back her sight. She pushed away with more strength than she knew she had. Caught off guard, Anita flew backward.

And Ardenne ran; away from temptation. Fighting the fire in her blood, the compulsion to drink, to be remade. Away from the things Anita had told her, had shown her, that just couldn't be true.

She stumbled over broken pews, scrambled sideways, toward the door. Gabriel. He was outside. She had to get to him. Away from this woman who was clearly insane.

Why had she come?

In the purple-velvet dark of her life, Ardenne thought she saw movement. The barest outline, a shadow in the dark.

"Come back to me, sweetheart. I remember the calling." Her mother's voice was luring, cinnamon and honey and sun on the hot sand. Ardenne fought the impulse to stop her flight, to turn, to give in. But it was impossible, her feet moving as if through tar. "It's already there inside you, living, pulsing. Like a song in your heart. Give in to the pull, Ardenne. You will never live in peace unless you do."

"I will never live in peace if I do."

Anita's laugh cracked in the air like a whip. "Oh, you are my daughter. Curse them for taking you from me."

Ardenne wished she could run as fast as Gabriel and escape the madness taking over her. "You're lying! You are not my mother. No mother would do what you just did to me."

"I *am* your mother. Don't deny what's so clear to your heart. You long to come to me. I can feel the rush in your blood. Let my blood give you back your sight. Come to me, beloved. Be one with me, a phoenix, arisen from the ashes."

Ardenne shook her head. If she drank anymore, the combination of the blood and her mother's venom would turn her. She didn't want to be made into a vampire. Not like this. Whatever Anita was, she wasn't good. Ardenne knew the biological facts. Lord Hei's blood and venom made his children good. The Wild and Dark Brethren's blood and venom made their children evil. Who had made Anita? And what would that blood and venom make her?

She didn't want to find out. But the pull was too strong. Anita's venom was a pulsing ache inside her. It had already addicted her. The blood already fired her veins, pain rising every moment she fought. Drawn like a wild animal to the sway of the cobra before she strikes, Ardenne turned. Already exhausted, further weakened by blood loss, numbed by shock, she couldn't stop herself. Sobbing, she took a trembling step back toward the woman who claimed to be her mother.

Muscled arms bound around her waist, swinging her up and away.

Anita's shriek of rage clung to the air as Gabriel sped out through the doors of the church. Moving faster than she ever thought possible, he ran, leaping over the crumbling ruins and down through the orchard. He didn't stop when he got to the road but raced over it and into the fields surrounding the old, ruined monastery, hiding the scent of their trail amidst the fetid stench of manure and animals and the sweet smell of growing produce.

Shocked, exhausted, injured, Ardenne clung to the safety of Gabriel. She buried her face in his neck, holding on to him like a lifeline to another safer, surer time.

They came to a stop. Sounds changed; the open echoing sound of wind and insects and animals muted. Ardenne realized they were inside a building. She thought at first it must be *Palazzo Maimoona*, but the scent was wrong. It was older. Dust clung to the air. There was no sent of wood polish. And the echoes were different. "Where are we?"

"Somewhere safe."

Gabriel's fingers curled into her flesh, not hurting, but possessive, as if he couldn't let go. She couldn't stop clinging to him either. Pain that had started as a hot ball in her stomach rose in her throat to choke her. But one thought overrode all others: "Is she ... f-following?"

He sat, settling her on his lap. "No. She ambushes. She'll never come at us in a straight fight. That's not the way she works."

Her fingers dug into him as the pain became a burn, a driving need.

Forcing her arms from around his neck, he muttered, "I'm sorry. I'm so sorry. I should have known, should have been able to tell. I don't know how she managed to cover her scent. I've searched ... so many years ... to keep you safe and she was right there."

"She's been speaking to me, in my dreams." Her teeth began to chatter as she fought the rising pain.

"Ardenne ... You were never meant to find out like this. I'm so sorry." His hands traced over her as they had before, stopping over the wound in her neck. "She fed on you. Did she blood you?" She said nothing, pain becoming a fire in her veins. His fingers tightened around her shoulders. "Did she blood you?"

Ardenne couldn't answer. Need clogged her throat. She wanted more of her mother's blood.

Shame flared inside her. She wanted what her mother offered. No, not want. Desire and longing seemed too trite to express the need burning like a hot brand. Was it the need that caused the terrible pain surging through her?

"Ardenne! Did you drink? Did you drink her blood?"

She couldn't answer, could only feel the pain growing inside her and Gabriel's worried gaze piercing her soul.

The shaking started, vibrating from her core, whiplashing through nerves and muscles, slashing, painful. She cried out, her body bowing back as every cell within responded violently to the blood and venom coursing through her veins.

"Ardenne! Ardenne!"

"Come back to me, my sweet Ardenne. Come back to me. I'm too weak. I didn't drink enough from you before you began to drink from me. There's no way I could fight him and win, but I've got so much more to tell you. So many more truths to share. Come to me. Come to me now and I will make all the pain go away."

Ardenne sobbed as pain screamed through her. She wanted to resist … wanted to shove Anita out of her mind.

Instead she pushed away from Gabriel, hard, spilling off his lap, sliding along the hard floor to slam up against the wall. Before she could get to her feet, he was there, holding her, stopping her from flying back to the waiting arms of her mother, stopping her from giving in to the thing that was like a fire in her veins. She kicked and punched in a flurry of arms and legs.

"Ardenne!"

"Let me go! Let me go!"

His body stretched over hers, pinning her down, making movement virtually impossible. Panting, she bucked under him, every muscle straining.

He reached up to cradle her head in his hands, thumbs stroking her cheeks. "I'm not prepared ..." he groaned, fear lacing his tone. "I don't have any human blood to give you, but that's not the worst. Fight her, Ardenne. Fight."

Ardenne didn't understand, but his touch brought back some form of sanity. Hot tears spilled from her eyes and into her hair. She didn't want to be made. She didn't. She might long for sight, but not this way.

Not this way!

"It hurts!" she said through clenched teeth, trying to hold back her scream.

"I know." He swore.

"Help me. Please help me. Don't let me go back to her. Don't let me turn."

He swore again, something deep and rough, and then his lips were against her brow as he said against her aching skin, "You know what I need to do? You know what's going to happen if I do what I need to do?"

Ardenne shook her head. She couldn't make sense of anything. Except the need to go back. Her body bowed and vibrated, pushing up and into Gabriel's against her will.

"I need to withdraw the fire in your veins. I need to suck out the venom she put in you. If I don't get it all, she can call to you, draw you back."

Ardenne nodded, a whimper escaping her lips as her mother's call sang through her. "She can ... control me ... through it," she whispered, her jaw so tight she could barely make her mouth shape the words. "She's trying ... now. She wants me to drink her blood. Why does she want to turn me?"

"She can't." Gabriel pulled in a deep, shuddering breath. "There's too much to explain right now, but it's different for you, because of who you are. Her blood won't turn you but it will cause you terrible pain." His voice tightened as he swallowed, hard. "I've fought all these years against just this. Lord help me ... I hope you'll forgive me. I need to drink from you. Get your mother's venom and blood out of you. Doing this will also allow me to meld with your mind and relieve some of the pain."

Ardenne didn't know what he meant, but she nodded while half her mind was caught by a siren's call, the other half burning with pain.

'They'll lie to you. Come back to me, sweetheart. Let me show you the truth.'

"I don't want to know the truth!" she screamed in her mind. But it was a lie. What she didn't want was more of this pain.

Gabriel's thumb brushed over her lips, across her cheek, sweeping away the tears coursing down her face, dampening her hair.

"Beautiful, sweet Ardenne. Do you trust me?"

Yes, yes, she did. She didn't know why after all he'd done, but she did.

"Don't trust him! Don't trust him! He'll give you his venom and then it will all be over."

"Your venom," she managed to mutter. "You can't."

"I won't bite you. I'll only suck. I promise."

"I trust you," she murmured.

"You shouldn't. Even without the venom, once I begin to feed, I'll be in your mind, sharing the pain, feeling what you feel. Are you prepared for that?"

Ardenne shook her head, the pain excruciating. "I don't care. Just ... do what you've got ... to do," she managed to say through clenched teeth. Her body spasmed as fire roiled through her—the pull to answer her mother's silent call so strong it felt like she would be broken in two. "N ... now! Do it now!"

She felt his reservation before he ducked his head. He still didn't want to touch her. But he had to. He had to. Or she would die. And she didn't want to die!

His lips, cold and perfect, pressed over the wound her mother had created. He began to suck. Exquisite excruciating pain filled her veins, swelling every pore. Heat and fire thrilled through her.

"Stay with me, Ardenne. Just hold on."

Gabriel's beautiful voice reverberated in her mind, velvet and warmth, longing and desire, taking the place of Anita's voice, pushing it aside. *"Just hold on."*

She held on as the sucking intensified. As he began to draw on the fire of the venom pulsing through her veins.

With a cry he reared back. The shock of his leaving reverberated through her.

"This isn't right. What did she do?"

"D-don't care," she gasped. "Don't stop." With his lips gone, the pain throbbed through her anew.

His lips returned along with his presence in her mind. Not just his voice this time, but him. All of him. His thoughts, his feelings, meshed with hers until they were one.

This was what he had meant when he warned her. That he could see everything she held inside.

Panic reared through her, overtaking the pain. No! He couldn't know how she felt about him! The pain was nothing compared to the thought of him really knowing how deeply she felt. She pushed against him, her hands mimicking the fight going on in her mind.

"Stop it, Ardenne. Let me in. Let me help."

"No! You'll use it against me like you did before."

"I'm sorry. I lied before. I lied to protect myself, to protect you. I don't want to hurt you again, but this is the only way. If you don't let me help, the pain could stop your heart. You must let me in."

The pain, hot and furious, burned through every synapse now. Her heart throbbed and strained under its weight. She had no power to keep him out even if she wanted to.

His lips returned to her throat.

At the feel of them there, soft and yet insistent against her skin, the fight in her died.

But in that moment of surrender, the rejection and torment she thought was coming her way never appeared. Instead, the pain was replaced with *his* fear, *his* worry, *his* struggle. He saw inside her, just like she'd feared, but she saw inside him too even more deeply than before. And her feelings, instead of making him laugh … By The First! Her love almost tore him in two.

He didn't hate her. He was afraid of her. Afraid of what she made him feel.

She'd thought herself mistaken before but … It was incredible. This knowledge. And as the pain ebbed, something else began to build inside her. Something hot and wild and full of need.

Every inch of him was pressed against every inch of her. The need thrumming through his veins fired her need to greater heights. Her hands moved, brushing along the muscles of his arms, over his sculptured back and shoulders, into his silky hair.

He groaned, pressed into her harder, his erection brushing against her core as she shifted her legs. Something wet and hot flooded between her thighs.

"Ardenne," he choked out, his lips moving on the wound on her neck. "Stop that. You must stop that."

She couldn't. Not feeling what she did. Not feeling what he did.

She breathed in, taking in his scent, her skin on fire with need for him. He was all around her, but it wasn't enough. Not nearly enough. Something had been started when they'd kissed both times before but now it had to come to completion. She wouldn't let either of them run away from it as they'd both done before.

This time she wanted more. Wanted it all.

She grabbed his butt as she arched against him, pushing his erection more firmly against her core, then began to scrabble at his clothes.

"Ardenne." His voice was a rumble against her throat. "Ardenne, no."

"Clothes. Too many clothes." Her voice was so breathy, so raw, it hardly sounded like hers.

"It's the feeding doing this to you. The aftermath of what she did, what I'm doing." His lips left her neck as he tried to grab her hands, but she slipped them from his grip.

"No. It's not the feeding. It's you. It's always been you." She didn't care if he knew exactly how she felt now. She wanted him to know. Needed it, with every ounce of her being. "I want you." She pushed closer to him, the sound of his groan a welcome song in her ears. "If I don't feel you inside me right now, I might die." Her heart was pounding so hard in her chest, she thought it might be true.

"It's wrong."

She grabbed his face, angling hers to look up as if she could see him with her own eyes. "I want you. I've always wanted you as you want me. That could never be wrong. Don't deny me now. Not now." Her voice trembled. If he said no, she would be destroyed.

For long moments he was silent, his breath brushing over her face.

"Am I mistaken? Don't you want me?"

"I want you, Ardenne." His voice was pained, as if he was in so much agony. Yet there was passion and a longing that was so great, she could feel it pressing into her. "I've never wanted anyone more."

The bliss of his words blew through her like a warm summer breeze, even though there was still no surrender in his voice. But she could make him surrender. She began to tear at his clothes again, pain replaced by a fever she didn't understand but wasn't ready to deny.

"Ardenne."

"Please, Gabriel. Please."

He held her head between his hands, stilling her. She knew his eyes raged over her face, could feel them like a deep caress. Then, on a moan filled with surrender and regret and passion that couldn't be denied, he dragged her head back and kissed the tears from her face. His lips were soft and perfect against her skin as they chased over her face then down her neck until they were where she wanted them the most.

He licked the wound and she writhed. His hands caressed her body. Her hips pistoned off the floor, searching, seeking for him to take her ...

Where?

She didn't know. Didn't care.

She wanted ...

He wanted ...

Their need was the same.

Gabriel tore her pants down her legs. She wrapped them around him, needing to keep him close.

"Forgive me." His voice rang in her mind. *"Please forgive me, but I can't stop."*

"I don't want you to stop," she said in his mind, unable to form the words with her lips.

His groan reverberated on her skin as her words imprinted themselves in his mind, in hers. Then he thrust into her in one strong stroke.

Ardenne was so wet, so ready, she barely felt it as her virginity was torn away.

His lips covered the wound on her neck again. The pain from what Anita had done subsided, pleasure increased, and he began to move inside her. Pleasure for him. For her. Rising and rising until she thought her mind would explode from the heat and sensations too intense to hold within.

His lips finished with her neck, made their way to her lips.

She opened to him. His tongue stroked and twined with hers as his hips moved in a rhythm between her legs, the pressure of him inside building, building. She rode on feelings, emotions, letting them have their way, open to him in a way she never thought possible, sharing his thoughts, sharing hers, becoming a part of him. Becoming One.

And in that Oneness, she felt everything.

Gabriel's needs were tearing at him like a clawed beast. Ardenne shuddered with the power of those needs. He wanted her. That wasn't in doubt. But even as pain from Anita's venom sang through his veins, his bloodlust raged through him, even stronger.

He wanted her blood.

He needed her blood.

He'd fill himself with her blood.

No!

Ardenne didn't know if the cry was hers or his. But it didn't matter. He denied the need just like he'd denied it all her life. He didn't feed, just moved with her, harder and faster, the burning deep inside building, building.

It was so much ... too much ... pleasure and pain entwined. She sank inside it, inside him, until she could barely understand the difference between them.

Then she felt it. His guilt.

It drove through him like an angry steed. Guilt for doing this. Guilt for lying. But not enough to make him stop what was happening right now. The scent of her surrounded him, blood and heat and sweat, all sweetened with sex and desire. He opened his eyes, and she looked down at herself through them and saw that to him, she was heartachingly beautiful. A beauty that spoke to secret places in his soul.

A beauty sent to torment him.

He reared up, taking her with him, her breasts crushed against his chest as he kept pumping into her, surrounding her with every part of his body, outside and in. It was the most amazing sensation. She'd never felt so full. So wanted. So needed.

"Gabriel, I need ... I need ..." she panted.

His lips left hers to cover the wound in her neck, sucking again, answering to the need she hadn't been able to voice.

The sucking wasn't hard, but it was just enough to pull the bow tight inside her and release.

She cried out as the orgasm took her, her muscles pulsing around him, bright light filling the dark void in her mind.

Crying out, he drove into her one last time and they shuddered together, drawn up and torn apart as one.

As the waves subsided, he fell back and rolled, cushioning her against the landing with his body and then his mind was gone from hers, his feeling torn away.

But, joined with him still in body, if not in mind, Ardenne couldn't make herself care. All she could do was ride the waves that took her up and away.

CHAPTER 32
AWAKENING

A secret will be revealed
A fate will be sealed
Love will be ignited
The blind will become sighted

All is not what it seems.
Extract from The Middleton Manifesto, Prophecy 43, Book 2

Ardenne came around slowly. The first thing she became aware of was the fact that Gabriel lay at her side, body slack, lost in the oblivion of sleep. The second thing was the horrible pounding in her head. She groaned and clutched at it, the movement making her aware of how much everything hurt.

Not a single part of her was immune to the deep ache.

On the bright side, the driving insanity was gone. She no longer felt the need to run back to her mother and beg her for more of her blood.

Ah hell! She'd let her mother drink from her. And had then drunk from her mother. If not for Gabriel coming and whisking her away …

Thoughts and feelings over what had happened with her mother pummeled her mind, making the pounding increase. She groaned again, clutched her head harder. Stop. Stop. She had to stop the thoughts and feelings from whirling around like this. But they wouldn't stop.

She was going to be sick.

She rolled over, away from Gabriel, and vomited. She had nothing much in her stomach to bring up, so simply heaved and heaved until, exhausted, she fell back to the floor, sweaty and weak and panting.

At least her thoughts had stopped swirling. And as she lay there, taking in deep, shuddering breaths, staring at the wall and the gauzy curtain fluttering against the cream plaster, the only thought in her head was that her life was built on lies.

He'd lied to her.

They'd all lied to her.

Lied to her for so many years about what she was. About what had happened to her mother; who she was and who she'd become.

Lord Hei, Papa, Piven, Carrington, even Sarita were liars. They all knew that Anita, Carrington's sister, was her mother. They all knew her mother, once a witch, was now a vampire who still somehow had some of her witch powers—how else could she come to her and speak in her mind like she did?

Did they know who her father was? Was he the vampire Anita had loved—although how that was possible she didn't know? Had they lied about his death too?

No. She couldn't think about that. The agony of it sliced through her, making her breath come in short, choppy gasps. Tomas was her papa. It didn't matter who her biological father was. He obviously wasn't alive, or Anita would not be working alone—hell it was so confusing!

The only thing that wasn't confusing was that her mother was the only person who had tried to tell her the truth.

Except ... Anita had tried to turn her into a vampire. She'd seen that memory of Anita killing those Dark Brethren; seen just how much her mother had hated vampires. How could she then turn her daughter into one of them?

And given that little piece of insanity, how much of what Anita said could be believed?

Gabriel had said they'd tried to keep her safe from her mother. Maybe that was true. Given what had happened, it probably was. Did that excuse some of the lies? Maybe some of them, but certainly not all. Never all. Because of what lay behind their lying to her: the fact they obviously thought her too weak to be able to deal with it.

Gabriel groaned behind her.

The sound made Ardenne's mind skitter away from impossible thoughts and center on something more impossible. The fog of pain that still shrouded her couldn't blanket the clarity of memory of what she'd done with him. Every action, thought, and emotion of the last six hours lay bare before her.

Her fingers fluttered to her mouth. She could still feel the imprint of his lips on hers. Still taste him on her tongue. Still feel the slide of him over her, inside her.

She'd made love with Gabriel!

It seemed like a dream, the memories of their coupling so vivid and yet shrouded in a cocoon of mist. But she knew it wasn't a dream. Her body was sore and well used and there was a warm stickiness between her legs. Not to mention the sensation inside her, building once again as she thought about what they'd done.

He had always caused a tremor inside her. The way he moved, his looks, his scent, his sensual presence; his voice, like warmed chocolate, caressed prickles of awareness over her skin and drew her in, making her long to be enfolded in the cold death of his embrace— she'd always tried to put that down to the fact he was a vampire. This was something different. Something more. He was no longer *L'angelo Solitario*, the Lonely Angel, foreswearing pleasures of the flesh in service to his Sire. He was Gabriel, her wild and passionate lover. When he'd been inside her, everything had exploded. Or imploded. Ardenne wasn't sure what description was more apt.

But why had he tried to make her think he hated her? How could he hide away from those astonishing emotions?

She decided to wake him up, ask him. She rolled back toward him, intending to push herself upright to give him a shake ... or to kiss him awake. But her muscles protested, head pounding. She flopped back. Her eyes flared wide against the rolling nausea and pain that threatened to pull her back into unconsciousness again, but she fought it, concentrating on the ceiling rose wavering above her.

Slowly, the nausea subsided. She turned her head, careful this time and tried to get a picture of where they were. They were lying on a rug on the floor. A bed stood close behind them.

How was it they'd never made it to the bed?

Memory was fuzzy about how they got here and what had occurred before Gabriel plunged into her. His voice, apologizing, echoed in her mind, his guilt, a raw slice across his heart.

He was sorry?

She sucked in a pained breath, the knowledge a shard of ice in her lungs.

He'd tried to fight the need to make love. Why fight so hard against something he wanted so much? She'd felt that need inside him as if it was hers. It had been overwhelming but he'd fought it, unwilling to give in.

Did he not think her worthy of him?

When she was inside his emotions, she had thought he did, but maybe she was just carried away by everything that had happened. Maybe—

He moaned again. She turned to look at him. A wave of nausea swamped her once more; she closed her eyes to ride it out. Finally, when it passed, she opened them again, her gaze drawn to Gabriel like iron to a lodestone.

By the Lord's blood, he was beautiful. His hair, the planes of his face, the color of his skin.

Still too sore and sick to move, she had to be content with looking at him. Her gaze caressed his face, his cheekbones, his straight nose, his blood-plum-colored lips. She remembered biting that full bottom lip last night, sampling, sucking, savoring. That beauty couldn't be wasted on someone unable to see it.

She gasped as the ice cold of startling realization chased embarrassment away.

She could see!

Holy crap! She could see. She could see Gabriel. Had seen the curtain flapping against the plaster wall. Had seen the ceiling rose above them. But how?

Was she seeing them from Gabriel's perspective?

No. She couldn't be. Because not only were his eyes closed, but she couldn't see him if she was looking out of his eyes.

Oh. Holy. Crap.

She could see!

She glanced around, the nausea lost in a sea of wonder as she took in her surrounds; the curtains fluttering in a light breeze were lit by the golden glow of the sun coming in through the window; the plush carpet under her hand was decorated with diamonds and stars; the ceiling rose above her head clasped the antique light fitting in a lover's embrace.

And the colors!

Colors so vibrant they pulsed with life. It was so beautiful, but ...

How could this be real? It couldn't be. Could it? Maybe someone else was here and she was seeing it through their eyes.

Fear gripped her as she looked around, frantic, wondering if Anita had tracked them down.

But they were alone.

Maybe she was dreaming. She'd always been able to see in her dreams for some reason. She dug her fingers into the carpet, the scent of the puddle of bile she'd vomited up only moments ago lifting in the air, thoroughly awful. And too real. Too mundane.

She looked down. Saw her own nakedness. Lifted her hand to her face, over her eyes, blanking out sight behind her hand. Her heart stilled as realization shook her.

Oh.

My.

Lord.

This was no dream. She wasn't seeing out of another's eyes. This was real. There was no other explanation for what was in front of her.

"I can see," she whispered. "I can see!"

It wasn't like in the Trial, or in shared memories or dream-visions. Seeing through her own eyes was like being outside after a summer storm with everything sounding and smelling suddenly more vivid. The range of colors was breathtaking; as if God-like she stood on a mountain peak, the world spread before her. Light glowed where it touched surfaces. Dust motes danced in the air. Surrounding everything was a halo, pulsing, like blood through veins.

Laughter gurgled out of her.

The motion brought the nausea on again like a rampaging flood.

Trembling, she rolled over and heaved and heaved until her muscles cramped and she could heave no more.

Face pressed to the cool floor beside the small puddle of bile, she closed her eyes, swallowing down the bitter taste in her mouth.

Vivid color paled to red-tinged darkness.

She breathed deeply. Then had to roll over, back toward where Gabriel lay, the smell of her own vomit making bile rise in her throat again. Everything pulsed and throbbed and she couldn't help groaning as she rolled, oh so carefully, over to her back. She breathed through the pain, long, low, purposeful breaths.

And in those breaths she smelled ... Dust. Blood. Something

warm and tangy with salt and a sweet muskiness that could only be the scent of sex.

Mingling with it was the scent of cool mountain air.

Gabriel.

The nausea subsided a little. She opened her eyes again. Bile raced up her throat. She jammed her eyelids shut. What was going on? How could her sight make her sick?

Maybe it was all too much. Sensory overload. Perhaps that's what this was. Something she just had to get used to.

Right now she didn't care. Trembles and a little vomit she could put up with. She had learned so much over the last eleven months. This was just one more thing to learn to control.

Ardenne pushed down the nausea, tried to still the trembling. It worked until she opened her eyes. The room rose and sank, and she went with it, a boat on a wave, tossed and turned, at the mercy of elements beyond her control.

Closing her eyes again she noted the lightness behind her eyelids. That was new. She examined the shades and textures of this new darkness. Concentrating on this one thing seemed to help. She opened her eyes, cautious. The world pulsed and she almost vomited again, but steadied herself, determined not to spill her guts once more—especially given there was quite literally nothing left inside her to spill and all it would do was make her hurt more.

Careful not to make too much noise and overwhelm her senses, she faced Gabriel, wanting to share this with him. She couldn't believe her vomiting hadn't woken him. But he was still asleep, lying there like the living dead.

The living dead ... she giggled, smothering the sound with her hand, but the world stayed still.

He groaned.

Why was he groaning? She edged forward slowly, still unable to move fast without the nausea and pain stabbing at her. Reaching his side, she put out a trembling hand and touched his shoulder.

And pulled it back with a jerk.

He wasn't cold. He should have been cold, but his skin felt clammy, heated. Her gaze roamed over him, assessing, looking for injuries.

There was no outward sign he'd been hurt except ... He wasn't just pale; he was porcelain white. His skin looked fine, breakable, his veins, a sickly green, tinged with purple around the edges, glowed and pulsed under that smooth white surface. Perspiration glistened on his skin.

He looked sick.

He looked close to death. Real, unforgiving, this-is-it death.

"Gabriel?" She shook his arm, the wonder of sight squashed under the weight of sudden fear.

He groaned again as if in terrible pain.

"Gabriel?" She clasped his hand in hers, panic coloring her tone. She pushed the panic aside because she had to think. What had caused this? It had to be something that had happened last night. But what?

What?

She wrangled her circling thoughts as Piven had taught her, making herself focus on the events of the previous night until they came into sharper focus.

Words flashed through her head. His words. Spoken as he sucked the venom out of her blood—"*This isn't right. What did she do?*"

He'd been speaking about Anita's venom; venom he'd sucked from the wound in her neck. A vampire's venom was a kind of toxin, but could it hurt another vampire? Could it kill?

She didn't think so except ... why would he have said that?

And if he'd known there was a problem with Anita's venom, why would he keep sucking it out of her system?

Her lips trembled as the reason slammed into her head.

She'd pleaded with him to save her. And he had. He'd saved her knowing Anita's venom was poison.

He was dying and it was all her fault.

Tears in her eyes, she gripped his shoulders and said, "Gabriel, please tell me. Tell me what to do. What do you need?"

He didn't answer. She shook him gently.

Nothing.

She shook him harder. "Gabriel! Please! I need help. I don't know what to do. I need ... I need ..."

"*You.*"

The word echoed in her head. She wasn't sure if it was her thought or his. "What? Was that you? Please, Gabriel?"

She touched his cheeks and instantly recoiled. His skin was so hot she was afraid it might melt at any second, sloughing off under her touch like rock melted before a flow of burning lava.

A sigh escaped his lips, dry, acrid. His eyes fluttered open, liquid pools of violet flame sucking her into hell.

Ardenne grasped her hands together, afraid to touch him again. Eyes stinging with withheld tears she asked, "What can I do?"

"*Sire's blood. I ... need ... Sire's blood.*"

His beautiful voice, a weak echo in her mind, brought comfort out of all proportion to its lack of strength. Wringing her hands in front of her, she said, "Don't worry, Gabriel. I'll get you to him. Don't leave me now. Just don't leave me now. I need you."

Ardenne leaped up, lurched forward, dry retching, falling back to her knees. *Pull it together!* She had no idea where they were or how she could help him, and right now, he was relying on her. She closed her eyes, trying to use her hearing, but all she could hear was the labored sound of his breath, the fluttering of his improbable heartbeat.

She opened her eyes again; her new sense had to be a positive.

Light flared, making her wince. Light coming from the window, filtered by the fluttering curtains.

Shit!—daylight. How long had he been like this? Was it just past dawn or later? She had to get him out of here. Had to get him help.

Think. Think.

Grabbing her clothes off the floor, she pulled on the tattered remains with trembling hands. It took too long to cover her naked-ness but when she was finally dressed, she looked around, uncertain what to do.

If only she knew where they were, then she could figure some-thing out. Kneeling back beside him, she leaned in close and whis-pered, "Gabriel. Can you tell me where we are?"

He didn't answer.

There was only one thing she could do then, although she was loath to do it without his permission. She'd already cost him so much pain.

But she had no choice.

Carefully, she used her power to press into his mind.

And found only swirling images of what they'd done last night mixed with nightmare images of a hut, blood all over the floor, the wailing cry of a baby and a woman, her face contorted in pain, begging, *"Guard her, Gabriel. Keep her safe."*

He bent over the woman, her blood flooding across his hands. He looked into the baby's glacial eyes. A bond snapped into place. A bond that forced him to act; to break a most solemn vow. Mortifica-tion and despair drove through him. He didn't want to do this, but what choice did he have?

His despair filled her, choked her.

Ardenne shook the images away even though she wanted to dive into them further.

The baby in his arms had been her. The eyes had given it away. As had the glimpse she'd had of a pale and dying Anita. Had Gabriel turned her to save her life?

Had he turned her because the baby she'd been had begged him to save her and it was the only way he could?

The thought was too big, too unsettling. It made her want to cry, to give in to the nausea that wouldn't stop pushing at her, to be nothing more than a trembling wreck on the floor.

But she couldn't let herself become that. Gabriel needed her. She was the only one who could help him now.

So she thrust all the questions and disturbing thoughts aside and concentrated on him. On what she could do for him.

The first thing was to make him hold on, to not give in to the desperation and darkness of his circling thoughts and to make him tell her where they were.

"Gabriel," she pleaded, hands clasped before her so as not to touch him. "Please, don't give up. I'll fetch help. I'll get you to Lord Hei. I just need to know where we are."

An image filled her head of the countryside.

An image that could be anywhere in central Italy.

"Come on, Gabriel. I need more. Please, give me more."

The vision shifted to show a town nestled in the hills nearby. The name *Gubbio* rang in her head. "*Gubbio*? Did you say we are in *Gubbio*?" He didn't answer.

But she definitely had heard the name of the hilled town in the heart of *Umbria*. How had he taken her so far from the crumbling monastery? Why had he taken her so far away?

Shit! Shit!

In a car it would take hours to get back to *Firenze* and *Palazzo Maimoona*.

Too long. Too long.

Tears welled. She didn't know how to drive, even if there was a car nearby.

Pounding her head with her palms, she stood, pacing.

Think, think.

Sarita and Piven. She'd been in both their minds. Could she use the mind speak she'd shared with her mother to get to them so far away? She'd never done anything like it before with anyone but Anita. And Gabriel. Although, she hadn't realized she'd been doing that then. Had thought them dreams.

She had to try. Had to figure out how.

Closing her eyes, she sank into that deep part of her mind where her powers were seated. Grasping it, she looked for an echo, an imprint, of the times she'd spoken to Anita and Gabriel in her mind.

Nothing.

There was nothing.

Perhaps it was them, not her, who held the talent for mind speech. Hopelessness folded over her like a shroud. Her shoulders bowed under its weight.

Gabriel groaned.

She snapped upright.

She couldn't let him down. Couldn't let him die. Couldn't. She tried again to find the part of her power that had allowed her to talk with her mother and Gabriel, and again, all the time aware of the heat surging from him. So hot. Too hot.

"Come on! Come on!" she screamed, pressing her knuckles into her temples. "Come on!"

Something rustled in the heart of her power. She didn't know if it was what she wanted, or if it would be enough, but she lurched toward that rustle and hurled her thoughts into it. "Sarita! Piven! Help. Help me. See where I am. Gabriel. He's dying. He needs help. He needs Sire's blood." She repeated it, over and over, speaking the words with her lips and her mind.

And as she spoke them, Gabriel began to toss and turn, his movements becoming ever more violent as the minutes slipped away.

Then suddenly, his body bowed rigidly up, his head and heels cracking against the floorboards with a loud snap.

His blood scented the air.

Then he flopped back down and began to shake and shudder as if having a seizure, his limbs, body, and head slamming into the floor over and over, the loud smacks reverberating around the room.

Ardenne had no choice. She gave up her mad effort to reach her friend and her teacher and stretched her body over his, desperate to stop his movements. His muscles vibrated beneath her, his stomach, his chest, his arms and legs flopping like caught fish. His head lifted again, but before it could slam back down, she grabbed his face, held it still. He went limp beneath her.

Her touch. Was it calming him? Or was it something else? Maybe the seizure had stopped.

Or maybe he was getting that much worse. He was so hot and sweat poured off his body. Blood rivulets were coming out of his eyes, nose, and ears. And his veins looked like they were about to burst out of his skin.

"Please, Gabriel, please." Her voice rang with grief and desperation. She cupped his face, ignoring the heat of him, the slick-sweat and blood covering his skin, willing him to open those flame-filled eyes once more so she could look further, deeper, into his mind. She kissed him, his brow, his cheekbone, his lips. She didn't care if he'd been part of the lie. She didn't care. "Talk to me. Tell me what you need. Tell me what to do."

He moaned, long, low, painful. Ardenne clenched her lip between her teeth, biting, cutting the soft skin. The copper taste of blood welled in her mouth.

Nostrils flaring, Gabriel bucked off the floor, his fangs elongating with a click. The tendons in his neck tightened so they looked like they might snap. Veins pulsed under his skin. His mouth opened. Words—harsh and frightening in their intensity, yet barely audible—shivered out. "Sire's blood. Need ... Sire's blood."

"I don't know how to reach Lord Hei," she said in a rush. "I didn't bring my phone and I can't reach Sarita or Piven." A sob hiccoughed out of her. "I'm useless. You were right ... I can't help you. I don't know how." Tears poured down her cheeks, hitting his skin with a little sizzle.

"No, no ... you ... more ... now it's ... pure." His voice died in a gasp, breath rattling.

She didn't understand. Crying hard, she bent over and kissed his hot, hot lips. The moment the blood beading on her lip touched his, he moaned and latched on.

Shocked, she stilled. He growled beneath her and let go. "More. More blood." He licked her lip, but the blood that had been there was gone. "More blood." He looked up at her, the heated coal of his eyes lessening for a moment, his skin looking less like wet glass.

Her blood. Had it made him better? But it wasn't Sire's blood. Maybe any blood would do for now. And if it would help ... Those few scant drops had made him slightly more lucid, although, as she watched, that lucidity waned, the life force leaching out of him as fast as it had been revived.

If she gave him more, would it be enough to make him lucid and able to move so they could get back home? She had no idea. But she had to try. It was her only hope.

Tearing away from him, she pulled a knife out of her vest, sliced it across her wrist and placed her wrist against his lips. He latched on, sucking hard, and by some miracle, his teeth and fangs never pierced her skin. Even this ill, he didn't chance exposing her to the poison of his venom. He just sucked on her wrist like a toothless baby at the breast, helpless, mewling because the flow was not nearly strong enough.

He reached up, fingers wrapping around her arm, pinching.

"Ouch," she muttered, but didn't pull away. This wasn't like last night, she mused as her head began to swim. But of course it wasn't. Without the venom thrumming through her, the pain wasn't turned to ecstasy.

No. The only sensation surging through her was panic.

Panic at the possibility of losing Gabriel.

Panic at the possibility of doing wrong.

Panic it wouldn't be enough.

Nausea swelled again alongside weakness. Having the blood sucked out of her, the feel of her life force draining away, was nothing close to sensual. Horrible, horrifying; the pulse as her heart pumped the precious blood out and away was painful, pitiful.

The room swayed and floated around her. She'd lost blood last night and hadn't eaten or drunk anything to replenish herself. She was already weak. She couldn't give much more.

She tried to tug her arm from his grip, but he didn't let go.

Surprised at the strength of his grip, she pulled harder, but he just growled and sucked harder. Panic clawed at her throat. If she didn't make him let go, she'd lose consciousness. If that happened, he could suck her dry.

Desperate, she swung her legs around, kicking out. He grunted and his grip loosened. She kicked again and pulled at the same time. Her wrist slipped from his grip. She scooted back as he growled, reaching for her, but she managed to crawl out of range of his grasping hands. "Don't follow. Don't follow." She wanted to save him and hoped he'd had enough, but she didn't want to die.

"Ardenne," he whispered and then shuddering, fell back to the floor, eyes rolling up in his head.

Long moments passed as she listened to his laboring breath, the stuttering of his heart that persisted in beating in an almost human way even though he was a vampire. She couldn't tell if her blood had helped. Inching forward to get a better view, she was surprised to see the floor coming up to meet her face.

As darkness rushed over her, one thought ran through her mind: *Let him live.*

CHAPTER 33
MOTHER'S BLOOD

Vampire blood could make her see
But vampire blood could bring her death
Do not drink the blood of the vampire.

The blood of the seer will bring him life
But the blood of the seer will bring him pain
Do not drink the blood of the seer.
Extract from The Middleton Manifesto, Section On Death,
Lesson 10

"Will she live?" Lord Hei's voice rang through the shadows shifting around Ardenne.

"Yes. But we can't give her more blood. The balance must be maintained. We won't know if the transfusion has done its job until she wakes." This voice sounded like her old pediatrician, Doctor Rosso. "I must go now. If she wakes, give her some of this to drink, but under no circumstances are you to give her more blood. Call me if there's a change for the worse."

"Thank you, Rosso."

Ah, so it was Doctor Rosso. Why was he here? And who were they talking about? She wanted to ask but a door closed, the soft click echoing like a drum in her head, taking over all thought.

"My Lord. I'm so sorry. I didn't get here soon enough." Sarita's voice, thick with tears, floated through Ardenne's mind amidst swirling lights, a shifting susurrus of sound.

"You called me as soon as you felt her in danger. You even thought to bring blood with you. By the time I got here with Doctor Rosso, you had her care in hand. Don't apologize for doing more than I could have expected of you."

"But she might—"

"Shh, don't say the words. You know how powerful words can be."

"My daughter is a fighter. She will survive."

Tomas Bartolli's voice brought the swirling lights and shifting sound into solidity. "Papa?"

Her voice was barely a croak, but he heard it. "Ardenne." She felt his weight on the bed beside her, the touch of his warm hand on hers. "Ardenne? Ardenne, speak my name."

She wanted to open her eyes but couldn't. Why couldn't she open her eyes? Or move? What had happened to her? "I feel terrible," she managed to say, her throat so dry, her tongue so thick, it was hard to form the words.

Even though she sounded terrible, her papa chuckled, the sound full of relief. "Of course you feel terrible, *cara mia*. What you did was foolish. Brave, but foolish."

Foolish? What was he talking about? She opened her mouth to ask, but his finger on her lips silenced her. "Shh, don't argue with your papa. You don't have the strength."

"He's not your papa," Anita's voice whispered in her mind.

And with that whisper, memories came surging back.

Anita. The monastery. The fight. Anita had fed on her. Had forced her to drink her blood in turn. Then ... She gasped. Pain. There'd been so much pain and then Gabriel had taken it all away. He'd ... Gabriel! Oh God, Gabriel. "Where's Gabriel?" She tried to sit up, but dizziness crashed over her, pushing her back. Voices wavered in and out and then became clear.

"... nearby."

"You can see him later."

"Yes, but first she must rest."

"Not for too long. We must get her back to *Firenze*."

"*Firenze*? We can't send her back there. She needs to be back home, with us. It's the only place she can truly be safe."

"Tomas, be reasonable."

"I am being reasonab—"

"Where are we?" Ardenne's voice broke across her papa's tirade, and he clasped her hand in his.

"Still in the safe house in *Umbria*. Dr. Rosso thought it was best to keep you here until you recovered."

"She won't recover if you keep bickering over her like that." Sarita's acerbic comment almost made her laugh. She could just imagine the expression on Lord Hei's and Papa's faces at being taken to task. But then Sarita's arm was under her head, lifting her. "Here, sweetheart. The doctor said you needed to drink this."

She sipped. It was sickly sweet and yet salty with an earthy aftertaste that was even worse. "Yuck."

"I know, but the doctor insists. Drink some more, Ari. You must get your strength up."

Ardenne did as bid. But only because Sarita asked ... and because she could feel it working on her almost immediately, adding warmth where there was none, soothing muscles that were screaming in pain.

Even so, she only had strength for a couple of sips. Swallowing was a struggle. "I can't," she muttered, pushing it away weakly.

"That's okay. Have some more later." Sarita lowered her against the pillows.

Someone pulled the sheet and blankets up under her chin. She tried to push them down. "Too hot." Fingers touched her aching brow. She longed for the cool of Gabriel's touch. Didn't want any other touch right now. She reached up to push the hand away. Something pulled on her hand. It itched. She pulled harder, trying to rid herself of the discomfit.

"Don't, Ardenne." Sarita's hand on hers. "It's the IV. You lost a lot of blood. The doctor gave you a transfusion and now you need fluid to help your body recover."

The site where the needle entered her skin itched like mad, but she stopped pulling.

"Good girl," Tomas said. "Now it's time to rest."

"Can I get anything else before you go back to sleep?" Sarita brushed loose strands of hair back from Ardenne's temple.

"Gabriel. Where's Gabriel?"

Tomas' disapproving sigh filled the air. "I knew this would happen."

"Hush, Tomas. He did what he did to save her."

Lord Hei's voice was a warm rumble to her right. She had to see him. Ardenne finally managed to open her eyes but saw only darkness. Where were the lights? Maybe there were no lights. The house might have no power if it hadn't been used for a while.

Through the haziness of her thoughts, she heard Tomas whisper, "I know he saved her, Hei, and I'm eternally grateful to him. But you know this can't be. *He* promised."

Her mind whirled. "Papa? What do you mean? Where's Gabriel?"

"Shh, my darling girl. You must rest. Doctor's orders."

"But, Gabriel?" She began to think the worst. "I tried to save him. I tried." Silent tears fell down her cheeks. "Is he ... is he ...?" She couldn't say the word.

"Shh, don't cry. You did your best. You fed him your blood," Sarita whispered, wiping her tears away with gentle fingers.

Ardenne looked up in the dark, could see nothing but a hazy outline. "But it was the wrong blood. He needed Sire's blood."

"He had no right to ask it of you."

"Tomas." Lord Hei's voice was a low warning before Ardenne felt him at her side. "You did what you could, my precious one. You gave him exactly what he needed. Nobody could ask more."

"But it wasn't enough. Not nearly enough." The words fell out of her, rambling, unsteady. "I called out for help, but I couldn't reach anyone. I couldn't do it. Hadn't practiced the right things. Nobody was coming and I ... and I ..." She began to weep.

"Hush, my child. You will make yourself sick." Lord Hei's cold hand grasped hers.

"But Gabriel ... he saved me and I failed him. I failed him."

"You didn't fail me." Gabriel's voice came from across the room, the door snapping closed behind him.

"Gabriel!" She lurched forward, desperate to see him, to touch him, but Tomas and Sarita held her back, pushing her down into the pillows. "Let me go!" she cried.

"You're not well enough to get up, Ardenne," Gabriel said, his voice a soothing balm, despite the fact it was husky and a little weak.

"Neither are you, Gabriel. You should be resting," Lord Hei said.

"I need to be here. Don't make me stay away any longer."

"Tomas, help him over." Tomas' grasp tightened on Ardenne's hand.

"I don't need his help," Gabriel said firmly. Lord Hei sighed.

Ardenne squinted hard as Gabriel moved closer, but the room was still too dark. She could only see the faint shadow of movement, the barest of outlines, but could hear by the jerking sound of his footsteps, the weak huskiness of his voice, that he was still recovering. She wanted to see if that terrible, green-tinged paleness had left his skin; that his eyes were no longer burning with a hellish flame. "Can someone turn on a light or bring in a candle. I can't see."

Uncomfortable silence.

Sarita shifted, allowing Gabriel to take her place. His hand enfolded Ardenne's and she gripped onto it, holding tight, wondering if perhaps the entire thing had been a dream.

Was being with him and gaining sight a delusion brought on by what Anita had done?

No. It couldn't have been a delusion. He was sitting beside her, holding her hand, not flinching away from her touch like he'd always done. He lifted her hand, pressed a kiss against her skin, rubbing her knuckles against his cheek in a way only a lover would.

If they'd been lovers, then she *had* been able to see. "Please turn the light on," she whispered.

"The light is on, Ardenne."

"But I can't see you." Her voice hitched.

"You're too weak to use your empathic talents, but you can feel me. And I can feel you. Nothing else matters."

At any other time, those words would have thrilled her to her soul, but he didn't understand. Of course he didn't. She'd been able to see with her own eyes, and now ...

Something was terribly wrong. To have sight and then have it taken away—

She couldn't bear the thought, but she had to check. Entering Sarita's mind, she flinched from the wash of bright light coming from the lamp on the bedside table illuminating the profile of the beautiful vampire sitting on the bed holding the pale girl's hand as he looked into her icy-blue eyes that were staring blankly up at him.

She didn't want to, didn't mean to, but she began to cry.

"Shh, Ardenne. Please, don't cry." Gabriel's cool fingers brushed her cheeks.

"I could see you after ..." She had no words for what they'd done. "When I woke up after you saved me, I could see."

The silence hissed with meaning.

"You imagined it." Gabriel's voice was a husky whisper.

"No, no! I saw the room, the Venetian glass light hanging from the delicate ceiling rose, the deep red brocade on the bed, the diamonds and stars on the carpet beneath us."

"Lord's blood! She's describing the room we found them in," Tomas blurted.

"She had to be using someone else's eyes," Sarita whispered.

Ardenne shook her head. "No. Gabriel was unconscious and nobody else was here. I know what I saw." She swallowed hard, concentrating on the vivid memory. "There's a casement window on the far wall. The sunlight fell through lace curtains that shifted and swayed in the breeze. Everything pulsed and glowed with life, with light. I looked down, Gabriel. I saw you. I thought my heart would stop."

"You saw me?"

Her breath shivered from her lips. "Yes. I saw you, the way the light caressed the planes of your face ... Your beautiful face. Now there's nothing but shadow."

He sucked in a sharp breath. She reached out, ran her fingers along his cheek, over his lips. "The day you came to take me to *Firenze*, I thought I imagined what you looked like. I thought it was just a fancy. Nobody could be that beautiful—an angel's face with eyes of luminous violet, a fire at their heart. But it wasn't a fancy. I did see you because, as I learned later, I saw you through Sarita's eyes. But last night it was different. Sarita sees you as a friend. I see you as a lo ..." She couldn't say it. Didn't know if he felt the same way about what they shared. He wanted her, she knew that, but he'd also felt terrible guilt and remorse. So she couldn't give him that piece of her until she was more certain about his feelings. She swallowed hard. "I see you as something else. I saw you with my eyes. I know I did."

Someone gasped.

"It's true. Blood is the key. Anita's blood—"

"Sarita!"

Sarita's outburst was cut off by Lord Hei's peremptory tone.

"Forgive me, my Lord, but what if the proph—"

"Enough!"

Lord Hei's angry tone rang through the room. She'd never heard him like that before. What was going on?

She didn't ask—couldn't ask. She was as tongue tied by his anger as everyone else seemed to be.

Finally, Lord Hei broke the silence. "I apologize for my anger. But your questions can keep. Ardenne must rest. We can get to the bottom of all this later. Now, everyone, leave."

"I want to stay," Gabriel said.

"My Lord," Tomas said, his voice stiff. "He can't stay. As you say, Ardenne needs her rest and I'm quite certain she won't go back to sleep with him here. Besides, what if he says something."

Fear rose in Ardenne's throat at the thought of Gabriel walking out and not coming back. He'd told her he'd tell her the truth. Not to mention, after what they'd shared, she had to know it meant something to him. Had to know what he was feeling behind that inscrutable facade of his. But she couldn't ask with everyone here.

Gripping tight to his hand, she said, "I want Gabriel to stay."

There was a heavy pause. She used Sarita's sight again so she could see what was going on, feeling the loss of her own remembered sight as a heavy weight in her chest. She hadn't dreamed it. She hadn't.

Lord Hei was looking between Gabriel and Tomas, a silent conversation seeming to pass between them. It made her shiver.

Fearing Tomas' obvious dislike of Gabriel might make Lord Hei send Gabriel from the room, she clasped her lover's hand tighter and said, "Please? I need him to stay."

Lord Hei looked at Gabriel and he nodded. "He may stay if he allows you to rest. Sarita? Tomas?"

Tomas swore under his breath, "I hope you know what you're doing," he shot at Gabriel before leaning in to kiss Ardenne on the temple. "Don't stay up talking. You need to sleep."

She nodded, even though she didn't feel like sleeping at all, her mind cleared of all fog, her limbs buzzing with all the questions unanswered.

Tomas stepped back and headed for the door. As he did, Sarita leaned in to kiss her. "Call if you need me." Then they were all gone, the door closing with a quiet snick as she pulled out of Sarita's mind.

Ardenne's thoughts spun with all that was said, all that was unsaid. The loss of her sight was a heavy weight in her chest; she had to know what Gabriel knew about it. Whether there was a way she could get it back. She knew he had to know something. Sarita's outburst told her that much. And the way the others had reacted, shutting her down, then Lord Hei's anger when Sarita persisted, told Ardenne it was something they didn't want discussed.

But Gabriel had promised to tell her the truth when he pulled her out of Filippo's mind. He couldn't keep lying to her now—could he? Not after what they'd shared. She had to find out.

"You said you'd tell me the truth."

"I never—"

She put her fingers to his lips. "Don't lie to me, please. I know you were protecting me then, but now, I know so much more. I know the danger. There's no need to protect me from knowledge of my mother and what she might tell me anymore."

He was silent. Too silent.

"Gabriel. Please. You believe me, don't you? That I could see?"

Silence once again. And then, "Yes. But it doesn't matter."

"Doesn't matter!" She pushed upright, away from him. "How can you even say that?"

"Sight won't make things better, Ardenne. Believe me. There are things I wish I'd never seen."

"Said as only a sighted person could. You have no idea what it's like, only being able to see through other people's eyes. It only gives me half a view. When I saw with my own eyes ... I can't explain it. And now it's gone, and ... I feel like if I can't see again, I might die."

"Shh." Cool fingers cupped her face, brushed over her lips. "Don't say such a thing."

She wanted to melt into his caress but couldn't let herself fold in that way. She shifted away, sat up straighter in bed, pulling her legs up, arms wrapped around them. "Why not say it? It's true. It's why everyone's protected me so much for all these years."

"That's not why."

"Then why? You can't tell me that the fact I can't see makes you all think I can't protect myself properly. I know you all think that. It's always hurt me because it's true. I'd fight better if I could see. Be a better Bartolli Prime. I wouldn't have to rely so much on others."

"You don't need to rely on others now."

"Don't I?" She uncurled her fingers from their tight grip around her legs, reached up, touched his face. "I don't just want to see through touch, through smell, through other people's eyes. I want to see with my own. What I saw when I woke after ... when it was just you and me ... the wonder and beauty of seeing the full spectrum of colors in the light it was ..." She sighed and shook her head. "To see that room, the light coming in through the window, to see you. How can I be happy knowing I might never see the gift of your face with my own eyes?"

"You see me in your dreams."

"It's not the same!" She slammed her hands down on the bed. "It's not the same."

He grasped her hand, held her fingers against his face once more. "What we look like is only part of who we are. Not seeing me again ... It doesn't matter. I'm here. Can you feel me here? You don't need to see me to know that. Don't need to see me to feel my care." He kissed her fingers.

Ardenne's lips trembled, his words tearing at her heart.

"See me in your mind like you did before. That was real. You know it was."

"Not real enough!" She pushed away from him, clambered out of bed only to be stopped by the drip in her arm. She wrenched it out, ignoring the quick jab of pain, the copper scent of her blood.

"Ardenne. Don't—"

"Don't what? Don't want more? Don't want the truth? Don't want to see when it's all I've ever wanted?"

"But you can see. Your power—"

"It's not enough. I'm not enough!" She turned away from where she could hear him standing on the opposite side of the bed, fist to her mouth to stop more words from spilling out. She was giving away too much.

Gabriel's fingers were gentle on her shoulders but still she jumped. Then, embarrassed, she didn't have the will to stop him as he turned her to face him.

His breath brushed over her face as he said, "You can't believe that's true. Not after what you did at that monastery. Not after everything you've accomplished."

The scent of him ... it was almost like a drug. But she wouldn't let it cloud her mind like it had before. Because there was too much she needed to know. And he had the answers. So she cleared her throat and focused on what he'd just said.

"What I did at that monastery was because I had Seer's Blood." She laughed at his sudden tension. "You don't think I worked it out? I wasn't sick with a migraine, was I? That was Seer's Blood, wasn't it? It took me over, didn't it? That's why I can't truly remember what happened, and why there was such terrible pain, such terrible loss afterward. It was a part of me for a while. But I remembered when I felt that again last night. Seer's Blood ... It's alive. It speaks to me. It's the great fighter, not me." She gasped a little as she realized something. "Is it part of you in there? Did you give it to me as a way to help poor little blind deluded Ardenne?"

"Of course not. I never saw you that way." He sounded hurt.

She didn't care. She snorted. "That's hard to believe."

"It's true. I have never felt that way about you, no matter what you think."

She frowned. "Then why give me Seer's Blood if not to keep track of me in some other way?"

His fingers tightened on her shoulders a little. "I gave it to you because you are strong, because I knew it belonged to you. Seer's Blood is a living soul, but not because it has any part of me in it. It worked with me for a while, but the minute you were born, I knew it wasn't truly mine. It told me that."

"It speaks to you?"

"Yes."

"Does it speak to everyone?"

"No. Only those who are worthy."

"Worthy of being taken over."

"No. Worthy of wielding control. It only took control that first time you tried to wield it because I'd kept it hungry for too long and you weren't ready. I'm sorry about that. But that night, at the monastery, you were its master, not the other way around. It didn't take you over. If it had, you wouldn't remember what happened, would you? And you would have been sick again, like you were before."

"I was sick last night."

"But that was different, wasn't it?"

She nodded slowly. It had been different. And he was right, she did remember every moment of what happened at the monastery and after. "But I've never been trained to fight like that. Piven has taught me much, but some of what I did ..."

"It guided you, that is all. I saw what you did. That was all you. Seer's Blood just complemented your already prodigious skill."

His words stopped her racing mind. "Prodigious skill?"

"Yes. Why do you think Piven agreed to train you? He has only ever trained a handful of people, and never anyone outside the coven. You are special."

"Because I'm Anita's daughter and he was in love with her."

Her words hung bitterly between them. He sighed. "I'm sorry you think that, but it's not true. Not entirely. Piven would never have trained you if it was, even though you are Anita's daughter. You are special."

"I could be more special if I had my sight," she said stubbornly.

"You have no idea what you are talking about."

"Then tell me." She gripped his hands before he could pull away, held them tight to her chest. "Tell me. You promised you'd tell me about my mother. But I found out about her the hard way."

"I'm sorry for that. I never intended you to find out that way."

"No. I don't doubt that. But don't you see, if you or someone else had told me, I would never have gone out last night to save her. She would never have been able to trick me, to feed on me and give me her blood." She gasped as Gabriel stiffened. "Her blood. That's it, isn't it? Her blood gave me sight."

Gabriel was so still he could almost have been frozen in time, but then, almost too soft to hear, he said, "Yes."

His affirmation hit her like a blow. She staggered back. Legs hitting the edge of the bed, she sat down with a plop. "Is it just hers or any vampires?"

"It has to be blood from a certain bloodline."

"So not just hers then. And you kept her from me? Kept this knowledge from me? Why?"

"You met her last night. She fed on you. Surely, I don't need to explain why we wanted to keep her from you."

"She's insane."

"Yes."

"How? Lord Hei's blood wouldn't turn someone insane. In fact, it would help cure insanity, wouldn't it?"

"Perhaps. It would depend on the mental illness."

There was an edge to his voice that told her he wasn't being entirely truthful. "She said Lord Hei isn't her Sire. That's true?"

"Yes."

"She said she wasn't Wild or Dark Brethren."

"She isn't."

"Then who?"

A pause and then, "She is something else entirely. Different from any of the cults or Lord Hei's children."

"You're still not telling me the truth, are you?"

"I'm telling you what I can. What I definitely know. I can't do any better than that."

She took a moment to take that in. Fury was a tight ball in her chest, and she wanted to deny his words, yell at him for lying, but his voice was so full of pain, of sorrow, of guilt, that she realized he was doing the best he could. Swallowing the fury down, she asked, "Why is she insane?"

CHAPTER 34
PROPHECY

The Blind One comes, this I see clearly
And Seers Blood, it comes to her dearly
The loss of her love will darken her soul
The gaining of love will make her whole
Both of these futures could be true
To know which, there is no clue

Maybe both of them should be.
Extract from The Middleton Manifesto, Prophecy 44, Book 1

Gabriel paused so long, she thought he wasn't going to answer. But then he said softly, "You don't need to know this."

The angry spark lit in her chest again, her hands fisting at her sides. "You promised to tell me about her."

He swore, something soft and fierce she didn't catch. "You're still so weak. You don't need to hear something that might upset you."

"Gabriel." A warning; a plea. "I'm not breakable. Don't treat me like I am." She couldn't let him do that. Couldn't let him make her feel less. She'd spent too much of her life feeling that way already.

"I think you know I don't want to do that." He took her hand in his, curled his elegant fingers around hers, thumb brushing her palm. It sent shivers through her, made her mind haze, her attention waver so that she almost forgot what they were talking about.

Almost.

Pulling her hand from his, her body still shivery with expectation, she waited.

He sighed. "Something went wrong with her transformation. We think it might be partly because she didn't want to be turned. She hated vampires."

"She was forcibly turned?" Then she remembered the images she'd seen last night when joining with Gabriel. "You did it, didn't you? You were the only one there. There was so much blood. You saved her."

"Yes, but I did it against her will. I did it because the baby—you—begged me not to let her mother die."

"She didn't want to live?" It hurt. More than it should. Because if her mother hadn't wanted to live, that meant ... "She didn't think it was worth being here for her baby. For me?"

"She wanted to stay with you. More than anything. But she didn't want to become one of us either. In turning her to save her life, I condemned her."

His voice, so utterly bitter with self-condemnation. It made her hurt deep inside. But she couldn't let her empathy distract her. "How did turning her condemn her?"

"What I said before about her not wanting to be turned having an affect ... well, it's only part of what we think caused her to be like she is."

"What do you mean?"

His fingers squeezed around hers compulsively and for a long moment he was silent. Then he said softly, "Whatever makes me different from the others is now in her too. I was never supposed to make another. The prophecies are quite clear on that. It is Forbidden."

There was so much in that sentence, too much to tackle in one go, so she latched onto the only thing she could understand. "And you think that's why she's insane? Because of your blood?"

"Yes." He cleared his throat. "That, mixed with her attitude to vampires and the fact she never agreed, created the Anita you met last night. It's my fault. I am to blame for the danger she poses to you."

She couldn't believe it. She'd seen, in his own mind, felt the terror and hatred for what had been done to him, the never-ending regret that Lord Hei had saved him without truly explaining what he was to become. Knew he would never do that to another, except ... "You said you did it for me. That I asked you. How? I was a newborn baby."

The tension in him became even tighter, so tight, the air between them crackled with it. She thought he wasn't going to answer but then he said, "When you were born, a bond snapped to life between us." There was a shifting sound. On anyone else, she'd say it was the sound of someone shifting nervously. "I think you've overheard enough to know what I'm talking about."

Her skin heated and she lowered her head. "Yes."

"I never wanted you to know about that. I never wanted you to feel bound to me or obligated in any way. I tried to stay away so it wouldn't strengthen. Tried to allow you the choice I was never given."

"Choice? You mean about me? About being bound to me?"

"I didn't want you to think you felt something because of the bond. I didn't want you influenced in any way by it."

"As you are influenced?"

"Yes. No. I ... I'm not explaining this right. The bond ... it doesn't need to mean anything other than it binds me to you as your special Guardian. That's what it is meant to be. That's what it should be."

"But for you, it's more."

He paused for so long she didn't think he'd answer but then he said softly, "Lately ... yes. I didn't want it to ... I didn't mean it to ... but yes."

His words were multiple barbed bolts to the heart, tearing and ripping. He was bound to her, but he didn't like it. She'd always known. Even when he'd made love to her last night, he'd been sorry, had fought against it.

She drew back. "Right." She wished her voice didn't sound so lacerated. "So, you're saying it's best if we ignore it."

He made a sound of frustration. "I don't know. I don't know what's right anymore."

"You're sorry we made love last night."

"Yes. No. I don't know. *Merda*, Ardenne. I don't want to talk about this right now."

"Right. Because hiding from it and running away has worked well so far for both of us."

There was a strange sound, like a choked laugh. "Christ, you are so like your father."

"You know who he is?"

Deathly stillness greeted her statement. The silence cut at her. For a moment, she almost thought he wasn't there, except she could still smell him, still feel the impact of his presence buzzing under her skin. "Gabriel?" A horrible thought crept over her. "It's not Piven, is it?" That would explain so much.

"Piven? Why on earth would you think that?"

"Because he loves her. Because he treats me like he has a right over me."

"That's because he's an asshole, not because he's your father. And I wasn't talking about your birth father, anyway. I was referring to Tomas. You're as stubborn as he is."

Tomas *was* stubborn. "He doesn't like you."

"No."

"Why?"

"Because he's afraid that if you're with me, the rest of the prophecy will be true too."

The prophecy again. "You keep mentioning a prophecy. What are you talking about?" Silence again. She was getting sick of it. "You can't mention it and then not tell me. You promised. The truth."

"Yes, I did. Didn't I?"

He moved then. She was certain of it, even though he moved too silently for her to hear. She felt it. Then his voice came from over near the window. "Long ago, Lord Hei helped a witch called Mary Middleton. It was a time when women were accused of being witches and were put to death, burned at the stake for little more than playing with herbs. Many witches were caught up in the witch hunts and rather than give away their entire covens, allowed themselves to be taken and killed. Others used their powers to escape, creating even more fear and panic. Some lashed out, killing the humans that should have been under their care so as to not risk one of the humans turning on them. It was a terrible time rife with superstition, mistrust, and fear for human and witch alike."

His voice had shifted, soft and far away somehow as he spoke. "Mary had been clever. She'd stayed clear of the witch hunters without endangering or turning her back on the humans in need of her help. But that left her open to other hunters, equally as vicious and hateful of those with power."

"The Wild and Dark Brethren."

"Yes. Lord Hei saved her from a group of Wild who were hunting her with the intention of making her their sex slave and forcing her to use her powers on their behalf. When she realized what Lord Hei was, she wasn't shocked as most would be to discover there were vampires out there who were good, who had humanity's best interests at heart because she had read in her family grimoires of the Vampire King who had helped her coven in the past. She had actually been looking for him to talk him into a more permanent agreement to help her and her coven fight the demons that would destroy our world. She managed to bring other covens into the fold and together they created the Cousins —warriors and scholars from fading witch bloodlines who would be intermediaries between the Middleton Coven and his vampires."

Ardenne felt like a light had gone on inside her mind. "Carrington and Anita are her descendants."

"Yes."

"But what does this have to do with the prophecy you keep mentioning?"

"Mary Middleton, while a powerful witch with control over the elements, was first and foremost a seer. Her Sight was triggered by her meeting with Lord Hei, and she began to speak prophecy about the future with a frequency and accuracy that she never had before. The future she saw mostly involved Lord Hei, his family, his followers, the Cousins, her coven, and the war that is to come."

"War? What war?"

"Between the cults and witches and humanity. Mary foresaw a time when the world would be brought to ruin because of this war. Humanity becomes aware that the myths of vampires and witches are not myths, they discover us and, fearful, try to destroy us all, Dark Brethren, the Wild, witches, and Lord Hei's family alike. In this future, she saw us fighting back, joining with those we would never usually join with to survive. Once that happened, humanity would lose and those with the greatest power would come to rule the world."

"Lord Hei would never join the Dark Brethren and Wild."

Gabriel chuckled. "That's what he said. He also said that prophecy is not set. It's just one possible future. And yet, Mary was adamant that it was a very definite possibility if certain things came to pass."

Her mind spun at the thought. "What things?"

A long pause and then, "You. Your birth. Your life. Your decisions."

"What?" The word stuck in her throat. Surely she hadn't heard him right?

"She saw you. The blind witch. You were the nexus around which all might stand or fall."

"Me? But that ..." She couldn't take it in. They had to be mistaken. "That can't be true. I can't be the reason for the war."

"You're not," he said gravely. "Not entirely. But the prophecy does state that the blind witch given sight would make or break the war."

"Given sight? Do you mean ...?"

"Yes. Mary saw that by drinking a certain bloodline of vampire blood, the blind witch would gain unique sight."

"But ... but how do you know that's me? Surely there have been other blind witches?"

"Yes. There have. But there were other things in the prophecy that indicated who this might be. Your parentage, how you came to be, was part of it. That you were born of vampire and witch was one." Her father *was* a vampire! She wanted to ask about that, but he kept talking before she could. "The other was that once this blind witch was born, a bond would snap into place at birth with a certain singular vampire who had been made by one cult but was tied inextricably to another."

All thought of who her father was flew away. "You? She meant you?"

"Yes," he said, something hesitant and almost shameful in the sound. "It was for these reasons that Lord Hei perpetuated the idea that witches and vampires could never be friends and certainly not lovers. He was trying to ensure that part of the prophecy would never come true. That you would never be born. Because if you were never born, a bond would never snap into place between you and me, you would never gain your sight, and there would be no war."

"That doesn't make sense. How could a war break out because a blind witch gained sight by drinking vampire blood?"

"Because in gaining sight you would be the proof that a being could be created who was more powerful than anything that had come before. And neither witch nor vampire could allow such a being to be drawn to one side more than the other. For to gain control over the hybrid would mean the ability to destroy the other side in the fight."

"But I ... that can't be ... it can't be me. Because I was born. And you don't have ties to another cult." Except a horrible, scratchy sensation rising from her stomach and raking over her nerves told her that wasn't true.

"But I do. You saw how I was born into this world. Lord Hei turned me when I still had Wild blood and venom in me. He had no idea what it would do at the time, but it made me different from my brothers and sisters. Made me crave human blood and need Wild and Dark Brethren blood to sustain me. Your mother is the same, because of me."

The panic was rising, setting fire to her nerves. There was a hot burning in her chest, and she realized she'd stopped breathing. She dragged in a painful breath through a throat thick with burgeoning fear and said, "That's not possible. You say my father is a vampire but ... I'm not part vampire. I eat. I don't need blood. I can't be this nexus thingy. It's not true." She was standing. She couldn't remember standing. And her voice was rising, shouting. "It's not true. You're lying. Why are you lying?"

"Ardenne." He cupped her face, his breath a cool brush over her heated skin. "It's okay. It's okay." He pulled her to him, wrapping her shaking body in the cool steel of his embrace, his hand brushing over her hair.

And Lord's blood, she couldn't push away like she knew she should.

She wrapped her arms around him, fingers clawing under his shirt to touch skin, to dig into his muscles, as if she could draw strength from him.

He held her closer, tighter, his lips brushing over her hair as he soothed her with body and voice. "I know. I know it's a lot to take in. We don't have to talk about it anymore right now. You probably need to rest anyway."

"No." The word came out muffled, her lips mashed up against his chest. She shifted a little, still unwilling to move out of his embrace, but needing to make herself heard. "No. I'm sorry. It just took me by surprise. It's ..." she cleared her throat, "kind of hard to believe. You're telling me I'm part vampire. It's ..." She shook her head a little, her cheek rubbing against his chest. She wished she could burrow closer, nest inside him where his heart pounded with that strange, unearthly beat that shouldn't be. "Is that why you have a heartbeat?"

"Probably."

"And why you act like you do to my blood?"

"Yes."

She took a moment to let that sink in. "And why you've fought the bond?"

"Partially. Mostly. Yes. If it wasn't real, the rest of it couldn't be true."

"My father ..." She swallowed hard, tasting the bitter bile of the question that needed to be asked. "Did he rape my mother?"

"No. You were made from love."

"But how? Anita hated vampires. How did she fall in love with one?"

"Love is blind. That's all Anita ever said when asked about it. I don't think she ever fully understood it herself."

"So, she never spoke about him?"

"When she realized what had happened, she knew it must be kept a secret, because if it ever got out she knew the cults would be after her, not to mention other witches. She knew, if her baby was born blind, she would be the key to everything. If she was raised in the right way, she could make the right choices to stop the war to come. She focused on the fact the prophecy said you could make or break the war."

"So I could stop the war?"

"Yes."

Ardenne shook her head. It was too hard to take in. "But I'm nothing. Nobody. Not important."

His cupped her face again, lips brushing over her forehead. "You are more important than you can possibly know."

"To the prophecy?"

"Fuck the prophecy." His lips met hers for a brief caress. "I meant to me."

"Gabriel," she breathed.

"Ardenne." His voice was a whisper of breath across her face just before his lips met hers.

It was a soft kiss, but brutal in the way it tore her resistance apart and took her under. Every part of her centered on the heated point of contact of his lips on hers, his tongue sliding into her mouth, stroking along her tongue. She opened wider, pushing harder against him. His groan vibrated through her hands which were splayed on his chest. "I thought you didn't want this," she muttered when his lips left hers to burn a path down her throat.

"It wasn't this I was fighting."

No. He was fighting something so much bigger. So big, she felt crushed under the weight of it. "We shouldn't do this." Certainly not when she felt so uncertain about everything.

He pressed his forehead against hers, breath brushing over her face in an intimate caress. "Sire's blood, Ardenne. Do you have any idea what you do to me?"

The evidence of it was pressed against her stomach. She smiled even though she knew she shouldn't be thrilled by the knowledge. Every nerve tingled, racing, tightening toward the center of her just at the thought of what they could be sharing if not for this terrible thing he'd just told her. "Perhaps you were right to fight it."

"Perhaps I was a fool. Perhaps Anita is right that the dye was cast at your birth and all we can do is ensure we are the ones who end up on top." His voice was bitter as he pulled away from her.

She ached with the loss of him, wanted to cry out, to reach for him, to pull him back and lose themselves to the madness of passion they felt for each other. Instead, she tucked her hands under her arms, determined to be as stoic and strong as he was. She pulled her thoughts away from the grief screaming in her mind and concentrated on what he'd just said.

"Is that why she wants me? Because she can use me?"

"Yes. The prophecy isn't always clear on the details, but it is clear on one thing. That the vampire's blood that is used to give you sight will help mold your decisions. That your power will ensure that cult or coven will end up on top when the war is won."

"And Anita intends to end up on top."

"Yes."

She bit her lip, trying not to feel the betrayal of that, the hurt. "Is that why Lord Hei has me? Does he intend to use me too?"

"No." His fingers gripped her shoulders again. "Never. He's never wanted any part of the prophecy to come true."

"He should have killed me at birth."

Gabriel's fingers tightened. "He would never have done that." The horror in his voice told her that was true, at least. "Others wanted to do exactly that, but he kept you safe from them. He loves you. He would never see you hurt by something you can't control."

"But he has plans for me?"

"Yes. But not to fulfill the prophecy or make him stronger. It's always about protection. Protecting you from those who would try to see it come true."

"Like Anita."

"Yes."

"And who else?"

"Only a chosen few know of your birth and connection to the prophecy. Lord Hei has made certain of that."

Ardenne shivered. He'd killed for her. "What else?"

She didn't need to explain, knew Gabriel would understand what she meant. "He brought you up in his house to keep you safe and to watch you, see who you were, what the influence of your bloodlines might mean. But you were just a beautiful child. A little mischievous and headstrong, but intelligent and so good. You won the heart of everyone who met you. It was hard to see how something so pure, so good, could be influenced to bring such evil."

"But he still thinks I can."

"Not because of you. But because of what others might do. It's the real reason your powers were kept from you for so long. Why you were kept so sheltered."

"And why I must be kept blind."

A pause then, "Yes. At the moment only a few people know what happened and none of them will speak of it, ever. And for your part well … you must never drink from another vampire again. To keep you safe, to safeguard our secrets from the world, to protect the humans, and to ensure the war never begins, you can't gain true sight."

She winced at the harsh truth of his words, wishing she could go back to a time when she knew none of this. To the time before she knew exactly how hard the loss of that wonder would be. It cut deep into her heart and soul in a way that would never heal. For a bright moment, she'd had the world and everything in it, everything she'd ever wanted, right there, ready for her to scoop up and create the most remarkable life out of and now … now she had nothing. Now she had less than nothing, because having had a true glimpse of what she was missing, she couldn't go back and be happy with her lot ever again.

She wanted to rail against the cruelty of it. Wanted to scream at Gabriel, tell him he was wrong. She wanted to tear apart the cruelty of fate that would stop her from reaching for the thing she wanted more than she'd ever wanted anything else—except him. Now she would always know that she wasn't quite whole.

And not being whole, she couldn't be with Gabriel. Because how could she be with him and fight at his side, and for his heart, knowing she could never be quite enough because she was stopped by fear and necessity from being who she was born to be?

The knowledge killed something essential inside her, the fluttering hope of her future a firefly, brilliantly ablaze for a second and then gone, the only reminder it was ever alive a ghostly imprint on the retina.

She was a ghostly imprint. That's all she could ever be because of a prophecy made hundreds of years before her birth. And unless she wanted to cause a horrifying war, she could never hope to be more.

"Ardenne. Did you hear what I said?"

She almost laughed at him then. Had she heard him? Nothing he'd ever said had had more impact on her. In one foul swoop, he'd taken away her hopes, her dreams, her determination, and had left nothing but a ghostly imprint in its wake.

Too tired to cry, too tired to even sigh, she just simply nodded and said, "Okay."

"Okay what?"

"Okay to everything you just said. To stop a war in the future, I will never seek to see with my own eyes again." She lowered herself back onto the bed and curled into a ball on her side, wrapping her numb fingers around her numb legs.

"Ardenne?"

His hand was on her shoulder, the cool familiarity of it sending arctic winter blazing through her nerves instead of summer warmth. She shivered. "I'm tired. I want to go to sleep."

"Are you okay?"

She shook her head, fighting tears. Voice thick, she said, "I don't know if I'll ever be okay again." She sniffed, desperate not to cry with him still here. "Please. Go. I want to be alone."

Hesitation and then, "I'll be just outside the door if you need me."

She couldn't answer, only managed a slight nod. The door clicked closed and she was alone. A shuddering breath escaped her, the tears a tight burn behind her eyes, across her forehead.

She closed her eyes against the final imprint of shadows that were the only thing left of her sight now and let the dark purple velvet of her blindness suck her under.

CHAPTER 35
TRUTHFUL LIES

*Truth and lies are difficult to encompass in a world so strange.
Some lies are truth and some truths are lies. Only time and
perspective will help us to discover that what feels like betrayal is
filled with good intentions, and what seems like good intentions
is a betrayal. Truth lies and lies tell the truth: a black hole we
must somehow navigate at the cost of our lives. At the cost of our
souls.*
Beware.
**Excerpt from Middleton Manifesto, Section On Truth & Lies,
Lesson 5**

Ardenne woke with a start, her mother's voice still echoing in
her ears.

Anita had been trying to get back into her dreams,
into her mind for the last two weeks since they'd returned to *Palazzo
Maimoona*. But Ardenne had been blocking her, using the techniques
Piven had taught her. She wasn't interested in hearing what her
mother had to say. Those cruel words of hope that just tore her soul
apart, piece by aching piece, with every treacherous insane utter-

ance. But her mother was nothing if not determined. She was starting to break through.

And The First help her, Ardenne wanted to let her. Which was why she'd only visited Filippo a couple of times since getting back because his belief in the vampire who had 'saved' him and his family made it harder to think of her mother as deranged and on the side of evil. His insistence that she go to her mother made her want to believe what her mother was whispering to her in the night. Those snatches and snippets she'd managed to get through Ardenne's blocks buzzed in her mind all day, raising hope again when Ardenne knew there could be none. It was killing her. She might as well pick Seer's Blood up right now and drive it through her heart as put up with this for one more night.

But tempting as that thought was, she couldn't do it. Couldn't bring herself to take her own life even though it would simplify matters for everyone. If she wasn't alive, they wouldn't have to be worried about the prophecy coming true. But she was just selfish enough not to want to die despite the fact everyone's worry and the need for secrecy scratched at her skin like an infection, spreading and shredding her nerves until she wanted to scream and scream and never stop.

It had to stop though. The only way she could get through this was if they stopped worrying and treating her like some broken thing. They had to stop the secret whispers. And she had to stop moping around like a dog who'd lost its master and its leg in one go. She had to pull her shit together and to do that, she needed to stop Anita and her poisonous whispers.

She sprang from the bed, jaw firm, a plan formulating in her mind. She stopped long enough to throw on some clothes and then headed toward the door. Opening it, she took a moment to breathe in deeply. Gabriel had been here not long ago. So had Sarita. They'd headed off to the left, the trail of their mingled scents stronger that way.

Following her nose, she decided to track them down. With luck, she'd find them together. With even more luck, Piven and Master Solari would be with them—or at least, nearby.

Smiling for the first time in weeks, she wished she could see their faces when she told them what she wanted to do.

~

"Come in. Ah, Gabriel and Sarita. Sit, sit."

Gabriel followed Sarita into Master Solari's study but didn't take the chair Vincente waved at. Instead, he stood, hands behind his back, trying not to let his growing agitation show. Sarita didn't sit either.

"This is most fortuitous. I just got off the phone from Lord Hei."

Gabriel nodded. He'd spoken to his Sire not long ago too. "He wanted to get my impression on how Ardenne is faring after what happened with Anita."

"I'm worried about her," Sarita said quickly, expressing Gabriel's worry.

Vincente nodded solemnly. "As am I, Sarita. She hasn't been herself, has she?"

Sarita's eyes darkened as she shook her head. "It's as if she's lost something."

"She has," Gabriel said. "She saw with her own eyes and now, to save everyone, she can never have that again. How would that make *you* feel?"

"Sad, then fucking pissed off."

Gabriel's lips twitched at Sarita's blunt answer.

Vincente waved his hand. "Yes. But she hasn't really got to the pissed off stage yet, has she? Piven tells me she is doing well with her training, but there is a spark missing. She hasn't even asked to use Seer's Blood again."

"I don't think she's even touched the sword."

Gabriel's hands tightened behind him. "She hasn't." He knew she hadn't. He'd been watching over her closely. Even when he was away, feeding, he kept the bond open, feeling for her. He'd have known if she'd so much as touched the sword.

"Do you think this lack of spark is because of what Anita did?"

"How can it not be?" Sarita said. "What her mother did was horrifying."

"Gabriel? What do you think?"

"I think what I said before: that the fact she'll never have her own sight is more an issue than specifically what Anita did. Her blindness has always made her feel different from everyone else, less—"

"Oh but that—"

He put his hand up, stopping Sarita. "Let me finish. It's not what any of us think or believe that matters. The fact is, her blindness—especially in the face of growing up surrounded by supernatural beings that for all intents and purposes are physically perfect—has made her feel isolated and alone and ... other ... to a great degree. It doesn't matter that we all love and cherish her and think her as capable and strong as she is proving to be. She has felt like this all her life. So when Anita gave her sight and it was taken away ..." He shook his head and tapped his fingers against the chair he stood behind. "It's a wonder she's not been more morose."

Vincente frowned, his fingers steepled against his lips in thought. He sighed deeply after a moment before saying, "True. But my greater concern is how she feels about Anita. I mean, she not only discovered she had a mother, but that mother had insane plans to use her to create a war," Vincente pushed. "That is certainly reason for her to be out of sorts as anything else. Maybe we just need to give her time to get a handle on that."

"I think she already has a handle on that, which is why the loss of her sight is even greater," Gabriel insisted.

"But she can still use other people's sight to see."

"It's not the same," Gabriel said, repeating what Ardenne had said, so heartachingly, to him.

"Sarita?" Vincente looked at her.

She shrugged, the worry creasing her brow, creating lines of tension around her mouth. "I think Gabriel is right."

Vincente's fingers tapped against his chin. "Hmm. That is worrying. I didn't realize her sight meant that much to her. I thought Piven's training had shown her just how extraordinary she was without it."

"I think, maybe in time, it will," Sarita said slowly.

"We don't have time though, do we?"

They both looked at Gabriel. He swallowed hard, shook his head. "No. Not with Anita still out there more determined than ever before. You know the Huntress side of her was exacerbated by the change into a vampire. Somehow either it or my blood has enabled her to keep some of her witch abilities too—I didn't realize until I sucked her venom from Ardenne. It was how she made it poisonous to me. How she's managed to evade me all these years too. My blood and her Huntress magic smacking up inside her is also a great part of the reason she is so unstable and difficult to reason with—as you know, Hei and I tried. We can't trust her to ever leave Ardenne alone."

"So, what are you saying?"

"He's saying we need to go after Anita." Ardenne's voice rang through the room.

Gabriel whipped around to see Ardenne standing inside the door. A door which he'd closed behind him when he'd entered. The fact she'd managed to enter without him hearing her, sensing her, just showed how off his game he was. He could tell by the expression on Ardenne's face that she had overheard more of their conversation than any of them would have liked. He also noticed that the spark that had been missing these last few weeks had come alight. Whether it was overhearing them talk about her that had whipped her anger up to light it, or if it had happened before she'd heard them talking, he couldn't know, but he was glad to see it, regardless of the cause.

Maybe the horrible itching ache he'd endured under his skin and around his heart would dissipate now she was more herself, and not the shadow of the woman he'd come to love.

Yes, he loved her.

How he ever thought to deny it when he'd accompanied her on her journey to *Firenze*, or that the bond had anything to do with his love for her, he didn't know. He was a fool.

He wished he could tell her but knew she wouldn't believe him. Not after what Anita had done, forcing his hand to tell her about the prophecy and her role in it. There was no way she could return his love. Hearing of his feelings would just make her feel worse, not better.

He had to keep his thoughts and feelings to himself. A torturous exercise over the last few weeks when all he'd wanted to do was take Ardenne in his arms and kiss her sorrow away. Explore the passion they'd touched on the night he'd sucked her mother's poison out of her veins. But he couldn't. He couldn't even try to discuss that night with Ardenne because more questions than he was willing to answer would arise. And he couldn't lie to her. Not again. Not after he'd promised her he wouldn't. So, he had to avoid while being never-endingly aware that he was the reason she was so horribly sad.

He'd taken her spark.

He'd do anything to give it back, but he didn't know how.

She turned her face toward him now, those glacial eyes finding him almost like she could see him. Her fingers fisted at her side, jaw firming as she took a deep breath and said into the continuing silence, "We can't let Anita stay free. She is too dangerous to everyone because of me. So, we need to capture her, bring her in. And the only way you can do that is by using me as bait."

Gabriel couldn't have been more stunned had an electric bolt hit him right then. Beside him, Sarita shifted, gasped, "Ari, no!"

Vincente stood and came around from behind the desk. "I'm sorry, but that is never going to happen, Ardenne."

Her blind eyes didn't move from Gabriel as she addressed

Vincente's statement. "I'm sorry, Master Solari, but you are wrong. Using me as bait is the only way it is ever going to happen."

"Do you know what danger that would put you in?"

"Ari, be reasonable."

"I am being reasonable. I'm just saying something you are all too afraid to say."

"Gabriel. Say something."

"Talk some sense into the girl."

Gabriel admired the way Ardenne's chin lifted, readying herself for him to agree with the others, to deny her what they all knew was the only way to capture Anita, to rid themselves of her threat. Readying herself for him to do what he'd always done, what they'd all always done—treat her like she was breakable. A victim. Someone to be pushed to the side, hidden away, never allowed to stand up for herself. Never allowed to be the strong, remarkable woman she had grown into. No wonder she'd always felt 'other'.

He would do that to her no more.

Smiling, he said, "I agree with Ardenne."

"Just close your eyes and think of Anita as you've done for the last week. Don't lower your blocks too quickly, or she'll sense the trap. Make her work for it. But once she's in, let her talk to you. Not just a whisper, but fully. This time you must let her talk you in to meeting her."

"I know the plan, Piven." She had come up with it after all.

She was still amazed by how quickly everything had turned around because Gabriel had agreed with her.

He'd agreed with her! It was still a stunning enough moment to take her breath every time she thought about it.

No questions. No doubt. Just surety that what she suggested was the right course.

Gabriel believed in her.

It was still too new a concept to feel real. She kept waiting for him to change his mind, to realize he'd been rash in trusting her. But he hadn't. He'd just been there, solidly behind her, as she'd outlined her idea to everyone. It had been his insistence that had changed Master Solari's stance, and then Piven's. Even Sarita had agreed to be part of the plan, though she was worried for Ardenne. Not because she didn't trust her—Sarita had never had any doubt about Ardenne or her abilities. But simply because she cared. Ardenne couldn't fault her friend for that.

Gabriel had even taken the argument to Lord Hei. She hadn't heard the discussion but given how Lord Hei behaved with her before he returned to *Casa Cinque*, she could only imagine. However, after Gabriel spoke to him, he agreed to the plan.

Tomas, however, was not happy. Like Sarita, his attitude stemmed from worry about her, but it was still difficult to deal with his disapproval when he'd never disapproved of anything she'd done before. Thankfully he was back at *Casa Cinque* and couldn't leave there because Lord Hei had gone on one of the secret trips he went on every few months. So Tomas had no choice but to stay where he was and content himself with phone calls. Nothing her papa said swayed her or any of the others, not with Gabriel standing firmly behind her, but still, she wished he wasn't so worried. She wished he could trust in her like Gabriel did.

It was still the most astonishing sensation to be trusted in that way. Especially when she wasn't quite sure she was worthy of such trust. There was a part of her that longed so much to have her true sight returned to her that she wasn't sure what she would do when confronted by her mother and the possibility of drinking her blood.

"Ardenne, calm your breathing. You won't be able to convince Anita you are giving in to her if you are too excited or nervous."

"Sorry."

"Don't be sorry. Be calm. Center yourself and try again."

Piven's breath brushed over her face as he leaned over her, his fingers cupping her cheeks as he entered her mind. "Good." He slipped back out quickly before he could leave more than the kind of trace that would be there due to his training her.

"You can do this." A hand gripped hers—Sarita—and squeezed. She squeezed back, wishing it was Gabriel. But he couldn't be anywhere near her for this part of the plan. Anita would be able to sense him if he was too close. She had to believe he'd left Ardenne with Piven and the Cousins to oversee her safety while he went hunting for Anita.

She tried not to think about how much she missed him, even though she knew he would be there on the night as backup. But she couldn't think of that either. She had to fill her mind with thoughts of grief and desperation. Had to make herself feel the desolation she'd been trying not to feel ever since Gabriel had told her the truth about why she could never gain her sight. Anita must think Ardenne was ready to be swayed. To be lured back to her side again. It was the only way this would work.

Opening to a pain she wished she'd never experienced, she sank into her mind and cried out into the darkness.

It didn't take long for Anita to respond. Didn't take long to ensure the first part of the trap fell into place. It was almost too easy.

Acting like she was giving in, she agreed to slip out the next night when she was supposed to be asleep. Agreed to meet Anita at the monastery where the beginning of the end of all her dreams had begun. She didn't play too easy to get though. She still made it clear she wasn't certain Anita wasn't simply insane—she had fed on her after all. But she let enough of her desperation show to make Anita think she had a shot to bring her over to her way of thinking.

An hour after she'd closed her eyes, she sat up and said, "Tomorrow night."

CHAPTER 36
TRUST

Trust is a strange thing I struggle to get my head around. As is true of love. The two are inextricably intertwined—which is perhaps why I've never truly experienced either. However, I know there can be trust without love, and there can be love without trust. The former is perhaps friendship. The latter ... well, that is a painful, deadly thing I would not wish on my worst enemy. I hope, despite my vision of last night, she will not discover the truth of the latter. Because if she loses all trust, none of what we fight for will matter. It will be the end of everything.

As I read back what I wrote, I know it sounds overdramatic. But it also feels true.
Extract from Mary Middleton's Diary, February 14, 1566

Gabriel lifted his head, took a deep breath and sighed as he took in that scent that was forever twined in his soul. Ardenne.

Her unique scent drifted back to him as she wended her way through the orchard back to the monastery where her life had changed so dramatically. There was a slight tartness to the scent now—not fear. No. Since deciding what had to be done, she had shown no fear. The tart bitterness he could smell in her scent now was more like tears washed away with determination.

She didn't like what she was about to do, but she was going to do it anyway, because it was the only way they could all stop Anita from wreaking havoc on the world.

His love was remarkable. He didn't know many young women, not yet twenty—her birthday was the end of next week—who would take such a weight on their shoulders and not complain. She'd had her night of tears, a couple of weeks of what could only be called depression, and then she'd pulled herself out of it and had come up with a plan to ensure everyone, not only herself, were safe.

She wasn't just remarkable; she was the best of everything he'd ever known. It was little wonder he loved her. He wanted to shout his love to the world, to claim her as his own forever, but he couldn't do that.

She wouldn't believe him.

Not now that he'd shattered her trust. Not when he'd been the one who had told her the truth she wanted to know and brought so much pain to her life. He'd killed her dream. He killed the idea that he could ever share his love for her. She might once have begun to feel something true for him, but that time was gone. He couldn't even blame anyone else. *He* was at fault. He'd known she should be told about her heritage years ago. About her mother and the prophecy. But he'd allowed his Sire—and everyone else who knew— to talk him out of telling her.

They'd wanted to protect her. Instead, they'd hurt her more piercingly than when Anita had sunk her fangs into her neck, shared her blood, and given Ardenne the sight she craved and could never have.

And there were still things she didn't know. Things he couldn't tell her.

At least those things centered mostly around him. She knew everything pertinent to herself.

Almost. But that wasn't his secret to tell.

An owl hoot pierced the air—Piven's warning that Ardenne had reached the top of the hill.

Silently, he slipped through the shadows cast by the overgrown orchard trees. Ardenne's honeysuckle and wild jasmine scent tantalized his senses as he ran up the hill, but now, he could also smell something else. A hint of jasmine with hot spices.

Anita.

And there was something else. Something that grabbed at him, stroking him sensually; warmed firs, the musk of sex and rare, night-blooming orchids.

The Wild.

She'd brought some of the Wild with her?

He still didn't know how or why she'd involved herself with them. She'd once hated the vampire cults with everything in her. This turnaround was as baffling as why they were allying with her. Why would they do such a thing when her ultimate goal was so different from theirs? How could they not know they were dealing with the devil?

Or maybe, they weren't here with Anita at all. Things hadn't turned out so well for her or them on the train and then again in *Firenze*. Maybe they were here to take revenge. He hadn't killed an even number on the train, or in *Firenze* the night they were trying to lure Ardenne to them. The two Ardenne had seen him kill weren't the first or last he'd taken out that day. If the ones who had died still had living partners, they would want to make whoever they thought responsible for the death of their mate pay. And Anita was most definitely responsible for putting them in his way.

Fanculo.

They couldn't be allowed to get anywhere near Ardenne. They couldn't be allowed to figure out who she was and take tales back to their Grand Sire. Or, The First forbid, capture her themselves.

A strange sense of doom surged through him, pulling at the bond, an insistent throb in his head, making it difficult to concentrate on anything except finding Ardenne and ensuring she was safe. But he couldn't do that. He had to let the trap spring. Had to support her plan. If he ran in there now, he'd not only ruin everything, but he would lose Ardenne's trust forever. It was already on a knife's edge. He'd almost lost her when he told her of the prophecy. He'd gained back some ground by backing her against everyone, including Hei. He couldn't stab at the healing wound now.

Gritting his teeth, he made himself stop.

He wanted to take care of Ardenne. The best way he could do that was to kill the Wild before they figured out what was really going on here. She wouldn't know they were here. And they most definitely couldn't be allowed to get away.

He stopped gritting his teeth and smiled in anticipation. He was hungry. The Wild who had foolishly come here tonight thinking to gain the upper hand with Anita would sate that hunger very well.

He sniffed the air. The Wild were moving in on the monastery. They might have followed Anita's scent here, but they couldn't fail to notice Ardenne's rich scent. Even though they couldn't know who she was, they'd find it difficult to ignore the enticement of such a scent.

Their smell was so thick in the air now. His throat tightened with thirst. His eyes burned with the fire of the hunt. His fangs distended with a sharp click. Venom, both bitter and sweet, welled in his mouth.

He came to the edge of the trees. Moonlight cast a pale glow on the tumble of stones from the crumbling wall. An owl hooted in the distance—a real one this time, not Piven's signal.

Piven. Had he spotted the Wild yet? He and Sarita were stationed across the plaza in one of the derelict buildings, their scent hidden by the mud and rust they'd rubbed over themselves. He wished there was a way he could warn them not to wade on in and ruin Ardenne's plan.

He just hoped that they understood if they tried to interfere now, Ardenne's confidence and trust in all of them might never recover. Worse, her confidence in herself would be destroyed. Given he couldn't warn them, he had to trust they would do the right thing.

Gabriel stood in the shadows, nostrils twitching as the sweet perfume of the Wild called to him. They were moving closer to the church now. They were moving stealthily—not a tactic they normally used. That wasn't the only unusual thing though. Now he was closer, he could smell multiple different scents.

There were more than the usual two or three couples that traveled together. This smelled more like a dozen couples.

Could they know what the prize truly was? Could they have divined the truth about Ardenne?

A growl erupted from him. They couldn't get her. They couldn't have her.

He sprang forward, flying up and over the debris of the crumbling wall. He landed silently on the other side. Heard something move to the left. Turning, he saw a male Wild crouched in the shadows.

The male hadn't seen him. He was gesturing to a female hidden in the shadows of the church wall directly opposite. The scent of other Wild was all around him. They surrounded the church. The one gesturing appeared to be the leader of this unusual group. If Gabriel took him out, it might send the others into disarray—they were pack animals after all.

Speeding forward, he was on the male before he knew he was there, sweeping out with his hand with such lethal force, the male's head was ripped from his body before he could utter a sound. The scent of his blood filled the air, creating a burn of thirst in Gabriel's throat, but before he could feed, a guttural cry of grief told him the male's partner had seen what he'd done.

She lunged at him, fingernails glistening like steel knives in the moonlight, ready to tear him to shreds. He darted to the left. She overbalanced and fell past him, her swing going wild. As he stepped up behind her he noted that none of the other Wild had noticed the scuffle—they were too focused on the church where Anita was waiting for Ardenne. He wrapped his arm around her, squeezing so hard she could barely move, then grabbed her hair in his other hand, tipped her head to the side and sank his fangs into her neck. A cry caught in her throat as she scrabbled at him, but it was too late for her—his venom was poison to the Wild and Dark Brethren. As she went limp in his arms, he grabbed her head and tore it from her body.

Licking the blood from his mouth, he noticed Piven and Sarita looking down from a window on the other side of the plaza. He cast the female's head aside like he'd done the male's and surged forward, intent on finding more Wild before they managed to interfere.

As he hunted, there was another sound that caught his attention —the sound of a foot scuffing on the cobblestones. A sound he knew so well. A sound that only meant one thing. Ardenne was in the plaza, not in the church like she was meant to be.

He saw her then, walking up to the portico of the church, standing there for a moment before turning and walking back to stand in the middle of the *piazza*. In the moonlight her skin shone like pearls, her glossy hair tied back in a tight bun looked like shimmering shadow and her eyes, those incredible glacial-blue eyes, focused unerringly on the church doorway.

A moment passed and then a figure appeared to stand beneath the portico.

Ardenne didn't move. She stood there, tall and certain, her scent calling to him more strongly than ever before. It had changed once again. It was no longer like honeysuckle and jasmine as it had been when she'd left *Casa Cinque*; or rich and sweet like honeyed *panna cotta* with a tinge of spice it had become during her training with Piven. It had deepened further in the last few moments since he'd left her, and smelled of everything it had plus more; summer-ripened wheat after the rain; wild orange blossoms on the spring air; long hot afternoons in the tropics where the kiss of seawater on a lover's skin brought a surge of heat that had nothing to do with the summer sun. The whole combination became something unbearably enticing.

He realized with a jolt, she had finally come into herself, into her powers. There was no more fear. No more self-doubt.

She was incredible.

And even though he knew the Wild moved to attack, he didn't move. Couldn't. He had to let her deal with Anita, deal with the Wild who were about to make themselves known. Had to let her make the first move.

Vibrating with the effort not to act, a growl tore at his throat. But he didn't move. Wouldn't.

Not until she had taken the lead.

ARDENNE STOOD in the middle of the *piazza*—she'd decided not to get caught in the church by her mother again. She'd walked to stand just inside the door, stood there long enough to be noticed, and then walked out. It was a risk. Her mother might have decided Ardenne changing the arrangement like that wasn't to her liking. But given all their interactions so far, Ardenne was willing to bet Anita wouldn't be able to stop herself from following.

She took in a deep breath, noting the mixed scents surrounding her—the dust of the broken walls, the tang of rust, a faint scent of mud and dried leaves she knew was Sarita and Piven. She'd been able to smell Gabriel right up the hill through the orchard, his scent calling to her, but the familiar freshness of him was no longer in evidence.

And there was another strange scent she couldn't quite grasp. Possibly Anita. Although, she couldn't remember her mother's scent being so sweet. Maybe because she'd been covered in blood.

She waited, sightless, until she heard her mother's footsteps as she walked out of the church toward her.

With an ease that no longer surprised her, she clicked into Sarita's sight. Her friend was perched in a window in the building behind her, hidden in the shadows, but looking right at them. She tracked Anita's movement from the church, slow and uncertain as she drew closer. Her mother's expression was hidden from Sarita's sight, which was annoying. Ardenne would have loved to have seen her face, seen whether her features resembled her mother's or if she looked more like her unknown father. But that wasn't to be.

"Ardenne."

"Hello, mother."

"Why have you moved out here?"

"I don't like to be hemmed in."

"Smart girl." She heard the smile in Anita's voice. "Sasha has taught you well I see."

"I don't want to talk about Piven. I want to talk about what you did to me. What you offer."

"Your sight. It's something only I can give to you. Something only I *will* give you. You understand that now, don't you?"

"Yes, but I—"

Her words came to a choked halt as the strange scent she'd smelled before suddenly became so much stronger, so much headier and a voice cried out, "Anita! You betrayed us. Tonight will be your end."

Through Sarita's eyes, Ardenne saw a figure dart out of the shadows beside the church and leap at Anita. There was a glint of something metallic in the moonlight.

"No!" She moved before she'd even realized she'd done so, pulling Seer's Blood from its sheath on her back and swinging it around in a wide arc. It connected, sliding right through the creature. Its blood flowed over her hands, stinging. Its scent all around her, pulled at her, sending writhing warmth through her. The stinging on her hands and the scent pulled her out of Sarita's mind, but she didn't care she'd lost her sight. Didn't care about the pain burning her hands. She wanted to step forward, into that scent. She wanted to breathe it in from here to eternity. She wanted to ride the pleasure it offered her until no more could be wrung from her.

Her fingers loosened on the sword.

Seer's Blood cried out a warning.

Her hands tightened on the hilt, not truly under her control—her sword had taken her over again just in time. Under its influence, she stepped to the side, and before the creature could do more than stagger forward, she sent the sword arcing through the air again, cutting off its head.

Breathing heavily, she tried to grasp what had just happened. What had made her lose control like that? But there wasn't time to think further about it as another screech sounded behind her.

"Ardenne. Watch out!"

Ardenne pushed into the closest mind to her—her mother's—and saw one of the Wild leap down from the roof of the building opposite the church, its face a twisted show of grief and rage. Another figure flew out of the shadows on the opposite side of the plaza toward them.

Anita leaped at the one heading straight toward her, pulling a compact crossbow from her back. She took two quick shots which hit the Wild male in the neck and chest, but it kept coming at her. She clocked it across the head with the crossbow when it reached her. As it staggered sidewards, she dropped the crossbow, drew a short sword from the sheath at her side and shouting to Ardenne, "We're surrounded! Take care of yourself," she engaged with the Wild male.

Howls sounded close by. The echoing sound of pounding feet across stone. More were coming. Ardenne tried to grasp another mind she could use and found one wide open and ready for her.

Gabriel.

Through his eyes, she saw two more coming around the left side of the church. Another howl. The sound of fighting and blood stung the air, and so much of that intoxicating scent—it was overwhelming. But she couldn't let it take her over. Couldn't.

She breathed through her mouth to minimize its impact and turned to meet the Wild female racing toward her.

Beside her, Corinna appeared, pulling out a sword.

"Let her handle it!" Gabriel shouted.

Ardenne ducked as a clawed hand sliced through the air, just missing her head. Seer's Blood screamed its rage. She let it do what it did best. Following the suggestions that flowed through her like air, like blood, she pivoted and stroked down with her hungry sword. A head flew through the air to the side.

A noise sounded from the roof above. Gabriel looked up and she saw through his remarkable sight a female Wild clinging to the gutter. A feral snarl exploded from his lips as she sprang, aimed at Ardenne. Uncoiling from a crouch, Gabriel sprang into the air, catching the female in mid-air just above Ardenne's head. Ardenne ducked, rolled, the female's clawed hands swiping at the air over her head. Fear and hunger pounded through her veins, drying her mouth.

Her fear for Gabriel. But not only her fear.

Gabriel's fear. For her. He couldn't lose her. Couldn't.

As she rolled to her feet, a smile bloomed inside her, pushing at her lips. She wasn't just a ward to him, a burden he was bonded to against his will. His feelings mirrored hers!

She could hear him grappling with the Wild female behind her. Struggling more than he should.

No!

If he couldn't lose her, she equally couldn't lose him. Turning, she lifted Seer's Blood, ready to swipe out in defense of him. Another two Wild had joined in the fray, with more merging on them.

"Kill him," one shrieked as he ran. "He killed Anton and Steph. He fed on Tiff. He's the cannibal."

Others cried out at this, their rage and grief piercing the air. They converged on Gabriel. Behind her, Anita's laughter pierced the air.

It was a scene from her nightmare. Gabriel about to be over-run. He fought them all, with sword and body, but there were too many. Too many. They were trying to mob him, hold him down. If they covered him with their bodies like in her dream …

"No!" Seer's Blood sang through the air and sliced through an arm raised to tear skin from bone, blood spraying wide. Gabriel's hungry growl fed the air alongside the female's shriek. She sliced out with the blade again, taking off the female's head in mid-shriek.

A few of the Wild turned on Ardenne.

She cut through them like a scythe through dried grass. Arms, legs, heads, bodies hewn in half, fell right and left. She tried to kick them apart as she moved, separating the body parts to stop them from re-attaching themselves. But more were coming at her now and she didn't have time. Just had to trust that the damage her sword wrought would keep them occupied long enough for her to save Gabriel from the mob.

She was only half in Gabriel's mind now, only half seeing with his sight. The other half was melded with Seer's Blood, using sound and scent and vibration as Piven had taught her, with Seer's Blood's guiding help, to take down those who would take from her the only person she had ever loved.

The only one she ever would love.

The half that was in Gabriel's mind saw him tear off the head of one attacker, throwing it aside to smash up against the church wall, before turning to a female coming at him, eyes wild, fangs and nails gleaming like viciously sharp diamonds in the moonlight. He caught her hands, spun her around and pulled, tearing off her arms as his fangs sank into her neck.

The shock of him feeding didn't make Ardenne pull out of his mind like she had before. The sensations of his feeding surged through her; the excitement of the fight, the heady sting of power from the vampire blood, the rich wild taste of it in her mouth, the salty floral scent of it wrapping around her, binding them all together in this stolen moment as one life fed another.

Just then, Piven and Corinna joined the fray around her, and Ardenne was surrounded for a moment by a strange calm.

Gabriel lifted his head, his eyes finding her in the dark. Fear surged through him for a second—fear of her reaction to how he'd fed from the Wild—but then he relaxed because he saw her. Saw the smile. The triumph. The trust. It glowed from her pale face. As did the strength and confidence in her stance. Seeing herself through his eyes, she felt more like the person she'd always wanted to be. She lifted her head, meeting his gaze, wishing she could see his expression.

No. She didn't need to see it. She could feel it. Feel the pride. The love. The passion. The Wild's blood may have fulfilled a basic hunger, but only Ardenne could fill the hole in his heart and succor his soul.

Gabriel tore the Wild's head from the body, throwing it far to the edges of the *piazza*, the body to the other. There would be little chance the Wild female would be able to pull herself back together with her parts separated like that.

Footsteps pounded toward them, breaking the moment. He turned, and through his eyes she saw Sarita engage a Wild about to take Ardenne in the back. Ardenne had no idea her friend could fight like that. Gabriel's gaze found Piven. The witch assassin fought like a demon, using all his talents to fight three at once. Then Corinna leaped into his line of site, descending with double swords toward two Wild, flame burning bright in the light blue-green depths of her eyes.

Ardenne's fear for Gabriel swirled away. He wasn't going to be torn to shreds like he'd been in her nightmares over and over. She and her friends had stopped that from happening. They were beating this incredibly large group of Wild who had come for Anita.

Anita!

She spun, trying to figure out where her mother was.

Seeming to sense her need, Gabriel swung around, searching in the shadows and mass of fighting bodies, past Piven, Sarita, Corinna and a few others in the distance she couldn't make out, until he came to a circle of half a dozen Wild converging on one person.

Anita.

"Gabriel!" Ardenne screamed as Anita ducked the attack of one only to be caught by a kick from another. "Help her!" She wanted to capture her mother. She didn't want her dead.

Gabriel didn't even falter. He raced forward, reaching the attacking Wild before she could, taking one of them from behind with his sword; the head sailed through the air. A female Wild screamed her rage, turning on him, fingers outstretched, nails glinting like blood-red diamonds in the moonlight. Gabriel met her attack, but another joined in the fight.

Ardenne threw herself at the attacking female, caught her around the middle and took her down. They rolled across the cobblestones. The Wild female scrabbled at her with razor sharp nails, but before she could do more than tear at Ardenne's clothes, Ardenne kicked out, her foot making crunching contact.

"My face. You broke my beautiful face!"

"I'll break more than that." She lashed out with Seer's Blood. Lacking the sight to see what she was doing now that Gabriel was engaged in his fight, the blade caught on something but then swung free. The bright sting of Wild blood scented the air, but not strongly. She hadn't hit anything major. She focused on her other senses and the instincts thrumming through her from Seer's Blood and swung around, blade high and in a position to stab. The blade caught on something, and she pushed harder until the hilt stopped. Warm sticky wetness gushed over her hands. It stung, but she didn't care.

The female made a gargling sound. Ardenne twisted the blade before pulling back to swing the sword where she now knew the Wild's neck to be. More blood sprayed. The gargling sound ceased.

There was a dull thump as the head hit the ground, the body close behind.

The sound of the fight was loud all around her. She quickly kicked at where she knew the head had fallen, making certain to put distance between it and the female's body, then ran into the main fray that was still centered around Anita.

CHAPTER 37
BECOMING ONE

The Bond is what brings them together, but it will not shape more than his need to protect and her need to stay safe so that she can learn what she must. Something more must occur to tie them together even more strongly so they can always find their way back to each other; something that is so rare in this world, it is akin to the most precious of gems. Nae, it is even more precious.

If there was a magic I could use to give them this precious commodity, I would use it, because they, more than any other, will need the comfort and surety of it in the future to come.

I cannot see if they will become truly One; I only hope that they do.

Extract from The Middleton Manifesto, Section on the Bond, Lesson 1

Gabriel almost got caught by a Wild with a sword in his hand as his gaze once again went to Ardenne as she fought. She wasn't the fighter Piven promised she could be. She was better.

At the last second, Gabriel came back to himself and ducked the sword swipe. He then spun and drove his fist into the male's chest, fingers crunching through bone and sinew to wrap around the fast-beating heart before tearing it out. The male looked down at his heart clenched in Gabriel's hand, eyes widening in incredulity before dropping to the ground.

Gabriel threw the heart far away, picked up the sword the Wild had dropped and moved to engage another. He didn't worry that the body would try to get to the heart that belonged to it. The fight would be over long before it managed to meld together again, and Gabriel could put heart and body to the flame.

Right now, he focused on Ardenne, fighting with another female attacker close to Anita. He spied another Wild on the roof behind her, waiting to pounce.

Gabriel surged forward as the Wild jumped at Ardenne. He wasn't going to get there in time. He didn't have to. She spun out of the way, the Wild she was fighting stepping into the place she'd been standing. The leaping Wild caught the female's head in his hands instead, wrenching it from her shoulders before he realized what had happened.

The scream that erupted from his throat told Gabriel one thing. The male had just torn apart his love. And as he cradled the body of his mate in his hands, looking around for the head he'd thrown aside, Ardenne sprang forward, Seer's Blood whipping through the air. The male's head went flying.

Her blind eyes found Gabriel in the shadows and a smile flashed across her blood-splattered face.

"Ardenne, the blood." He was at her side in an instant, wiping the blood from her skin. It had to be hurting her; even just on her skin, it was dangerous to her equilibrium.

She stopped his frantic movement, fingers wrapped around his wrist, the touch stilling the panicked beat of his heart. "I'm fine."

He could see that she was. The adrenaline of the fight and her sword's influence seeming to protect her now from the worst of the blood's effect on her skin.

"We need to save Anita."

The look on her face was so impassioned, he couldn't help himself. He leaned into her and pressed his lips against hers in a hot, hard kiss. Her gasp filled his mouth, her fingers trembling on his skin at the impact of the touch. It took him that way too. But neither of them could get lost to this right now.

Even so, his smile was wide as he took her hand in his and stepped back. "Come on." Together they turned and engaged two more Wild trying to get to Anita.

The sound of flesh hitting flesh, the clang of swords and grunts of pain filled the air of the old monastery as their small team fought the Wild intent on taking revenge on Anita and capturing what she had come here for—Ardenne.

It was ironic that he was now trying to save the life of the very person he had been intent on capturing and killing since Anita had run off eighteen years ago after trying to give her baby daughter her blood. But Ardenne had asked. It was her will that was important, her choices. The prophecies repeated that over and over. He had to protect those choices. Had to stop her doubting herself. Doubting them and their intent. Doubting him. He'd done such a bad job of that over the years, allowing Hei and others to talk him out of telling her anything. He'd done that because he'd put his need to deny the prophecies and their impact on him and Ardenne over the reality that was right in front of him. When Anita had taken her, he'd been so afraid it was too late; that he was too late to do the very thing the prophecies instructed him to do.

However, now he saw clearly it wasn't too late. Through this fight, he could sense his love's—his soul mate's—doubt falling away and in its place, a true sense of herself that was astonishing to see.

She was incredible. More than incredible.

He was no longer going to pretend to force away the fact that he was hers just as she was his.

The sour taste of fear that had filled him for the last few weeks disappeared as he fought side by side with his love to save her mother. It didn't matter that he believed Anita was more of a danger to Ardenne than all these Wild put together.

All that mattered was what Ardenne had always wanted.

He'd saved Anita all those years ago because baby Ardenne's need for him to save her mother had overridden all else, even the Forbidden. He'd given in to that need partially because of the bond, but also because a child should never be without a mother. Even a mother changed by vampire blood that had mixed disastrously with the magic of the Huntress that was welded into the core of her.

That need was still in her. And he would give in to that need and cope with what came after. It was all they could ever do.

He turned, warding off a blow that came at him from behind, flipping backward over the male Wild, sword slashing. The male fell back, flesh laid open from chin to groin. His mate howled and lunged, talons extended. With fury racing through him, blood lust high, he dispatched her with equal calm. Spinning, stabbing and tearing, he did what he had been trained to do, what was in his nature to do, losing himself to the fight and the glory of moving in step with the remarkable woman at his side.

He spun to face the next attacker, only to discover there were no more. The scent of blood, acrid with copper and power, hung in the air, a miasma of delicious smells, surrounding him as it dripped from his fingers and fangs, making him want to feed. But he didn't. Instead, he turned to Ardenne. "We did it."

Her face was a beam of sunlight in the darkness as she smiled at him. "Yes."

"Where's Anita?"

He turned to face Piven as he jogged over to them and realized Anita was no longer in the monastery grounds. "*Merda!*"

"She got away while we were saving her? Typical," Sarita said as she joined them.

"She got away? All of this was for nothing?" Ardenne asked as she spun around, obviously trying to feel which direction her mother had gone, her despair clearly marked on her face.

Gabriel squeezed her shoulder. "It was a good plan. None of us could have known the Wild were after her too."

"Certainly not in those numbers," Piven agreed.

"Any idea how that many of them came together?" Sarita asked. "There must have been two dozen or more of them. I've never heard of such a thing."

"They probably wanted revenge for the attack on the train," Gabriel suggested. "Many of them died that day too."

Piven chuckled. "They're not going to be happy with her now."

"Anita was behind that?" Ardenne asked. "How?"

"We're not sure, but from what that one said to you on the train, we know she was involved," Sarita said.

"Speaking of Anita, I saw her run off that way." Corinna, fingers dripping with blood, pointed back toward the crumbling wall as she joined them. "I couldn't go after her because two more Wild came at me. But I think I saw a few Wild go after her."

Gabriel shared a look with Sarita and Piven. "They can't be allowed to get away."

"What about Anita?" Piven asked.

He shook his head. "The Wild can't be allowed to get to others of their kind and spread any stories about what happened here." His gaze went to Ardenne and the others all nodded, understanding.

"Let's go after them before they catch Anita," Ardenne said, face still tense with worry.

She turned, but Gabriel grabbed her arm. "Piven and Corinna will go. They'll make certain Anita isn't in danger. Won't you?"

"I want to go, too, Gabriel." She winced, staggered a little.

He pulled her close to his side, noted her trembling. Now the adrenaline of the fight was passing and her soul sword was returned to the sheath on her back, the blood on her skin was starting to take a toll. "We have to get that blood off you."

"But Piven and Corinna won't be able to bring Anita back by themselves."

"Probably not. But they will stop the Wild from hurting her, if she hasn't already gotten rid of them herself. They'll track where she's going." He wanted to touch her face, hold her closer, but he was covered in Wild blood, his fingers sticky with it. He didn't want to hurt her more than she already hurt. "This mightn't have gone exactly to plan, but we have all survived to try again. And taken out more Wild in one go than anyone has ever done before."

He waited for her to argue, but she simply nodded, her expression tight. "Okay."

"Piven? Corinna?"

"I'm already gone." Piven threw him a mock salute before taking off into the night. He moved off in a blur like a vampire. His powers were obviously still at their peak despite the epic fight. Gabriel shook his head. If he didn't already know Piven was something remarkable, that would have told him right there.

"I'll call to let you know what happens," Corinna said before taking off after him. She'd have to move fast to catch Piven.

"Well," Sarita said, putting her arm around Ardenne. "How about we get home and clean off this mess. The smell is making my head swim."

"You didn't get it in your mouth, did you?" Gabriel asked.

"No. I was careful. What about you, Ardenne?"

"No. I didn't get any in my mouth. But it's really stinging now."

"I can imagine." Sarita winced.

Ardenne frowned, hand held out toward her friend. "You're hurt."

"It's nothing."

Ardenne pulled at Sarita's jacket to show a large gash in her side, her clothes blood-soaked. "Sarita!"

"I'll be fine."

"Yes, you will." Ardenne clapped her hands together and placed one over Sarita's wound and another on the bare skin of her forearm. Gabriel's skin buzzed as magic was summoned. A golden glow surrounded Ardenne's hand, covering the wound.

"Ardenne. Don't," Sarita gasped. But she couldn't stop Ardenne because she'd already done it. The long, nasty gash began to close before their eyes.

"How?" Gabriel said, gaze finding Sarita's stunned eyes.

"She's channeling my power. Using it on me."

"I didn't think that was possible."

Ardenne winced and the golden glow died. She staggered back from Sarita. Gabriel caught her before she fell. "There," she said, satisfaction clear even through her exhaustion.

"How did you do that?" he asked.

"Piven had mentioned I could channel other people's powers to help me fight. I did it the night I came here to save Anita from the Dark Brethren. I figured if I could do that, then I could do this." She winced again, staggering as she tried to take a step away from him.

"Ardenne!" Sarita grabbed her arm, held her steady.

"I'm fine." But she didn't shrug away Sarita's help.

Gabriel wanted to pick her up but knew she wouldn't like that. She was strong. She didn't need him to carry her. "I'll walk you back to the cars."

"You're not coming?"

"No. I must clean up the mess here. Make sure these Wild don't mesh back together."

"We'll help."

"No. You get back home and clean up. It won't take me long."

"Okay. A shower sounds good. Lead on, McDuff."

He smiled as he followed Sarita and Ardenne out of the ruins and down through the orchard back to the car. When their lights had disappeared around the bend, he headed back to the slaughterhouse that was the crumbling monastery and set about the task of burning the Wild.

Damn their interference. If not for them, Ardenne's plan would have worked. It was going to be even harder to catch Anita now she knew Ardenne wouldn't be tricked by her. He'd worry about that later, though.

He collected all the heads in one pile and all the body parts in another and then lit them on fire. They went up with a whoosh, the fire licking quick and hot at the Wild as if they were dried timber. Very soon, there was nothing but ash floating in the air. A good downpour, and no one would ever know what had gone on tonight.

Except Piven, Sarita, Corinna, and Anita. And none of them would say anything, not even Anita. None of them would ever discuss what had been proven tonight when Ardenne had been fighting like one born to it—that the prophecy spoke the truth about her.

Anita must be gloating right about now. Not that it would do her any good. She would never again get close enough to Ardenne to use the knowledge she now held. The others who were here would help him make certain of it. He'd seen it in their eyes before they left, the agreement to keep Ardenne safe.

Ardenne was the nexus, the center of everything. A step had been taken tonight, one that could never be taken back. It was up to them to ensure it was a step in the right direction, not the wrong one.

He sighed, the glow of the fires hot on his face. Ardenne had changed tonight, just like the prophecy said she would in battle, but the change was more than that. It was a choice she had made. A profound shift had happened inside her, a strength and confidence in who she was, who she could be.

"I have to encourage that to grow," he whispered into the night. "Have to help her achieve her goals." She must never wonder if she was good enough or chase after his love and trust ever again.

As he turned his back on the guttering flames, he looked up at the heavens above him and said, "I vow to The First that I will never shy from my love for her, or my duty to her, ever again."

It was a vow he would never break.

CHAPTER 38
RETURN

In her twentieth year, she will return to take up that which is hers
by birthright.
Fear her coming. She is a warrior born.
Extract from The Middleton Manifesto, Prophecy 1, Book 2

Ardenne showered as soon as she returned to the Cousins'
compound to wash off the Wild blood and the dirt and
sweat of the fight. Once done, she found Sarita waiting for
her to treat her injuries and insist she eat the meal she'd brought up
for her—sandwiches and a restorative tea. Sarita then made her go
to bed.

"I don't want to sleep yet. I want to wait for Gabriel to return."
She needed to talk to him.

"You need to sleep," Sarita insisted. "You can barely keep your
eyes open."

She was right, damn her. Because as the door snicked closed
behind her friend, Ardenne's eyes drooped closed. She sat up, grabbing one of her braille books from the bedside table to read, but

before she'd read more than a page, her eyes closed and sleep took her under.

In the darkness, her mother came to her. Not just a voice this time, she showed herself to Ardenne.

"Anita," she said as her mother, dressed in a flowing white dress, sauntered toward her out of the darkness, stopping only a few paces away.

"Can't you call me Mother? Or maybe even Mama?"

Ardenne regarded the woman before her, the fall of long dark hair, the perfect porcelain of her skin, the deep violet blue of her eyes —eyes similar in color to Gabriel's—that glowed with a fervor close to madness. "Mother."

Anita smiled, a genuine smile, the madness falling away to be replaced by love. "You did well tonight."

"I know."

Anita's smile widened. "You are the true daughter of the Huntress. I am so proud."

She would have asked what a Huntress was but her thoughts jagged on Anita's last words. "You are proud of me?"

"You doubt it?"

Ardenne shrugged. "I tried to capture you."

"You saved me. That speaks volumes more than why you think you came tonight." She reached for Ardenne's hand. Ardenne pulled away. Anita frowned. "Do you not trust me? Trust that I love you? That I want only what's best for you?"

Ardenne shook her head slowly. "No. I don't. I don't know you. I don't know what you want of me."

"Yes, you do."

Ardenne watched her, trying to gather meaning from more than the words being spoken. "Why are you here?"

"Because, despite what happened tonight, despite the fact you tried to trick me, I wanted to let you know I forgive you."

"I don't need your forgiveness."

Anita's smile dipped, her expression suddenly so sad, it was almost heartbreaking. "I know. I need *your* forgiveness. But it seems circumstances and prophecy will forever keep that from me." She sighed. "I do want your understanding though. I won't give up coming to you until I have it."

"I won't come to you. I won't do as you ask."

Anita tipped her head to the side, smiled again. "We'll see."

Ardenne bit her lip. "I wish things were different. Wish you could have been a true mother to me but wishes can't change the past. I'm sorry for what happened to you, but I can't give you what you want. And I won't let you in anymore. This is goodbye."

Anita reached for her, but she stepped back.

Anita hissed her frustration. "We are meant to be together. Don't you feel it? I won't let you cut me off."

"You have no choice." She let the power flow from her, building a wall around herself, around her mind. The vision of Anita began to fade.

"Ardenne! No. Don't do this! You need to listen to me. You need to know the truth." Anita's voice turned from a shriek into an echo as the wall built around her.

"I don't need to know anything from you." She pulled on more power, keen to see this done.

"They're lying to you."

"Gabriel has told me all about the prophecy."

Anita's eyes widened, panic flaring in their depths as she scrabbled around for something more to say, something to change Ardenne's mind about what she was doing. "They can't have told you everything. They are still keeping truths from you. What about your sight? And the blood. You're in danger. I'm the only one who can save you from the danger of your heritage. Don't do this. Don't believe them. You need to come to me. You need—"

Anita's words were lost as the final chink in the wall fell into place, the ghost of her presence disappearing, locked out forever from Ardenne's mind.

Ardenne woke with a sob.

"Ardenne?"

She turned in the direction of his voice—that glorious voice. "Gabriel. You're here."

"Of course. Where else would I go?" She felt his weight next to her on the bed as he sat beside her. "I didn't mean to wake you."

She wanted nothing more than to throw herself into his arms, lose herself to the madness of his touch. But she had to tell him about her dream first. "I just had a final confrontation with Anita."

"*Merda*, Ardenne." His hands captured hers, held them to his chest. "Are you okay?"

"I'm fine."

"What did she say?"

"The usual. Nothing I haven't heard before." She breathed in deeply, his scent filling her lungs, pushing away the sadness. She wanted to ask him about the Huntress comment, but now wasn't the time. Instead, she said simply, "I had to say goodbye."

"You've blocked her out?"

"For good."

He let out a sharp breath. "I'm glad."

"She loves me."

He paused, before nodding. "Yes. But her love is tainted with the madness that changed her when I forced her to become a vampire. If I'd realized what would happen, I would never—"

She freed one hand to place it against his lips. "You did what you thought was best. For me. I can never be angry with you for that." She dropped her hand from his mouth, the imprint of his lips still hot against her fingertips.

He didn't move. Neither did she. She still wasn't certain what he wanted where she was concerned. She'd spent a year fighting her feelings for him, then had spent the last few weeks resigning herself to the fact that their one night together was the last they'd ever have. But since he'd backed her plan, and after fighting with him side by side tonight, that passionate kiss they'd shared, she wasn't so certain.

Suddenly she was sick of sitting around torturing herself by wondering. Even though the thought of him not wanting to be with her hurt more than cutting herself off from her mother had, she could deal with it, just like she'd dealt with Anita.

She was strong. She'd survived against the odds tonight, had fought as an equal, had tipped the balance of the fight. And though Anita might have gotten away, not all was lost. She now knew exactly what she was capable of; that her blindness gave her strengths sighted people didn't have.

She wasn't less because she had a disability in a world of perfect supernatural beings. She was more. And if others didn't see that, it was their loss, not hers.

As this sense of herself filled her, she sensed that his gaze was roving over her profile, studying her. She knew she could shift into his mind, use his eyes to see what he was doing, that he wouldn't stop her. But she didn't need to do that. She just simply had to ask.

"Gabriel."

"Yes." His low, musical voice thrilled her, the breath that carried it a cool caress against her face.

"Do you love me?"

"Yes."

Her breath caught. She almost faltered, almost gave in to the need to be in his arms, her lips on his. But it wasn't enough. She needed to tell him all. "I love you, too."

He moved closer, hand gripping tighter to the one of hers he held. "You do? But—"

Her free hand splayed on his firm chest, stopping his words. "It's not because of any bond. I know that with everything in me. It's because for me, there will never be anyone but you in my heart."

"I know. I feel the same."

"You do?"

"Yes." His smile glowed in his tone. "I have been so stupid, so stubborn, not seeing the truth when it was staring me in the face. The bond that snapped into place when you were born doesn't make me feel what I feel for you. It is only there to allow me to fulfill my duties as a true Guardian; to allow me to gauge your wellbeing. It allows contact, but it doesn't feel." He cupped her face, his fingers tracking along her cheekbone, across her chin, jumping sparks left in their wake. "What I feel is because of who you became as you grew into an adult. Not because of the bond. Or because some prophecy says so. But only because you are my soul mate, the one I choose and who chooses me. I see that now."

He pressed closer, but she still held him at bay, her hand against his chest. "I love you, but I won't be looked after by you. I can stand on my own two feet."

"I know. I love that about you."

"Good. And I want to keep training."

"Of course. Although, I want to be in on that training now."

A smile curled the corner of her lips. Her heart pounded faster at the thought of being trained by Gabriel. "Of course."

"And there will be times I'll struggle not to protect you, even though you don't need it."

"As I will protect you, even though you don't need it."

"You saved me tonight."

"I only killed some Wild. We all did."

"I don't mean that. I expected that."

"As you should." The pleasure that filled her at his words expanded out of her skin like a golden glow.

His thumb brushed over her lip, and he managed to inch closer, even with her hand still pressed to his chest. "I meant you saved me. I have always been the Lonely Angel. The lost one among all my siblings. Since Lord Hei sired me, I have never felt like I belong; never had a home."

"But you do now."

"Yes. With you. Always with you."

His words wrapped around her, and she wanted to laugh, to dance, to sing. Instead, she smiled up at him and whispered, "I feel the same. Always with you." He pressed closer, but she held him back. "You no longer want to escape me?"

"Never."

"Good. Because you know I'd always chase after you. You are mine, Gabriel. And I'd do anything to stay with you."

"Me too."

He moved then, and she let him, her hand slipping up to his shoulders as he leaned in and kissed her brow, her nose, her cheeks, his lips finally coming to hover over hers. A low growl escaped him. Then his lips met hers and she was lost in the wave of desperate passion his touch always incited in her.

They tore at each other's clothes, eager to be skin to skin, heart to heart and then he was inside her.

She met him, kiss for kiss, touch for touch, rising with him, stroke for stroke, the pleasure of him deep inside almost too much to bear.

"I love you, Gabriel. I want you. I need you. Now. Always. Forever."

"Now. Always. Forever," he repeated.

Then there were no words, nothing but mingled sighs and skin sliding over skin and a joy so profound, Ardenne knew she would never be the same again.

Hours later, after making love twice more, she lay snuggled in his arms, too exhausted to move. But that was okay, they had forever— although she didn't know if she was ever going to get enough of Gabriel's touch, the feel of him inside her.

Gabriel's hand brushed lightly along her arm, and despite the tingles it created, she slipped into an exhausted sleep.

In her mind, she flew through the velvet dark to burst out into the vibrant visual landscape of her dreams.

The visual resolved into one she knew so well. She stood on their hill above *Firenze*. Gabriel walked toward her, gaze searching her face. She held her hand out to him and he took it, his beautiful face glowing with love as he came to stand beside her.

She turned, breathing in deeply, content for the first time in her life to be who she was. She smiled now to think she'd ever thought of herself as blind Ardenne, dependent on everyone around her. She had never been that.

She was a powerful warrior-witch capable of anything she put her mind to. And she was in love with, and loved by, one of the most powerful vampires on Earth. She could fight against the darker side of the prophecy alone if she wished, but with Gabriel by her side, she would never need to.

In the distance the sky grew dark. Thunder rolled, closer and closer. But as Gabriel's arm slipped around her, and she slipped hers around him, holding him close, protecting as she was protected, she knew they could weather the coming storm.

Together, there was nothing they couldn't do.

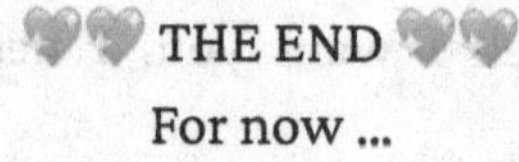 THE END

For now …

I HOPE you enjoyed Ardenne and Gabriel's story as much as I enjoyed writing it. If you did, Stay tuned for more of their adventures and their fight against the coming war in:

The Blood of the Sire
Due out 2026

But if you can't wait for that, I have something special for you right now: free exclusive bonus chapters from **_The Blood of the Seer_** —turn the page for more information on how you can get access to this amazing bonus content.

· · ·

BUT BEFORE YOU do turn the page, if you've got a moment, I would love it if you could leave a review for ***The Blood of the Seer***. Reviews can help readers find books, and also help tell me where I'm going right and where I'm going wrong. I am grateful for all honest reviews. Thank you in advance for taking the time to let others know what you've read, and what you thought—you can leave your review at **Goodreads**, **BookBub** or the ebook retailer where you bought your copy. You can find links to the ebook retailers **HERE**.

NOW TURN the page to find out how you can access your free and exclusive bonus chapters of ***The Blood of the Seer*** right now!

WANT TO READ MORE OF THE BLOOD OF THE SEER?

If you want to read the emotional and hidden truth of what happened when Ardenne was born, then use the QR code, fill in your details and these exclusive bonus chapters will be winging their way to you soon after.

What is the exclusive bonus about?

Well, the scene that first came to me when I began to write *The Blood of the Seer* was the one where Ardenne was born. That scene morphed into two over the various iterations and even inspired me to write *The Huntress and the Vampire King*—the prequel novel.

These birth scenes were so important to me and stayed through every iteration of the book until the final edits where I realised they no longer belonged in the book.

They are still important though and I wanted to share them in some way with readers who have loved TBOTS as much as I do.

Don't miss out. Grab your exclusive bonus scenes from the original beginning of TBOTS through the QR code or the link below:

GIVE ME THE EXCLUSIVE ACCESS BIRTH SCENES
https://www.subscribepage.com/tbots-newsletter-signuppage

But wait! There's more …

If you're not into newsletters but think you might be into subscriptions that give you serialised content, exclusive chapters to new books, exclusive bonus content, signed print books and much more, then turn the page to find out about **Leisl's Legends** - you can also get exclusive early release chapters of the prequel novel to *The Blood of the Seer*.

Read on …

JOIN LEISL'S LEGENDS

Subscribe to (or follow) me (via the QR code) at my Leisl's Legends page on REAM—a new subscription app like Patreon except it's designed especially for readers and authors for an amazing reading experience—and you will get early access to ***The Huntress and the Vampire King***, my hot enemies to lovers, witch-and-vampire-licious urban fantasy romance that readers over there are already in love with. It's the prequel novel to the first book in the Blood-Rites Series - ***The Blood of the Seer***.

Be the first to find out where it all began with Anita and Hei's love story.

BECOME A LEGEND NOW!
https://reamstories.com/leislleightonauthor

You will also get exclusive early access to *The Middleton Manifesto* as it's updated with new prophecies, Middleton Coven Librarian notes, and so much more.

You will also find serialised chapters of the next book in my popular **Gods Cursed Series** there and can comment on the story as I write it! Not to mention you will also get extra bonuses like exclusive NSFW Bonus Epilogues, Bonus Prologues and cut scenes and chapters from all of my books.

Be part of creating the stories you love AND get exclusive access to a whole range of goodies including other WIPs, bonus content, voting rights, signed books and more.

Read on to find out more about The Huntress and the Vampire King PLUS read the opening chapters …

THE HUNTRESS AND THE VAMPIRE KING

She hates the vampire who saved her; he holds the key to her fate …

Hunter-witch Anita Middleton wants revenge against the violent vampire cults that murdered her father and has worked hard to become one of the best vampire hunters there is. But on a difficult hunt she is caught in an ambush and is mortally wounded ... only to be saved by a mysterious warrior. A warrior with brilliant blue eyes and long silver-blonde hair who fights with a grace and violence like nothing she's seen. It is only after she wakes in the heart of his palazzo that she realises her saviour is a vampire - and according to her brother and mentor, this vampire king is their ally.

Lord Hei rules over an empire of witches, humans and vampires who have been trying to keep the vicious vampire cults, the Wild and Dark Brethren, at bay for centuries. Then he saves Anita and knows with one look she is the prophecied Huntress who could be his downfall or his salvation - and she is also his fated mate. But she struggles to trust him as her hatred of vampires is deep-seated. And she *needs* to trust him because only he can offer the specialised training a Huntress needs so her power won't overwhelm her.

But with the Dark Brethren mysteriously amassing, he has little time to win her over. And Anita must go on a crash course to learn how to control her Huntress magic ... or go slowly and violently insane.

The Huntress and the Vampire King is the exciting action-packed prequel novel to *The Blood of the Seer*.

If you love your vampires hot with a bit of The Witcher thrown in and your heroines as kick-arse as Buffy and even more tortured, if you love fated mates, enemies to lovers, chosen ones and epically hot romance mixed with action and mystery, then *The Huntress and the Vampire King* is what you've been waiting for.

Sign up to Leisl's Legends and start reading exclusive early release chapters of it now!

BECOME A LEGEND NOW! https://reamstories.com/leislleightonauthor

Want a little taste of **The Huntress and the Vampire King** before you head over to **Leisl's Legends**? Then read on for the first few chapters ...

THE HUNTRESS AND THE VAMPIRE KING

A BLOOD-RITES SERIES PREQUEL NOVEL

PROPHECY

A prophecy of love
A prophecy of hate
A prophecy of will
A prophecy of fate
One made him for duty
But Five's soul is bound
To the broken Huntress
Once her magic is found
Neither will wish for it
Neither will see
Their love is eternal
So mote it be.

Extract from The Middleton Manifesto, Prophecy 2, Book 1

CHAPTER
ONE

Anita thrust with the sword then caught the sneaky attack with the hilt of the dagger she held in her other hand. Spinning to the left, she dropped her hand, flicking out a small thrust of power as she went. The clang of her opponent's knife hitting the floor made her smile, as did the growl in his voice as he said, "Sneaky."

"I learned from the best," she said, swinging her blades around, one low, one high, aimed at stomach and neck.

And almost fell over when her opponent disappeared and her swing brought her around 360 degrees, her movement only stopped by the arm that pinioned her to a body as hard and honed as the steel blade in her hand.

She started to struggle but stopped when he pressed the sharp blade of his knife to her neck. "Not sneaky enough," Sasha whispered in her ear knocking her blades from her hands with his powers.

She laughed, looking up at him as the sound rang through the room. "At least not as sneaky as you. Or am I?" She pricked his thigh just above his femoral artery with the knife she'd palmed—dropped there from where she'd hidden it in the brace up her sleeve before their session started.

Sasha's lip curled at the corner. "There's my girl." Then he let her go as abruptly as he'd caught her, stepped back and bowed. "I believe you have bested me."

"I told you I could." She couldn't help the smile that beamed from her face as she span to face her brother, Carrington, who still stood just inside the door of the training room, arms crossed over his chest, a displeased scowl on his handsome face.

"It would count—except he let you win."

"Sasha would never be so crass." Anita was pleased her voice was so even—it would do nothing for her cause to lose her temper with her brother now—although, she couldn't stop her hand from tightening around the knife. "Especially not for something this important."

"He would for you. He'd do anything for you if you asked."

She wanted to yell at him, deny it was true, but ... he was right. Sasha wasn't only her instructor, he was one of her best friends. Actually, he was her best and only true friend. And she would like to think she was his best friend, except there was Carry of course.

Nothing she could do would ever create the bond they had. She'd been too young when her mother had brought Sasha home with her after tracking down a rogue witch assassin—an assassin which turned out to be Sasha. Her mother, Sarah, would have stilled his magic and imprisoned him—or killed him if necessary—but he was only fifteen and had been used by an evil coven of witches to do their bidding. Her mother had decided he was young enough to be retrained and so she had brought him home and into their family, calling him their brother, and taking him under her wing for the special training she was putting Carry through.

Carry, being the earnest and kind sixteen year old that he was —had embraced Sasha as a true brother and treated the lonely, scarred—mentally and physically—boy as a friend and confidant. It had taken a while, but eventually Sasha had responded in kind and given Carry his full love and loyalty and did everything with him.

Anita had wanted to be a part of their private group but her mother had said that at age ten she was too young and her brother—and Sasha—had treated her like an annoyance for some years. Persistence had paid off with Sasha however, who, while still treating her like a younger sister, stopped seeing her as annoying and saw the potential in her. He had even gone behind Carry's back after their mother died and trained her in the way of the witch hunter, seeing the desperate need in her to do something to avenge her parents.

Sasha had even worked on Carry to make him see how good she was as a hunter until he had no choice but to allow her to train formally. It had been the best few years of her life up until then, feeling like she was finally doing what she was meant to do. She'd done so well, she'd been invited to join the most elite team that Sasha had created—he assured her it was not his decision to ask her to join, but the team as a whole—and she'd hunted far and wide with them, chasing down and killing the vampire cult menace that was a scourge to witches and humans alike.

But then on a hunt without Sasha, their leader had led them into an ambush and half the team had been lost before they'd even realized what was going on. She'd almost lost her arm and had been stabbed in the stomach and only got away because a few of the surviving team mates had used their powers and pulled her out of there.

Carry of course had gone mental when he'd seen her and forbidden her to hunt ever again.

It had taken a year of healing and training in secret by herself, and then with Sasha who she had finally managed to rope in before Carry had come around to even thinking about letting her hunt again. But he'd set her a series of almost impossible tasks—which she'd set about passing one by one, today's being the last: that she best Sasha in a fight.

She actually hadn't been certain she could manage it. Sasha was the best fighter and hunter anyone had ever seen and his telekinetic skills were rather hard to beat. But then, she had something special too. Her ability to track people was extraordinary, as was her speed. Not to mention her powers lent themselves to battle magic—not something her mother or Carry for that matter had ever liked to admit. But her father had. He'd always called her proclivity for battle magic and her tracking abilities her little bit of special sauce that made the whole work.

Her heart throbbed at the memory.

She hadn't meant to think of him now; usually was much better at keeping any of those painful memories away. But her emotions were high today because of how much was at stake. It was much more difficult to keep the door shut on the bits of her past that could make her lose her shit—and her control—when that was the case.

She bore down hard though before the hounds of grief and ruin could come snapping at her heels and shoved the door closed to her memory vault once more—a trick she'd learned from Sasha. And masking all her emotions just like he'd taught her, she met her brother's eye and said, "Sasha would never lose to me even if I asked it of him. Not for this. Not when winning means I'm ready to go out hunting again. He would never put me out there if I wasn't ready. You do him a disservice by even suggesting as much."

Carry's gaze flickered to his friend—Sasha didn't so much as blink, but she was certain something passed between them. Not surprising given they were both so good at mind-speaking—something she really needed to work at perfecting so they couldn't keep having discussions she couldn't hear right in front of her.

But she didn't show her annoyance with them both. She just straightened her shoulders and waited for the verdict.

CHAPTER

TWO

Finally, Carrington sighed and nodded once. "Fine. You win. You can be a hunter."

"You mean, I am fit to go out hunting again. I already am a hunter."

"Are you really pelting semantics at me right now? Do you want me to take back my decision?"

"No." She grasped her hands behind her back and tried to look apologetic, but by Sasha's snort, she failed terribly. "So, can I join the hunt that's going out today?" A few of her old squad were in the team who were heading out to hunt a particularly nasty pack of Dark Brethren who had brazenly made a nest in Manchester. She was desperate to go with them. Killing Dark Brethren always gave her an extra thrill.

"I supposed so." He lifted his finger before she had a chance to squeal her excitement and jump at him to hug him. "But only because Sasha is going. In fact, over the next few months, you can only go out if Sasha is going, and you must pair with him at all times."

"What? That's ridiculous!" she argued, even though she actually liked hunting with Sasha. But it was a point of pride. She glanced at him to see if he would say something about this, but he looked steadfastly ahead and didn't even give a flicker of response over what was being said. "I don't need a babysitter," she said through gritted teeth as she returned her attention to her brother. "Only new hunters are placed under such a restriction—and I am well past my probationary period."

"Firstly, Sasha is not a babysitter," Carry said, his voice annoyingly calm and even. "And secondly, you *are* on a kind of probationary period given you are starting again after recovering from a serious injury and an extended period away from hunting."

"It was extended because of *you*, not me!"

His lips thinned and his nostrils flared as he breathed out a deep sigh then said, "With good reason. I almost lost you. My only sister. I could not bare—" He cleared his throat and shook his head, but not before she saw the hint of extra moisture in his eyes.

It brought a lump to her throat too, the thought of what Sasha had told her about how Carry had been in those days after she was brought back and, despite the many magical healings that were done on her, her life had hung by a thread. She hated the thought that she had brought such pain to him. But even so, he couldn't deny her the right to do the very thing she was born to do—the thing that came roaring even more to the fore after she watched their Papa slaughtered at the hands of those monsters. She stepped forward and touched Carry's arm. "Me too," she said softly.

He met her gaze for long, emotional seconds before nodding sharply. "Yes, well ... it's why I would feel more comfortable if you were hunting in a pair with someone I fully trust to look after you."

She understood the sentiment but it could make her look weak in front of the others, so she said, "That's not f—"

"Would you like me to make it six months?"

She bit her tongue and shook her head before saying belligerently, "No." She let out a steady breath and met her brother's determined gaze. Working with Sasha really would be no hardship—in fact, she could get so much better out in the field at his side than she ever would with any other member of the squad. She could concentrate on that and overlook the fact that Carry meant for his Second to babysit her and keep her on a tight leash—probably far away from the action.

But he forgot that the accusation about Sasha doing anything for her was right. And her Sasha would never hold her back from any aspect of a hunt—in fact, he'd be right there beside her helping to take down as many of their enemies as they could. He'd make a game of it as he always did, vying with her for the most kills. Kills that would not only save human and witch lives, but that to her, were justified revenge.

She wanted to slaughter those blood-sucking bastards just as they'd slaughtered her parents and half their household before her mother had saved them with her magic, helped by Carry and Sasha and their squad who had arrived back in time to help her.

She'd vowed that night, as she'd watched them cart her father's body away to be burned—along with all the others who'd been murdered—that she wouldn't stop until every single motherfucking bloodsucker on this earth was dead. By her hand and design if she had anything to do with it.

So, she simply nodded as she thrust out her hand and said, "Fine by me. I'd love to work with Sasha."

Carry's brows rose, his surprise quickly overshadowed by suspicion as he took her hand. "You will follow his every instruction."

"Of course."

He stared at her for a long moment, her hand still clasped in his as he searched her face and eyes for anything that would allow him to recant his permission. But finally, after an interminably long pause, he let go of her hand and nodded. "Don't make me regret this."

"I won't."

"Look after her," he said to Sasha.

"With my life."

One final glower in her direction then he spun on his heel and left the sparring room.

Unable to contain her glee any longer, Anita spun to throw her knife at the target on the wall—hitting it dead in the heart as Sasha had trained her to do—then threw herself into his arms with a laugh of joy.

Sasha, to his credit caught her and spun her around and around as if filled with the same joy as she—and why not? He'd worked hard with her to get to this point so it was as much his celebration as it was hers.

Finally, he put her down but held on to her shoulders until her head had stopped spinning. "So, Ms Huntress. What do you want to do until it's time to leave?"

"Sharpen my weapons so they'll slice through our enemies like a hot knife through butter."

His eyes gleamed as he held out his arm to her. "Then let's go do that, shall we?"

Five hours later, armed to the teeth with knives and her two swords strapped across her back, Anita hopped out of the SUV with Sasha and three other members of their ten witch team and unable to hide her smile, turned to Sasha who had just rounded the vehicle.

He smiled back and said, "Ready to go hunt down and kill some vampires."

"I've been ready for the last year." She pointed to the docks that lay in front of them. "Are we certain they are here?" It wasn't like Dark Brethren to come so close to a city in such a large group as they'd heard were here.

"You tell me." He gestured for her to take the lead.

She took off, using a little push of power to leap over the fence ahead of them, aware of Sasha and the rest of the squad following her. A few paces in she caught a scent of blood and death and something inherently rotten—it was faint but it was there. The scent that always surrounded and followed Dark Brethren in particular was hard to miss even when they hadn't been there for days, weeks. She'd smelled it in Middleton Manor for months after the attack. It was a scent she would never forget.

And it wasn't old here. Not even a day or hours old.

Even as faint as it was, she could tell it was fresh.

They were here. Maybe not in the numbers that had been reported, but there was a small pack here at least. Feeding. Torturing. Killing.

She turned to Sasha and the others and grinning grimly, nodded.

Sasha grinned back and pulled his katana from his back.

Anita echoed his movement with her own swords, one for each hand, then nodded in the direction the scent was coming from.

Quietly, they raced through the shipyard containers towards dealers of death that had nested among them.

Senses heightened, she wasn't surprised at all when a Dark Brethren landed in front of her, his bald, tattooed head glinting in the faint moonlight. He hissed at her, baring his mouthful of pointed teeth but before he could even lunge at her, she'd swung her swords, taking his head clean off his body. She kicked it far away when it landed in front of her just as ten other Dark Brethren rushed out of a large shipping container—the horror of the mass of body parts inside glinting in the light of the fire they had lit.

"For Papa," she yelled—as she always did—and raced forward, Sasha at her side, the rest of the squad at their backs, ready to mete out justified death.

CHAPTER

THREE

Hei tapped his fingers on the carved arm of his chair, diamond hard fingernails click-click-clicking on the polished dark wood in time to the song running through his mind.

A song that wouldn't leave his head. He had no idea what it was or if it even had lyrics, but it was annoying. Pretty, but annoying. Mostly because he couldn't get the damned thing out of his head since he woke in the middle of the night.

Something about it was oddly familiar though—like he'd heard it before but couldn't remember when. Not surprising given his long life. He could remember most things but small, inconsequential things were difficult to bring to mind with any specificity.

He wished he could remember why this song felt familiar though. He was certain if he could, it might leave him alone.

"Sire?"

His head jerked up at the polite whisper, his gaze going to Gabriel who was seated at his left. One of his oldest—and most troubled—sirelings, and his vampiric right hand, Gabriel had surprised him with his presence last night when he appeared as if from air in

Hei's study. He'd sent no notice of his arrival like he usually did—which usually meant nothing good.

Although this time he—

"Sire!"

Hei raised his brow surprised at his Second's tone. "Yes?"

Gabriel's gaze went to where Hei's hand was tapping on the wooden arm of his chair.

A wooden arm that was now splintered, the fine carvings that had flowed like silk under his hands for over a hundred years since that talented carpenter in Gubbio had made it for him, now chipped and cracked under the impact of his nails. On both sides. "Oh crap!"

He loved this chair. Far more comfortable—and far less of a throne than the one he'd had before it—it should have lasted him centuries of use. And now he'd ruined it.

Because of that blasted ear worm of a song. He'd tapped so hard to its rhythm he'd all but destroyed his chair. "Do you think it can be fixed?" He asked Gabriel.

Gabriel's generous mouth quirked and he nodded towards Tomas who sat on the other side of the round table—the very round table that had created the myths of Arthur and Camelot.

His Prime, the new leader of the Bartolli, closed the report he'd been reading from and stood to come around and view the damage. He pressed his lips together, his brows furrowed as he assessed the damage in that careful and considered way that had caught Hei's attention when Tomas was but a boy and singled him out as the one he wanted trained to be his next Bartolli. The brow furrow deepened and Hei was certain Tomas was about to tell him the chair was nothing but kindling, but then he met Hei's gaze and nodded. "I know of an artisan who can replace the arms if you have images of the original design."

"I can draw them for him."

Tomas waved his hand. "Then it will be no worry. Leave it with me, my Lord."

"Good. And how many times must I tell you, Tomas, that you are to call me Hei when we are in council alone?"

"We are not alone, my Lord," he replied, gaze flicking to Gabriel who still sat—sprawled might be a better word for it—in the chair next to Hei.

"He is about to say I do not count," Gabriel said, humor lightening his tone.

"I wasn't about to say any such thing," Hei said, allowing a smile to touch his lips. "But given you and Gabriel are my closest councilors, along with my twelve, I need for you to feel you can always speak truth to me. That begins with us coming together in this room, at this table, as equals."

"Nobody can be your equal, my L—"

Hei raised his finger. "Hei. Please."

Tomas blanched. "But I—"

Gabriel chuckled again. "Give in, Tomas. We might know none of us can ever be my Sire's equal, but he believes we are. Best to humor him. Also, it's good for him to be taken down a peg or two every now and then."

"Is that what you think your most important task is?" Hei said, enjoying the uncharacteristic levity in Gabriel this morning.

"It is the single most important aspect of my existence," his sireling said, hand over his heart, eyes dancing. "Ensuring your nearest and dearest don't treat you like a god."

"Well, as long as it's that." He huffed out a laugh. "I wouldn't want anyone thinking I was a god."

"A bit late for that my ... Hei," Tomas said.

He and Gabriel stared at Tomas for a silent second, then burst into laughter. Gabriel stood and slapped Tomas on the back.

"You have promise," he said as his laughter died.

Tomas's gaze moved from Gabriel to Hei. "I aim to please."

"Then go and sort the repairs on my Sire's chair."

"But the reports ...!"

Gabriel glanced at Hei then at the pile of reports, his mouth turning down. "Can you go over them later?"

"I suppose ..."

"Good." Gabriel clapped him on the back then was around the table in less than the flicker of an eye and back again, the reports in his hand. "Hei will call you when he's more in the mood." And very gently, he escorted Tomas from the room.

Hei pushed up out of his chair and strode across to the fireplace to stare at the flames. "You didn't need to do that, my son."

"I did because you weren't paying attention. And your Prime would only have had to go over everything again."

"Why would that bother you?"

"It doesn't—especially given I will not be here having to put up with the boring drone of things best left in the other hands. But it would bother *you*. You would not wish to double your new Bartolli Prime's workload, especially not when he is still settling in to the role."

Hei sighed. Gabriel was right. His people already worked hard enough on his behalf to keep his empire running smoothly so that he could concentrate on keeping the scourge at bay and doing as his maker had bid of him upon his making.

A terrible mistake had been made and it had been given unto him to right it. At times, he'd been grateful for his purpose, but at others ... well. He wished the duty had fallen to someone else.

Especially now. When he was worried about certain ... prophecies that were looming. Not that he believed in prophecies in the sense that they gave a complete telling of an immutable future. He believed they were a suggestion. Something that could happen but didn't need to.

But some beings of the magical and fanged variety put a lot of stock in certain prophecies and trying to keep the Wild and Dark Brethren from bringing certain prophecies into being was becoming a more urgent part of his job. Not only because of the death and destruction that would increase as they worked to make the prophecies real, but because it would most definitely bring them all to the attention of the humans. His maker had told him that one of his most sacred duties was to make certain the humans never realized their kind were more than myth and legend, because upon such a discovery, the world he so loved would be ruined by terrible and unending war.

And that could never be allowed to occur.

The problem was, he never knew that after thousands of years of working toward his goal, that his birthright duties would begin to feel like they were fraying him at the edges in the way they now were so that he couldn't even get a simple tune out of his head. It was playing and playing and playing around, whispering to him in his sleep over the last few weeks and coming to him during the day until it was nearly all that filled his mind and …

"What in all the seven hells is that tune!"

I HOPE you enjoyed that little taster of **The Huntress and the Vampire King**. If you did, you can read more now over at Leisl's Legends. Follow me there or subscribe for other amazing bonus content, exclusive extras and more.

Become a Legend Now!
https://reamstories.com/leislleightonauthor

Also by Leisl Leighton

Blood-Rites Series

The Blood of the Seer

The Blood of the Sire

The Blood of the Son

(Coming 2027)

~

Blood-Rites Prequel and Bonus Material

The Huntress and the Vampire King

The Middleton Manifesto

(Available now via Leisl's Legends subscription)

~

Gods Cursed Series

A Love Cursed Christmas Wish

Love Cursed

Soul Cursed

Blood Cursed

Hearts Cursed

Fates Cursed

Witch Cursed

Dragon Cursed

(Coming 2026)

~

As well as writing sexy, epic and romantic paranormal novels, I write mysterious and emotional romantic suspense novels too. Check out the following titles for amazing, suspenseful reads:

STORM HAVEN SERIES

Need You Tonight

The Devil Inside

～

COALCLIFF STUD SERIES

Climbing Fear: Book 1

Blazing Fear: Book 2

～

ECHO SPRINGS SERIES

Dangerous Echoes: Book 1

Books 2-4 in this series, (written by Daniel deLorne, TJ Hamilton and Shannon Curtis) are also available now at all ebook retailers.

About Leisl

Leisl Leighton is a tall red head with an overly large imagination. As a child, she identified strongly with Anne of Green Gables, and like Anne, is a voracious reader and born performer.

It came as no surprise when she went on to a career as a performer, script writer, script doctor, stage manager and musical director for cabaret and theatre restaurants.

After starting a family, Leisl stopped performing and began writing the stories plaguing her dreams. She now writes emotional stories mixed with mystery and a little bit of what goes bump in the night.

Her novels have won and placed in writing contests here and overseas. She is a passionate advocate for the romance genre, was President of Romance Writers of Australia from 2014-2017 and when she's not writing romantic stories of redemption, she is helping other authors reach their dreams with her Author Services.

You can contact Leisl through her website:

www.leislleighton.com

And if you want to stay in touch and be the first to find out about new releases, appearances, special deals and exclusive content and giveaways, sign up to her Newsletter and pick up your free copy of **TBOTS Exclusive Bonus Birth Scenes.** Or sign up to Leisl's Legends subscription to get them plus serialised early access stories, bonus content and more.

You can also follow her on social media:

facebook.com/LeislLeightonAuthor

instagram.com/leislleightonauthor

bookbub.com/authors/leisl-leighton

amazon.com/stores/Leisl-Leighton/author/B00DBYRGZY

ACKNOWLEDGMENTS

Writing this book has been a labour of love—one that has taken many years more than any other book I have ever written. It has gone through so many iterations over the years as I worked on it and worked on it—one even had a first person viewpoint from Gabriel's perspective; another skipped all the training Ardenne did with Piven.

That version was when I realised the book I had written really needed to be 2 books, and even though I'd already started on what I thought was the second book, I went back to the drawing board and thought for a year about what I could do to split that one book in two and make it work.

So many questions swirled in my head though: Where was I supposed to cut it in two? What should be in the first book and what in the second so it worked with what would now be the 3rd book that I'd already written? What scenes did I need to add, what needed to be changed and what needed to be axed? I could come up with no answers. Everything seemed wrong. I was too close to it after working on it for years already and couldn't see the forest for the trees.

But finally in 2019 I had a dream where the answer came to me—hallelujah for my story dreams!—and I started writing what you have just read. It took me a long time to finish it though—I had two other series to work on for my publisher and started down the self-publishing path as well which was a huge learning curve and included writing two new paranormal/urban romantasy series. Every time I returned to it though, it felt like I was coming home.

It was a journey of discovery—as much for myself as Ardenne and Gabriel—and was equal parts joy and frustration when my characters (especially the very stubborn Ardenne) wouldn't play ball. But I finally managed to pull it off and finished it.

Worry didn't subside though. This book, of all my books, had been an agony to write and yet I loved it so much and wanted it to be just right. So I decided to test it out in serialised form to my newsletter subscribers and my subscribers and followers over at Leisl's Legends to see what other people might think.

I got such a wonderful response I knew I had managed to finally pull off what felt like a miracle—turning this labour of love book into something not only I enjoyed, but others did too.

So many people, both family and friends, helped out during all these years and filled me with love and the encouragement I needed to keep pushing on. Thanks to all of you—you are superstars!

Of course, special thanks have to go out to my hubby, Mark, and my two beautiful boys, Jacob and Nathaniel, and to my parents, Kerrie and Jim, whose support has never wavered and whose love I could never do without. Love you all.

Aside from great family and friends, a writer needs a Coven of writing peeps all their own. Thanks need to go to these special people for encouraging me in this endeavour and giving me the strength to push on through all the highs and lows of doing this crazy writing thing—Anita and Marnie (my writing retreat buddies), Samantha and Helen (my fellow lovers of sparkly unicorns), Laura, Chris and finally Frana. I couldn't have gotten here without you.

Thanks once again to the insanely talented Samantha Marshall for her brilliant covers. Every day I thank the universe for bringing us together and for being able to count you friend.

A big thank you to to my editor on this one, Brooke Halliwell, who took on this huge project and did a beautiful job of helping me get it to the finish line. It helped too that she loved this book as much as I did—in fact, she was even so bold as to announce it was her favourite of all my books that she's worked on, which at the time, when I was full of worries, was just what I needed to hear. I can't wait to work with her again on the rest of the series.

During the writing of this book I lost my best friend, Helen, and the first writing friend I ever had, Liz. Both of these beautiful women are always with me and forever in my thoughts. And my thanks are eternally with them as I would never have got published without their encouragement, helpful feedback and constant cheering support. Both of them will always be a part of my stories.

And of course thanks have to go to the newsletter subscribers and followers over at Leisl's Legends who lapped up every chapter release and let me know how much they were loving Gabriel and Ardenne. This book would not be here without your encouragement—so thank you.

And a big shout out to all my friends in Romance Writers of Australia—you are inspiration and mentor rolled into a big ball of supportive writerly love. Thank you.

The final person I have to thank is my agent, Alex Adsett, for believing in me and my work and always backing every decision I make. Your confidence in me helps me believe I can actually do this writing thing no matter the path I take. Eternal thanks.

* 9 7 8 1 9 2 2 8 3 6 2 4 3 *